The Dead Man's Dame

The Dead Man's Dame

A Novel

Kevin Obike

KCN Press

The Dead Man's Dame
© 2025 Kevin Obike

Published by KCN Press
www.kevincnoel.com

Cover design by Art2knockout

ISBN: 979-8-9934858-0-5

Printed in the United States of America

10 9 8 7 6 5 4 3 2 1

To My Dad

There is nothing the eyes will see
that will make them shed blood.

-Igbo Proverb

PROLOGUE

The following events do not occur chronologically…

The Admiral

Admiral Alex Maduagu hurried down Ikeja's narrow alleys, hand pressed to his side, the streets a blur. Blood seeped between his fingers, staining the crisp linen of his shirt. Each step sent a sharp jolt of pain through his ribs, but he couldn't stop. Not yet.

Somewhere behind him, the echo of rapid footsteps grew louder, relentless in their pursuit. The city around him carried on as if oblivious: distant shouts of hawkers peddling their wares, the occasional honk of a danfo bus, the metallic clank of gates closing for the night. Lagos was always loud, but tonight, its noise felt far away, swallowed by the pounding of his heart and the churning of his stomach.

He darted into a narrow alley. His breath came in short, wheezing bursts as he paused, pressing his back against the cool, wet concrete. For a moment, he let his gaze drop to the phone in his trembling hand. The cracked screen reflected his own terrified face, the weight of everything he had done staring back at him.

Time was running out. They wouldn't stop until they had what they wanted.

His free hand moved to the pocket of his shirt, where he felt the outline of an SD card tucked inside. He hesitated, his mind racing. He couldn't let them have it. If it fell into the wrong hands, all that he had worked for, the crusade to dismantle the rot at the core of the system, would unravel in an instant.

He believed disclosing the reality would be sufficient. The documents he had gathered, the names and accounts they contained, were supposed to bring justice. But he had underestimated how deeply the corruption ran. Those he once trusted had turned on him. Now, he was alone.

The sound of footsteps snapped him back to the present. They were closer now. He glanced at the alley, then down at the phone again, his decision made in an instant. He slid the SD card out of his pocket and clenched both it and the phone in his hands.

"Admiral," a voice called, smooth and mocking, cutting through the night.

Alex straightened, pushing away from the wall as two figures emerged from the shadows at the other end of the alley. The faint glow of a distant streetlamp obscured their faces, but their intent was clear.

"You've made this harder than it needed to be," one of them said, stepping forward. His tone was conversational, almost friendly, but the glint of black metal in his hand suggested otherwise.

The Admiral didn't respond. Instead, he looked back at the phone.

"Oga, you think you can outrun us?" the second figure said, his laugh low and humorless. "Nobody go help you." He stretched his hand out. "Just give us what we want. Then you can go."

Alex's chest heaved as he took a step back, his eyes darting to the alley's far end. The shadows there seemed deeper, impenetrable, but they were his only chance.

"Did she send you?" he asked with equal parts desperation and defiance.

The shadowy men did not respond, but inched closer to him, their intent undoubtedly deadly.

For a little while, Alex's mind drifted to the one person who had made all of this bearable. Her face flashed before him, her smile, her voice, the way she often looked at him with love and trust. "I just need to see her again," he thought to himself, steeling his resolve.

"Go to hell," he spat at the men.

The first man moved fast, and Alex turned and ran, his heart pounding in his ears as their footsteps followed, echoing down the alley like a death knell.

The Ex-Minister

Mmachi Alex-Maduagu observed the skyline of Washington, D.C. from her hotel room, the city's glittering lights spreading out before her like a map of possibilities and failures. The weight of her situation pressed against her chest, heavier than the silk robe she wore. She clenched the edge of the marble counter, her thoughts racing.

Losing leverage wasn't merely an inconvenience, it was a death sentence. The documents Alex had stolen were more than mere digital information; they were her shield. Names, dates, transactions. Evidence of a system so corrupt it would completely shut down an entire country if those secrets ever

3

surfaced. Without them, she had no protection, no way to stay ahead of the vultures circling her exile.

She heard the buzzing of her phone on the table. She read the text message from an unknown number: "It would be in your best interest to find him and make him see reason."

Her jaw tightened as she deleted the message. They wouldn't let her rest without those documents. And Alex, with his self-righteous delusions, imagined he could use them to fix the system. She almost laughed at his naivete. The system was designed to be navigated, not fixed.

She picked up the phone and dialed a +234 number, one she hadn't called in years. The line rang, and for a moment, she thought he wouldn't answer. Then a low, growling voice came through.

"Mmachi."

The way he said her name sent a shiver down her spine— not from fear, but from the memory of how much power this man wielded.

"I need your help," she said steadily, though her hand trembled.

A low chuckle echoed through the line. "Help from me? I didn't think you'd ever stoop so low."

"I wouldn't call you if I had a choice," she admitted, hating how vulnerable she sounded.

"And what do you think I can do for you?"

Her grip on the phone tightened. "You can find him before he does something he will regret. I know you can."

There was silence on the other end, and for a second, she imagined he'd hung up. But she could still hear his low breathing.

"How much can I give you to make this happen?" She asked quickly, the words spilling out before she could stop herself.

The man laughed humorlessly. "Do I appear to be the sort of man who needs your money, Mmachi?"

She closed her eyes, forcing herself to breathe. "Then what do you want?"

Another pause, heavier this time. Then he did the unthinkable. He recommended someone. Her eyes snapped open, and she almost dropped the phone. "What's so special about him?"

"He is smart enough to find him and solve all your problems, Your Excellency," he said, the honorific falling out of his mouth like a joke and half an insult.

Mmachi thought for a moment.

"Fine," she said at last, the word cool and flat. "Where can I find him?"

The Dame

She leaned over her vanity, her hand steady as she swept a brush of golden highlighter across her cheekbones. The faint shimmer caught the light, accentuating her already striking features. She leaned back and admired her work in the mirror. Perfection.

The emerald-green bodycon dress she wore hugged every curve, its sequined fabric catching flecks of light with her every movement. The neckline plunged close to her midriff, crossing the line into vulgarity, and the slit along her thigh offered a tantalizing glimpse of even more skin.

She adjusted her curls, the loose waves framing her face in a way that felt effortlessly glamorous. As she smoothed the dress, she glanced at the tiny room around her. It wasn't much: a one-bedroom apartment tucked into a corner of Marina—but she had decorated it to fit the life she was building. A faux-fur rug softened the floor beneath her, and carefully chosen decor added a touch of elegance she hoped would distract from the cracks in the paint.

Tonight's livestream was an investment in her future. She had learned long ago that life didn't hand opportunities to women like her. If she wanted something better, she'd have to create it.

Moving to the corner of the room, she adjusted her livestreaming setup. She mounted her phone on a tripod with a glowing ring light attached, which perfectly illuminated the sleek red-and-black accent chair positioned in the background. The chair gave her setup an air of effortless sophistication, a calculated contrast to the gritty reality of her surroundings.

She slid her phone into the tripod's holder and tapped the screen. The camera's preview sprang to life, showing her reflection. She adjusted the ring light until her skin glowed, the background softened, and her dress sparkled just right.

Her fingers danced across the screen as she opened Slago, the livestreaming app that had turned her bedroom into a stage. As the app loaded, she leaned back in the chair, crossing her legs at just the right angle.

Within seconds of going live, her audience poured in, a flurry of usernames and comments scrolling up her screen. *"Angel!" "Perfect queen!" "Are you single?" "Show me your armpit." "360, abeg!" "Hi, beautiful. Can I take you to Dubai?" "I so much love you." "Check your DM." "Wow, you are so sexy."*

She ignored the ridiculous ones with the ease of a seasoned coquette. She had mastered the art of engaging just enough to keep the gifts coming. When a viewer asked for a "360," she smiled coyly, tilting her head toward the camera. "Hmm," she replied. "You know the rules. Spin the wheel first."

On the side of the screen, the digital wheel glimmered. Each quadrant promised something different: a 360, a shy wave, a moan, or even her WhatsApp number. She watched the comments grow more frantic as viewers raced to send her virtual gifts to unlock a spin.

From the corner of her eye, she noticed Candy leaning against the doorframe. Her housemate dressed down in a tank top and joggers, but her sharp gaze remained sharp and calculating. Candy winked before slipping out, leaving her to her work.

Moments later, a new username popped up on her screen: King Investor.

Her lips curled into a knowing smirk. She leaned closer to the camera, letting the glow of the ring light catch her lined eyes.

"Hi, papi," she whispered.

The comments exploded in response, but her focus stayed on her top gifter. She was a professional, after all.

CHAPTER 1

I've never been fond of cheats or the corrupt, but somehow, I always ended up working with them—or worse, for them.

I slammed the door behind me. They didn't deserve my words. Those backstabbing bastards. As I stepped out onto Georgia Avenue, my chest still heaving with rage, I thought about how my old man would've told me to keep my cool, to show some restraint. But he wasn't here. It was just me and the burning desire to tell Patrick and Bikram to go straight to hell.

It wasn't the fact that I got fired that pissed me off. It was on account of my getting canned before I could really tell them what I thought. After everything they'd put me through, I didn't even get to give them a proper piece of my mind.

Now, don't go thinking I'm some bigoted xenophobe for saying that about my immigrant bosses. I'm an immigrant myself. Born in Nigeria. My old man made sure I got my bachelor's degree there too. Said it'd build character, toughen me up for all the rocks life was gonna throw my way. He figured it'd teach me humility, seeing how my peers lived without half the chances I had. And most of all, it taught me restraint. In Nigeria, you learn to choke down the urge to snap when you see some fat politician breeze by in his convoy, or when a cop shakes you down for a bribe. When I was younger, I hated him for it. But he was right. Restraint's what kept me from walking back into that office and smashing a desk over the boss and that Nepali kiss-ass's head.

I was an insurance fraud investigator, but don't let that title deceive you. I wasn't solving crimes or busting major fraudsters. Most days, I was up to my neck in the filth of fraudulent claims, from people faking injuries to twisted paperwork. Sure, some of it was justified desperation, and I didn't blame those folks for trying to get one over on the system, but Patrick, my boss, a slick, fast-talking conman, couldn't care less about the human side of things. He just wanted to save the company money, or worse, fatten his own pocket. He had me chasing potential issues and fixing problems everywhere. And the worst part? It wasn't just the company cases. No, Patrick had me doing legwork for his personal side business, chasing claims that had nothing to do with my job.

Do you suppose I earned one cent for it? Of course not. Every time I asked him for the money he owed me for these little "off the record" gigs, he'd throw an arm around me, slap me on the back, and promise, "Next week, Dozy. Next week, I'll take care of you." Except next week never came. I was earning "trust," he'd say. I was learning the ropes. Truth was, I was getting hustled. And I knew it.

It was vexing.

The tipping point for me wasn't one of Patrick's dirty side jobs, it was an actual case for the company. A guy had lost his leg in a legitimate accident. The paperwork was a mess, but the claim was clean. Yet, Patrick wanted me to find something to deny the payout, some technicality. He knew there was nothing, but it wasn't about justice, it was about saving money. He didn't care if it ruined the man's life. That was it for me. I wasn't about to let this company screw over a guy who actually deserved something.

When Bikram handed me the case, I was already at my breaking point. The unpaid side hustles, the endless claims, and the constant visa threats had created weight, which piled up until I was enraged. I'd read once about something called resenteeism. It's when you hate your job so much, but you stick around for the paycheck. That was me, down to the letter. My patience snapped like an old, worn-out rubber band, and before I knew it, I was saying, "No!" louder than I should have. Louder than anyone should, especially in an office where stepping out of line meant more than just a slap on the wrist.

I didn't wait for a reaction. I grabbed my jacket, stormed out, and hit the streets to investigate another case. I needed to cool off, to walk off the rage. I'd always prided myself on keeping it together, being the one who didn't make a scene, even when I had every reason to. But that day, I just couldn't. I was at my boiling point, and I didn't care who saw it.

For a few hours, the cold air and the methodical rhythm of walking through the city streets calmed me down, and my mind settled. Upon returning, I felt calmer, figuring perhaps I had overreacted. I could fix it. After all, I wasn't a troublemaker. Hell, I'd been the model employee. I handled cases and didn't stir the pot. So, I figured at most I'd get a warning, a mild reprimand. A "don't do it again" from Patrick, maybe a smirk from Bikram.

When I returned, Bikram didn't even look at me. His eyes stayed glued to the screen, that dull, robotic tone slipping from his lips: "Patrick sent you an email."

My heart sank.

Patrick never emailed me outside of the usual work nonsense. I was certain that whatever awaited me in that inbox would be unpleasant. I knew it. Bikram knew it (probably composed it himself). The way everyone in the entire office fixated on their screens, trying to avoid the fallout, showed that they knew it.

I walked to my desk like I wasn't standing at the edge of a cliff. Sat down. Opened my laptop. There it was.

The subject line told me everything I needed to know.

Subject: Termination.

Alvan,

It has taken me some time to arrive at this decision, but after careful consideration and my observations from yesterday, I have made up my mind.

It has become increasingly evident that you are unwilling to participate actively both in field investigations and in-office analysis. You also seem unwilling to follow instructions from senior members of the team, which was particularly apparent today when you abruptly left the office, disregarding the task at hand.

It seems that your role here no longer aligns with your interests, and you no longer wish to contribute effectively to the ongoing investigations. This is not sustainable for the company, and after careful thought, I've decided that we cannot continue to engage you as part of this team.

Today will be your last day with us at the firm. Please return all company materials and equipment by the end of the day.

Regards,
Dr. Patrick Antwi
Senior Claims Manager

At the risk of sounding like a disgruntled ex-employee, fuck them. Fuck their job. And fuck the little power trip they were on. I grabbed my stuff and walked out without a word.

— ◆ —

A year before, I had a conversation with Jasmine, a friend from grad school. She saw the writing on the wall before I did and came up with the idea of marrying me temporarily, just so I could get a green card and secure my future here. We agreed it would be a quiet arrangement. Simple. Businesslike. And it worked. A few months after the paperwork filing, I received the green card. Freedom, right?

Wrong.

After I got the card, I found myself standing in front of a series of closed doors. Overqualified for entry-level, too risky for anything higher up. And with each rejection, the walls closed in tighter.

With each passing week, the sense of purpose I thought I'd find with the green card vanished. Instead, I realized that mounting bills, constant rejections, and the "better job" I had envisioned weren't waiting for me at all.

After one month of being jobless, I started seeing things differently. One evening, sitting in my car, I wondered if I could get my old job back. Maybe I could suck it up, smile, and keep my mouth shut like they wanted. But the thought of their smug faces made me snap my fingers in rejection of the idea. No, not a chance. Still, the fact that they had so much control over my mood made my stomach churn. I hated that more than losing the job itself.

I decided to head to the gym. The idea of punching a sandbag felt like the kind of therapy I needed. The image of Patrick's smug face helped channel my frustration. Bikram too, with his fake grins and double-dealing ways. I aimed each jab and hook at them; every punch released a bit of the anger that had been festering. The sound of my fists landing hard against the sandbag was satisfying, but the aggression left me more drained than I expected.

As I went through my routine, drenched in sweat, a trainer who had been watching from the sidelines approached me. He was lean, muscled, and had that unmistakable aura of someone who knew their way around a ring. "You're hitting the bag like it's personal," he said with a slight smirk. "How about you spar with me? See if it does you any good."

I should have said no, but the challenge stirred something old in me. There was a time when I was decent in the ring, when I could hold my own. Maybe this would help shake off the frustration, I thought. Maybe this was what I needed.

We suited up and moved into the ring. From the moment the bell sounded, I knew I was in over my head. The trainer was fast. Too fast. I threw a few punches, but they barely grazed him, while his jabs were precise, landing squarely on my face and ribs. My body was slow to react; my reflexes dulled. I staggered back after a solid punch to the gut, winded. He knocked me down once. Then again. And again.

I used to be better at this. I could almost hear my old man's voice in the back of my head, barking orders, reminding me to hold my hands up, to never let myself get backed into a corner. I wish I could blame my poor performance on a distracted mind. But I wasn't much of a

13

fighter anymore. My muscles were out of practice, my technique sloppy.

The last knockdown left me staring at the ceiling, gasping for breath. The trainer leaned over me, offering a hand, though the smirk never left his face. "Not bad," he said. "But you're rusty. Did you receive training?"

I nodded, though the movement made my head spin. "A long time ago," I muttered. "Krav Maga."

"Yeah, thought so," he said, helping me to my feet. "But Krav Maga's all about balance, right? Attack and defense are supposed to be seamless. You're too focused on hitting. You need to think about protecting yourself at the same time."

His words hit harder than the punches. He was right. Somewhere along the way, I'd let myself lose touch with the fighter I once was. And it wasn't just about the gym. It was about life. I wasn't sharp anymore. I'd let myself grow soft, complacent.

I limped out of the ring, bruised and battered, but with a strange clarity settling in. If I wanted to take control of my life again, I had to toughen up, mentally and physically.

After that, every other day found me back in that gym, pounding through the routines my old man used to swear built character. Back then, I called it torture. Now, it was therapy. Each drill, each breath, peeled away a layer of weakness I didn't know I'd been carrying. The same discipline that once made me hate him was now the only thing keeping me sane.

Four months of sweat and bruises later, I could feel the old instincts waking up: the quick hands, the sharp eyes, the reflexes that used to keep me alive. But there was something else too, something missing. A ghost of who I used to be. No matter how much strength I built, I couldn't shake the feeling that the best version of me had already seen his last fight.

I needed a break from all the self-pity, so I figured it was time to dig up another old routine. Every Friday night, I used to bar hop along U Street with a couple of friends. I hadn't done it since I got canned. Money was too tight for blowing on drinks, but I had to get out. I had to clear my head.

U Street was buzzing as always, a carnival of neon lights, thumping music, and the smell of grilled food wafting from local restaurants. It was alive, almost too much so for a man who had been drowning in his own thoughts for months. Girls from Howard University, strutting like they owned the place, rolled through in impenetrable packs, their laughter echoing off the walls. Every few steps, a guy would pop out of a shadow, pitching knock-off merch and weed like they were part of the nightlife package. White folks were out in force too, throwing down bills at the bars, nodding their heads to rap lyrics they wouldn't dare say out loud. And then there were the random clutches of foreigners moving together like a tour group, cameras hanging around their necks as if this was some kind of urban safari.

It was chaos, the kind that makes you forget your problems. At least for a while.

I pushed into Filosofer DC, my old haunt. Inside, the air was thick with hookah smoke and the scent of sweat mixed with cheap perfume. The tightly packed crowd swayed to the rhythm of a song by a hypersexual rapper that I did not know. I squeezed my way to the bar and ordered a Long Island Iced Tea. I wasn't the type to drown my sorrows in a glass, but that night? I figured maybe I'd understand why so many people did.

Half an hour passed before I noticed her. She sat a few seats down, wearing a nude-colored bodycon dress that hugged every curve just right. Her golden-brown braids draped down her back, resting over a perfectly rounded bottom that didn't need any enhancements. She ordered a drink, something colorful, and sipped it slowly, eyes glued to her phone like she was somewhere far away.

I couldn't take my eyes off her. Everything about her, the way she carried herself like she knew she was the center of attention, whether she wanted to be or not. It had been too long since I'd been with a woman. The last time was the night things ended with Jasmine, my friend-turned-wife. We parted ways right after I got my green card, as agreed. She gave me a hell of a goodbye gift, and once I dove into my savings to pay her what I owed, she was out of my life. Since then? Nothing. So it wasn't a shock when this chocolate-skinned goddess had my member nudging me to action.

Still, I was never the type to approach women in clubs. There was no way someone like her was here alone. She had to be waiting for someone. But then her eyes flicked up from her phone and caught me staring. Shit. I turned away fast, but not fast enough. From the corner of my eye, I could see her smirking as she stood up.

She started walking toward me. Her scent hit me first, vanilla and lavender, subtle but intoxicating. She leaned in, close enough for her breath to brush my ear. For a second, I thought she might kiss it.

"Hi," she shouted over the music.

I grinned, nodded, and managed to get out a "hi" back.

Her smile was blinding, teeth gleaming under the club's neon glow. "Haven't seen you here before."

"Funny, I was thinking the same about you," I said. "Used to be a regular, but I've been away for a couple of months."

"I've only been coming here for about two months," she said, taking a slow, satisfied sip of her drink. "The mixologist is great."

"The mixologist, huh?" I took a sip of my drink. "I started coming here back when I was at Howard. The mixologist's good, I guess," I lied. Truth was, I just liked sticking to what I knew.

She stretched her hand out. "I'm Giselle."

I took it, making sure not to squeeze too hard. "My friends call me Dozy."

She chuckled. "Dozy? What, you lazy or something?"

"Inside joke," I said.

She laughed, and we chatted a bit longer, trading light banter, but I couldn't help noticing how her eyes kept scanning the room between sentences. Was she bored? Looking for someone else? Or maybe she was waiting for me to make a move.

Then she leaned in again, those feline eyes locked on mine. "Wanna go somewhere else?" she asked.

My gut twisted. It was more than just nerves, though. Something about her just seemed... off. I listened to enough true crime podcasts to know you shouldn't just up and leave with someone you don't know at two in the morning. But then again, it had been a long time since I'd been intimate with a woman, and I wasn't going to let paranoia get in the way of a good time.

"Sure," I said, trying to sound cool and collected, even though my pulse was racing.

She grabbed my hand, and we pushed our way through the crowd, out into the cool night air. I wasn't sure what I was getting into, but for the first time in months, I didn't care.

CHAPTER 2

I woke up in a king-size bed, head throbbing and mouth dry as sandpaper. The roar of a nearby vehicle told me it was time to leave. I glanced around. no sign of Giselle. It was strange, though. I'd never had a one-night stand at a woman's place before. The idea of doing the walk of shame in broad daylight almost made me laugh, but I shook my head in silent judgment. This was a one-night stand. If it were something more, she'd have been in the room waiting for me to wake up, maybe with breakfast or some awkward post-coital conversation. No, she'd taken a good look at me and decided I wasn't worth the morning small talk. Fair enough. God bless her for letting me sleep in, at least.

The night: wild, truly. I licked my lips, remembering her skin against mine, soft and warm. I couldn't help but chuckle. Seemed like my plan to forget my woes had worked out after all. Who cared if I was unemployed?

I buttoned my shirt, ready to slip out, when the smell of eggs hit me. Maybe she was downstairs. I figured I should show some dignity, tell her I had a great time, wish her well, and walk out like a gentleman. No asking for numbers, no "see you around," just clean and easy. I might've been down on my luck, but like the typical Igbo man, I still had my pride.

I walked down the stairs, trying to act indifferent, though I was curious about the house itself. Lavish was an understatement. I'd barely noticed it last night, too distracted by her lips on mine to care. But now, in the daylight, it was obvious. This place oozed money. Plush furniture, expensive artwork, everything in its place. I wasn't sure if Giselle owned or rented it, but it was clear she had access to some serious cash.

As I reached the bottom of the stairs, I was startled to see an older woman seated on a plush couch, with a cup of tea resting in her hands. This was not Giselle.

She had to be in her fifties, but damn, she looked incredible. Her skin was smooth, with the same warm brown tone Giselle had, but with a certain maturity that only made her more striking. The ensemble, dark violet netting which glimmered subtly, suited her perfectly, accentuating a physique that rivaled women half her age. She looked fit, elegant, and, dare I say, predatory in a way that some might call "cougar material." The head wrap, folded and tied in a perfect crown of purple, added an air of sophistication, but it was the glint in her eyes behind those low-sitting glasses that made me pause.

She didn't seem surprised to see me. In fact, she looked me over with a calm, knowing gaze, the kind that told me she was used to situations like this, maybe even expecting it.

"Good morning," she said, her voice laced with veiled sarcasm. "I trust you had a restful night."

Her tone alone made me dislike her. But it wasn't until I recognized who she was that the dread crept in. At first glance, she looked nothing like the woman I'd seen all those years ago on Nigerian news. Time had softened her edges, but that voice—rich, commanding, Igbo, polished by years of wealth and Western influence—it hit me like a slap.

"You..." I spat, the venom in my words surprising even me. "You're Giselle's mother?"

She raised an eyebrow, her expression a mockery of confusion. "Giselle?" She repeated, drawing out the name as if it tasted foreign. "Oh, you mean the young lady that brought you here." She smiled, but there was no warmth in it. "She was a call girl, Mr. Dozy. A rather expensive one. I do hope she was worth every penny."

I cursed under my breath, my stomach turning. Of course. Everything about her had been wrong from the start, and I'd been too horny to see it.

"I can tell from that look of absolute scorn you know who I am," she said calmly.

I swallowed hard, my gaze narrowing as the pieces fell into place. "Yeah, I know who you are. Mmachi Alex-Maduagu." The words tasted bitter on my tongue. "Former Minister of Petroleum, now living in exile. You were the focus of a political witch-hunt against the former administration. Your corruption was the worst of the lot."

She smirked, but I detected sharpness behind her eyes. She did not take offense. In fact, it seemed to entertain her.

I had grown to despise people like her. People who abused their power, who had everything handed to them and still wanted more. People like my former bosses, immigrants who clawed their way into management and thought that gave them the right to exploit others. Exploit me. And now here she was, in the flesh, a symbol of everything I hated.

Still, it seemed strange. The elaborate scheme. Sending me a high-priced escort. Luring me to her place. It didn't add up. "So, what's the angle here?" I asked, suspicion in my squinted eyes. "Why go through all this just to get me here?"

She smiled. "Tea?" she offered, gesturing toward a teapot on the table between us.

"I don't drink tea."

"Something stronger, perhaps?" She raised an eyebrow, her lips curving into a knowing smile. "It's only nine in the morning, I know, but I've had to start my day with far worse."

"No thanks," I muttered, but there was no denying the cleverness of her offer. She was testing me, feeling me out.

She stood up, her movement fluid and precise as she walked toward the kitchen. "At least let me fix you some eggs. I assume a night like the one you had would leave a man famished."

My eyes followed her. She was even more striking on her feet, her body somehow looking even better with the way she moved. Every curve was well-defined, her dress hugging her figure just right. I hated myself for noticing, for letting my guard down even for a second.

But she saw, obviously. Mmachi Alex-Maduagu wasn't the type to let anything slip by unnoticed. As she began plating the eggs and sausages, she spoke without looking at me. "You know," she started, her tone casual, "I've always been... good. Growing up, I excelled at everything I did. My father taught me ambition early. He drilled it into me." She glanced back at me. "I never used my gender to achieve anything. I worked hard for every success, every position."

I crossed my arms, observing her as she continued, "By the time I became an executive at Chevron, I was at the top of my game. I was sure no one would ever accuse me of sleeping my way to the top, so I dressed more... freely." She smiled, a slight lift of her lips, as she placed the plate of eggs and sausages on the table before me. "I suppose I got used to the attention, the male gaze. In fact, I encourage it."

She turned to face me now, her eyes locking onto mine. "So, Mr. Dozy, your wide-eyed lusting shouldn't embarrass you. I'm not offended. Far from it."

Her words caught me off guard, and I felt my face flush, the heat rising as I tried to gather my composure. She had read me like a book, and here I was, exposed and irritated by how easily she'd done it.

I clenched my jaw, fighting the shame creeping up on me. I hated her more for being right, for toying with me while I was still trying to piece together why I was even there.

I eyed the food in front of me, the smell hitting me like a freight train. My stomach growled, loud enough to remind me I had eaten nothing in what felt like forever. Maybe it was the neglected dinners from the past few days, or maybe it was the too-many-to-count Long Island iced teas I'd downed the night before, but hunger was gnawing at me, and this plate of eggs was mocking my attempts to keep up appearances.

Of course, Mmachi noticed. She was sharp like that, always watching. "Relax," she said, with a smooth, almost condescending tone in her voice. "If I wanted you dead or drugged, I had all of last night to make it happen. Trust me, the breakfast is safe."

I didn't respond, but her logic made sense. If she had any darker plans, I'd already be on the other side of them. I nodded, and she watched as I sat down on the couch opposite her, facing the plate of food like it was some test of will. The eggs in front of me weren't just breakfast, they were a memory, the kind that pulled me back to my mother's kitchen in Enugu. They were colorful, mixed with bright tomatoes, peppers in every shade: green, orange, red and yellow. They smelled of spice, of home. The kind of food that reminded me why I never quite got used to the bland, too-creamy scrambled eggs here in America. I wanted to stay composed and keep the hard, unamused exterior. My pride was no match for my hunger, and before I knew it, I was eating, my thoughts clouded with confusion and anger. Silence hung between us, save for the quiet clink of fork against plate as I shoveled food into my mouth. Mmachi said nothing. She just watched me, the way a mother watches a child devour the food she cooked. Maybe there was a sense of satisfaction in her eyes; I couldn't tell. I wasn't looking at her. The food held my focus, and I savored every bite despite the circumstances.

When I was done, I put the fork down and leaned back in the chair, feeling more human than I had in days. Mmachi's voice broke the silence.

"Did you enjoy the meal?"

Years of home training kicked in. No matter the situation, my parents didn't raise me to ignore hospitality. "Yeah," I said. "Thanks."

She smiled, like she knew I couldn't say anything else. Then, with no fanfare, she reached over to the arm of the couch and opened a small compartment. She pulled out a file, thick and heavy, and turned it so I could see the words written on the cover. It was my full name.

Alvan Chidozie Agu.

"I've been looking for you," she said, like she was discussing something as casual as a misplaced phone number. "I found out where you worked, only to discover that you had been fired. Looked for you at the forwarding address they gave me. Turns out you moved out. Then I learned you were a regular at the Filosofer DC bar, so I had

Giselle scope the place out for months, waiting for you to show up."

Her words baffled me, but I did my best not to show it. She'd been planning this, hunting me down for God knows how long, and I'd walked right into her trap. I clenched my jaw, feeling the heat rise in my chest, but I kept it together. I wasn't about to give her the satisfaction of knowing she'd rattled me.

"Why?" I asked, trying to keep my voice steady.

As if changing the subject was the most natural thing in the world, she asked, "By the way, what have you been doing these past five months? For a living, I mean."

"I don't see how that's relevant," I snapped.

She was unfazed. "You're free to leave, Mr. Dozy. I won't tell you what you want to know until you answer."

I scoffed, leaning back against the couch. "Uber driver."

She nodded, waiting for more. I could tell she wanted details, and something in me gave her a glimpse.

"Yeah, I've been driving Uber. Not exactly living the dream, but it pays the bills... barely. Some rides are alright, y'know? Sometimes I pick up people who want to talk, people with stories, people who share my interests." I paused, the memories of countless passengers running through my mind. "Other times, though, it's annoying as hell. You get folks who act like you're not even there, or worse, the ones who never stop talking. The drunks are the worst. College kids who can't handle their liquor or middle-aged women who've had one too many glasses of Chardonnay. They'd slur some promise of a 'wild night' if I followed them home."

Mmachi chuckled, a sound that made my skin crawl, though I couldn't say why. "A perk of the job, I suppose," she said.

I shook my head, smirking despite myself. "Not my thing."

She leaned back, observing me through those glasses of hers, expecting something. I didn't know what game she was playing, but it was clear I was already a part of it. The question now was: how deep was I in?

CHAPTER 3

"Does driving pay enough to send money to your mother and siblings back in Nigeria?"

I froze. My spine stiffened as her words settled. How the hell did she know about my family? The thought of someone like her knowing something so intimate made my blood run cold. My mind raced for answers, but none came fast enough. She was already reaching into the folder, pulling out something that made me realize just how deep this rabbit hole went.

She handed me an old photograph. It was one of those that had the yellowed edges and glossy sheen from back when Kodak was still a thing. I looked at it, and my heart nearly stopped. There they were, my parents, but younger than I'd ever seen them. My mom, probably in her twenties, holding a baby swaddled in a white blanket. Me. My father stood beside her, looking like a version of himself I barely remembered. One could only describe his perfectly round, neat haircut as the remnants of an afro he must've let go at the end of the '70s. He wore brown aviator shades and his Nigerian military uniform, a lieutenant colonel. Standing next to him was another man, one rank higher, a colonel by the insignia on his uniform. The guy had a bit more weight on him, with a balding head and a thick mustache that screamed authority. And by his side was a young woman, no older than twenty-one.

I looked back up at Mmachi, my hands holding the photo tighter than they should. I flicked my eyes between her and the image, trying to make sense of what I was seeing.

"That was your christening," she said, her voice cutting through the fog in my head. "That's my father there," she added, gesturing to the Colonel. "He and your father were good friends back then. Sadly, they drifted apart."

I couldn't respond. My mind was stuck on one thought: Why the hell hadn't my father ever mentioned any of this? I sat there with the weight of the photo pressing down on me. General Agu was a hard man, not the type to talk about his personal life, but something like this? A connection to the most corrupt politician in all of Nigeria? It was too important to leave out, but he had. And that picture of my mother… she looked so much younger, happier, lighter than I ever remembered.

Mmachi must've seen the gears turning in my head because she didn't rush me. She just let me sit with my thoughts for a while. Eventually, she spoke again.

"I met your dad some years after we took that picture," she said, her tone shifting into something more conversational. "I'd just been appointed Minister of Housing. He was a general by then. He told me about you."

I blinked, coming out of my stupor. "What did he say?"

She smiled a thin, knowing smile that didn't reach her eyes. "He said you were the black sheep of the family."

I snorted involuntarily. Of course, that's what he would've said. She went on.

"He told me you joined a campus cult back when you were at university."

I sat up straighter. Of all the things my father could have mentioned, that's the one he'd focus on? I shook my head and cleared my throat. "He was wrong about that," I said, looking Mmachi dead in the eye. "I never joined a cult."

She raised an eyebrow, her interest piqued. "No?"

Campus cults. For anyone outside Nigeria, that might sound like a fraternity: guys partying, making memories, maybe hazing the new recruits. But not back home. In Nigeria, campus cults were a different beast entirely. They weren't about parties or brotherhood; they were gangs, violent and territorial. Groups like *Black Axe, Eiye, the Buccaneers*. They weren't just kids playing around. These were organizations that ran on blood oaths, initiations that could leave a man broken, and turf wars that sometimes ended in murder.

Back then, joining a cult gave you power and control over the campus, over your peers, over anyone unlucky enough to cross your path. It was protection, too, from rival groups, from authorities who couldn't, or wouldn't, do anything. And the members? They didn't hesitate to wield that power, to exploit it. Friends of mine had gotten caught up in that life, good people who turned bad fast. It wasn't long before the violence swallowed them whole.

I thought back to those days. Days when I had to navigate a minefield of friends and enemies, keeping my distance from the madness but never quite escaping its shadow. I hadn't joined, but I had been close enough to feel its pull. My father wouldn't have known the difference, though. To him, I was just another disappointment.

I shook my head, snapping out of the memory. "I had a lot of friends mixed up in that life, but I never joined," I said, voicing my thoughts.

Mmachi nodded, the corner of her mouth twitching into an almost playful smirk. "So, you were an honorary member, then?"

I let out a dry chuckle. "Some might say."

I could still feel the weight of her gaze, as if she was trying to unravel me bit by bit. And maybe she already had. The past was a knot I hadn't planned on untangling today, but there it was, laid out on the table in front of me. And she wasn't finished yet.

"With friends like that, you must have connections in that world, right?"

Her question wasn't casual. It had a certain edge to it, like she was looking for something specific, testing the waters. She was gathering intel, trying to see if I was the right man for whatever twisted game she was playing. By now, I'd had enough. Whatever she was after, it didn't involve me.

I stood abruptly, my patience worn thin. "I'm leaving. I don't know what this is, but I'm not interested."

Mmachi didn't flinch, didn't even bat an eyelash. She just watched me, perfectly composed, as if she had expected this reaction all along. That damn smirk never left her face. I took a few steps toward the door, determined to put her and this whole bizarre situation behind me, but my momentum faltered. I couldn't remember where I'd left my shoes. Were they upstairs? The thought of trudging back up made my head spin. And where the hell was my phone?

That's when I felt her presence behind me. I hadn't noticed her move, but there she was, standing a few feet away, hands clasped in front of her like some aristocrat watching the help fumble about. She was quiet, not threateningly, but like she held all the cards and was simply waiting for me to realize it.

She pointed across the hallway to a shelf, and there, in a transparent basin, I spotted my shoes and a few other things. My belongings, neatly arranged like I'd been staying at some hotel.

I walked over and retrieved the basin, sitting on a nearby chair to put on my shoes. As I tied the laces, she spoke.

"I heard a story about you," she began, her tone casual, like she was recalling some distant gossip. "When your father passed, your aunts were... eager to claim a share of his property. You couldn't attend the funeral because of your immigration status, no doubt. But, somehow, you got them to leave your mother alone. All the way from here. How did you manage that?"

Her words made me pause, fingers frozen over my shoelaces. I hadn't thought about that mess in years, hadn't wanted to. Funerals in my culture are complicated affairs, especially for someone of my father's standing. They're supposed to be about honoring the dead, but more often than not, they're about power, control, and inheritance. My aunts saw my father's death as an opportunity, a chance to lay claim to things that didn't belong to them. It's common. Relatives swoop in, try to take advantage of the grieving family, see what they can walk away with. And my aunts? They were relentless.

I finished tying my shoes, stood up, and looked at her. "They thought I was a kid they could push around," I said, standing a little taller. "My absence emboldened them. All I did was show them they were wrong."

Mmachi raised an eyebrow, her curiosity piqued. "How?"

I gave her a slight smile, one that didn't quite reach my eyes. "I'd rather not talk about it."

She nodded slowly, a look of understanding crossing her face. She didn't need the specifics, and I would not give them. But I'd learned early on that everyone has secrets, especially family. And in a culture like ours, where reputation was everything, skeletons were leverage.

"Impressive," Mmachi said. She stepped closer, her eyes locked on mine. "You investigated insurance fraud for your previous employer. And from what I hear, you were effective. You have a knack for uncovering things, don't you?"

I didn't respond. There was nothing more to say.

I gathered my things and moved toward the door, determined to get out. For the first time since this strange encounter began, I heard something in Mmachi's voice that hadn't been there before: unease.

"I'd like you to find someone for me," she called out.

I didn't break stride, didn't hesitate as my hand wrapped around the doorknob. "I'm not interested," I replied flatly.

But her next words cut through the air like a serve in a tennis match, swift and sharp. "I'll pay you fifty thousand dollars!"

I froze. Fifty grand. That was more than I made driving in a year, hell, in two years if you factored in the dry spells. For a moment, the doorknob felt slippery under my palm. The response I had lined up died in my throat, replaced by a knot of indecision. I tried to keep my hand steady, tried to keep my resolve intact, but my mind suddenly flooded with the weight of that number. *Fifty thousand dollars.*

What that kind of money could do for me... for my family. Pay off debts. Help my mother with the medical bills she was always too proud to talk about. It would get my sisters, Nkechi and Amarachi, out of the financial hole they had been trapped in since my father died. That sum of money was freedom, the kind of freedom I hadn't had in... well, ever.

I gripped the doorknob tighter, trying to shake off the pull of it, but Mmachi's voice slipped in again, more piercing than before, almost like she could sense the conflict brewing inside me.

"I represent everything you detest," she said, calm and calculating. "So naturally, you're conflicted."

Her hand rested on mine gently, as if this was all just some polite negotiation over tea. She gave the knob a slight twist, opening the door for me like she was granting me permission to leave.

"Go," she said smoothly. "My driver will take you anywhere you want to go. But if you change your mind, if you decide you're willing to work for me, return by 6 PM tomorrow."

I stood there, staring at her outstretched hand. Her entire demeanor had shifted, not the untouchable, powerful figure she'd been just minutes ago. There was something else in her eyes now. Something closer to desperation. She was offering me a way out, but I couldn't shake the feeling that she wasn't as calm about it as she wanted me to believe.

"If I don't see you by then," she said, that smile returning to her lips, "it was a pleasure chatting with you, Mr. Dozy."

I hesitated for a moment before taking her hand and giving it a reluctant shake. She gave me a slight nod, and I stepped outside, the cool air hitting me like a splash of cold water. A silver Chrysler waited at the curb, and the driver leaned over the passenger seat, glancing back at me through the rearview mirror.

"Where to?" he asked.

I didn't answer right away. My eyes stayed fixed on Mmachi, who was still standing by the door, watching me leave. But her mask had slipped. She didn't look powerful or untouchable anymore. She looked... helpless. The sight of her like that unsettled me in ways I couldn't explain.

"Great Hope Road," I muttered, tearing my gaze away from her.

CHAPTER 4

Great Hope Road in Southeast D.C. wasn't the kind of place you'd see on a tourist map. It wasn't the postcard version of Washington with its monuments and museums. No, this was the real D.C., where life was gritty, and people scraped by. Old brick buildings lined the streets, a mix of low-income housing and run-down storefronts with faded signs. Graffiti was everywhere, marking territory or just the passage of time. The streets themselves were worn; cracks and potholes filled patches that never seemed to hold.

When the driver dropped me off in front of my apartment building, I stepped out and looked up at the familiar, chipped facade. Humble would be putting it generously. The place had seen better days, if it had ever had better days to begin with.

Inside, my studio apartment was no different. Cramped, but functional. A 35-inch TV sat against one wall, with a PlayStation 4 hooked up underneath. I'd had my eye on a PlayStation 5 for a while, but that kind of luxury wasn't in the budget anytime soon. Across from the TV was my full-sized bed. Simple, with just enough room to stretch out after a long day. Next to it were a small fridge and a futon that doubled as a couch. Everything had its place, but nothing was more than what I needed. It was a far cry from the comforts I'd known when I was living with Jasmine, but there was no point in dwelling on the luxuries of the past.

Above the bed hung the only real decoration in the room was a family photo. My father, dressed in his military uniform, stood tall and proud, his aviator shades concealing eyes I'd learned not to challenge. My mother stood beside him, smiling a soft, contented smile that only mothers seem to master. My two younger sisters, Nkechi and Amarachi, flanked them, grinning as though life hadn't yet taught them its harsher lessons. And there I was, a beardless seventeen-year-old, standing at attention, unconsciously mimicking my father and subconsciously seeking his approval. It was a snapshot from a different time, a simpler one, when we still believed in the comforting illusion that everything was going to be okay.

I poured myself a glass of ginger ale; the bubbles fizzing angrily in the glass. I downed it quickly, letting the carbonation burn my throat, a sharp reminder that I was still here, still fighting. After setting the glass down, I dragged myself to bed, exhausted.

As I lay in bed, my mind ran in circles. Fifty thousand dollars. A year's salary in one shot. I couldn't pretend it didn't appeal to me. I'd spent my life trying to scrape by, trying to make sure my family back in Nigeria didn't suffer because of my mistakes. That kind of money would fix everything, or at least, a lot of things.

But it wasn't just about the money. It never was. Mmachi was a symbol of everything I despised. Corruption. Power wielded without consequence. She'd stolen from the Nigerian people, from my people. I hated her, hated what she stood for. And yet... fifty thousand dollars.

The more I thought about it, the more twisted my reasoning became. The money in her hands wasn't hers. Not really. It had been stolen, siphoned off through years of corruption. And technically... technically, that money was mine. Mine, my mother's, my sisters'. She'd taken it from the Nigerian people, and now I had a chance to take some of it back.

I turned over in bed, staring at the ceiling.

I wasn't a saint. I never pretended to be. Life had forced me to break rules, to bend the lines of morality when it suited me. But this? This was different. I hated corruption, hated what it did to people like me. But fifty thousand dollars...

"Technically, it's my money," I muttered to myself, the words sounding less convincing each time I said them.

I could feel the pull, the seduction of the offer. But was I willing to dive into Mmachi's world? Could I do it and still look at myself in the mirror afterward?

I'd barely closed my eyes before sleep took me. My dreams weren't peaceful. They were full of faces—my father's, my mother's, and Mmachi's—watching me, waiting for my decision.

— ◆ —

I woke up feeling more rested than I had in days. The hangover that had been gnawing at the back of my skull had mostly faded, leaving just a dull throb as a reminder of the night before. The guilt hit almost as soon as I sat up, memories of overpriced drinks and partying pushing their way to the front of my mind. I reached for my phone on the nightstand.

Sighing, I pulled up the money transfer app and sent a hundred dollars to my mother back in Enugu. It wasn't much, but it would help keep things steady for her and my sisters. The price of guilt.

Just as I hit send, my phone rang, buzzing in my hand. Gbenga. I stared at the screen for a second, debating whether I had the energy for whatever teasing he had lined up. Gbenga was a detective with the Metropolitan Police Department who I had worked with a few times as a fraud investigator. He was also an inveterate joker and party animal. Against my better judgment, I answered.

"Oga Dozy!" Gbenga's voice was already filled with laughter. "Bro, you won't believe this, but we were about to meet up with you on U Street last night when we saw you staggering like a madman, cozying up with some honey in a tight dress!"

I cursed under my breath. As if I needed a reminder of the mess I'd gotten myself into. "Nah, man. She just shared a taxi with me. I came straight home after that."

There was silence for a beat, then Gbenga's laughter burst through the speaker. "Yeah, sure, whatever you say. Anyway, you coming out tonight? The guys are trying to do a round two, and it's my last night off."

I rubbed my face, trying to shake the remnants of my hangover. "Can't. I gotta work. Driving Uber."

"Man, you're getting old!" Gbenga teased, but there was no real malice in it. He knew things had been tough for me. "Alright, catch you later."

The phone went silent, and I tossed it back on the nightstand, staring at it for a second longer than necessary. I needed to keep my head on straight, stay focused. And almost immediately, I picked it back up.

I swiped over to my email inbox, skimming through the new messages. Three emails from jobs I'd interviewed for in the past few weeks. I already knew what they said. The first few words were always the same: "*We thank you for taking the time to apply...*" followed by some pre-packaged excuse about being overwhelmed by "many *talented candidates*." Same crap, different day. I didn't even bother reading them all the way through.

I sat there staring at the rejection emails, my body sinking deeper into the bed. It had become routine at this point. The steady stream of "nos" and "unfortunatelys" that greeted me every time I dared to hope things might turn around. But routine or not, it still stung, like being punched when you were already down.

After a minute, I shook it off. Sitting around wasn't going to change anything. I tossed my phone onto the bed and stood up, making my way to the bathroom. A hot shower would do me good. Wash away the remnants of last night and whatever shame still clung to me.

The shower was quick, and the hot water did its job, loosening the tension in my shoulders. I scrubbed away the grime of the night, letting my mind clear under the steady stream. Once I was out, I got dressed in my usual. A pair of jeans, a t-shirt, and sneakers. Nothing special, just something comfortable enough for a day spent driving around picking up strangers.

I grabbed my keys, phone and wallet. The essentials for a day in the city. Then headed out the door. Uber driving wasn't glamorous, but it was what I had, and if I was lucky, I'd catch the brunch crowd. They were usually generous tippers, especially after a few mimosas. I needed the money more than ever now, especially with what Mmachi had thrown into the mix. *Fifty thousand dollars*. It was still ringing in my ears, tempting me like the devil's whisper.

I shook off the thought, focusing on the job ahead.

It started as a typical Uber Pool, always a recipe for chaos. First pickup was a quiet guy, mid-twenties, brown-skinned, earbuds jammed in. He mumbled, "Good morning," and sank into the backseat, eyes fixed out the window. I appreciated that. Silence was a gift on these rides.

The second passenger? Whole different story. White girl, brunette, maybe twenty-five. She opened the door and looked at me as if I'd personally offended her.

"You ordered a pool?" I asked, keeping my tone even.

Her eyes narrowed. "I didn't ask for a pool."

I checked the app. Her name and Uber Pool beneath it, plain as day. I could've shown her, but it wasn't worth the energy. I just nodded and waved her in.

"Right," I muttered, "not a pool."

She climbed in and started tapping furiously on her phone, sighing every thirty seconds like I owed her an apology. Earbud Guy stayed lost in his music.

I dropped him off without a hitch. The moment he was gone, she piped up again. "Can you, like, drive faster? I'm running late."

I bit my tongue. No point in arguing with someone who doesn't know how to read her own app. I got her to her stop. She stormed out without a word.

Good riddance.

The next few passengers were normal. A chatty brunch couple, quiet older guy. Things were finally settling when a message popped up from the platform:

We've received a report from a recent rider regarding a breach of protocol. Someone reported you had a "friend" in your vehicle. Rider has also rated you one star.

My blood boiled. It had to be her. She must've thought Earbud Guy was my friend, as if I drove around with buddies for fun while working.

I pulled over and called customer service. After an eternal hold, someone actually listened. I explained the trip, her attitude, the whole thing. Thankfully, they believed me. Said they'd clear the report.

Still, while I was parked outside a convenience store handling that mess, things worsened.

A D.C. cop approached. He was black, overweight, and looked like he'd rather be anywhere else.

"What are you doing here?" he asked.

"I'm an Uber driver," I said, hoping that would be enough.

It wasn't.

He squinted at the back window. "Where's your Uber sticker? That's required by law."

My stomach dropped. I'd forgotten to put it up that morning. I usually removed it when off-duty. In the rush, I'd completely spaced.

"Look, officer, I normally have it…I just forgot…"

He waved me off, already writing. "It's the law. Seventy-five-dollar ticket."

I took the ticket without a word, thanked him through gritted teeth, and watched him waddle back to his car. Then I logged off the app.

I was done for the day.

I drove a few blocks before pulling over again, away from the store, and screamed in the car. Just a guttural release of anger and frustration. Nothing was going right. Not the jobs. Not the driving. Not anything.

Then my phone rang again. This time, it was my mother.

"Alvan," she said, her voice warm and full of life. "Thank you for the money you sent. It will help with Amarachi's school fees this term."

I leaned back in my seat, running a hand over my face. "You're welcome, Mama."

"Are you alright? You sound… tired."

She always knew. I could never hide my frustration from her. "I'm fine, Mama. Just a rough day. I got a ticket."

"Oh no! How much?"

"Seventy-five dollars," I muttered, the words tasting bitter.

Her response was immediate. "Do you want me to return the money you sent?"

"No, Mama. Keep it. I'll be fine."

There was a pause, and I knew she wasn't convinced, but she let it go. "Okay, my son. But if you need help, don't be afraid to ask. God will provide."

I nodded, even though she couldn't see me. "Thanks, Mama. I'll be okay."

After she hung up, I sat there for a long moment staring at nothing. I couldn't shake the feeling that I was stuck. No matter how hard I worked, no matter what I tried, things always seemed to go wrong. Meanwhile, most of my friends—fellow immigrants—were thriving with their corporate jobs, big salaries and stability. They'd all found a way to make things work here in the States, while I was stuck driving an Uber and getting slapped with tickets for forgetting a damn sticker.

I looked at my watch.

An hour and a half left before Mmachi's deadline.

CHAPTER 5

I felt the bitter sting of shame gnawing at me as I drove up to Mmachi's house in Forest Hills, Northwest DC. It was the kind of neighborhood where even the air seemed cleaner, more expensive. The houses sat on sprawling lawns with manicured hedges, the kind that probably had gardeners trimming them twice a week. The trees lining the wide streets were tall, old, and full of history, providing shade to the Bentley or Range Rover or Tesla parked in nearly every driveway. This was the sort of place people pointed to when they talked about making it.

And here I was, driving in with my 2015 Honda Civic, which rattled like an old man's cough when I stopped at the gate. I couldn't shake the feeling of embarrassment. It wasn't just the car or the fact that I had returned to Mmachi, it was the speed with which I came back. I'd barely let a day pass. If it had taken me a week or two to mull over the offer, maybe I could've convinced myself that I was in control. But the tight grip of that fifty-thousand-dollar carrot dangling in front of me made me swallow my pride faster than I liked. Mmachi's timeline didn't give a damn about my ego.

I pulled into the driveway and killed the engine, sitting there for a moment longer than I needed to. The house loomed large before me, quiet and imposing. With a deep breath, I stepped out of the car, walked up to the door, and knocked. I knocked hard like a cop about to serve a warrant. I wanted to make it clear that I wasn't exactly thrilled to be here.

A few moments passed before the door swung open, revealing someone I hadn't expected. A young woman stood in front of me. What struck me first was the odd contrast. Her body was thin as a rail, almost childlike, with barely a chest to speak of. It was as if she were a teenager trying to play dress-up in clothes too mature for her frame. But her face, that was something else entirely. It was an almost perfect replica of Mmachi's, sharp eyes and all.

Her expression, however, was nothing like her mother's. She stared at me with clear irritation, her lips pursed like I'd interrupted something important. "Who are you?" she demanded.

She probably wasn't more than five years younger than me, but the arrogance in her tone made her seem like she was trying to establish some kind of dominance. All I could see was a sixteen-year-old brat talking down to me. My hand clenched, the disrespect grinding at my patience.

"You must be Mrs. Alex-Maduagu's daughter. Her *real* one this time," I said, my voice laced with sarcasm.

Her brow furrowed, and she raised an eyebrow. "Huh?" She clearly didn't catch the jab.

"Tell her Dozy is here," I said, trying to keep the tone of my voice from showing just how much this whole thing was pissing me off.

Her irritation only grew. "Look, Mister, I don't have to do anything," she snapped. Her accent was pure American, sharp and clipped in the way kids born and educated here sounded. Clearly, this bubble raised her far from the struggles her mother once knew. If she had ever been to Nigeria, I could bet she never saw past the luxury of Lagos Island or the polished streets of downtown Abuja.

Before I could say anything else, a voice floated from behind her. "It's okay, Adaora," came the calm, commanding tone of Mmachi.

Adaora—so that was her name—glanced over her shoulder as her mother approached from the hallway. I could feel a shift in the air. Mmachi's presence had that effect. This time, she chose a different style of clothes. Gone were the regal fabrics, the traditional lace and head wrap that had made her look like a queen. Soft beige layers wrapped around her today. A shawl was draped over her shoulders; she wore loose-fitting pants, a beret, and round sunglasses perched on her nose. If I hadn't known better, I would've thought she was merely some well-to-do D.C. local stepping out for a stroll.

"Good to see you again, Mr. Dozy," she said, a small smile playing on her lips as she eyed me. "I was just heading out. You're welcome to join me."

The casual invitation startled me. "Join you? Where?"

"I've got a few errands to run," she said, glancing at her watch. "I'll bring you back here when we're done."

I hesitated, my eyes drifting from her to Adaora, who was still standing there, arms crossed, glaring at me like I was an intruder in her world. Everything about this felt off, as if I were being pulled deeper into something I couldn't fully see yet. But then I thought about the fifty thousand dollars again. That kind of money didn't just fall into your lap every day. And besides, there were still things I needed answers to.

I nodded. "Alright. I'll come with you."

She smiled again, wider this time, and gestured for me to follow.

This wasn't the same car that had dropped me off earlier. No, this was something else entirely. A white Lincoln Aviator, gleaming under the sunlight, looked like it had just rolled off the assembly line. It was the kind of car you didn't just drive, you *arrived* in it. The sleek curves and chrome accents gave it an air of understated luxury, the kind that whispered wealth rather than screamed it. The paint was flawless, catching the light just right, and the massive grille at the front made it clear that this was a vehicle meant to command attention on the road.

The interior matched the exterior's promise. Cream leather seats, soft to the touch, and the smell of newness clung to the air, a mix of rich leather and something crisp and clean. Everything about it was pristine, from the polished wood trim to the state-of-the-art touchscreen that seemed to float on the dashboard. It was the kind of ride that made you sit up a little straighter, conscious of the comfort, the wealth it represented. A far cry from the rattling Honda I'd rolled up in.

"Do you feel you always have to rub your stolen wealth in my face?" I asked.

Mmachi sat next to me, unbothered, the same smug look playing on her lips. "Have you ever stopped to think that maybe the charges against me were entirely fabricated? That this wealth you despise so much is the fruit of my hard labor?"

I didn't answer right away. The evidence presented against her by the current administration and the Economic and Financial Crimes Commission (EFCC) had been damning, no doubt. They had paraded her as the face of corruption in the previous administration. Billions of naira had gone missing under her watch, linked to fraudulent oil deals, shady allocations of crude oil contracts, and accusations of laundering money through luxury real estate purchases in London and Dubai. They had accused her of siphoning off funds from government projects, sending money via offshore accounts, and using public wealth to fund an extravagant lifestyle. Private jets, designer clothing, luxurious properties, and a rumored $20 million worth of jewelry.

But I knew, everyone knew, that there was more to it than just her guilt. There was sexism, plain and simple. She had been the convenient scapegoat. Plenty of her male colleagues kept their jobs or were shuffled into cushy positions. Sure, there had been arrests and dismissals, but not like what they did to Mmachi. Still, it didn't absolve her. Just because the system was rotten doesn't mean she wasn't part of it.

"As far as I know," I said, breaking the silence, "you're all the same. Even if they threw you to the wolves, it doesn't make you innocent. Now, who do you want me to find?"

Mmachi sighed, more out of boredom than frustration, and gestured to her driver. He was an attentive man, too attentive. He'd been watching us through the rearview mirror for most of the ride, like he was in on the conversation. Without a word, he reached into the glove compartment and pulled out a thick folder, the same one I'd seen earlier. He passed it back to me.

I opened it, and my eyes landed on a photograph. The man in the picture was tall, maybe in his late sixties, clean-shaven, with thinning black hair that had more than a few strands of silver mixed in. I recognized him immediately.

"Your husband," I said. "Admiral Alex Maduagu, retired."

Mmachi nodded, her face calm, emotionless. "He left for Lagos four months ago. He said he was homesick and wanted to reconnect with old friends. Since no one implicated him in anything, he could move freely in Nigeria. But I haven't heard from him in six weeks. Then something happened. Look at the next document."

I flipped the page, and what I saw made my stomach tighten. It was a handwritten note:

Alex Maduagu is secretly getting married to someone else on September 7th.

"What the hell?" I muttered under my breath.

"Craziest thing," Mmachi said, her tone dry. "No one seems to know who this girl is. Not his friends, not his family. Now, my lawyer reached out. He's suing for divorce."

"And who sent this note?"

She shrugged. "Anonymous. Someone dropped it off at my lawyer's. He handed it to me with the divorce papers."

I glanced at her, expecting to see some sign of emotion. Anger, betrayal, something. But her face remained cold, almost calculating. The divorce wasn't what hurt her. What bothered her was how it all looked. It was a blow to her pride, an insult to the image she'd built, even in exile.

As I stared down at the note, something clicked. Slowly, the realization crept in, heavy and unwelcome. "Wait a second," I said, shaking my head. "I can't do this. You want me to go back to Nigeria."

Mmachi's lips curled into a knowing smile, as if she'd been waiting for this moment. "All expenses paid," she said, her voice almost singsong. "And a generous stipend on top of the fifty grand I already promised."

She made it sound simple. But it wasn't simple. It was far from it. I couldn't return to Nigeria. Sure, I wanted to make

47

enough money to bring my family down here, to get them out of that mess. But I couldn't go back myself. Not now. Not ever.

I started to shake my head, my thoughts racing, but before I could say anything, Mmachi let out a chuckle. A knowing, almost taunting laugh.

"You have concerns about Chief Obidi," she said.

The world around me seemed to freeze. My jaw clenched, and I turned to her, my eyes locked on hers, anger bubbling just beneath the surface. My voice dropped low, cold. "How the fuck do you know about Chief Obidi?"

She raised a hand, almost as if she were calming a child. "I don't know much. Just enough. I know that you had a... disagreement with Chief Obidi. And that your father had to get you out of the country immediately."

Chief Obidi. The name was like a corkscrew in my chest. I hadn't even allowed myself to think about him in years. He was no mere man of power, he was a kingmaker. A true political godfather. The kind of man who controlled cities, who had politicians and business executives at his beck and call. He was untouchable, with connections in every corner of Nigeria, and even beyond. And I had crossed him.

I swallowed hard, my mind racing with memories I thought I'd buried. "So, you know why I can't return to Lagos. Why I can't return to Nigeria," I said.

"From what I understand, Chief Obidi controls Southeastern Nigeria, not Lagos."

"His connections stretch much further."

Mmachi nodded, her face betraying nothing. "Normally, I'd find someone else. But you're the only person with the kind of connections I need. You know the dark side of Lagos, the underworld, the people who move without being seen. But you know the other side as well. Being the son of a renowned General afforded you those privileges. Alex hides somewhere between those worlds.

"That doesn't make any sense," I shot back. "You clearly have competent investigators on your payroll. Why do you need me?"

She leaned forward, her gaze locked onto mine. "Because you're more competent than any of them, Dozy. The dirt you dug up on your aunts, not even the EFCC could manage that. You may not be a cultist, but you're connected in ways that I appreciate. Members of rival cults don't just 'respect' anyone."

I felt the weight of her words settle on me, heavy and suffocating. She wasn't wrong. I had always managed to keep myself at arm's length from the worst of it, but that didn't mean I hadn't dipped my toes in. I knew how to navigate the dangerous waters of Lagos' underworld, how to get things done when others couldn't. But going back meant risking everything. Crossing Chief Obidi once had been a mistake. Going back would be suicide.

But fifty thousand dollars.

I stared at the folder in my lap, my mind spinning with possibilities, fears, and, most dangerously, temptation.

CHAPTER 6

I leafed through the remaining documents in the folder, each page a window into the tangled world of Admiral Alex Maduagu. The documents listed his known associates, especially the ones Mmachi claimed she knew little about. People who had slipped into her husband's orbit in recent years. They ranged from fellow ex-military men to shadowy business figures with enough wealth and influence to shape the country's future behind closed doors. There were names I'd heard of and names I wished I hadn't.

Admiral Alex Maduagu was a figure of renown in Nigeria. A former military governor, his reputation had been defined by one pivotal moment—the time he openly defied Sani Abacha, the man whose name still sent shivers through the spines of anyone with even a passing knowledge of Nigerian politics. Abacha, the patron saint of corruption, set the gold standard of malevolence by which all other corrupt officials were measured. Alex Maduagu had called him out publicly, an act of defiance that had sealed his fate.

The blatant corruption that ran rampant during Abacha's regime had deeply disturbed the Admiral, but it was the murder of Ken Saro-Wiwa that finally broke him. After that, he could no longer sit idly by, watching the country choke under Abacha's iron fist. Speaking out had cost him his position as governor and landed him in jail, where he languished until Abacha's sudden death from a heart attack. He often remarked, with a grim sense of humor, that Abacha would've had him executed if not for his cardiac arrest. The man had escaped death by the skin of his teeth.

His defiance earned him the respect of the people. In a country where history forgave the right kind of mistakes, people conveniently erased whatever wrongs he might have committed during his time in government. Unlike many of his peers, retired military men turned self-proclaimed champions of democracy, Alex Maduagu stayed far from the political arena. He'd left all of that to his ambitious wife, who had her own aspirations in that realm.

I didn't know enough about the man to form a solid opinion of him. But I could respect his desire to stay away from the circus that is Nigerian politics. Anyone with sense would.

I glanced over at Mmachi, who sat beside me with the calm, calculated composure of someone who had already considered every angle. "Tell me about him," I said.

She didn't respond immediately. Instead, she turned to the window, watching the world outside in silence. Finally, she spoke. "Alex is a good husband and father. But... last year, he had an epiphany."

"What kind of epiphany?"

She sighed, the sound heavy with the weight of untold memories. "Alex found God."

"Oh." It was all I could manage. I'm a Christian, too, but in Nigeria, religion wasn't always a good thing. My father used to call it the ultimate piece of corruption. Truly, an opium for the masses.

"After the reports about me came to light, he couldn't see me the same way anymore. He believes that I failed God." She hung her head slightly, wiping what seemed like a tear, though I couldn't be sure because her face was still turned to the window.

There was a long pause, and I sensed the conversation had hit a sore spot. Time to change the subject. "Do you have any property in Lagos?" I asked. "Anything the EFCC hasn't touched?"

She hesitated, a flicker of reluctance crossing her face, but she seemed to understand that being upfront with me was in her best interest. "Yes," she finally said. "A bungalow on Banana Island."

Banana Island. Of course. Only the wealthiest of the wealthy had homes there, tucked away in one of the most exclusive spots in Lagos.

"Does anyone live there?" I asked.

"My caretaker stays in the boy's quarters. Otherwise, it's free."

"Good," I said, still flipping through the documents, taking in the details. "I'll stay there for the duration of my investigation."

Mmachi nodded, as though this was all part of some business transaction. It probably was to her.

"What are you hoping for, exactly?" I asked. "I can't guarantee I'll be able to bring him back."

She scoffed, her expression tightening. "I don't care what you have to do. Make him come back. And make sure this travesty…," she pointed at the wedding note in my lap, "…does not happen."

I glanced out the window. We were cruising down Wisconsin Avenue, the familiar storefronts and tree-lined sidewalks blurring past us. "Why chase after a man who doesn't want you? You're a beautiful woman. I'm sure you could find some young fool to satisfy you."

She raised an eyebrow at that, a smirk forming on her lips. "You think I haven't?" She pulled off her sunglasses, her eyes locking onto mine with an intensity that shut me up quick. "Alex cannot divorce me. My reasons are my own. He knows I won't let him, so he's hiding. Your job is to find him and stop him."

There was something in her voice now, an edge that told me not to push. I was somewhat interested in understanding the actual reasons, but I wasn't gullible. I knew when to leave things alone. Her gaze pinned me to my seat for a moment longer before I finally nodded.

"I'll see what I can do," I said, glancing again at the note. The date caught my eye. September 7th. I had two weeks to find the old simp and somehow stop this.

I looked up from the folder and realized we were looping back toward Forest Hills. The well-manicured lawns and opulent homes reappeared, and I raised an eyebrow. "I thought you had errands?"

Mmachi smiled. "I didn't have any errands. I just needed to get out of the house. Adaora is nosy, and I prefer that she doesn't know what's going on."

Of course. Everything with Mmachi was planned down to the last detail. That didn't surprise me. As we pulled up beside my car, Mmachi reached into her bag and handed me a small card. Her full name and number were scribbled on it.

"Send me your banking details. I'll transfer your allowance today," she said, her tone businesslike. "And, Dozy?" Her voice softened, almost conspiratorial. "Be discreet. No one can know I sent you."

I nodded, taking the card from her hand, feeling the pressure of the task settling onto my shoulders. Fifty thousand dollars. A house on Banana Island. And the burden of a mission that seemed doomed from the start.

I stepped out of the car, stretching slightly, and before I could take a step toward my Honda, Mmachi's window slid down with a soft hum. She leaned slightly toward me, her face still holding that same unreadable expression.

"Tell me," She began. "That accent of yours. It's not quite American, but it's also not fully Nigerian either. I wonder how discreet you can be if that makes you stand out."

I smirked, feeling the challenge in her tone. She thought she had me pinned. "Don't worry," I said, and without missing a beat, I slipped effortlessly into a different voice, my accent now perfectly mimicking the slightly Igbo-tinged yet educated English of a middle-class Nigerian. "I can code-switch faster than a politician at a campaign rally."

That did the trick. Mmachi laughed, a genuine sound that I hadn't expected. It was sharp, and knowing, the kind of laugh that told me she appreciated a good game of wit. "Of course you can. I love our people," she said, still smiling as her amusement lingered. "One last thing, Mr. Dozy, don't trouble yourself over Chief Obidi. Although no one will know you work for me, I might still be able to whisper in a few ears and keep him off your scent. So, don't worry, my boy."

I watched her closely for a moment, taking in the brief glimpse of levity before it vanished behind her usual composed mask. She gave me a final nod before her driver eased the car forward, the quiet hum of the engine punctuating the space between us as they pulled away. The Lincoln Aviator disappeared down the tree-lined street, fading into the sea of wealth and privilege that was Forest Hills.

What did she mean by that? Did she really believe her influence, even in exile, could keep a man like Chief Obidi at bay? I shook my head. No matter what she said, I was going to worry. My only hope was to find the Admiral and get out before Obidi even caught my scent.

Hopefully.

CHAPTER 7

The flight was long and uneventful, just the way I hated it. I've never been one for flying. Doesn't matter how many times I traveled as a kid, or how many stamps filled my passport, that sense of anxiety never left. Something about being packed in a steel tube at 30,000 feet, with no control over my fate, didn't sit right with me. It's the certainty that if something goes wrong, you're done for. No miracle landing, no hero story. Just a nosedive into oblivion.

So, I did what I always do. I downed a hefty dose of ZzzQuil and forced myself into unconsciousness. Sleep is better than panic. By the time the plane landed at Murtala Mohammed International Airport, I was well rested, but I was nursing a stiff neck that felt like someone had taken a wrench to it.

I never pack much, just a small carry-on and one piece of luggage. Traveling light makes it easier to move, to disappear if needed. As soon as I stepped off the plane, I slipped on my sunglasses and started scanning the scene. The airport was as chaotic as I remembered, maybe worse. The vultures were out in full force. Hustlers circling the entrance like predators eyeing fresh meat, ready to pounce on any naïve foreigner stupid enough to make eye contact. I could hear them before I saw them, the endless calls of "Oga, you need taxi?" and "Oga, I fit help you carry your bag?"

I swatted them off like flies. "No need," I muttered, waving them away, but the closer I got to the exit, the more intense their offers became. One guy even grabbed my luggage, trying to strong-arm me into letting him carry it. I shot him a look that said all he needed to know, and he backed off quickly enough.

Finally, I found my Uber parked just outside, blending into the cacophony of the street. I slipped into the backseat and exhaled. But the second we hit the road, the scorching heat of Nigeria overwhelmed me like a wave. It was dry, oppressive, the kind of heat that clung to your skin and made you want to shower three times a day.

As the car pushed through the streets of Lagos, the memories started to flood back. It had been over ten years since I last set foot in this city, but nothing about the mainland had changed. The roads still had potholes deep enough to swallow a compact car, and the smell of petrol fumes and dust thickened the air. Street vendors lined the roads, hawking everything from bottled water to fake designer bags. It was the Lagos I remembered—dirty, chaotic, and alive with a kind of energy that you either loved or hated.

But as we crossed from the mainland to the island, everything shifted. The grime gave way to glass-fronted buildings and wide, clean streets. The further we got onto the island, the more obvious the wealth became. This was the Lagos they showed in tourist brochures. Mansions behind tall gates, fancy restaurants, and private schools with names that sounded foreign enough to charge obscene fees.

It was a different world, one I didn't belong to but was forced to enter.

All I could think about was finding my mark and getting the hell out of this godforsaken country. Truth was, despite the circumstances of my departure a decade ago, I'd always planned to leave Nigeria. The chaos, the rot, the unrelenting grind of it all, it had worn me down. I'd tasted life in a place where systems actually worked, where traffic lights meant something, and a man could trust the ground beneath his feet. Coming back here, it was like waking from a dream into a nightmare I'd been trying to forget.

Every little thing annoyed me. Cars barreling down the wrong side of the road like death was offering discounts. Others weaving without warning, no lane discipline, no signals, no damned rules. Sometimes the lines weren't painted on the asphalt, so who knew where the lanes were? The whole place moved to a rhythm I couldn't follow anymore.

I told myself I was just passing through. Get in, find the target, disappear. But deep down, I knew it wasn't just about the job. I wanted out and back to the cold, efficient sterility of the West. Back to anonymity. Back to peace.

Finally, we pulled up to Banana Island, Lagos's most exclusive neighborhood. It was quiet. Too quiet. The kind of place where money bought you security, privacy, and peace. The house wasn't huge by Banana Island standards, but it was more than enough. A small bungalow, but no less ostentatious. High walls surrounded the property, topped with barbed wire, the universal sign of wealth in Nigeria. No one rich enough to live in a place like this left protection to chance.

I stepped out of the Uber and knocked on the gate, my knuckles rapping against the iron with a deliberate force. It was a good minute before I heard movement on the other side.

"Who be dat?" a gruff voice called, irritated, like I'd interrupted something important.

I glanced over my shoulder, still cautious, making sure no one was lurking nearby. Lagos wasn't a place where you could afford to relax, not even for a second.

"Na the person wey you dey expect," I replied in Pidgin.

There was a pause, then the sound of hurried footsteps and metal scraping. The gate clanged open, revealing a tall man dressed in a slacked wife-beater and a pair of threadbare three-quarter shorts. His skin clung to his bones, and the broken smile on his face told me everything I needed to know about how long he'd been working here.

"You're welcome, sah! My name na Akaneme. Welcome oh," he said.

I nodded, not in the mood for small talk, but I managed a polite smile. I always made it a point to be polite to working people. "Could you please help me with the bags, Akaneme?" I asked, keeping my tone steady but respectful.

The caretaker, Akaneme, scrambled to grab my luggage with an exaggerated eagerness to please me. Meanwhile, I scanned the compound, taking everything in. The place was well kept, but I wasn't merely looking for signs of luxury. I was looking for anything out of place. Security cameras, hidden microphones, anything that could suggest Mmachi was keeping tabs on me. I might've been working for her, but I didn't trust her. Not for a second.

Akaneme led me to the entrance of the house, his broken smile still plastered on his face, a mask of servitude worn too long. I followed him in silence, taking mental notes as I went. The house itself was exactly what I expected: comfortable, understated, but with just enough touches of luxury to remind you that you were on Banana Island and a world away from the chaos of Lagos.

As we walked through the main hallway, I noted the layout. Spacious living room, modest kitchen, a few framed paintings of landscapes that were probably bought more for status than taste. It wasn't over the top, but it was comfortable. The kind of place you could lie low in, unnoticed, but still live well enough to forget the heat and noise outside.

By the time Akaneme led me to the bedroom, jet lag had begun creeping up on me, the weight of the long flight pulling at my limbs. The moment I saw the queen-sized bed, any thought of planning or scanning the streets for the Admiral went straight out the window.

It had been years since I last set foot in Lagos, and I knew I'd need all the energy I could muster to chase down the Admiral's trail. But that would have to wait. Right now, sleep was calling, and I wasn't about to fight it.

I dropped my bag by the door, took one last look around the room—clean, simple, nothing out of place—before collapsing onto the bed. The soft mattress felt like a luxury after the cramped economy seat on the plane. The pillow cradled my head, and before I knew it, jet lag took full control despite my drug-induced nap on the plane. I barely managed to kick off my shoes before I was out cold, lost to the world.

— ◆ —

A hot shower after I woke up brought me back to the land of the living. The water beat down on me, washing away the jet lag and tension from the long flight. By the time I was out, toweling off, I felt like a new man. Seated on the edge of the bed, with nothing but a towel around my waist, I reached for the folder on the nightstand and started flipping through it again. I needed to make a call.

Osita. We went way back. He was my boy from university, someone who knew the streets and the players better than anyone. I dialed his number and held the phone to my ear, listening as it rang. When he picked up, all I could hear was the deafening noise of Afrobeat blaring in the background.

"Hello," he said, his voice so chill I could practically hear the smile on his face. I wouldn't be surprised if he had taken something. Osita always had a knack for "enhancing" his good mood.

"*Odogwu*, speak up," I said, mocking him.

"Wait..." He paused, and I could tell he was trying to place my voice. "Dozy?"

"Yeah, boy."

There was a sudden yell of excitement from the other end of the line. "Motherfucker! This is a Naija number! Tell me you did not just enter this country without telling your boy!"

A grin tugged at my lips. Typical Osita. He had always been the boisterous type, and he had no qualms about calling me out. We had a history; a good history. We met during orientation at university when we were both fresh-faced undergrads, clueless and navigating the ridiculous bureaucracy that defined Nigerian academic institutions.

I could still remember the scene that sparked our friendship. There we were, standing in line at the registrar's office, trying to get our documents signed. The woman behind the desk was typical of the old ladies who occupied administrative roles: miserable, with a permanent scowl on her face, and taking her frustration out on the timid freshmen who needed her approval. She barely glanced at me before barking, "Oga, buy me banana first."

"Ba... banana?" I stumbled. It caught me off guard. I had just come back from the UK, where I'd gone to secondary school, and I wasn't used to the casual bribery that was a part of everyday life here. It sounded like a joke at first, but when I realized she was dead serious, I froze.

That's when Osita, who had been standing behind me, stepped forward. He was already hardened in ways I couldn't understand. A Enugu boy, recruited into a campus cult straight out of secondary school. The swagger and confidence that came with it were undeniable. He walked right into the office, sat on the edge of the desk, and looked directly at her.

"To hell with your banana," he said. "Give the man what he wants."

The woman didn't argue. She knew better than to cross someone with that kind of confidence. Anyone who could talk like that had power behind them. And just like that, I got my documents signed without buying anyone anything. We'd been tight ever since.

"Bro, I just got in. This was a last-minute trip," I said, pulling myself back to the present.

"Aha, my boy's making mad cream if he can just enter Lag like that without stress," Osita laughed.

I ignored that. While Osita and I were close, I didn't want him to know too much about my business with Mmachi. Some things were better kept under wraps. "I need to see you, man. I'm gonna need some help with something."

"That one no be wahala," he said, sounding as carefree as ever. "I dey club. Come through."

I could already imagine the scene. A packed nightclub with music blasting, neon lights flashing, and bottles popping. But I wasn't in the mood to be seen. "I'm gonna need to pop in incognito," I said.

Osita chuckled knowingly. "Relax, bro. Chief Obidi no dey Lag."

I felt a knot tighten in my stomach at the mention of that name. Chief Obidi was not someone you took lightly. "Osita, I don't want anyone to see me."

"No wahala," he said, sensing I wasn't joking. "I'll meet you out back. Just come to the club."

"Okay. Before I get there, see if you can find anything about Admiral Alex Maduagu."

"The old Admiral? Heard he's getting married again. To some woman nobody knows."

I smirked. Of course, Osita already had the inside scoop. He always did. His network stretched all over Lagos, from the high-rises of Victoria Island to the slums of Ajegunle. Information flowed to him whether he wanted it or not.

"I need to find him," I said. "Chances are, he's with this person. Can you look into it for me?"

Osita didn't hesitate. "I'll make a few calls. Come to the club, *alobam*."

I ended the call, my mind already working through the logistics of the meeting. I wanted to phone my mother and sisters too, to let them know I was back in the country. But I knew that wasn't smart. Not yet. The last thing I needed was my mother calling me every day, asking when I was going to visit. There would be time for family later. Right now, I had to focus on why I was here.

Work first. Handle Mmachi's business. Then maybe I'd have enough to make all their dreams come true. And mine too.

CHAPTER 8

I considered the blistering heat outside, the kind that stuck to your skin and made every breath feel as if you were dragging in fire. It was Lagos, after all. Heat was a constant companion. I settled on a white short-sleeved shirt, khaki chinos, and brown loafers. It was a look that made me feel like James Bond, minus the tailored suit and MI6 credentials.

Stepping out of the bungalow, I caught sight of Akaneme hosing down a pearl-white Range Rover Sport. The paint was flawless, the pearl white gleaming under the sun like a jewel. The headlights, sharp and predatory, angled slightly as if they were daring anyone to stand in their way. The 21-inch alloy wheels sparkled with a finish that made the vehicle seem like it was gliding on air rather than rolling on Lagos's pothole-riddled streets. It was the epitome of luxury meets power, an SUV built to conquer both urban jungles and actual ones.

Inside, I could only imagine the leather upholstery, polished wood trims, and the state-of-the-art infotainment system that would wrap any driver in comfort. This was the kind of car designed for people who lived above the noise and chaos of the streets. A mobile fortress for the elite.

At the sight of me, Akaneme gave his usual broken smile and bent his head slightly in greeting. "Good afternoon, sah."

"Evening," I corrected, but my eyes were still on the vehicle. I shook my head, realizing I was staring at yet another symbol of ill-gotten wealth. This car alone could feed entire villages, but here it was, another fruit of corruption parked in the driveway. There was no escaping it in this town.

"She tell me make I give you the keys to this car, oga," Akaneme added, handing me the keys like it was just another casual errand.

Akaname's pidgin caught me off guard. It was something in the accent. Too polished for someone in his line of work. Or maybe it was me. Too many years in the States turning me into the kind of snob who expected the hired help to sound rough and uneducated. The thought made me shudder.

"She told you to give it to me?"

Akaneme nodded, the broken smile never wavering. I looked down at the key in my hand, considering my options. I could take a taxi, keep a low profile. But driving around Lagos in a brand-new Range Rover Sport? The idea had its appeal. It wouldn't be discreet, sure, but vanity always had a way of winning over discretion.

As I admired the sleek lines of the vehicle, my mouth slightly ajar, something in my peripheral vision caught my attention. I glanced over toward Akaneme's quarters by the gate and noticed a figure lounging comfortably. At first, I thought it was a guy, given the casual, relaxed posture and the oversized t-shirt, but the soft curves, the fullness of her cheeks, and the quiet grace of her presence told me otherwise. She had dark, coiled braids that fell around her face, framing her with a casual confidence. The way she checked her wristwatch with an almost nonchalant air added to her laid-back style, highlighted by the loose-fitting jeans and red-and-white sneakers that complemented her effortlessly cool vibe.

I wasn't about to get in the middle of Akaneme's personal life, but I couldn't help but find his choice of girlfriend peculiar. She wasn't the type I would have pegged for him— her androgynous appearance, mixed with her casual style, made her stand out. But that's the thing with people; they're full of surprises.

I slipped into the driver's seat, the leather cool beneath me despite the oppressive heat outside. As I pulled onto the road, I rolled down the windows, letting the warm air whip through the cabin and enjoying the fresh air with sunglasses on, I headed toward the Lekki-Ikoyi Link Bridge, one of those moments where Lagos actually felt like a modern city. The bridge was sleek, its cables stretching up like fingers grasping the sky. Below, the water glittered under the relentless sun.

I headed for *The Diamond Ballot*, Osita's luxury adult entertainment club, tucked deep in the heart of Victoria Island. As I pulled into the neighborhood, the contrast was sharp. Victoria Island was a world away from the chaos of the mainland. Here, sleek glass buildings, high-end restaurants, and clubs lined the streets, catering to the city's elite. The Diamond Ballot was no different. It was subtle yet eye-catching, with the kind of lettering that whispered exclusivity.

I parked the Range Rover a street away, blending into the shadows as best I could. No point in showing off more than necessary. As I made my way to the back entrance, dodging dirty puddles and sidestepping trash bags that I had no interest in identifying, I heard the unmistakable click of a gun's hammer. I froze, the feel of cool metal pressing against my back and stopping me in my tracks.

I raised my hands slowly, my heart steady. "Calm down," I said. "No need to be hasty."

"This one dey speak English," said a voice from behind me. I didn't turn around. Sometimes it was best not to see the face of an *agbero*—street thug—who had decided to make you his next payday. Lagos was full of them, low-level criminals scraping by on fear and intimidation. "My friend, your money or your life!" he demanded.

I winced, more out of irritation than fear. Couldn't these guys come up with something more original? "Make I give you my wallet," I said. "Just dey calm. I no want wahala."

"Oya na," the agbero grunted. "Bring the wallet."

Slowly, I reached for my right pocket, but I wasn't about to hand this piece of shit anything. Instead, with a practiced motion, I turned sharply, grabbing his wrist and twisting. The gun dropped to the ground, and before he could react, I had it in my hand, the barrel now pointed at him. I stared at him for a second, both amused and angry.

And then, from behind me, a familiar sound. That of laughter, loud and uncontrollable. Osita stepped out of the shadows, doubling over like he'd just heard the best joke of his life. He slapped his thigh, stomping his foot as he tried to catch his breath.

"This guy!" Osita howled, still laughing. "Oh my God, I honestly thought you'd piss your pants!"

"You son of a bitch," I muttered, shaking my head.

He finally got himself together, wiping away tears of laughter, and pulled me into a tight hug. "Bro, you look good!" he said, still catching his breath.

Osita was just as lean as I remembered him, his frame wiry but solid. He had shoulder-length dreadlocks which was new to me. He was wearing a glossy suit, the kind of material that shimmered under the light, and somehow, he looked impervious to the heat, like he belonged in some swanky 70s nightclub, completely unfazed by the weather.

"Man, you haven't changed a bit," I said, shaking my head, grinning.

"Neither have you," Osita shot back, still smirking. "You can give Jack his gun back. He's part of my security team here."

The fake agbero, Jack, was already on his feet, smiling sheepishly, though I could see the surprise in his eyes. Clearly, he didn't expect me to disarm him so easily. I checked the clip of the gun. It was empty, just as I had suspected from its weight. I handed it back to him with a smirk.

"Don't mess with this guy!" Osita declared, laughing. "His popsi probably taught him how to kill before he could walk."

Osita led me through a back door and into his swanky office. The moment I stepped in, I was hit by the rich scent of chocolate, thick and lingering in the air. The air-conditioning was on full blast, and the soft hum was barely noticeable over the sound of my footsteps. Two girls were lounging on the couch, dressed in skimpy outfits, eyes glued to their phones, completely absorbed in whatever TikTok or Instagram video was holding their attention.

Behind Osita's desk, a large Biafran flag hung openly. It was bold red, black, and green stripes with a golden rising sun at the center. Right beside it were framed pictures of Emeka Ojukwu and Nnamdi Kanu, two symbols of the struggle for Biafran independence. Ojukwu, the military leader who led the secessionist state of Biafra during the Nigerian Civil War in the late 1960s, had become a martyr in the eyes of many Igbo people. And Kanu, the controversial modern-day figure and leader of the Indigenous People of Biafra (IPOB), had reignited the fight for a sovereign Biafran nation, though his methods and rhetoric had sharply divided opinions. Together, their images represented both the past and present of a struggle that refused to die.

I raised my eyebrows. "You're still on this Biafra thing? You know this is treason, right?"

Osita sucked his teeth, loud enough to startle one girl from her social media scroll. "Biafran thing? Bro, fuck Nigeria," he spat, waving his hand dismissively. "One day, we'll be free."

I shook my head. "You? Free? You've made your fortune in Lagos, Osita. My guy, you're freer than most."

He chuckled, walking over to a small bar in the corner of the room. He poured two glasses of Jack Daniels and raised a can of Coke, his way of asking if I wanted it mixed. I nodded, and he added the soda, handing me a glass.

"Dozy, my guy, the Igbo will always make money, no matter where he finds himself," Osita said. He jabbed a finger at the veins running down his arm, his tone rising with fervor. "Ọ dị n'ọbara anyị, Chidozie! It's in our blood to hustle. We thrive in adversity. We'll turn even a desert into a marketplace if we have to. And that's exactly what they hate about us. The fact that no matter what they throw at us, we find a way to rise, to build, to profit."

He leaned back in his chair, a self-satisfied smirk playing on his lips. "But let me tell you something, Dozy. This country doesn't want to see us succeed. Lagos? Abuja? They'll take your money, they'll let you play their game, but they'll never really accept you. And that's why we need Biafra. A place where we can be in control of our own destiny."

I almost rolled my eyes. It was hard to take him seriously when I knew just how deeply he'd planted himself in Lagos nightlife, profiting from the very system he claimed to despise. I took the drink and sat down in the chair opposite his desk. The leather was cool and soft, a small luxury in this hot city. I raised the glass to my lips. "You're still a funny man, Osita," I said, shaking my head. "You talk about Biafra like it's some promised land, but let's be real, it wouldn't be any better than the mess we've got now. You think independence will magically solve all our problems? The same kinds of leaders who are running Nigeria into the ground would be the ones in charge of Biafra. Corruption doesn't stop at tribal lines. Whether it's Abuja or Enugu, these politicians are all cut from the same rotten cloth."

I leaned forward, locking eyes with him. "You're smart enough to know that. Power corrupts. It doesn't matter if it's Igbo, Hausa, Yoruba, or anyone else. We'd just be trading one set of thieves for another."

Osita grinned, eyes glinting. "Ehen, and that's where people like you come in, alobam."

We both laughed, knowing damn well I wasn't the political type. I was more likely to rob a politician than run for office. The room settled into a peaceful rhythm as we caught up, the usual back-and-forth between two old friends who hadn't seen each other in years. The girls on the couch hadn't moved, still buried in their phones, completely ignoring us.

Eventually, the conversation shifted. I glanced at the girls, who had perfected the art of pretending we didn't exist, then turned to Osita, my expression more serious. "We need to talk."

Osita didn't miss a beat. He clapped his hands twice, signaling for the ladies to leave. They didn't need to be told twice. One of them shot an icy look at me as she passed by, pissed that I had interrupted her fun. I didn't care. I was here for business, not entertainment.

Osita lit a cigarette, took a deep drag, and leaned back in his chair. "Alex Maduagu?" he asked, blowing out a cloud of smoke.

"Have you found him?"

Osita raised an eyebrow, his interest piqued. "Must be important if you came back to Lagos while Chief Obidi is still breathing."

I clenched my jaw, grinding my teeth at the mention of that name. "Didn't you say I didn't need to worry about Obidi?"

Osita chuckled. "Relax, Dozy. I'm just messing with you. My man will call with information any moment now. Why are you looking for him?"

I shook my head. "I can't tell you."

Osita placed a hand on his chest, feigning offense. "Ah ah, Dozy! Is that what we've become? Secrets?"

I stood up, adjusting my shirt. "Two thousand dollars for the information," I said. "Somebody's eager to see him again. That's all you need to know."

Osita chuckled, his fingers drumming lightly on the table. "*Omo*, you're still a sharp guy. Fine. I'll ask no more questions."

I smiled, extending my hand. "My guy."

He shook it firmly. "How's your sister?" I asked, unable to resist the tease.

71

Osita pulled his hand back, his face twisting in mock irritation. "Forget about my sister, Dozy."

"She married now?" I asked, smirking.

"I said forget about my sister."

I laughed. "Come on, man. You act like I was the one breaking hearts in university. That was all you."

Osita pointed at me, grinning. "I don't care. Forget about my sister."

"Fair enough," I said.

Osita's phone buzzed and vibrated on the table, breaking the casual flow of our conversation. He glanced at the screen and, without looking at me, picked it up. His voice dropped to a hushed tone, the kind people use when they don't want you eavesdropping but know you will, regardless.

"Did you put him on the list?" he asked, then nodded a few times, grunting softly in approval. "Good man. He'll be there. Bye."

The satisfied grin that spread across his face told me something big was brewing.

"You got something?" I asked, trying not to sound too curious.

"The Governor's throwing a birthday gala for his wife this evening," he said, the grin widening. "It's on a yacht, just off the coast."

"A yacht?" I frowned, trying to picture the kind of floating palace the Nigerian elite would use for such a spectacle. "Where exactly? Marina?"

Osita shook his head. "Nah, further out. Lekki Phase 1, out of Five Cowries Terminal. And my informant tells me the Admiral is on the guest list."

I couldn't hide the surprise on my face. "Hold on. That can't be right. It's too easy. You sure he's going to be there?"

Osita's smirk remained, but his eyes narrowed slightly, studying me. "My man is certain."

A knot of suspicion twisted in my gut. Mmachi had given me the impression that her husband was in hiding, off the radar. Why would he show up at a public event? A high-profile gala, no less, with the Governor and all his cronies? This smelled fishy, but if the Admiral was there, I couldn't afford to ignore it.

"The earlier I find him, the better," I muttered, more to myself than to Osita. I turned to him. "You've got a way to get me on that yacht?"

Osita chuckled, leaning back in his chair, his grin now smug. "Already done, my guy. I had you added to the guest list. I'll have someone take you on the yacht tonight. Just be at the terminal by 9 PM. Impressive, no?"

I raised an eyebrow, genuinely impressed. "You don't waste time, do you?"

"I told you, man. It's in our blood to hustle. I'll get you in. You just gotta do the rest."

I gave him a nod and shook his hand. "On that note, I'll go drop in on someone else."

Osita threw his hands up in mock outrage. "Ah ah! Why now?" he said. "You no wan hang with your guy? Na wa o!"

I chuckled. "Trying to catch Oge."

His head jerked back, then he snapped his fingers as the realization hit. "Ah! I forgot she dey town." He grinned and nodded. "No wahala. Just make sure you swing by later tonight—after you finish finding your Admiral."

— ◆ —

The Lagos Oriental Hotel rose from the ground like a stack of money. I stepped through the revolving doors, the AC slapping the heat off my back. It was very nice in there.

I followed the signs up to the Skyline Terrace Halls, where a conference was already in full swing. A vertical banner stood by the entrance, all purple and white, screaming optimism:

SheIsEmpowered Conference 2022: Building Brighter Futures for the Nigerian Girl Child. Presented by The Nwa Ada Institute.

Underneath, in smaller print:

Keynote Speaker: Ogechi N. Nwankwo, Founder & Executive Director.

Oge.

I hadn't seen her since our NYSC days ended in a hurried blur. Now here she was, standing at the front of a packed hall, wrapped in a sharp purple blazer and loose-fitting trousers that said power without screaming it. She hadn't changed a bit. Sure, maybe a few lines here and there from the years gone by, but she was still Oge. The same warm eyes, the amiable smile that could break through even my worst moods. Hair braided and pulled back, glasses perched on her nose. Not the thick, nerdy kind she used to wear, but something sleeker now. She was speaking into a wireless mic.

"...we know education changes everything," she was saying. "And when we invest in young girls, we invest in entire communities. Today, I'm proud to announce a new scholarship program that will cover tuition and provide free laptops for fifty girls from underserved secondary schools across Nigeria. Because potential should never be limited by a where you're from or a gender."

The crowd clapped as if they meant it. I joined in, slowly and deliberate. She spotted me somewhere between her thank-you and her next breath. Her face lit up and not just with recognition, but with something deeper. Warmer. Like someone had just unzipped a piece of her past and draped it over the present.

She finished her remarks, let the applause wash over her one last time, then subtly pointed toward the glass doors at the back. I got the message.

Outside the hall, with the Lekki horizon somewhere behind the hotel's silhouette, she stepped into view and didn't say a word. Just walked straight into me and wrapped her arms around my waist like she never wanted to let go. I held her back, grounding myself in the moment.

"Dozy Agu, is this you or your ghost I'm seeing?" She murmured into my chest.

"Barrister," I chuckled, the sound low. "It's good to see you too."

She pushed back, blinking like a thought had just slapped her. "Wait oh, you didn't even tell me you were in Lagos?"

"I believe the whole point of a surprise, Oge, is *not* telling," I said, pulling back to take her in. "Look at you, still glowing like we're back on campus."

"Abeg, leave that matter," she said, swatting my arm. "I don old small."

"Old ke?" I shook my head slowly. "You're looking better than all of us."

She rolled her eyes, but the smile stuck around. Then, just as quickly, it softened. She gestured toward a pair of cushioned chairs lining the hallway, and we sat. Her tone dropped as she said, "I was really sorry to hear about your father. I reached out but... never heard back."

I nodded. "I'm sorry. I just…" I exhaled through my nose. "I couldn't talk. Not to anyone."

She placed a warm hand on my shoulder and gave it a light rub. "It must've been hard… not being able to attend."

I didn't answer. Grief was a language I still hadn't learned to speak. But she knew me well enough to change the subject. "So, what's been happening? Last I heard, you were still in the States, making money and living the American dream."

I shrugged. "It's not been easy, but I'm getting by."

"You don marry oyibo, abi?"

"I no even fit handle oyibo, abeg," I said. Jasmine did not count as oyibo, she was not white.

We shared a quiet laugh, the kind that bubbles up from somewhere deep, born from years of familiarity and understanding. It was the kind of laugh that reminded me how much I missed this. Missed her. Missed having someone in my life who didn't want anything from me but my company. No betrayal, no hidden agendas, no complications. Just pure, unfiltered friendship.

A woman with long dreads poked her head out of the conference hall and scanned the hallway until her eyes found Oge. "Excuse me, ma, we need you for the presentation."

Oge nodded and turned to me. "I've gotta get back. How long are you in town? We need to catch up."

"I'm not sure. But I'll reach out. Go do your thing, boss lady."

She hugged me again quickly and disappeared into the light of the conference hall.

I sat back in the chair for a moment, letting the memory of her linger like perfume in a warm room. Then I stood. Time to find Mmachi's man, and with any luck, convince him to go home.

— ◆ —

A few hours later, I was speeding across the water in a small boat, courtesy of one of Osita's many connections. The wind whipped at my face, carrying the scent of saltwater and gasoline as we cut through the waves, heading toward the yacht in the distance.

I glanced down at my outfit, a sharp suit Osita had lent me. A dark gray one, tailored to fit just right. No tie. He'd insisted on that. "You want to look like you belong," he had said, "not like you're trying too hard. The last thing you want is them thinking you're about to show them your CV." The suit was probably unnecessarily expensive, and it felt strange wearing it. But if I was going to play this game, I needed to look the part.

As we neared the yacht, my irritation began to simmer. The vessel was massive, gleaming under the evening sky like a beacon of excess. Gold railings, polished decks, and an upper level that looked more like a rooftop lounge than anything that belonged on the sea. It was the kind of floating palace that made it clear Nigeria's wealth wasn't in the hands of the people. No, it was right here, in the pockets of the political elite, who flaunted it without a care. Stolen money dressed up in champagne and caviar.

I gritted my teeth as the boat came to a stop beside the yacht, a crew member tossing a rope to secure us. A few guards at the entrance eyed me, their well-fed faces showing no interest in stopping anyone who looked like they belonged. I climbed aboard, feeling the weight of it all. This obscene display of power and wealth, these corrupt elites who had bled the country dry.

This party was a reminder of how far removed they were from the people they claimed to represent. I noticed how brazen this all was, how these men and women could parade their ill-gotten wealth without a care. And now, I was stepping into their world, searching for a man who supposedly didn't want to be found.

As I made my way across the deck, I took in the scene. Lavish doesn't even begin to describe it. Servers in crisp white uniforms floated around, carrying trays of expensive champagne and hors d'oeuvres I couldn't name. Guests, draped in designer clothes and dripping in jewels, laughed too loud, their voices competing with the soft jazz music floating through the air. It was a surreal kind of elegance, the kind that only the rich and powerful could afford to take for granted.

One server, dressed in a crisp white uniform with a spotless black bowtie, approached me, balancing a tray in his gloved hand. "Would you care for some suya, sir?" he asked.

I glanced down at the tray. This wasn't the suya I had grown up eating on the streets of Lagos. The suya I knew was served in makeshift kiosks, wrapped in old newspapers soaked in grease, with that unmistakable peppery, earthy scent, garnished with raw onions and tomatoes, rough around the edges but full of flavor. This version was something else entirely. A Western knock-off. Neatly skewered pieces of meat, onions, cucumber, and tomatoes presented like a kebab for the overly sophisticated. Leave it to the super-rich to gentrify even suya.

But despite my disapproval, I took one stick, curious about how this "posh" suya would hold up. I bit into the meat, expecting to be disappointed, but to my surprise, the familiar taste hit me. The smoky, tender beef, perfectly spiced with suya pepper, had just the right amount of heat. The pepper tingled on my tongue, intensifying with every bite, and the crunch of the onions added a satisfying texture.

It wasn't street-side suya, but damn, it was close. The spices danced on my palate, leaving a lingering warmth, and I couldn't help but nod in approval.

"My compliments to the chef," I said, turning to the server, who still stood by me as though he had been waiting for that very compliment. His face lit up with a grin and a respectful nod, pleased with himself.

I picked up two more sticks and made my way through the crowd, the taste of the suya still sparking a rare sense of pleasure. Maybe these high-class types knew a thing or two about flavor after all.

"I haven't seen you before," said a voice from behind. I turned and saw a woman in a striking red dress. She was tall, slender and elegant, her posture perfect as she stood before me with an air of confidence. Her skin was light chocolate, glowing under the soft lights of the yacht, and her hair, styled in loose waves, framed a face that could only be described as stunning. She wore minimal makeup, save for a bold red lip that matched her dress. Her eyes, dark and sharp, studied me as if I were an interesting puzzle. Her British accent was as polished as her appearance, betraying her expensive education, most likely somewhere in the UK. Maybe Cambridge.

"And I know everyone," she added, her lips curling into a playful smile.

I chuckled, adjusting my posture to appear elegant, more at ease. The last thing I needed was for anyone here to sense I didn't belong. "That's bound to happen when you're new in town," I said. I extended my hand. "Alvan Agu. My friends call me Dozy."

Her smirk widened as she took my hand, her touch lingering for a moment longer than necessary. "And how does one become a friend of Mr. Agu?"

I grinned, sensing the game she was playing. "You can start by telling me who everyone is," I replied smoothly. She arched her eyebrows, clearly enjoying the challenge. With a slight tilt of her head, she gestured toward the crowd. "Alright, let's start with the usual suspects," she said, leaning in a little closer. "That's Senator Bankole," she pointed to a short, stocky man in an expensive agbada, surrounded by a cluster of sycophants. "Powerful man, real estate mogul, owns half of Victoria Island. He's also rumored to have a mistress in every city from Lagos to London."

I glanced in the senator's direction, noticing how he commanded attention with a mere wave of his hand. He looked every bit the part of a man used to getting what he wanted.

"And over there," she continued, "that's Major-General Adebayo. He's with the military elite. He oversaw security during the last election. Some say he's the reason the current administration is still in power."

The Major-General stood stiffly, his uniform sharp and crisp, his medals catching the soft glow of the yacht's lights. His eyes darted around the room, as though he were on high alert even in the midst of luxury.

"Those two," she nodded toward a well-dressed couple sipping champagne by the bar, "are Kunle and Ijeoma Balogun. Nollywood royalty. If you've watched any Nigerian film in the past decade, chances are they either starred in it or produced it."

I had seen them before on magazine covers, in TV interviews, always playing the perfect power couple. Tonight was no different, with Ijeoma's glittering gown drawing eyes from all corners of the room.

As we moved through the sea of names and titles, she paused, her voice dropping to a near whisper. "And over there," she said, nodding subtly toward a group gathered at the far end of the yacht, "that's Mother C, the Prophetess."

I followed her gaze and spotted a woman in a flowing white gown, her hair covered in a matching head wrap. Even from a distance, there was something magnetic about her, the way she stood at the center of the group, commanding attention without saying much. She was older, perhaps in her late fifties, but radiated an energy that seemed to pull people in.

"The Prophetess?" I asked, intrigued.

"She's a preacher," the woman in red explained. "Has a massive following in Lagos, Abuja, and even London. People go to her for blessings, healings, miracles. You know the type."

I nodded. I definitely knew the type. In a country where religion and power often went hand in hand, it wasn't surprising that someone like Mother C had wormed her way into this elite crowd. There was always a prophet or pastor lurking around the edges of Nigerian wealth, offering divine favor for loyalty and, of course, hefty donations.

"Don't be fooled by the holy robes, though," she added, a hint of cynicism in her voice. "Mother C is as much a businesswoman as she is a preacher. Some say her prayers come at a price."

"I can imagine," I muttered, my gaze still fixed on the Prophetess standing across the deck. She exuded confidence and control, but I knew there was always more than met the eye. I turned back to the lady in red. "However, you missed someone."

She arched an eyebrow, playing coy as if she didn't know what I meant. "And who might that be?" I didn't answer, holding her gaze. After a beat, she gave a small, conceding sigh. "Fine." She stretched out her hand to shake mine, her grip firm. "Funlola Alakija. You can call me Lola."

I nodded. "Alakija? As in the hotels?"

"The same," she said with a smirk that spoke volumes about her wealth and connections. Her tone had an air of satisfaction, as if she enjoyed the fact that her family name carried that much weight.

She began talking some more, going on about herself, but my attention drifted. My eyes had found someone else. A woman was standing near the bar. Her long braided hair cascaded down her back, and she wore a sleek, form-fitting black dress that accentuated every curve. The dress was sleeveless, and the cut-out sections on the sides revealed just enough of her midriff to leave a lasting impression. There was something magnetic about her presence, and I had to know who she was.

"Who's that?" I asked, interrupting Lola mid-sentence. She paused, clearly annoyed by the shift in my attention.

She turned to look and then shook her head. "I don't know her. But she came in with Alex Maduagu."

The name hit me like a punch to the gut. The Admiral. I stood there, processing the information. Alex Maduagu. So this was the mystery woman he was going to marry. It had to be! Before I could approach her, a heavy hand landed on my shoulder. I turned and met the intense gaze of Admiral Alex Maduagu himself. He wore a white blazer over a black shirt, an effortlessly elegant yet commanding ensemble. He looked like a man who knew how to make an entrance, and judging by the look in his eyes, he had been expecting me.

"I see you've met my friend, Lola," he said. He turned to her with a smirk. "Were you aware that Mr. Agu here is related to Alvan Ikoku?" he asked. "I think they are cousins."

Lola's eyes widened in shock, her cultivated air of superiority slipping for a moment. "Shut up!" she exclaimed, her incredulity clear. "As in, the Alvan Ikoku?"

It startled me. How the hell did he know about that? My connection to Alvan Ikoku, a key figure in Nigeria's academic history, wasn't something I flaunted, and it wasn't common knowledge. Yet here was the Admiral, using it as if it were an ace up his sleeve.

The Admiral's gaze held mine, and I realized I was caught in something far more complex than I had anticipated. This job had turned into a game, and the Maduagus were playing it with a precision I hadn't accounted for.

"If you don't mind, Lola," the Admiral said smoothly, "Mr. Agu and I need to have a little chat."

Lola, still stunned, handed me a business card, winked, then drifted away without a word, leaving me alone with the Admiral. I wasn't sure what to say, but there was a part of me that felt oddly relieved. My task of finding him seemed to be moving along faster than I had expected.

"Admiral," I began, extending my hand, "it's a pleasure."

He didn't take my hand. Instead, he inspected me, his eyes scanning me from head to toe like I was some specimen under his microscope. He glanced around, checking for anyone else who might be with me, probably trying to figure out if I had an accomplice hidden in the crowd. Once he seemed satisfied, he turned his focus back to me.

"You don't want to be dancing with Mmachi, young man," he whispered. "She knows I've been onto her, and now she sends you. You don't look like the usual type of person they send after me."

I raised an eyebrow. "They? I don't understand, sir. Your wife heard about your upcoming wedding. My job is simply to find you and convince you to return home."

I glanced over at the woman by the bar, still curious. She hadn't turned to face me yet, and it was frustrating not knowing what she looked like.

The Admiral leaned in. "And how do you plan to manage that, Mr. Agu?"

His attempt at intimidation didn't escape my attention, but I wasn't one to back down easily. "With all due respect, sir, I've been hired to do a job, and I intend to complete it."

He glared at me for a few seconds, then let out a sharp laugh, his tone laced with bitterness. "I like you, Mr. Agu. You've got guts. But you're wasting your time. Mmachi is the worst kind of sinner. The kind that doesn't believe she's done anything wrong. I will not, cannot, go back to her. The only way you'll get me to return is if I'm dead." He straightened up, adjusting his shirt as if to emphasize his finality. "Now, if you'll excuse me, my fiancée and I have lost our taste for the sea."

I watched as he walked away. He approached the woman at the bar and placed a possessive hand on her lower back, whispering something in her ear. Then, for the first time, she turned and looked at me, her face stunning. She gave me a curious look before turning back to the Admiral, and together they left.

His reluctance wasn't unexpected, but I had a job to do. I wasn't about to walk away just because he said no. I needed to follow him, convince him, or at the very least, learn more about this fiancée of his.

As I made my way through the crowd toward the exit, three large men appeared out of nowhere, blocking my path. One of them, a hulking figure with a stern expression, grabbed my shoulder. "The Admiral says you're disturbing him," he said flatly.

Before I could respond, they grabbed me. One clamped his thick hand around my arm, and before I had a chance to protest, they were dragging me through the crowd. No one seemed to care, or maybe they just chose not to notice, too busy clinking glasses and murmuring over their exorbitantly priced champagne. I struggled, but it was useless. These guys were professionals, dragging me along as if I weighed nothing more than a sack of rice.

The crowd thinned as they pulled me toward the back of the yacht, past the glittering lights and laughter, until we reached a shadowy, secluded area near the rear deck. I could hear the water sloshing against the hull, and the smell of salt and seaweed filled the air. It was darker here, away from the bright lights of the party, the perfect place for something like this to go unnoticed.

Before I could even muster a full protest, they hefted me up by the arms, and with one swift motion, they threw me overboard. My stomach dropped, and for a brief second, time seemed to slow as I flew through the air. Then, cold water slammed into me, engulfing me with a splash. The shock knocked the wind out of me, and I thrashed in the dark, frigid sea, disoriented for a moment.

I kicked instinctively, fighting the panic that clawed at my throat. My arms worked through the water, pushing me to the surface. I broke through, gasping for air, coughing up saltwater. My heart pounded in my chest, but I managed to right myself, treading water. I looked up at the deck, seeing the silhouettes of the three goons still standing there, watching me with detached amusement.

"You fucks!" I shouted, struggling to keep my head above water. "What if I couldn't swim?"

One of them snorted, clearly entertained by my predicament. "Just get out of here, my friend!" he called down, laughing. They turned and disappeared back into the party, their job done.

I muttered curses under my breath, the cold seeping into my bones as I looked around for my next move. That's when I spotted the jetty not far off, illuminated faintly by the dim lights from the yacht. It wasn't close, but it was reachable. I forced my body to swim toward it, each stroke cutting through the cold, salty water, my muscles aching with every movement.

After what felt like an eternity, I finally reached the jetty, gripping the rough wooden beams and pulling myself up. My clothes clung to me, soaked and heavy, as I collapsed on the wooden platform, panting from the exertion. I lay there for a moment, catching my breath, the cool breeze off the water biting at my skin. My teeth started to chatter, but I willed myself to get up, shaking off the water as best as I could.

I was fuming. Those bastards had made me lose track of the Admiral, and now I'd have to start all over again. This wasn't how I'd expected things to go, but I had no choice but to regroup. I knew I couldn't let this lead slip away.

As I stumbled down the jetty, my wet shoes squelching with every step, I decided my next move. I'd go back to the Diamond Ballot to retrieve my car, dry off, and head to Surulere. According to the folder Mmachi had given me, the Admiral had family over there. There was no way I was giving up now. Not when I was so close. Fortunately, I had made a new contact.

The game was afoot.

CHAPTER 9

Funlola "Lola" Alakija was the kind of woman who didn't just host parties, she made them elaborately staged spectacles dripping with opulence and casual excess. The only daughter of Chief Babagbenro Alakija, a billionaire hotelier who treated Banana Island like his personal Monopoly board, Lola saw herself as Nigeria's answer to Paris Hilton, but without the scandalous sex tape and questionable movie career. That didn't stop her from reveling in the spotlight, though. Every gathering was an audition for her next headline-grabbing performance, and everyone in Lagos who mattered, or who thought they mattered, wanted an invitation.

Since meeting her on the yacht, I'd spent the night piecing together everything I could find about her. Socialite. Heiress. Serial Instagram poster. Her life was an open book, filled with flashy cars, exotic vacations, and a revolving door of high-profile companions. But under the glittering surface, I sensed there was more. That wink she'd thrown my way, the subtle brush of her fingers against my arm. It could've been meaningless flirtation, or it could've been something else. Something useful. She had connections, and more importantly, she seemed perfectly positioned to help me cross paths with Admiral Alex Maduagu again.

The next morning, I tested the waters, calling her under the pretense of thanking her for the previous evening. She didn't miss a beat, inviting me to a luncheon at her home without hesitation. She said that she had invited the Admiral, but she couldn't guarantee that he would come when I casually asked if he would be there. It wasn't the answer I wanted, but it was better than nothing. After a fruitless detour to Surulere the night before, where the Admiral's supposed family residence had turned out to be occupied by wary but polite strangers, Lola felt like my last solid lead.

Her home on Banana Island was the kind of place that screamed wealth with a megaphone. As I drove up the winding road, the Range Rover's tires crunching over the pristine gravel driveway, I caught my first glimpse of the house. It was a sprawling modern masterpiece, all clean lines and expansive glass, perched like a crown jewel amidst a lush green lawn. The main building stood tall, its white facade gleaming under the Lagos sun. Floor-to-ceiling windows framed a luxurious interior that I could only imagine was designed by someone whose idea of subtlety started at six figures in US Dollars.

I parked my car in the already crowded driveway and stepped out, adjusting my shirt collar as I made my way to the back where the music was coming from. The house was a palace disguised as modern art, and I was a fish out of water, walking into its gilded depths.

The backyard was a masterpiece of luxury, every detail meticulously crafted to dazzle. Two infinity pools cascaded gracefully into one another, their crystal-clear waters shimmering like liquid diamonds in the sunlight. Surrounding the pools was a sleek wooden deck, adorned with sun loungers straight out of a travel magazine. Beyond that, a carefully landscaped garden added vibrant splashes of green and bursts of color, the flowers in full bloom as though they'd been rehearsing for this very moment. In one corner, an elegant outdoor seating area shaded by a modern awning hosted a cluster of well-dressed guests, sipping champagne and trading gossip.

Lola greeted me at the entrance, her smile radiant, as if she'd practiced it to perfection. She wore a loose-fitting top that somehow still hinted at elegance, her hair swept up with an ornament that screamed money. "Dozy," she purred, extending a hand with manicured precision. "You made it."

"Wouldn't miss it for the world," I replied, keeping my tone smooth even as her gaze appraised me with the precision of a jeweler examining a diamond.

As I surveyed the opulent scene, my eyes flicked to the guests scattered about the garden. They were impeccably dressed, and their conversations were an intricate dance of shallow flattery and thinly veiled digs. Exactly the sort of atmosphere one could expect from an Alakija soiree.

"Your home is exquisite," I said, layering my words with a polished, Americanized accent.

"Thank you," Lola said, her grin widening with self-satisfaction. "I had it modeled after a villa I saw during a vacation in Portugal two years ago. Worth every penny."

I nodded, taking another casual glance around the garden as I searched for my target. Still, I kept the small talk alive. "I've never seen anything like it. The country feels far more Western than I remember."

She plucked a glass of champagne from a passing server and handed it to me. "How long have you been away?"

"Just over ten years," I said, savoring the smooth drink. Expensive, no doubt.

"Ah, yes. Things must seem very different to you," she said with a knowing smile. "Nigeria has come a long way since then. Our film industry is booming; our music dominates the global stage. Some of the greatest minds and personalities are Nigerian."

"Truly impressive," I replied, though my attention was divided.

"And then, of course, there's the other kind of Nigerian," she added.

I raised an eyebrow. "The other kind?"

Her expression shifted to something sharp, almost predatory. "Certainly not like you. You mentioned last night you were born here, spent part of your life in Lagos, and even went to school in Enugu. No, I mean the Nigerians who have never lived here. The ones who've maybe visited once or twice in adulthood, yet cling to the claim of being 'authentic.' The 'I'm Nigerian by way of insert random American city here' crowd. They talk about traditions they barely understand, using our culture for clout."

I chuckled, though it wasn't without incredulity. "This sounds personal."

She rolled her eyes dramatically, swirling the champagne in her glass. "When you move in my circles, you meet a lot of fake bitches like that. What can I say? It grinds my gears."

I listened as she spoke in her flawless RP English accent, her words laced with indignation. And there it was. The irony. Here was Lola, raised in the UK by her wealthy father, her polished British tones practically dripping with privilege, lamenting the inauthenticity of others. She'd spent more time sipping champagne in Kensington Gardens than walking the streets of Lagos, yet she had the audacity to decry others for not being "authentically Nigerian."

She came across like a spoiled child, upset that all the other kids in class had the same toy as her.

I didn't point it out, of course. I simply smiled, took another sip of champagne, and let the quiet hypocrisy linger between us as I searched for the Admiral.

I didn't find him, but arguably, I saw someone better. Turning to Lola, I tried to make my exit as smoothly as possible.

"Please don't neglect the rest of your guests on my account," I said with a polite smile.

Lola tilted her head slightly, her sharp gaze cutting through the pleasantries. "I've known everyone here for far longer than I've known you," she replied smoothly. "It only makes sense I chat with you a tad bit longer."

Her persistence was both flattering and unnerving. I quickly thought of an excuse. "In that case, perhaps you'd be kind enough to direct me to the restroom? I shall be with you again momentarily."

For a moment, suspicion flickered in her eyes, but she finally motioned toward a brightly lit hallway. "Down that way," she said, her tone clipped but gracious.

I bowed my head courteously. "Thank you."

As I walked away, I glanced back briefly. Lola had turned her attention to a small group of guests by the pool, her smile lighting up the conversation as effortlessly as her chandelier earrings caught the light. Seeing my opportunity, I detoured toward the elaborate makeshift bar set up on the patio. Its backdrop was a beautifully draped trellis with climbing plants and strings of fairy lights which gave it the look of a pop-up lounge at a luxury resort.

My focus, however, turned to a woman sitting at the bar. She held a colorful cocktail in her hand and was scrolling through her smartphone. Her vibrant pink dress, with its intricate texture and flattering fit, hugged her figure like it had been custom-tailored just for her. Her dark, sleek ponytail cascaded down her back, while the minimal ornament in her hair added a subtle touch of elegance. Her heels sparkled faintly under the warm patio lights, and a small, glossy handbag rested on her lap. Everything about her appeared polished, poised, and utterly magnetic.

She was undoubtedly the most beautiful woman in the room, but I was working. Distractions could cost me more than time.

I moved to stand beside her. "Hello," I said, keeping my tone casual but deliberate. "It's good to see you again."

The woman turned slowly, her eyes sweeping up and down my frame with an air of measured disinterest. Her lips curled slightly, acknowledging my presence but little else, before she turned back to her phone.

"I don't know you," she said flatly.

I leaned against the bar, undeterred. "Perhaps not. But I've seen you before. Last night, to be specific. You were with the Admiral."

Her gaze flickered toward me, quick and sharp, but she didn't fully turn. Instead, she spoke with a calm, practiced detachment. "Of course. You went for a late-night swim," she said, her tone coolly mocking. "How was it?"

I chuckled, appreciating her sharpness despite myself. "Definitely not the most pleasant experience. The water was filthy."

She finally turned to face me again, her lips curling into a subtle smirk. "I doubt you were supposed to enjoy the experience, Mr....?"

"Alvan," I offered.

Her smirk deepened, a faint glimmer of amusement flickering in her cat-like light brown eyes. "Is there something you wanted, Mr. Alvan?"

"A name would be nice," I said, leaning into my best Lothario impression.

She tilted her head slightly, studying me with the detached curiosity of someone who knew her worth. "I'm not in the business of giving my name to strangers, Mr. Alvan."

I nodded slowly, thinking over my next response. Girls like this—poised, enigmatic, and with an edge sharp enough to cut through glass—had a way of disarming men without lifting a finger. I'd like to think I had more control than that, but the flutter in my stomach betrayed otherwise. "You are the mysterious fiancée of retired Admiral Maduagu, aren't you?"

This time, she turned fully to face me, her posture regal yet teasing. Her ample bosom moved with an almost exaggerated bounce, like something out of a hyper-stylized anime. "And so what if I am?"

I shrugged, masking my intrigue with casual indifference. "A man like the Admiral is getting engaged, and yet no one knows the name of the woman he's about to marry. Of course, he's already married, which makes you doubly mysterious."

She smirked, the curve of her lips a calculated response. I might've been getting through to her, or perhaps she just enjoyed the banter. "Mysterious, huh?" she echoed. "Marriages fail every day, Mr. Alvan."

"You're right about that, Miss...?" She scoffed, deliberately ignoring my invitation for her name, and took a slow sip of her colorful cocktail. "I guess it's also typical for the old man to leave his wife for someone young enough to be his daughter," I added, testing her patience.

Her smirk widened into something almost triumphant. "If it works for Regina, it works for me," she quipped, her tone cutting and self-assured.

The name threw me off for a moment, but I understood the reference. A young Nollywood actress who had become the talk of the country after becoming the sixth wife of a billionaire decades her senior. It was a scandal that had fueled endless gossip columns and polarized public opinion. It struck me as an odd comparison to wear with pride, but it told me everything I needed to know. She was unapologetic, ambitious, and completely indifferent to anyone's judgment.

"You don't look like the judgy type," she added, cocking an eyebrow. "Are you the judgy type, Mr. Alvan?"

I opened my mouth to respond, but before I could answer, a deep, commanding voice interrupted us. It carried the weight of authority yet held a hint of familiarity that sent a chill running down my spine.

"I think you'll find everyone in these circles is the judgy type, my dear," the Admiral said, his presence impossible to ignore as he approached. He leaned down and placed a soft, deliberate kiss on her cheek.

Her demeanor shifted instantly. "Hi, papi," she purred, her tone a mix of adoration and playfulness. "Where have you been? I've been waiting."

The Admiral's eyes remained locked on mine, even as he spoke to her. "I'm sorry, my dear. I had a rough night."

The young woman, with her perfect poise and disarming beauty, moved to hug him, but he winced and subtly held her back. It wasn't overt, but I noticed the slight flinch, the way his muscles stiffened. He tried to cover it up with a soft, reassuring caress of her cheek, his thumb brushing against her flawless skin. "Darling, please excuse us," he said, his voice gentler now. "I owe this man a conversation."

She hesitated, her gaze darting between us, as though trying to assess what kind of business we could have together. Finally, with a small nod, she turned and strolled toward the garden, her heels clicking softly against the stone patio. She didn't look back.

I turned to him, a faint smirk tugging at the corner of my lips. "We've got to stop meeting like this," I said. "With me trying to talk to your... girl."

The Admiral let out a weary chuckle as he eased himself onto the barstool beside me. The movement wasn't smooth. There was a stiffness in his posture, and the way he adjusted his weight suggested discomfort. "Is that a dig at our age difference?" he asked.

I shrugged, keeping it casual. "The age gap didn't go unnoticed, but that's how it usually goes, isn't it? Old man, young trophy wife. Everyone knows she's in it for the money and the lifestyle. I've seen enough *Real Housewives* to recognize the setup. My ex-wife's favorite show."

I pulled a business card from my shirt pocket and slid it across the counter. It was from my old job, but I'd crossed out the work number and email, scribbling in my personal contact info instead.

The Admiral picked it up and let out a dry, knowing chuckle. "You presume too much, Mr. Agu." Still, he slipped the card into his pocket. A good sign.

"And you, sir," I said, leaning slightly closer, "you seem to have me at a considerable disadvantage. You know quite a bit about me."

He leaned toward me. "Did you follow me home last night?"

I raised an eyebrow. "I was too busy fishing myself out of the water your boys so generously threw me into." The Admiral nodded slowly, as though confirming something only he understood. His reaction made me curious, and I pressed on. "What happened to you, though? You've been wincing since you got here. Are you hurt?"

He didn't answer immediately. His eyes scanned the bar, checking our surroundings with the precision of a man who had spent a lifetime looking over his shoulder. Satisfied that we were alone, he finally spoke. "To answer your earlier question, I was informed that Mmachi hired you to find me."

My curiosity deepened. "And who's your well-informed snitch?"

He leaned back slightly, his expression hardening. "My daughter, Adaora."

I couldn't help but chuckle, the memory of Adaora's disinterested expression flashing through my mind. "Have you even thought about how your actions might affect her?"

"There's hardly a decision I've made in my life that didn't take my daughter into account," he retorted defensively. "But even she is old enough to know that her mother and I are over."

"I guess she's taken Daddy's side in this divorce?"

"Sides," he scoffed, the word dripping with disdain. "My daughter knows my wife is desperate. And Mmachi... well, she isn't the most rational when she's desperate."

"Maybe that's all the more reason for you to go back home," I said. "Come on, you've had your fun with the Instagram hoe."

The Admiral's reaction was instantaneous. His hand shot out, gripping my arm with a strength that belied his age. His fingers dug into my skin, and his eyes burned with a cold fury. "Don't you ever call my fiancée a hoe."

I froze, every instinct screaming at me to shove his hand off and let my temper take over. But I didn't. I thought of the last time I'd let anger get the best of me, the spiral of poor decisions that followed, and forced myself to stay calm. I nodded once, deliberately slow, and he released his grip. The tension between us was stifling.

The Admiral turned to the bartender and ordered a glass of brandy, his voice calm again, as though nothing had happened. He took a long, measured sip before speaking. "Mmachi and I are done," he said simply. "There's nothing left there anymore. You should know." His eyes flicked toward me, assessing, calculating. "You've been divorced."

I shrugged, suppressing a smirk at the irony of his assumption. My situation was obviously different. My marriage was always going to end in divorce because that was the plan from the start. The vows were not legit, and the ceremony, if one could call standing in a courtroom in jeans a wedding ceremony, was barebones and far from memorable.

"I have a job to do, Admiral," I said matter-of-factly. Inspired by his composure, I raised a hand to signal the bartender. "Scotch with a splash of soda water."

The bartender paused, his gaze flickering toward me with the faintest glimmer of curiosity, as though silently appraising my choice. Then, with a nod, he reached for a tumbler. The pour was precise. A measured stream of amber liquid pooling in the glass. The hiss of soda followed, the bubbles rising and dancing like tiny fireworks. He slid the drink toward me, and I took it without a word.

I brought the glass to my lips, the smoky warmth of the scotch and the effervescent bite of the soda sharpening my senses. For a moment, I let the flavor settle, then set the glass down with purpose, ready to prod the Admiral further.

He watched me and chuckled softly, swirling the brandy in his glass. "I knew your father, you know. He was a fine general."

I blinked, caught off guard. "Through Mmachi?"

His laugh was sharper this time, almost bitter. "Mmachi barely knew him," he said, shaking his head. "Though I'm sure she gave you the impression they were close. Everything she knows, she got from me." I wasn't sure how to react to this. Did everyone know my father?

The Admiral leaned closer. "Be careful who you trust in this game, Mr. Agu. Mmachi... she may want me back, but not because she wants us to be one happy family."

This revelation caught me off guard. Was he implying that Mmachi wasn't to be trusted? That much wasn't news. Trusting a politician was as naïve as playing poker with a loaded deck. But there was something in his tone, in the way his sharp eyes locked onto mine. The warning carried an air of something deeper, darker, almost sinister. His words gnawed at me, as if they concealed a truth I wasn't ready to confront.

My gaze instinctively shifted to the left side of his ribs— the spot he had clutched earlier when his fiancée had tried to hug him. His awkward posture now seemed deliberate, almost like he was guarding something beneath his ornate brocaded top. Was he hurt? Wounded? The possibility only deepened my suspicion. "Why did you ask if I followed you home last night?" I probed, my unease growing. "Did something happen?"

He smirked and took a deep gulp of his drink, his eyes glinting like he was in on some private joke. "Look," he began, his tone shifting into something almost paternal, "I believe you're a man of integrity, even though you're working for a criminal like Mmachi. That tells me you must be in dire straits."

I stiffened; his words hit a nerve. "And what makes you think I'm a man of integrity?" I asked, trying to keep my voice steady.

He tilted his head, his smirk widening. "I could be wrong," he said with casual confidence. "But any man who unconsciously tries to emulate his father is bound to hold true to his values, good or bad."

I frowned, unsure of where he was going with this. Before I could ask, he gestured lazily toward the glass in my hand. "Take your drink, for example. Scotch and soda water. That's not a typical choice, especially not for a man of your age. It's old-fashioned. A rare combination, straight out of 1950s cinema. The kind of drink that would've been sipped by men who wore tailored suits, carried leather briefcases, and looked like they belonged in American boardrooms. Men who were measured, disciplined, and commanded respect with no need to raise their voices. It's not a drink for everyone. It takes a certain kind of man to enjoy it."

I glanced down at my glass, the amber liquid swirling under the dim light. I hadn't thought much about it before. It was just what I drank. Something about it had always felt... right.

The Admiral leaned forward slightly. "You know who else drank scotch and soda water? Your father. General Sylvester Agu. It was his favorite."

His words hit me like a punch to the gut. I blinked, surprised by the mention of my father. "What exactly do you know about my father?" I asked.

He chuckled, a low, knowing sound. "He was a respectable man, respected by all under his command, and fellow soldiers regardless of their rank. He had a vision for this country, a dream of what Nigeria could become. And not seeing that dream actualized. I'm sure it broke his heart."

I felt a swell of emotion rise in my chest, a mix of pride and something heavier. Grief, maybe. "And what does that have to do with me?" I asked, though I already sensed where he was heading.

The Admiral's gaze bore into mine, sharp and unyielding. "Everything," he said simply. "Whether you realize it or not, you carry pieces of him in you. The way you talk, the way you walk, it's all there. But it's clearest in your choices, in the values you cling to. The man you are, the man you're trying to be. It all circles back to him."

I opened my mouth to argue, but the words wouldn't come. He leaned back, his expression softening just slightly, and gestured toward my drink again. "That's what I mean when I say you're a man of integrity. It's not just about what you do. It's about who you are. And who you are is a reflection of the man who raised you."

The silence that followed was heavy, the weight of his words settling over me like a thick fog. I swirled the scotch in my glass, my mind flashing to memories of my father. The sternness in his eyes, the quiet strength in his voice, the way he'd sit in his chair with that same drink in his hand, his gaze far away as though he were wrestling with the weight of the world.

The Admiral broke the silence with a sigh, his tone softening. "I'm not saying you're your father, Dozy. But I've seen enough in my time to know that a lion does not give birth to a house cat." He pulled a box of cigarettes from his pocket and put one in his mouth. "I won't even offer you one. Your father didn't smoke," he said as he lit the cigarette and puffed out a few clouds of smoke before continuing.

He turned to face me, the smugness that had been so prominently etched on his face a moment earlier suddenly replaced by one of sternness and caution. "You're a smart young man," he said. "The smartest thing you can do now is head back to Washington, D.C. Trust me when I tell you. What she offered you isn't worth it."

The cryptic response set my mind racing. What wasn't worth it? What had Mmachi dragged me into? I opened my mouth to press further, determined to break through his wall of evasion, but before I could, Lola appeared between us, her presence commanding attention.

"This isn't what we're going to be doing, gentlemen," she said, her tone light but firm. "Mingle."

The Admiral chuckled, as though relieved by the interruption, and rose from his seat. Without another word to me, he motioned for his fiancée, whose name I still didn't know, and they headed toward the parking lot.

I made a move to follow, but before I could take two steps, a group of older women intercepted me. Lola, ever the perfect hostess, gestured toward me with an air of pride. "This is the gentleman," she said. "Dozy, my friends here are keen to meet you."

"It's you," said a skinny woman in a yellow sundress, her eyes narrowing as she studied me. I barely had time to respond before she clarified. "You're the man who cost Eneh his election in Enugu. Alvan Chidozie Agu."

My heart stuttered, then dropped like a stone. A wave of heat rushed to my face, and for a moment, the room seemed to tilt. Any mention of Dr. Eneh conjured memories of his godfather. The one man I hoped never to cross paths with again. Chief Obidi. The name itself was a trigger, a doorway to memories I'd spent years trying to bury.

I forced a tight smile, muttering a polite excuse as I stepped back from the group. My chest felt tight, and I couldn't tell if it was anger, fear, or some toxic mix of both. The mention of those days threatened to pull me under, but I wouldn't let it. Not now. My focus had to be on the Admiral and getting him back to Mmachi.

I closed my eyes, inhaling as I willed my composure to return. The dizziness eased, and my head cleared just enough for me to move again. When I stepped into the parking lot, I glimpsed the Admiral's sleek BMW speeding away, its taillights disappearing into the distance.

I stood there watching the car vanish. It wasn't over, not by a long shot. Whatever this was, whatever tangled web I'd stepped into, it was only just beginning. I wandered back into the party and rejoined Lola, not out of interest but necessity. I sipped my drink and nodded at her stories, biding my time until the conversation drifted to the details I could use.

Finally, after an hour of painful conversation, she revealed a valuable clue: an address. So, I excused myself with a polite smile, but inside, my instincts were kicking into gear. Whatever this lead was, it was better than standing around pretending to care about designer shoes and overpriced champagne. Time to get moving.

CHAPTER 10

Later that evening, I navigated the familiar chaos of the Lagos mainland. Ikeja was a far cry from the polished streets of Banana Island. Here, the roads were narrow, bustling with life even in the late hours, but the energy was different. More raw, grittier. As I drove deeper into the mainland, the streetlights became fewer, and the once orderly lanes gave way to a more unrestrained flow of traffic.

I reached the neighborhood in Ikeja and parked a suitable distance away from my target, just far enough to keep a low profile but close enough to monitor the house. It was a typical duplex, nothing too flashy, but well-maintained. The surrounding streets were quieter than I expected, but maybe that was a good thing.

I pulled out Mmachi's folder from the glove compartment and flipped through it once more. The photograph caught my eye again. Admiral Maduagu, standing beside a woman. She had an undeniable presence about her, even in a still image. Her short, silver-streaked hair was natural, cropped close to her head, framing her strong features. She wore a white blouse, the kind that spoke of elegance without trying too hard. Around her neck hung a string of coral beads, thick and bold against the simplicity of her outfit. Her smile was gentle, but her eyes were sharp. The kind of sharpness that came from years of experience and wisdom. As I studied the photo, my phone buzzed in my lap. It was my mother.

I sighed, knowing what was coming. "Mummy?"

"Nna, how are you?" Her voice was warm, familiar, and with a layer of concern. I could hear the love in every word, but there was something else. A seriousness, a sense of urgency.

"I'm good. What's up?"

"I just woke up and had this powerful urge to pray for you," she said. "So I am going to do just that, my dear."

There was no arguing with my mom when she felt like this. A devout Catholic, she believed in the power of prayer like nothing else. I wasn't one to question it.

She began. "Heavenly Father, I bring my son Alvan before you. Protect him, guide him, and help him find his way. Grant him peace of mind, a job he can be proud of, and a good woman to share his life with. Keep him safe from harm, Lord, and lead him on the right path. Amen."

Her prayer was calming. It grounded me, even if only for a moment.

"Amen," I whispered as she finished.

"Love you," she added.

"Love you too, Mom." I was still staring at the duplex, and my thoughts were split between her words and the job at hand. Just as I was about to hang up, headlights cut through the darkness, and a sleek black Mercedes pulled up in front of the house.

I straightened in my seat, observing. The timing was too perfect.

"I've got to go, Mom," I said, ending the call as quickly as possible. The night just got interesting.

I considered stepping out of the car to meet whoever was in the Mercedes, but that might've appeared threatening, especially at this time of night. I decided to start the engine and drove toward the house instead. The Range Rover I was driving might offer a sense of ease. No criminal would roll up in a car like this for a hit.

When I reached the gate, a man in a sharp suit stepped out of the Mercedes, the driver. He stood guard, and he didn't waste any time.

"Excuse me! May we know you?" he called out.

I alighted from the car, careful not to make any sudden movements. My eyes flicked to the tinted window in the backseat of the Mercedes. "My name is Dozy Agu," I said, making sure my tone was calm but direct. "I'm looking for your brother."

For a moment, there was nothing but the sound of the evening wind. Then the window rolled down, revealing the woman from the photograph. The one standing beside Admiral Maduagu. Her short, silver-streaked hair glistened under the streetlight, and the same coral beads hung around her neck. Despite her collected demeanor, her eyes reflected a silent warning.

Dr. Onyeka Okonkwo, the Admiral's younger sister, eyed me with suspicion, her sharp gaze sizing me up like I was a puzzle she couldn't quite solve.

"I've never heard of you, Mr. Agu," she said. "What do you want with my brother?"

I smiled, keeping my tone as neutral as possible. "I think this is a conversation best had inside, Ma."

Her eyes flicked to the Range Rover parked behind me—a symbol, no doubt, that I could play in her league. Nigerian elites had a tendency to feel comfortable only when they believed you were on their level. The car was my ticket in, and it seemed to have passed whatever unspoken test she had for me. I was soon sitting in her living room, holding a glass of orange juice.

The grand room was tastefully understated, implying wealth rather than flaunting it. Onyeka had softened, adopting the familiar, almost motherly tone of an African auntie. She asked if I'd had dinner, how my family was doing. The usual small talk designed to ease into whatever more serious matters were at hand.

"Now that we've gotten the pleasantries out of the way," she said, setting her glass down, "let's focus on why you're here. My brother doesn't live with me."

"I'm looking for him," I replied, leaning back in my chair and crossing my legs, trying to channel the cool confidence of Sam Spade. "I had the...pleasure of his company earlier. Sadly, we were interrupted."

She raised an eyebrow, taking a slow sip from her cup. "And why are you looking for him?"

I could already sense she knew the answer to her own question, but I played along. "Your sister-in-law," I said.

Onyeka scoffed, her lips curling in a slight sneer. "Mmachi," she said, her voice dripping with disdain. "I should have known. That woman can't stand not being in control."

"Control?" I echoed, sensing something deeper at play.

"Yes, control." She leaned in, her tone lowering. "You're here because of this wedding, aren't you? No one leaves Mmachi. Mmachi is the one who leaves."

"And you don't think she might still be in love with him?" I asked, though I didn't believe it myself. I just needed to get a sense of Onyeka's true feelings about Mmachi.

Onyeka laughed, a sharp, humorless sound. "Love *gini*? Mmachi doesn't know what love is. Her marriage was as fake as any Hollywood one. Everything she does serves her career. She loves only herself."

There was no love lost between these two women, and it rubbed me the wrong way. Maybe it reminded me too much of my father's sisters. Bitter women who seemed to despise my mother for no reason other than their own twisted jealousy. Onyeka's venom toward Mmachi triggered something in me, and it showed in my face, my entire demeanor shifting.

"Where is the Admiral?" I asked.

Onyeka leaned back, feeling the shift in the atmosphere. "I have no idea," she said, her tone suddenly defensive. "Believe it or not, I'm just as surprised by all this as you are."

I narrowed my eyes. "I don't understand."

"I didn't even know he was back in the country," she said. "He hasn't been picking my calls."

A sinking feeling settled in my gut, heavy and unsettling. Something was off. My hand, still holding the half-empty glass of juice, began to tremble. I looked down at it, then back at the glass. The realization hit me like a punch to the gut. I'd been drugged.

"Shit," I muttered under my breath, trying to rise from the chair, but my legs felt like lead. My vision blurred as I stumbled toward the door, but before I could reach it, Onyeka's driver from earlier appeared, blocking my path. And behind him, another man. A tall, well-built figure, older, with a frown on his face. He wore a traditional *isiagu* top, the kind with gold lion heads embroidered across the chest, and a red cap tilted on his head. His presence was commanding, almost regal, but there was something cold in his eyes.

They grabbed me as my body grew weaker, the drug taking full effect. My muscles slackened, and my knees buckled. I could feel the world spinning out of control, the room fading in and out of focus.

Before everything went dark, I glimpsed Onyeka's face, her expression unreadable. Then, everything slipped away into blackness.

CHAPTER 11

I felt consciousness returning in waves, though I kept my eyes shut. Groggy, yes, but my head was clear. Whatever drug they gave me wasn't enough to cloud my thinking. I could hear voices in the room, low and tense. Onyeka was arguing with a man, and it didn't take long to figure out that the man was the second person who had restrained me earlier. Their conversation, though quiet, revealed a lot.

From the way Onyeka spoke to him, it was clear she respected him, like a traditional Igbo wife respects her husband. She called him "*nna anyi*," meaning "our father," and "*di m*," "my husband," terms of respect that showed a deference I hadn't detected earlier.

"Listen, woman," the man's voice growled, deep and impatient. "Your brother has brought enough trouble to my doorstep!"

"But it's not my brother who sent him here. It was Mmachi," Onyeka replied, trying to keep him calm.

"*O bu nwunye ya!* She's his wife!" he barked.

"Listen," Onyeka said more calmly now, "all we need to do is wait for him to wake up, then we'll find out why he's really here and if he's connected to the others."

Others? I thought. *What others?*

A heavy silence followed her words, broken only by footsteps. Someone else had entered the room. I kept still, bracing myself for whatever was coming next. This wasn't good. I came here for answers, but I was tied up in a room with people who clearly did not intend to play nice.

I heard the soft click of heels against the floor—Onyeka was leaving. Her departure left me with two men, her husband and the other figure, likely the driver. I could feel their presence in the room, but they hadn't noticed me stirring. That was good. I needed the time.

I took a deep breath, subtle but significant enough to steady myself. Being tied up was not a position I enjoyed, but it wasn't unfamiliar either. General Agu had made sure of that. My father was the kind of man who believed in teaching you to survive, even in extreme circumstances. As a kid, I had to wriggle out of restraints more times than I cared to count while he timed me. I hadn't needed those skills in years, but they were coming back to me now.

I flexed my wrists, feeling the rope. They'd used a clove hitch knot. Interesting. The clove hitch is a basic knot, one that even a half-decent sailor could work free from if they had the patience and dexterity. I remembered reading about John Nevil Maskelyne, the legendary British magician who engineered some of the most intricate escape tricks of the 19th century. Maskelyne's expertise with locks and knots was renowned. He once exposed the famous Davenport brothers, proving that their "spirit manifestations" were nothing more than clever escapes from simple restraints. He always said the key to any escape wasn't brute strength but knowing how your bindings worked against you.

I rotated my wrists, testing the rope's give, feeling for any slack. The thing about a clove hitch is that if you work it just right, creating the smallest amount of space, you can slip out. I twisted my hands, careful to keep the movement smooth, pushing my thumb against the loop. Slowly, the knot began to loosen, the tension easing with each subtle motion. The men were across the room, preoccupied. I could hear them sorting through metal tools on a table. Tools that were likely meant for me. They hadn't noticed a thing.

With one last tug, I slipped my hands free. No need for theatrics or dislocated joints, just a little knowledge and patience. But I didn't move immediately. I took stock of the room and my captors. The two men stood over the table, murmuring to each other, inspecting what I could only assume were instruments meant to make my next few hours very painful. This was when I stood up and they noticed me.

For a moment, the room went still. Nothing happened. It was like the calm before the storm, a pause where both sides were calculating their next moves. Then I saw Onyeka's husband reach for a machete on the table. The polished steel glinted under the dim light, and that was all I needed. I moved.

I charged him, low and fast, my shoulder slamming into his midsection in a spear-tackle that sent him crashing backward into the table. It shattered under our combined weight, wood splintering everywhere. He grunted, gasping for air, the machete slipping from his grasp as we tumbled to the floor.

Before I could recover, I felt strong arms wrap around my chest from behind. It was the driver. He tried to pull me back, but his grip was sloppy, desperate. I shifted my weight and flipped him over my shoulder, sending him sprawling to the ground with a thud. He hit the floor hard, winded.

I stood quickly, sizing up both men. Onyeka's husband was struggling to get back on his feet, groaning as he pushed broken pieces of the table off him. The driver was down, dazed but not out. Neither of them was a skilled fighter. They might have had numbers, but they didn't have technique, and that was all I needed.

Onyeka's husband lunged at me, swinging a piece of the broken table like a club. I sidestepped, grabbing his arm and twisting it behind his back in a lock. He yelped in pain, his knees buckling, and I shoved him face-first into the nearest wall. His head bounced off the concrete with a satisfying thud, and he crumpled to the floor.

The driver was back on his feet, rushing toward me, fists swinging wildly. I ducked under his punch and delivered a sharp jab to his ribs. He doubled over, and I followed it up with a knee to his face. Blood sprayed from his nose as he staggered backward, collapsing onto the remains of the shattered table.

Both men were down now, groaning in pain, outmatched.

I stood over them, catching my breath. My skills in Krav Maga might have been rusty, but I'd been in enough scraps to know how to handle myself. These guys? They were just muscle—brutish and uncoordinated. They never stood a chance.

I wiped the sweat from my brow, glancing at the wreckage of the room. The quiet that followed was unnerving, but it gave me a moment to reflect. This wasn't part of the plan, but then again, very little ever goes to plan in Lagos.

Footsteps echoed down the hallway, catching my attention. I turned just as Onyeka burst into the room, her eyes wide with fear, roused by the sounds of the scuffle. She froze when she saw me standing there, her gaze darting toward the heap that was her husband, slumped against the wall. Panic spread across her face.

I took a step toward her, slow and deliberate, closing the door softly behind her. The quiet click of the latch felt like a gunshot in the silence. I leaned in close. "That was unnecessary, Doc. I just had questions."

Her eyes were frantic, flicking between me and the unmoving figure of her husband. "Did you kill Nkem? Is he dead?"

I followed her gaze and shook my head, giving her just enough calm to prevent a full-blown meltdown. "He's taking a brief nap," I said. "But he won't be asleep forever. So, if you don't want me waking him up with more pain, you better give me some answers."

The fear in her eyes told me she understood. I wasn't going to touch her. I wasn't raised that way. You don't lay hands on older women. But her husband? I was more than ready to take my frustrations out on him if it came to that.

"Where is your brother?"

She hesitated, defeated. "I don't know!" she said, her voice trembling. I gave her an icy glare that cut right through her, and she flinched under it. "He was here just last night," she added, the words rushing out. "But I haven't seen or heard from him since."

"Why was he here?" I asked, sensing she was holding back something.

"He dropped by unannounced," Onyeka said. "I had no idea he was even in the country. He seemed... upset. Agitated, as if something was eating away at him. Then he told me he had just escaped an attempted armed robbery. So, he gave me his things to keep for him and said people might come looking for him. Dangerous people."

"The others?" I asked, keeping my tone steady, though inside my mind was racing. "That's who you were referring to earlier?"

She nodded, her hands trembling as she continued. "Yes, earlier today, two men showed up. They were terrifying. They said they were looking for Alex too. Claimed they only wanted to talk, but something in their eyes..." She trailed off, shivering. "I told them I would let them know if he came back, but Nkem..." she glanced at her unconscious husband, her voice lowering to a whisper."...Nkem decided if they ever came again, we would deal with them ourselves."

A chill ran through me as I absorbed her words. My mind was a storm of questions. "Who were they?" I pressed, but her face tightened with fear.

"I don't know," she whispered, shaking her head. "They never gave a name. They didn't have to. Something about them... it felt wrong. Everything about them was intimidating. The way they were dressed. The way they talked." Her voice wavered as her fear became palpable. "Please, I'm really sorry. I thought you were one of them. I thought you were here to harm us."

I turned away, letting her words sink in. During my tense exchange with the Admiral, he'd made a passing remark that seemed strange at the time but now gnawed at me. *You don't look like the usual type of person they send after me,* he'd said. *They.*

Who the hell were *they*?

My mind raced. There were layers to this I hadn't seen before. People after Alex, people willing to hurt those close to him to get what they wanted. Dangerous men who operated in the shadows. I wasn't the only one tracking him down. Far from it. And the other players? They weren't going to be as gentle.

"His things," I said. "Give them to me."

She didn't argue. The fear had worked its way into her bones, and she wasn't about to resist anymore. A few minutes later, I was back in the driver's seat, pulling away from her house before more shit hit the fan.

Driving out of the mainland at this hour had a strange calm to it—deceptive, almost. Lagos by day was a relentless force, loud, chaotic and always moving. But at night, in places like this, the city felt different. Quieter, yes, but with an edge. People like to say Lagos never sleeps, like it's some African cousin of New York. But that's a lie. Lagos sleeps. And when it does, you better stay sharp, because this city can make you disappear into the kind of darkness you don't come back from.

I crossed the Third Mainland Bridge, the skyline of Lagos Island stretching before me like a promise and a threat. The city lights blinked against the darkening sky, the chaos of Lagos hidden beneath the surface, waiting for the sun to rise and reveal its true nature. Once I was off the bridge, I pulled over and parked in a quiet spot. My eyes scanned the surroundings, instinctively cautious, even though I was alone. You could never be too sure in this city.

I fished out my phone and scrolled through the unsaved numbers until I found hers: Mmachi Alex-Maduagu. I pressed the call button and listened to the steady hum of the dial tone, half-expecting her not to pick up. But she answered quickly.

"Mr. Dozy," she greeted me, no warmth in her tone. "You have an update?"

"I met him," I said, cutting straight to the point. "Your husband. He didn't seem eager to return to you."

Silence hung on the line for a moment. I could almost hear her grinding her teeth on the other end, fighting back whatever anger she had at the situation. She was probably expecting excuses or delays, not results this soon. "You found him already. I suppose I did hire the right man," she said, the compliment dripping with more sarcasm than praise.

"He wasn't exactly hard to find," I said, glancing around at the passing cars. "He's been out partying."

That earned a chuckle from her, a sound that was more bitter than amused. "Alex never could say no to a party."

"Seems that way." I leaned against my car, lowering my voice just in case. "But here's the thing, Mrs. Maduagu. Who else is looking for him? Your sister-in-law mentioned other people. Dangerous people. She seemed scared out of her mind. And the last time we spoke..."

"You had a conversation with Alex?" she interrupted.

"Yes," I said. "And he seemed hurt then. It was almost as if someone had attacked him the night before. It adds some weight to his sister's concerns."

"Onyeka is scared of dragonflies," she replied. "Whatever she told you, I wouldn't put too much stock in it. As for Alex, I have no idea what mess he's gotten himself into over there."

I didn't buy her indifference, but I pressed on. "So, you didn't send anyone else after him? No one besides me?"

She sighed, a long, exasperated sound that told me she was getting tired of this line of questioning. "Mr. Dozy, I'm paying you a significant amount of money to bring my husband back, not to interrogate me. Now, when can I expect results?"

I clenched my jaw. "You didn't hear me. I said he's not eager to return. He made that very clear both times!"

"That's not my concern," she snapped. "Your job is to bring him back to me, whether he's willing or not. I don't care if you have to drug him and ship him back to me like Umaru Dikko. Just do it."

And with that, she hung up. The click of the line going dead was like a slap in the face. The cool, composed Mmachi I had met was nowhere to be found. Her patience had worn thin, and it showed.

I stared at the phone, resisting the urge to throw it. For a moment, I wanted to tell her exactly what I thought of her, but she wasn't wrong. She had hired me for a job, and so far, I'd let myself get sidetracked. I didn't care about what she and the Admiral were caught up in, at least not yet. I had a job to do.

Time to take a look at what Onyeka had given me. I opened the brown leather bag and rummaged through its contents. A few clothes, a wallet, and a phone. The battery on the phone was dead, so that would have to wait. I made a mental note to charge it as soon as I could.

I flipped open the wallet, a fading black leather piece, worn from years of use. Inside, I saw a few crumpled receipts, an SD card tucked into one of the folds, and some mint naira notes that seemed untouched for weeks. I thumbed through the receipts, most of them from restaurants and gas stations in DC. It seemed the Admiral was the kind of man who held onto everything, possibly out of habit. I almost dismissed them as junk when something caught my eye. It was a receipt that didn't quite fit.

It was thinner, the paper different, the ink smudged but still legible. This one wasn't from the States. It was from a place I knew all too well. *Lorel Luxury Hotel.* A receipt for an extended stay, dated just two days before he visited his sister.

I sat back in my seat, staring at the receipt, a slow realization dawning.

I knew where I needed to go next.

— ◆ —

117

Lorel might have called itself a luxury hotel, but it was more of an understated spot tucked away in Ikoyi, one of those places where discretion was the true currency. From the outside, it looked like nothing special—a nondescript building that could have been mistaken for any run-of-the-mill business hotel. But the longer I observed it, the clearer it became. It wasn't the type of place tourists or families checked into. No, this was a sanctuary for Lagos's upper crust, a hideout for chiefs, Alhajis, and wealthy people who wanted to keep their side dealings hidden. I'd seen more than a few older men walk in with mistresses who could've easily been their daughters. The hotel was perfect for illicit liaisons. A little-known gem that provided privacy for those who preferred to keep their dirty laundry behind closed doors.

I walked through the entrance into the lobby, which was surprisingly upscale compared to the bland exterior. The floors gleamed, and soft ambient lighting gave the place a warmth that felt both inviting and deceptive. A young man at the reception desk looked up, a smile spreading across his face as he spotted me. He wore the hotel uniform: a plain white shirt, black tie, and slacks. Simple, clean-cut.

"Good evening, sir," he said, his voice deep and polite. "Welcome to the Lorel Luxury Hotel. How may I assist you?"

I gave him a casual smile and raised the dead phone from the Admiral's bag. "My uncle told me to bring him the car," I said, nodding toward the Range Rover Sport, which I had parked right out front like a Trojan horse. "But my phone's dead, so I can't call him down. Can you let me know what room he's in so I can hand him the key?"

The receptionist's smile didn't falter, but he shook his head. "I can take the key for you, sir. I'll make sure he gets it."

A small wave of annoyance crept in. "Do you see that car? My aunt was very clear. I need to hand it to him directly. I'm sure you understand." I slid my hand casually across the wooden counter, the edge of a crisp twenty-dollar bill peeking out, green enough to make my point clear.

For a second, his face was blank, possibly expecting it to be just a twenty-naira note. But then I saw it. The unmistakable spark in his eyes when he realized it was a dollar bill. The dollar still reigned supreme in these parts, which is exactly why I hadn't converted all the pocket money Mmachi had given me to naira. "Of course, sir," he said, his tone suddenly smoother. "And what's your uncle's name?"

I glanced down at the crumpled receipt from the Admiral's wallet. The name on it was false, but it was good enough for this situation. "John Richards," I said.

He typed something into the computer and nodded. "Room 202."

I thanked him and made my way to the elevator, keeping my pace calm even though my instincts were telling me to stay sharp. Something about this place wasn't sitting right with me, and the fact that the Admiral had used a fake name only added to my unease.

The elevator doors slid open, and I stepped out onto the second floor. The corridor was dimly lit, the carpet a deep burgundy that muffled my footsteps as I approached room 202. I knocked once, listening for any signs of movement inside.

Nothing.

I knocked again, this time harder. Still nothing.

That's when I noticed the door was slightly ajar, just enough for a sliver of darkness to seep out. A warning bell rang in my head, but I pushed it open anyway, slow and cautious. The room beyond was drenched in shadows, except for the faint orange glow from the security lights outside, spilling through the half-drawn curtains. I stepped inside, my senses on high alert.

The place was a disaster. Clothes lay scattered haphazardly across the floor; the bed sheets were tangled like a twisted mess of fabric; and a chair lay tipped over with a leg bent awkwardly. It didn't take a detective to know there had been a struggle. But it was the subtle details that caught my eye such as the slight stains of blood on the doorknob, the fallen chairs, and, most notably, three glasses of red wine on the bedside table. Lipstick smudges rimmed the edges of two.

I stepped further in, my fingers brushing against the wall in search of the light switch. When I found it, I flicked it on, and the fluorescent lights buzzed to life, casting a harsh glow over the room's disarray. Everything was clearer, and the chaos looked almost deliberate, as though someone wanted to cover their tracks. Yet, there was a certain precision to the scene that gnawed at me.

Then I looked at the bed.

A body lay there, sprawled on its back, clad only in a bloodied wife-beater and boxer shorts. Two bullet holes had punctured the center of his chest with surgical accuracy just like a professional's work. His eyes were wide open, fixed on the ceiling with that eerie, empty stare only the dead can manage. His face was also swollen, as if he had been beaten up before being shot.

I swallowed, the shock rippling through me, but I forced myself to steady my breath. Despite the scene's brutality, my mind switched into observation mode. Something felt off. The room was messy like someone had staged it. Too obvious, too chaotic. The chair did not appear as if someone had thrown it in a heated struggle. It looked placed, the legs perfectly spaced as if the fight had been a little too clean.

The faint metallic scent of blood hung heavy in the air, but there was something else, too. Something sweet. The scent lingered in the air—floral, feminine—yet oddly familiar. A woman's perfume? At first, it was a subtle smell of lavender, but then it was more like vanilla.

And then there were the faint impressions in the carpet, the indentations from high heels that hadn't fully settled back into the fabric yet. One was a bigger shoe, its impression much heavier. Something clicked in my mind, though I couldn't place it yet. There had been more than one person here. Women, too. The Admiral wasn't alone when he died.

But there was no time to dwell on that now. As the subtly sweet scent dissipated, the room still smelled faintly of gunpowder, the metallic tang mixing with the floral notes, and if I could smell it, others would too. Someone would come looking.

The admiral was dead. This was bad. Real bad.

I took one last look at the scene. The wine glasses, the scattered clothes, the footprints. Pieces of the puzzle started forming in my mind, but I'd have to deal with that later. Right now, there was only one thing to do. Get the hell out of there.

I didn't need to be a genius to know that sticking around would be a mistake. The longer I stayed, the deeper I was sinking into a mess I hadn't signed up for. My pulse quickened. I was still on time. I could get out of this, but I had to move fast.

With one last glance at the Admiral's lifeless body, I turned and slipped out the way I came, quietly closing the door behind me.

CHAPTER 12

I didn't hang around. I wasn't a cop, and I definitely didn't have training in crime scene investigations. What I did know was that this mess wasn't for me, and I needed to get the hell out of there before things went from bad to worse. The last thing I needed was to be caught up in a dead man's business, especially in a place like Lagos, where things like this didn't get solved, they just got buried.

I moved quickly, but I made sure not to rush. If anyone saw me, I didn't want them to think I had just stumbled upon a murder scene or worse, caused it. But I also didn't want to look like I was taking a leisurely evening stroll through a luxury hotel. Balance. That was key.

The receptionist greeted me with the same wide grin as I stepped back into the lobby, his smile almost mocking now. I approached the counter, maintaining my composure. Another crisp twenty-dollar bill appeared in my hand. This time, I didn't bother hiding it under my fingers. I slapped it onto the counter, making sure he saw it clearly.

"Call the police. There's a dead man in room 202. I was never here." I was cold and direct.

The receptionist's grin faltered, confusion crossing his face as he processed what I had just said. His eyes widened slightly, but he didn't panic. Not the overly hysterical type, it seemed. He gave me a curt nod and reached for the phone, his movements slow, deliberate.

That was my cue to leave.

I slid into the Range Rover and gunned it, driving away from the hotel as quickly as I could without drawing attention. My hands gripped the steering wheel tighter than I realized, and before I knew it, I was pounding on it, hitting it over and over in frustration.

"What the hell did this old bitch get me into?" I muttered.

Inside my head, it was like a storm had kicked up. The dead body, the fake name, the shady hotel. This wasn't what I signed up for. I came here to find the Admiral, not to walk into a damn murder scene. And now I was right in the thick of it. I cursed under my breath, the weight of the situation bearing down on me like a lead weight.

I thought about turning back, about ditching this whole mess and going back to the States. Hell, I could even try to get my old job back. Before they fired me, they practically begged me to help with more cases. They were definitely short-staffed. If I swallowed my pride, I could probably swing my way back in, even if it meant eating some humble pie.

But the very thought of it made me curse out loud.

"Fuck no!" I yelled at the steering wheel.

There was no way in hell I'd go back to those vultures. The people who exploited me, bled me dry, and tossed me aside like I was nothing. I'd rather take my chances in Lagos than crawl back to them, cap in hand, begging for another shot.

I realized then that I didn't have a plan. I was confused, angry, and neck-deep in a situation that had spiraled way out of control. There was only one person I could think of who might help me make sense of this. Osita.

I needed a drink, and I needed answers. The Diamond Ballot was the place for both.

When I pulled up to the club, the bass from the music inside vibrated through the walls, even in the back alley. This time, I walked up to the door without any hassle from security. I knocked, waiting for someone to let me in. The door swung open after a few moments, revealing Osita in another one of his flashy suits. This one was a sharp navy blue number with a subtle pinstripe pattern. His jacket was perfectly tailored and hugged his broad shoulders, while his trousers tapered just right. A cigarette dangled from the corner of his mouth, the ember glowing faintly as he took a drag.

"Sup, bro?" he greeted me, his eyes glinting with that usual cocky grin.

I didn't answer him at first. I walked straight past him and headed for the minibar, pouring myself a generous glass of scotch and soda water. I downed it in one go, the burn in my throat grounding me, pulling me back from the mess I had just left behind.

Osita watched me, his grin fading as he noticed my state. "Guy, wetin happen?" His tone shifted, concern creeping in.

I looked him dead in the eyes. "He's dead, man."

"Who be that?"

"Maduagu."

Osita's eyes went wide, his cigarette nearly falling from his lips. "Ewo! How the fuck?"

I took another long sip, letting the warmth of the scotch settle in my chest. "Someone shot him. Two in the chest. Found him in a hotel room, half-naked and bleeding out."

Osita let out a low whistle, shaking his head. "Damn, Dozy. This is some real shit."

I nodded, staring into the glass. Real shit didn't even begin to cover it.

Osita paced back and forth, flicking the ash from his cigarette into the glass ashtray with an air of practiced indifference. To him, it was just another day in Lagos. People die, bodies drop, life moves on. Maybe for him, this was the norm. For me? It was the kind of mess I had spent years avoiding, and now, here I was, neck-deep in it. Seeing a dead body is never something you get used to, no matter how much you try to act tough about it.

He finally stopped, snuffing out the cigarette before turning to face me. "Did anyone see you?"

I exhaled slowly, running my hand over my jaw. "Receptionist."

"You give am something?" He didn't need to clarify. Everyone knew what *give am something'* meant in this town. A bribe. The unspoken language of Nigeria. I nodded. Sure, I had been out of the country for a while, but some things you don't forget. Greasing palms was survival 101 around here.

"Then you'll be fine," Osita said with a shrug, like it was the most obvious thing in the world. "You wanna come into the club?" he asked, gesturing toward the door leading back to the pulsing bass and neon lights of the Diamond Ballot.

I shook my head, the exhaustion creeping into my bones. "I need to get the hell out of here," I muttered. "I'll call the person who sent me looking for the Admiral, tell her he's dead, and then I'm gone. Done."

Osita sucked his teeth, clearly irritated. "So, you'll just leave? After all this? You won't even hang out with your friends before you dip?"

I stared at him, incredulous. "How the hell am I supposed to do that? It's bad enough I've had to look over my shoulder since I touched down. Hanging out with you guys will just paint a target on my back."

Osita stepped forward, placing his hands on my shoulders, giving me that reassuring, almost brotherly look. "Bro, relax. Forget about Chief Obidi for now. Let's have some fun before you bounce. I'll arrange something codedly."

Codedly. That word was practically Osita's mantra back in school. He loved organizing things on the down low, always pulling strings behind the scenes. He got off on the secrecy, the thrill of operating in the shadows. Me? I was too tired to argue anymore. The events of the day had drained whatever energy I had left. What I needed more than anything was a good night's sleep.

I muttered something about catching up later and made my way out. By the time I got back to Banana Island, it must've been a little past midnight. Akaneme, groggy but obedient, shuffled out to open the gate for me, his eyes half-closed. He didn't say a word as he pushed the gate open, and I wasn't in the mood for conversation.

"Cover the car for me," I said, handing him the key to the Range. He gave a tired nod and muttered a soft *'goodnight, sah'* as I made my way inside.

I was exhausted, sure, but sleep wasn't going to come easily. My mind was racing. Visions of the Admiral's lifeless body, the mess I'd stumbled into, and the looming question of what the hell I was doing here.

The bed felt too soft, too luxurious for the situation I found myself in. I tossed and turned, my paranoia creeping in as I stared at the ceiling, wondering if someone was watching me, waiting. Events of the night replayed in my head.

— ◆ —

I'm not sure how much sleep I got, but I woke up with that eerie feeling you get when you can sense a presence around you. It was as if the air in the room had shifted, disturbed by something or someone. My eyes were sticky from sleep, but I forced them open, and I noted several men in black uniforms, standing over me, rifles pointed right at my face. Dirty rifles, the kind that looked like they hadn't been cleaned in years.

One of the policemen stepped forward. "If you try any nonsense, I go blast you."

I didn't doubt that for a second. This wasn't the States where people argued with the police, talking about rights and lawyers, throwing around phrases like, *'I'm an American, I know my rights!'* No, this was Nigeria. When a cop pointed a gun at you here, you didn't argue, you didn't hesitate. You obeyed. Otherwise, you'd find yourself in a shallow grave. No elaborate stories about your being armed or resisting arrest like dirty American cops might spin. Here, they didn't bother with lying. Just a simple, cold explanation: *accidental discharge.*

Funny how that phrase used to crack me up when I was a teenager, *accidental discharge* was something we joked about regarding premature ejaculation. Not so funny when it's a rifle aimed at your head.

They dragged me out of bed, my chest bare, wearing nothing but a pair of boxers. Without ceremony, they threw me into the back of their black truck. Comfort wasn't part of the deal. The rusted, ancient metal inside the truck made the floor burn hot under my bare feet, searing my skin as if trying to melt right through. Two policemen sandwiched me in the back seat. One sat behind the wheel, another in the front passenger seat, and we rattled down the road like that, heading toward whatever hellhole they were taking me to.

I glanced at the uniforms—black, with red insignias stitched onto the arms. Corporals. In the Nigerian Police Force, a corporal's uniform wasn't particularly fancy. Just a plain, well-worn black shirt with a red stripe running down the sleeves, the rank displayed just below the shoulder. I could tell these guys had seen action. They weren't the rookie types. These were the ones who did the dirty work, the ones who didn't mind getting blood on their hands.

After what felt like an hour of uncomfortable driving, we arrived at the station. They hauled me straight into a small room, no windows, a tiny bed shoved into one corner. The room reeked of sweat and stale air. They didn't tell me how long they planned on keeping me there, but I wasn't going to stick around to find out.

As the last corporal was about to leave the room, I made a sharp hissing sound to get his attention. He turned, glaring at me with bloodshot eyes.

"Wetin be that?" he snapped, clearly not in the mood for games.

I rattled off the number. "07067013997. Call that number and tell am where I dey. Don't worry, he go find you something. Just do am sharp sharp."

The cop stood there for a moment, sizing me up, eyes narrowing as if trying to gauge if I was playing him for a fool. "Wetin he go find me?"

I clenched my fists, keeping my voice calm but firm. "You go discuss that one with am. Abeg, hurry up. 07067013997."

He gave me a long, hard look, his eyes raking over me from head to toe. But then he turned and stepped out, leaving me in the suffocating silence of that windowless room.

I leaned back against the wall, exhaling slowly. If this worked, I'd be out of here in no time. If it didn't... Well, I wasn't ready to think about that just yet.

CHAPTER 13

I had no idea how long I'd been stuck in that room. Hours felt like days, each second crawling slower than the last. The small bed they provided felt like it was made of rocks. The thin mattress sagged in the middle, and the heat was unbearable. No fan, no ventilation. Sweat poured down my face and back, soaking into the ragged excuse for a pillow. The walls were bare, and the single flickering bulb above me cast long, eerie shadows, making the cramped space feel even smaller. It was like being locked in an oven, except here, the only thing being cooked was my patience.

I shifted uncomfortably, trying to ignore the sticky feeling of my skin clinging to the cheap fabric of the mattress, but it was useless. My throat was dry, my head pounded, and the scent of mildew mixed with the sour odor of sweat only made everything worse. Every minute in that room stretched my nerves tighter and tighter, and I kept going over what had happened earlier at the Lorel Luxury Hotel.

Footsteps echoed down the hall. Heavy, deliberate. The kind that didn't belong to your average uniformed cop. The door creaked open, and a man stepped inside. He wasn't in uniform, at least, not the kind the others were wearing. No, this one was different. He had on a striped shirt with the sleeves rolled up, a shoulder holster slung under his arm like something straight out of a crime movie. His face was dark, unreadable, and the sort that had seen things. He looked like a man who enjoyed his job a little too much.

"Good morning. I'm Detective Inspector Bayo. State CID," he said with a smile that didn't quite reach his eyes. "Are you comfortable?"

I didn't bother answering. It was clear as day that this was all part of the game. False pleasantries meant to throw me off or maybe just to amuse himself. Either way, I wasn't playing.

"Can we get you something to drink?" he asked, like he was offering me room service.

I leaned forward. "Why the hell am I here?"

The man's smile tightened at the edges, but he didn't seem too bothered. He crossed his arms, leaning casually against the wall as if we were having a chat over beers, not in a dingy interrogation room.

"Where were you last night between 10 and 11 pm?" he asked, his tone casual.

I didn't flinch. "The Diamond Ballot on Victoria Island. I was with the owner, Osita. You can ask him; he'll back me up."

He didn't blink, didn't move. Just stared at me for a few seconds longer than necessary. "Is that so?" he said, dragging out the words with a hint of skepticism. "Were you at the governor's wife's birthday gala the night before last? The one on the yacht."

I weighed my response. Asking for a lawyer would only make things worse and guarantee me a few more hours in this room. I had to thread this needle carefully. I kept my tone light. "Now that you mention it, yeah. I stopped by. Got thrown overboard for my trouble."

He arched a brow. "By Admiral Alex Maduagu?"

"So I was told," I said. "I never got the chance to meet him formally."

He scribbled something down, which I knew was for show. Then, his eyes locked onto mine again. "What was your issue with the Admiral?"

I leaned back. "Can't say I had one. Maybe he didn't like the way I was staring at his girl.

"Did she have a name?"

"Didn't get that far. His men tossed me before introductions."

Bayo chuckled, his first proper show of emotion. "You looked at his girl. I suppose that would make any man see red."

I sensed an opening, so I threw in a question of my own, keeping my tone casual. "Surely, you've got a guest list for that event. Her name should've been on there, right?"

His eyes locked on mine, sharp and calculating. For a moment, I thought I'd overplayed my hand. But he shook his head slightly, lips curling into a faint smile. "No plus one listed for the Admiral. For all I know, you're making her up."

I raised my eyebrows. "Ask anyone on that yacht. She wore the skimpiest dress imaginable. Believe me, no one would've forgotten her."

He scribbled something in his notepad and then fixed his gaze back on me. I considered mentioning that I'd seen her at Lola's party, but an instinctual voice in my head screamed against it. The last thing I needed was to draw a line connecting me to every place the Admiral had been. "So, you're telling me you weren't anywhere near the hotel room where the Admiral was found dead?"

My pulse quickened, but I kept my face as blank as a slate. No tells. No cracks. "I've got no idea what you're talking about. I told you, I was at the Diamond Ballot enjoying."

Another pause. Then he chuckled. "You know what I think?" he asked, leaning in. "I think you didn't like being embarrassed. Maybe you followed him later. Found out where he was staying. Maybe you wanted revenge."

There it was. The shift. The escalation. I'd seen this sequence before. The cozy approach, the strategic pauses, the carefully chosen phrasing designed to corner you emotionally and psychologically.

I exhaled sharply and gave him a small, almost amused smile.

"Detective," I said, "I used to work fraud in D.C. Sat in on a few interrogations with MPD. Good people. One of them, Detective Gbenga, swore by a particular method. I remember the whole pattern. Build rapport. Ask baseline questions. Then you start with the soft accusations. Subtle guilt trip. Good cop stays good; bad cop is nowhere to be found. It's all right out of the manual."

His brows knit together slightly.

"Use the Reid interrogation method on someone else," I said. "I know the script."

He said nothing. Just stared. And I could see he didn't like that I'd taken the mystique out of his performance.

Bayo's silence told me this wasn't over. He was waiting, circling like a vulture, but I wasn't about to give him more than he already had. If he wanted to pin the Admiral's death on me, he'd have to claw his way through a lot more than a vague timeline and a bad mood. His eyes narrowed slightly, fingers tapping rhythmically on the wall, as though he was weighing his next move.

Then he reached into his pocket and pulled out a small green booklet. The kind every Nigerian knew by sight. He flipped it open like it was a game, deliberately slow, eyes flicking to me just long enough to enjoy the look on my face. I knew exactly what it was.

My passport.

Damn.

He thumbed through the pages with all the subtlety of a customs officer on a power trip, hawkish eyes scanning each visa stamp like he might uncover some buried secret in the ink. I clenched my jaw and cursed under my breath. That little booklet was an annoying reminder. A tether to this country.

"Why are you really here, Mr. Agu?"

I didn't flinch. "Do I need a reason to visit the city I grew up in?" I shot back.

Bayo nodded slowly, the kind of nod you give when you know exactly where the conversation is headed but are letting the other person walk right into it. He leaned in, closing the space between us, his eyes never leaving mine. "But you didn't grow up here, did you?" he said. "Your father was a military attaché, hopping from embassy to embassy. Our records show you spent what, maybe six years in Lagos between the ages of ten and sixteen? But Japan, Israel, the UK, France, the U.S., those were your playgrounds. You went to university in Enugu, did your NYSC in Nasarawa, but here's the curious part: you left before completing your year of service, yet somehow you still passed out and received a certificate. I suppose you have your father to thank for that."

His tone had shifted. There was a bitter edge to it now, a hint of resentment laced with something almost personal. Maybe it was envy, or maybe it was something deeper. Something about me that rubbed him the wrong way. He was done digging for facts; he was looking for a reason to hate me. I've seen it before. Guys who resented anyone who seemed to have an easier life than they did. In his mind, I probably looked like some spoiled son of privilege, bouncing between countries while he stayed stuck in Nigeria, fighting his way up the ranks.

He would pin the assassination of Dele Giwa on me if he could, never mind the Admiral.

"Why don't you tell me why you're really here? You flew in, went to see an old friend, and just happened to be spotted near a dead man's hotel room. Not just any dead man, mind you. A retired Admiral. Important guy."

I ignored his statement about being seen near Lorel and folded my arms across my chest. "Like I said, I was at the Ballot. That's it. You want to arrest me, do it. Otherwise, stop wasting my time."

He smiled again, but this time it wasn't the rehearsed kind. It was dark and sharp enough to make the hairs on the back of my neck rise. "Tell me, are you a U.S. citizen, Mr. Agu?"

The question caught me off guard. I shook my head. "No. I'm a permanent resident."

"Hmm! Green-card holder! You dey enjoy oh!" he said, the mockery dripping from his voice. But the smile didn't last. It vanished as quickly as it had come, replaced by that scornful scowl. "So don't forget, you still be Naija boy. No U.S. embassy to run to here. Watch how you talk to me."

He wasn't wrong. I'd let myself get too comfortable. Forgot where I was for a second. This wasn't D.C. This was a Nigerian police station where rights were negotiable and broken bones were cheaper than paper. The reminder hit hard. I gave a slight nod, sobered by the reality.

"As for your involvement in this case. The receptionist from the Lorel Luxury Hotel is on his way in. We'll see if you're as innocent as you say when he gets here."

"Go ahead," I said, trying to keep my voice steady, though I could feel my pulse quicken. "I'll wait."

Bayo nodded, still smiling. "I admire your resolve, Mr. Agu" He left the room, closing the door behind him with a soft click. The moment he was gone, I started pacing.

This was bad. Real bad.

There were two things gnawing at me now. First, the police had found me too damn fast. Almost as if someone tipped them off. Maybe I wasn't just meant to find the body. Maybe I was being set up to take the fall for it. But who? Was it Mmachi? Had she somehow known what would happen and planned to throw me under the bus the whole time?

I shook my head, trying to push those thoughts away. I couldn't focus on that right now, because the second thing was far worse. The moment I set foot in the police station, I knew Chief Obidi's network of informants would be buzzing like a hive of hornets. The man had eyes and ears everywhere, especially in the Lagos police force. It was only a matter of time before he found out I was here, and when he did... Well, let's just say I wouldn't be walking out of this station.

I had to get out of here before Obidi got his hands on me.

I scanned the room, my mind racing for an escape plan. The door was solid; the window too high to reach. There wasn't much in the way of weapons, either. No chairs to break, no metal rods. Just a rusty nail peeking out from under the bed. I crouched down, pulling the nail free. It wasn't great, but it was better than nothing.

Footsteps echoed down the hall, growing closer. My heart pounded in my chest as I pressed my back against the wall, the nail clutched in my hand like a makeshift dagger. Whoever was coming wasn't friendly, I was sure of that. Obidi's men, probably. Sent to make sure I didn't leave here breathing. I braced myself, ready to strike as soon as the door swung open.

The door creaked open, and I froze.

A tall, dark-skinned man stepped through the door, his silhouette filling the frame. His head was clean-shaven, and his face was calm and composed. Almost too calm for someone stepping into a powder keg like this. He wore a black tactical vest strapped tightly over his broad chest, the letters *DSS* emblazoned in stark white across it. The Department of State Services, Nigeria's secretive intelligence agency. I recognized the uniform vaguely, but it was the man behind it that brought a rush of relief flooding through me.

He grinned when he saw me, that familiar, lopsided grin that had gotten us out of more trouble than I could count back in the day. "Let's get out of here, Dozy," he said, like it was the most normal thing in the world.

Relief hit me so hard I almost laughed. I dropped the rusty nail I'd been clutching like a lifeline and let out a long, shaky breath I hadn't realized I was holding.

"*Calvin*," I breathed, a grin spreading across my face despite the situation. "*Thank God.*"

CHAPTER 14

Calvin Asogwa was the last piece of our puzzle, the last member of our little group back in university. Me, Osita, and Calvin. We were tight, closer than brothers. Like me, he never joined the campus cults that circled around like vultures, waiting to recruit students. He didn't need to. He was a philosopher and bibliophile. But his appearance? That was another story. Built like an African god, his muscular frame made people assume he was deep in gang life. His body alone was a deterrent to trouble.

One particular incident that really showcased how much people feared Calvin's physique happened during our second year at university. Unlike Osita and me, Calvin preferred the cramped and poorly maintained university dormitories. Being a curious Nigerian-American, he was determined to get what he called the authentic Nigerian campus experience.

One night, nature called. Most students avoided the dorm's toilets because they were infamous for being filthy, with piles of shit in every stall left untouched for days. It was a revolting place, and those who could would often go outside to relieve themselves in the bushy areas behind the dorm, where the tall grass offered some privacy and a cool breeze made the experience somewhat tolerable. But people rarely did this at night for obvious reasons—fear of being robbed, or worse.

But Calvin? He didn't give a damn. Armed with toilet paper, his phone for light, and a novel he was reading, he made his way to the back of the dorms long after midnight. As he squatted, oddly at peace with his surroundings, he heard footsteps approaching through the tall grass. He calmly cleaned himself up, not in the least bit concerned by the sound. According to him, he figured from the faint glow of their flashlights that they were carrying cheap mobile phones. There were three of them, boys wielding makeshift weapons. Chains, shanks, and the like.

"Who be dat?" one of them called out as they approached.

"Na me," Calvin replied in his heavily Americanized Pidgin, still completely unfazed.

"Who be you?" the thug asked, his irritation clear. He swung the flashlight directly onto Calvin's torso, and when the beam caught sight of his massive, bulging chest, the boy froze for a second before blurting out, "Oh shit."

And just like that, they retreated, muttering something about looking for someone else.

That's just one of many Calvin stories, but easily my favorite. It summed him up perfectly. He was calm, fearless, and built like a walking deterrent. Funny thing is, I never expected us to be close friends, but somehow, a shared love for 1940s American film noir brought us together.

Straight out of university, Calvin had joined the DSS, putting all that brute strength and intellect to good use. The man was basically an African Terminator. A force of nature, unstoppable once he set his mind on something. And thank

God today that something was getting me out of this hellhole.

We got into his black Jeep, and before I knew it, we were speeding away from the station, the city flashing past in a blur. I leaned back in the seat and let out another deep breath, the tension in my shoulders slowly unwinding. That had been too close. Way too close.

After I recounted everything that had happened since I met Mmachi, neither of us said anything. The silence was comfortable, broken only by the hum of the engine and the occasional beep of a horn as Calvin weaved through Lagos traffic like he was born for it. I let my head rest against the seat and stared out at the chaos of the city. The longer I stayed, the deeper I was getting pulled in.

I broke the silence. "I need to get out of this country, man."

Calvin glanced over at me with a sharp look. "Well, that won't be happening soon."

"What do you mean?" I asked.

"Your passport," Calvin said, his tone flat but the weight of his words heavy. "Detective Inspector Bayo never handed it over. You're not getting out of the country any time soon."

Of course. My chest tightened. Bayo wasn't playing around. The Nigerian police system might be slow in some areas, but they become very efficient at their job when they want someone. I was trapped, and the realization punched me in the gut.

"Great," I muttered, rubbing a hand across my face. "Just great."

Calvin didn't respond right away, but he glanced at me from the corner of his eye. "You really think running back to the States would solve anything? If they want, they'll come after you there."

141

I wanted to argue, but Calvin was right. Hell, I'd just get flagged at Dulles and arrested, anyway. Of course, Bayo wouldn't let me skip town without a fight, not with a murder charge hanging over my head. And then there was my family to consider. If I bolted now, would they be safe? What would happen if the police, or someone worse, dragged them into this mess? Running wasn't an option.

I was boxed in, backed into a corner with no real options. Escape wasn't on the table, and facing Bayo without answers was just as bad. If I wanted to clear my name, I'd have to untangle the mess myself, solve the damn case, and close it on my terms. There was no other way.

I sighed heavily. "Looks like I'm stuck here."

Calvin turned to me, giving me that knowing look. "You're not stuck," he said. "You're home. Now do what you must to make it feel that way."

A wry smile tugged at the corner of my mouth. He was right. Sitting around feeling sorry for myself wouldn't solve anything.

"And now I just have to figure out where to start," I muttered.

Calvin nodded thoughtfully. "What about the girl?"

I flinched. "What girl?"

"The dead man's dame," he said in his best Bogart voice, a smirk playing on his lips. "She was with the Admiral that night, wasn't she? Plus, you mentioned smelling a woman's perfume when you found the body. She might know more than we think."

Realization dawned on me. He was right. "Yeah…you're onto something."

Calvin switched gears, his tone lighter. "How about I take you out for lunch?" He looked me over and added with a grin. "Maybe get you some clothes first. You're looking a little rough."

I blinked, then remembered I was still sitting there in nothing but my boxers. I looked down at myself, feeling ridiculous. We both burst out laughing. It was one of those rare moments where the absurdity of the situation caught up to you.

"Man, I'm tired of the police," I said, shaking my head. "How the hell are you even here? I thought you were stationed in Abuja."

"I am," Calvin replied, eyes focused on the road, though that smirk never left his face. "But I was in town, and Osita called. Told me to get you out of jail."

I exhaled a long sigh of relief, grateful that the cop I'd given Osita's number to had followed through after all. That was one hell of a stroke of luck.

"What have you gotten yourself into, my friend?" Calvin asked, the tone of his voice more serious now, his eyes flicking back to me.

"I don't even know," I muttered, shaking my head. "But I need to figure this shit out, and fast, before Detective Inspector Bayo comes knocking again."

Calvin nodded, keeping his gaze forward, his jaw set. "Where do you want to go after lunch?"

I thought about it for a moment, my mind running through the possibilities. Where would I even start unraveling this mess? And then it hit me. The Admiral's bag. There had to be something in there, some clue that could lead me to whatever the hell was really going on. I had to dig through it, put the pieces together before I ended up even deeper in this nightmare.

But then I thought of another pit stop. If I planned to figure out who killed the Admiral, I needed to know how he died.

"I don't mean to be that guy, Cal," I said. "I'm going to need you to pull some strings for me one more time."

— ◆ —

The coroner's office in Ikeja smelled of antiseptic and something faintly metallic, like the lingering scent of blood that refused to be masked by chemicals. The chill in the air hit me the moment we stepped inside. A sterile cold that seeped into the bones and whispered of death. Calvin led the way, his stride confident, his air of authority enough to deter questions from curious eyes. He was a man who knew his way around places like this, and his demeanor made it clear we weren't here to waste time.

At the entrance, a young coroner named Femi greeted us, his lab coat pristine, though his eyes betrayed a weariness that only came from spending too much time among the dead. He gave Calvin a polite nod before leading us deeper into the facility, his footsteps echoing off the tiled floor. The fluorescent lights overhead buzzed softly, casting a clinical glow on the room ahead.

We entered a large, cold chamber lined with stainless steel tables. At first glance, they appeared ordinary, but as we moved closer, the grim reality became clear. White sheets draped each table, covering the motionless form of a body, hinting at lives that had been ended suddenly.

Femi stopped at one table near the center of the room. "We'll need to make this quick, gentlemen," he said as he positioned himself beside the body. With a practiced motion, he pulled back the sheet, revealing the Admiral's lifeless form. His face was pale, his expression frozen in an unsettling stillness. The once-imposing figure now looked small and vulnerable under the harsh light.

"Two gunshot wounds to the chest," Femi began, gesturing to the small, neat entry points that marred the Admiral's torso. "Both shots penetrated cleanly, striking vital organs. Based on the trajectory and depth, I'd estimate he bled out within minutes."

Calvin nodded, his jaw tightening, but Femi wasn't finished. He pointed to several dark marks on the Admiral's ribs and arms, bruises that stood out against the pallor of his skin. "There's also significant contusion along the ribcage, forearms, and upper thighs. The bruising patterns suggest blunt force trauma, likely inflicted before the gunshots. These aren't postmortem injuries."

"Tortured?" I asked as I studied the Admiral's body.

Femi hesitated, then nodded. "That would be my assessment. The distribution of the injuries suggests an attempt to inflict maximum pain without immediately incapacitating the victim."

I swallowed hard, my gaze lingering on the Admiral's still face. "Why would they torture him if they were just going to kill him?"

Calvin shrugged, his detachment practiced but not indifferent. "Could have been for information. Could have been to send a message. Or maybe it's just the way they do things."

I leaned in closer, my eyes narrowing as I tried to piece together the puzzle. "Any defensive wounds? Did he try to fight back?"

Femi moved to the Admiral's hands, carefully lifting one to show faint abrasions on the knuckles. "There's evidence he resisted. Not much, but enough to indicate a struggle."

"Whoever did this, they wanted to break him before they pulled the trigger," Calvin said. "Any other findings? Something that might tell us more about what happened?"

Femi glanced at the clipboard on the counter nearby, flipping through the pages with practiced efficiency. "No signs of drugging or poisoning. Bloodwork came back clean except for elevated cortisol levels, which is consistent with extreme stress or fear prior to death." He pointed at a dark patch around the abdomen of the corpse. "He seemed to nurse a bruised rib, but the bruise suggests it was from before last night. Maybe two or three nights ago. Painful but not life-threatening. But no, nothing more."

My stomach churned at the thought. Tortured, terrified, and then executed. But why? The Admiral wasn't some petty criminal. He was a man of power, of influence. What could they have wanted for them to have resorted to this?

I stepped back, rubbing my temples as I tried to make sense of it. Calvin's hand on my shoulder brought me back to the present. "Let's go," he said, his tone firm but not unkind. "We've seen enough."

"One more thing," Femi said. "One other finding that might be relevant," he said, his clinical tone softening as though bracing for our reaction. "We found traces of semen on the Admiral's body, along with faint lubricant residue. Based on its location and the absence of significant time-related degradation, I'd estimate that he engaged in intercourse shortly before his death."

I blinked, momentarily caught off guard by the revelation. "You're sure about that?"

Femi nodded, his expression professional but firm. "Yes, the evidence is consistent. The biochemical markers, specifically, oxytocin and prolactin levels, also suggest recent sexual activity, which strongly supports the conclusion."

Calvin leaned back slightly, folding his arms across his chest as he let out a low whistle. "So, the old man got busy before he got dead. The dame?"

"Maybe," I said cautiously, my mind racing. "Although I find it hard to expect. She did not seem the type."

"You knew her well?" Calvin asked, sarcasm sharp in his tone. "You don't even know her name."

"Yes, I know. But I got the impression she was highly dependent on him. Torturing and killing him doesn't make sense." I turned to Femi. "Are you sure someone was with him right before he was murdered?"

"It's definitely possible," Femi admitted, his tone matter-of-fact. "Or it could have been unrelated. A private encounter before the attackers got to him. But based on the timeline, the two events seem close enough to warrant consideration."

I processed this additional layer of complexity. The Admiral wasn't simply tortured and executed, there was something intimate in the hours, or perhaps even minutes, before his death. It painted a grim picture: whoever he had been with wasn't just a passing stranger. They could've been a piece of this convoluted puzzle, a pawn, or maybe even the hand that set it all into motion. On the other hand, they might've been unwitting participants, caught in a web they didn't see coming. Regardless, they were essential to the investigation.

"Anything else?" I asked, my mind racing to connect the dots.

Femi shook his head, his gloved hands snapping off the disposable coverings as he gestured toward the exit. Without another word, we left the cold, sterile room behind, stepping back into the dry Lagos air.

As we made our way to Calvin's jeep, he spoke up, his tone casual but his words probing. "Do you need help finding her?"

I shook my head. "You're a man of the law," I said. "I don't want to involve you any more than I already have, unless I don't have a choice."

Calvin scoffed, his dry laugh a mix of camaraderie and frustration. "Sounds like you'll be using Osita, then."

I gave a slow nod. "I need his network for this. They know where to look, and they're not... constrained by the system."

Calvin paused, resting his arm on the roof of the car as he looked at me from across the bonnet. His expression shifted, growing serious in a way that made me take notice. "Watch out for him," he said. "He's my friend, and I love him, but Osita's never fully walked away from the life he lived back in university."

I exhaled deeply, weighing his words. He wasn't wrong. Osita had always operated in shades of gray, blurring the line between what was legal and what was necessary. Back in school, his underground connections weren't just useful, they were life-saving. But those same connections came with risks. I respected Calvin's warning, but I knew I couldn't afford to play it safe.

"Admittedly, I'm worried about that too," I said, meeting Calvin's gaze. "But I need his brand of effectiveness. Someone was murdered, and I'm being dragged into it. I don't have the luxury of waiting around for the system to work."

Calvin's jaw tightened, but he nodded. He understood, even if he didn't like it. "Just be careful."

I nodded in return and climbed into the jeep, my mind already racing ahead to the next steps. Calvin was right about one thing: finding her was essential.

CHAPTER 15

Calvin took me to a restaurant for lunch, where we caught up a bit. It was the kind of place that served overpriced jollof rice and boasted of being "authentically African" while catering to the elites who wouldn't know true authenticity if it slapped them. After the meal, he dropped me back at the house. He didn't come inside; he had some business to handle.

When I got to the gate, Akaneme was waiting, but a more muted expression replaced his usual broken smile. He let me in without a word. He probably didn't like that I brought the police into his peaceful little bubble. Nigerian cops, not known for their accuracy or restraint, rarely cared whom they roughed up to make their jobs easier.

I grabbed the Admiral's bag from under the front seat of the Range Rover and headed straight for the bedroom. I dumped the contents onto the bed, plugged his phone into the charger, and slid the microSD card into my laptop. Retrieving a flash drive from my things, I plugged that in as well, starting the file transfer of everything. While the files copied over, I headed for the shower, eager to wash off the grime of the police station. The stench of sweat, fear, and corruption had clung to my skin like a second layer.

As the water hit me, I ground my teeth, trying to suppress the anger building inside me. I'd never been one to chant "fuck the police," but Nigeria had a way of twisting your perspective. Here, it wasn't only about crooked cops or a few rotten apples, it was the whole damn system. Rotten from the inside out, corrupted at every level. Every encounter reminded me that the law wasn't about justice; it was about power and who could wield it.

Stepping out of the bathroom, I dried off and powered up my laptop, eager to sift through the contents of the SD card. As I began scrolling through the files, my initial excitement dulled. Most of it was mundane. Personal documents like bank statements, invoices, and scanned passports. Nothing leaped out as a smoking gun or even remotely intriguing at first glance.

However, as I delved deeper, something caught my attention. The bank statements revealed a surprising detail: the Admiral had been living off regular transfers from none other than his wife, Mmachi. The transactions spanned at least a year, painting a picture I hadn't expected. For a man like him, a proud, quintessential African alpha male, being financially dependent on his wife must have been a bitter pill to swallow. I couldn't help but wonder how it had chipped away at his pride, his sense of control.

But as intriguing as that psychological thread was, it wasn't the point of my investigation. I filed the observation away in the back of my mind and kept searching, determined to find something more relevant. Something that would actually move the needle on this case.

Then came the family photos. There were plenty of those. The Admiral and Mmachi, always at some exotic location or lavish resort. No doubt part of their endless vacation from responsibility. Adaora was in a few of them too, her petite frame and stony expression much warmer in the photos. She looked... happier, softer, like the world hadn't hardened her yet.

After nearly an hour of sifting through mundane pictures and documents, I came across a folder with a peculiar name: *G2JO2*. I raised my eyebrows. The folder contained over a hundred gigs of data. Jackpot.

I opened it, and what greeted me was a sea of video files. Row after row of them. The filenames were generic, just dates and timestamps. The first was eight months ago. Curious, I clicked it.

The video was a screen recording from a phone. The interface was immediately familiar. It was a live-streaming app, one of those platforms where young women sit in front of the camera, doing little more than existing, while men throw money at them as digital tokens called rubies. The layout was typical: at the top of the screen, you had the host's username and a list of her most recent "gifts" from viewers. Below that, the woman sat in a chair, the kind you'd find in a gamer's setup. It was black and red, reclining, ergonomic, all that crap. She wore a highlighter-green top that was so tight, it left nothing to the imagination. Her breasts were practically spilling out of it.

At the bottom of the screen was the chat, an endless barrage of thirsty comments.

I love you. Marry me. How can I get your number?

It was pathetic, really. Grown men blowing their hard-earned money on women they'd never meet, trying to buy a moment of attention. And for what? To feel special for all of two seconds before the host moved on to the next sucker in the chat. I scrolled through the comments, noticing a recurring word: *pvt.*

How much for pvt? Do you do pvt? 3k rubies for pvt?

It didn't take long to figure out what *Pvt* meant. Private. As in a private video call where things got a bit more... intimate. A sexual interaction that the live-streaming platform itself didn't allow. But for the right price? Well, everyone's got their hustle.

As I scrolled through more videos, I noticed the Admiral's attention seemed to gravitate toward one specific woman. Her screen name? *TequilaDream.* She had a caramel complexion that Nigerian men can't seem to get enough of, and an hourglass figure that looked suspiciously fake. Her waist-to-hip ratio would have looked almost cartoonish on most, but somehow suited and added to her allure.

It was her. The Admiral's fiancée.

In the videos, she'd always start the same way. "Hey, papi," she'd say in that sultry, rehearsed voice, her lips curling into a seductive smile. The Admiral, under the username *King Investor*, was her regular. Every time she called him *papi,* she probably wanted to make him feel special, as if she cared. It was all an act, of course.

I clicked on one of the later videos; this one was clearly more personal. The live-streaming sessions had turned into private video conversations. TequilaDream was standing now, wearing a black tank top that dipped low in the front, showing off more cleavage than anyone should see on a scorching afternoon. No bra, naturally. Her hips swayed as she moved in front of the camera, and I could see the Admiral's face on the bottom of the screen, his mouth slightly open, eyes wide with desire. The man looked completely mesmerized.

And there he was. Retired Admiral Alex Maduagu, a far cry from the stern military man I'd met. He was grinning like a fool, his thinning salt-and-pepper hair swept back, his dark skin shining under the dim light of the camera. His wide, weathered face looked almost boyish, like he was seeing heaven on earth.

"Hey, papi," TequilaDream cooed. "It's great to see you again."

"Baby girl," the Admiral gasped, his breath coming in shallow bursts. "I don't want to chat on *Slago* anymore. Hope you don't mind my calling here?"

Slago. That was the name of the livestreaming app. I wrote it down in my notepad, acting the professional sleuth. I also picked up my phone and typed in a quick text message to Osita:

Do you know anything about an app called Slago?
Looks like the Admiral met his fiancée on it.

TequilaDream smiled, slow and deliberate. "Not at all, papi. I know you got me."

The Admiral's breathing grew heavier. "Are you ready?"

She nodded, her smile widening. "Of course. Are you?"

The Admiral nodded wildly, his face a picture of raw anticipation. What followed was... well, let's just say it started off pleasurable but turned uncomfortable to watch. TequilaDream had begun to strip, one article of clothing at a time. She revealed everything.

On any other day, the sight might have been titillating. But the Admiral's grunts and shakes, the way he fumbled with himself on the bottom half of the screen, turned the whole thing into something grotesque. A man of his stature, reduced to a quivering mess by a woman half his age, and not even in person.

I shut the laptop, disgusted.

I leaned back in the chair, taking a moment to process everything I had just seen. The Admiral, once a military man of principle, or so I thought, had clearly fallen into something dark, something hidden beneath the surface of his respectable life. Whether it was a failing marriage with Mmachi, an unchecked addiction, or simple perversion, the man had spent more time and money than I could comfortably count on a livestreaming app that had morphed into a digital playground for prostitution.

TequilaDream, with her caramel complexion and surgically enhanced body, was undoubtedly his favorite. Sure, he had interacted with plenty of other girls on the app and thrown gifts their way, but none got the same attention as her. She had him wrapped around her finger—papi this, papi that. It was both sickening and fascinating.

I rubbed my temples, trying to figure out what this meant. Mmachi must have known something was off with her husband, but I doubted she had any idea about the depths of his addiction. Or maybe she did and just didn't care. IT was hard to say with her. Either way, it didn't change the fact that I was sitting on something huge.

I needed more. I needed something that would connect the dots. That's when I remembered the Admiral's phone. I took it off the charger and pressed the power button, silently praying he hadn't locked it with a passcode. But of course, the screen lit up with a numeric lock.

I groaned. Surely, the Admiral would be cautious enough to use a passcode. But now I had a problem. How the hell was I going to get in? I couldn't afford to waste time trying every combination under the sun.

I leaned back in the chair, staring at the Admiral's phone as if the answer would magically appear on the screen. It was encrypted by a man who lived his life with a certain code.

Disciplined, precise, and far too smart to use something obvious like a birthday or anniversary. Or was he?

I glanced at my laptop, where the videos from the microSD card were still uploading. There had been plenty of uncomfortable content in those videos, but a few conversations between him and TequilaDream had stood out. They were less overtly sexual, and more conversational. They were like tiny windows into the Admiral's mind, moments where he spoke freely, maybe even carelessly.

I pulled the laptop closer and scrolled through the list of video files, looking for the ones where his tone had shifted. There had been one in particular where TequilaDream had asked him about his life outside of their torrid exchanges. I found it, clicked play, and fast-forwarded past the initial flirtation until I landed on the part I wanted.

TequilaDream asked him what his proudest moment was. Without a moment passing, he responded. It was the birth of his daughter, Adaora. And his words to me also rang in my head: *"There's hardly a decision I've made in my life that didn't take my daughter into account."*

My heart raced as I keyed in a combination: Adaora's birthday.

02-15-98.

Incorrect Password. Please Try Again.

I swore under my breath. It had to be right. Then something occurred to me. This wasn't America. In Nigeria, they swap day and month. I stared at the screen, then entered 15-02-98.

The lock clicked open. Nothing more to it.

I exhaled sharply. There wasn't any time to congratulate myself. I needed to move fast.

I navigated through the phone's apps. There it was. SLAGO LIVE. The icon was a cartoonish white lion, one of those cutesy chibi characters that the Japanese seemed to love. A small splash screen popped up as I opened it, featuring an ad that promised "more rubies, more gifts, more fun!" I ignored it and moved straight to the primary interface.

Thumbnails of various hosts filled the screen, each one posing provocatively, waiting for their next "papi" to come along and throw rubies their way. There were many women: light-skinned with hair that looked expensive enough to pay my rent, dark-skinned natural beauties with curves that wouldn't quit, some with tattoos that snaked across their skin like vines, others with faces that looked fresh out of a cosmetic surgery catalog. There were men too, buff and shirtless, clearly catering to a female audience. Even a few transgender hosts, because apparently, Slago catered to every taste imaginable.

I clicked the profile button in the top corner and saw the Admiral's friend list. Twelve hosts. All Nigerian, from what I could tell. I clicked through the profiles, scrolling past their bios, some boasting thousands of followers, others still grinding for attention. And there she was. *TequilaDream,* with that signature sultry smile in her profile picture. She was the star, the queen of his digital fantasy.

I tapped on her profile and began scrolling through her pictures. It didn't take much to figure out what her game was. She knew exactly how to play to the weaknesses of men. Every photo was a carefully constructed trap. High angles, sultry stares, and skin on display. This was a girl who made her living by making men lose their common sense. I could tell just by looking. Her "assets" were front and center in every shot, and there was no doubt that she used them to keep men like the Admiral hooked.

She wasn't online, though, so I couldn't see her in action. That might have to wait. For now, I settled on watching more of the recordings from the app, trying to avoid the videos that were too... *personal.* I wasn't about to spend more time watching a man in his late sixties jerk himself to sleep.

I resumed my investigation, the screen flickering with clips of TequilaDream pulling the same moves again and again. The same seductive voice, the same sultry smiles. Men threw money at her, promising her the world for a little attention. It was almost pitiful how predictable it was, but I couldn't help but admire how well she worked them. She knew exactly how to bait them, and they were more than happy to be caught.

I was just getting into the rhythm of things when my phone buzzed loudly on the table, pulling me out of the dark world of livestream seduction. I glanced down and saw Osita's name flashing on the screen.

I picked up, expecting him to be his usual laid-back, joking self, maybe calling to ask if I wanted to swing by the club for a drink.

"Guy," his voice rang out before I could say anything. Osita usually didn't sound rushed or serious, which surprised me. My gut tightened. Whatever this was, it wasn't good. "Drop whatever you're doing. Come to the club, quick!"

The urgency in his tone hit me like a cold slap. I opened my mouth to ask what was going on, but he'd already hung up.

I stared at the phone for a second, the uneasiness settling in my stomach like a stone. Something was wrong, *really* wrong. Osita never sounded like that unless shit was about to hit the fan.

158

I quickly closed the laptop, put the flash drive in my coat pocket, threw on a shirt, and grabbed my keys. Whatever this was, I had to deal with it now. I couldn't afford another crisis, but in Lagos, it seemed like crises were all I ever got.

I rushed out of the house, tossing the bag with the Admiral's things into the back seat of the car, and peeled out of the driveway. As usual, the traffic clogged the roads to Victoria Island, despite the time of night, but I weaved through them like a madman. Horns blared, pedestrians cursed as I raced, but I couldn't slow down. My mind raced faster than the car, trying to piece together what Osita could need me for so urgently.

As I sped toward the club, the sinking feeling in my gut only grew worse. Something was happening, and if Osita was involved, it couldn't be small. Whatever this was, I had a bad feeling that I was about to get dragged even deeper into the mess I was already in.

And I wasn't sure if I could handle where this was heading next.

CHAPTER 16

I walked into the Diamond Ballot feeling like something heavy was hanging over my head. I worried about what Osita might say, given the prior events. As I moved through the back, the bass-heavy beats from the club pounded against my chest. The whole place seemed normal, but my instincts told me something was up. Osita was waiting for me in his office, or so I thought. I pushed the door open, half-expecting him to be sitting there, waiting to drop some fresh hell on me.

Instead, the lights flipped on, and the entire room erupted in shouts.

"Surprise!"

I froze, caught off guard. For a second, I didn't know what I was looking at. My brain was too slow to process the scene in front of me. But then, it hit me like a train. These weren't just random faces. These were *my* people.

Osita was front and center, grinning from ear to ear, his arms spread wide like the showman he was. "Guy, relax! You too dey form James Bond! We just wan make you feel at home."

I couldn't help laughing. The weight I'd been carrying on my shoulders seemed to melt away as I took in the sight of old friends. Calvin was there, of course, leaning against the wall with his usual smug expression, a glass of whiskey in hand. Familiar faces from university filled the room. People I hadn't seen in years. They were talking, laughing, and drinking like we hadn't been apart for nearly a decade.

Then there was Victor. He used to go by the name "Dark Snow" back in uni. It was a self-styled alias from his days as a cult member. He was always cool, always calculated, and spoke with an exaggerated American accent he'd adopted somewhere along the way, probably to compete with Calvin's effortless drawl. He greeted me with a firm handshake, his smile just as smooth as it had been all those years ago, then moved on to fraternize with a couple of strippers who were lounging near the bar, slipping back into his old ways with an ease that was almost impressive.

"My man, Dozy!"

It was a voice I'd heard recently.

I turned and there was Oge. She stood draped in a bright yellow off- the -shoulder dress that hugged her slender frame. The dress, stylish yet understated, had a playful ruffle at the hem that swayed with her every movement, showing off her long, toned legs. She paired it with black strappy heels. Her dark, neatly braided hair was pulled back, giving full view of her soft, oval face. She didn't scream for attention, never had. But somehow, Oge always commanded it effortlessly.

"Barrister!" I grinned and walked over, pulling her into a tight hug.

Oge shook her head, still grinning as she glanced at me. "So, Osita tells me you're a detective now, Mr. Agu. Solving crimes and catching bad guys?" She arched an eyebrow, the teasing in her voice clear.

I couldn't help but chuckle at the thought. "Ah, please, he's not being serious. I'm not exactly Sherlock Holmes. But I'll tell you all about it later. It's not as glamorous as it sounds."

"Uh-huh," she said, giving me a playful nudge. "Don't worry, I won't make you spill all your secrets tonight. Just don't disappear before we get a chance to catch up."

I smiled, feeling lighter in that moment than I had in days. "I promise."

Then Osita appeared out of nowhere, throwing an arm around my shoulders, grinning like he'd just won the lottery. "Guy, wetin una dey yarn wey una no invite me?" he teased, lifting his glass like he was toasting to the reunion.

"Osita, you dey craze," I said, shaking my head. "How dare you act like you were in trouble? What if I had come here looking like a bum?"

They both burst into laughter, but it was Calvin, who had just joined us, who spoke next. "There's no way in hell Dozy Agu will ever leave his house looking like a bum," he said with a smirk.

"Not in a million years," Oge added, nodding in agreement.

"Doesn't even matter if I was dying," Osita chimed in, still chuckling.

I glanced around at them, bewildered. "What are you guys even talking about?"

"You remember that Politics and Law in Africa exam?" Osita asked, looking from Calvin to Oge.

"Chai!" Calvin exclaimed, laughing even harder.

I ducked my head in embarrassment as I realized exactly what they were talking about. During our third year at university, I was so determined to ace all my classes and avoid spending an extra year that I started attending night classes. You know, the kind where students would head to school late at night, like around nine, and study until the early hours of the morning. I got a little carried away with it, especially for the Politics and Law in Africa exam. I didn't make it home until a little after six in the morning, utterly exhausted. The exam was at eight, and I figured I'd just rest for a few minutes before heading out.

Big mistake.

I woke up at four minutes past eight.

Now, a regular person would've dashed out of the house in a full-on panic. After all, the exam hall was a fifteen-minute walk, but I could've made it in five if I ran. I would've been late by ten, maybe fifteen minutes tops, probably forgivable. But my obsessive disdain for leaving the house without looking presentable pushed all that out of my mind. Instead, I hopped into the shower, put on some freshly ironed clothes, and walked—yes, walked—to the exam hall. By the time I arrived, I was a good thirty-five minutes late. The invigilator gave me a death glare as if I were insane. All I could do was mutter, "Please, sir," over and over until he got so irritated by my persistence that he handed me the exam.

I still got an A.

I glanced down at my outfit. Black chinos, a grey short-sleeved shirt, and polished leather shoes. Despite all the chaos, I had unconsciously dressed up again. They were right about me.

I laughed, letting the tension of the last few days slide off my back. For the first time since I landed in Lagos, I didn't feel like I had a target on me. I wasn't just the guy running from one mess to another, I was Dozy Agu, surrounded by my people.

A few drinks and tasty bites later, only four of us remained at the Diamond Ballot. Me, Osita, Calvin, and Oge. The club's energy had cooled, leaving us basking in the mellow afterglow. A half-empty bottle of whiskey sat between us. Oge, usually able to out-drink any of us, was pacing herself, more drawn to the stories than the booze.

"Remember Usanga?" Calvin asked, leaning back with a grin.

That name alone sent us into laughter. The story was legendary.

It happened back in our first year. We were in the canteen one morning, packed with students, the air thick with the smell of akara, fried eggs, and plantain. I was halfway through a plate of okpa when a loud *smack* cut through the noise.

Everyone froze.

Usanga, who was 5'2" and wild-haired, stood there holding his face, stunned. Beside him, Ruth, taller and furious, glared down at him. The slap had echoed. A guy near us, still chewing meat, muttered, "Shiiit," like his brain couldn't compute anything else.

At first, we didn't laugh. Just stared. Then it hit. Wave after wave of laughter as Usanga bolted out of the hall like a wounded cartoon character.

"That should've been the end of it," I said, sipping my drink. "But no."

"Yeah," Calvin chimed in. "We saw him that afternoon marching to Mass Comm with a squad like he was leading a coup."

The entire campus saw it. A dozen guys hyping him up, pushing him toward some grand revenge. Ruth was with her friends, probably still laughing. Usanga stormed in, silent. Then, without warning, he unbuckled his belt.

The girls stared, stunned.

"And then he just started belting her!" Osita howled.

"Belting the hell out of her!" Calvin added.

Chaos erupted. Her friends lunged, and Usanga's boys rushed in. An all-out brawl broke out. Chairs flying, boys and girls swinging. We just stood there watching, as if it were prime-time drama.

"Only God knows what he said to her before that slap," Oge said, still wiping tears.

"Someone dared him to hit on her," I offered. "Probably thought he was being charming."

"I heard he insulted her after she turned him down," Osita said. "That's why she slapped him."

We exploded with laughter again. No matter how many times we told it, the absurdity never got old.

— ◆ —

As Ogechi and Calvin headed out, Osita gave me a subtle nod, a signal to hang back. I knew him well enough to know this wasn't going to be a casual chat. We waited until the sound of their laughter faded into the distance, leaving the two of us alone in the now-quiet club.

"Alobam," he said, using the nickname he always reserved for me. "I got your message. There's someone I'd like you to meet."

He motioned for me to follow him, leading me toward one of his girls, who had just emerged from the dressing room. She wore a plain t-shirt and leggings, with her hair in simple cornrows rather than the sleek wig she had on the last time I saw her in his office focused on her phone. It took me a moment to recognize her.

"Ene," he said, nodding toward her. "Tell him what you told me."

Ene glanced at me and then at Osita, shifting uncomfortably before straightening her posture. "I know about Slago," she said matter-of-factly.

My interest piqued immediately. I leaned in, my voice betraying my excitement. "What do you know about it? What can you tell me?"

She hesitated, clearing her throat and crossing her arms. Her eyes scanned me, and her lips curled into an unreadable smirk. For a moment, I thought she might be sizing me up. Confused, I turned to Osita, who simply chuckled.

"Find am something," he said, the Lagosian code for *pay up* unmistakable.

"Oh, of course," I said quickly, kicking myself for forgetting the golden rule: in Lagos, nothing comes free. I pulled out five crisp one-thousand naira notes and placed them in her waiting palm.

She looked at the money, unimpressed. "Are you not coming from Yankee? This is small, na."

Before I could retort, Osita's tone shifted. "My friend," he snapped. "Will you tell the man what he needs to know before I show you a side of me you won't like?"

Ene flinched and straightened up, her attitude dissolving as quickly as it had formed. "Errrm," she began cautiously, "most of the girls you see on Slago have agents."

"Agents? Like the way actors have agents?" I asked, the comparison striking me as odd.

"Yes," she confirmed. "Slago doesn't pay hosts directly. They go through agencies. At the end of every month, agencies pay the hosts a salary based on the rubies they earned that month.

"Rubies are converted to cash," Osita chimed in. "The agents handle the payouts after taking their share, of course."

I cupped my chin, processing this new information. "Why do these agents sound like they're...?"

"Pimps?" Osita finished bluntly. "Maybe because they are."

Ene nodded. "The hosts have monthly targets. If they don't meet them, their payout is way less than what it should be. And the targets aren't small."

I shifted my focus. "What about this girl I'm looking for? If she is a big host in Lagos, she must have connections to one of these agents, right?"

Ene hesitated for a moment before leaning in slightly, lowering her voice. "If she's big, only one of the three agents here in Lagos can manage her."

"So, we need to find these three agents and see if they have information about her?" I pressed, already planning my next steps.

"Not exactly." Ene's voice dropped to a conspiratorial whisper, as if the walls themselves might be listening. "The three agents don't work independently. They all answer to one person. If you can get to that person, you can access the clients of all three agents."

I leaned back, impressed. Ene's information might have been worth more than the cash I'd given her after all. "Interesting," I said with a faint smile. "Who is this man?"

"Not a man, but a lady," she corrected, a wry smile creeping onto her lips. "Her name is Funlola Alakija."

CHAPTER 17

The Opal Heights Hotel, the Alakijas' flagship masterpiece, was nothing short of a modern marvel. Its cream and glass facade stretched skyward, reflecting the Lagos sun like a shimmering beacon of wealth and exclusivity. Perched strategically along the Lagos shoreline, the hotel offered a sweeping view of the lagoon, with its still, endless expanse enhancing the hotel's pristine allure.

As we drove up, the grandeur was palpable. Osita, seated beside me, whistled low in awe, astonished at my connection to Lola Alakija. "I can't believe you know her," he muttered, his eyes glued to the architectural masterpiece before us.

A smartly uniformed valet, dressed in crisp white and navy with a gilded emblem of the hotel embroidered on his chest, waited at the entrance. He stepped forward with practiced precision, opening the doors of the Range Rover. Osita and I stepped out, and the valet handed me a yellow ticket and then slid into the driver's seat, smoothly steering the vehicle toward an underground parking lot.

Another impeccably dressed man, with a demeanor suggesting he'd mastered the art of discretion, approached us. He gave a subtle bow and motioned us toward the entrance. I advanced, keeping my eyes on my surroundings, when a flicker at the edge of my vision froze me in my tracks.

Bayo stood on the other side of the street. His lips curled into a smug smirk I'd come to dread. He lifted a hand in a slow, deliberate wave. No surprise at all, just cold certainty that he'd been shadowing me since I left the police station.

My pulse thudded against my ribs. I straightened, even as my gut turned itself inside out. The usher cleared his throat, fingers still pointing at the revolving door. I gave a curt, polite nod, swallowed the tension, and stepped forward. Every breath I took reminded me: one wrong move and Bayo wouldn't hesitate to close the trap.

Inside, the lobby unfolded like a gallery of cultural opulence. A fusion of European sophistication and African heritage defined the space. Polished marble floors gleamed under chandeliers that sparkled with thousands of crystals, each refracting light in a kaleidoscope of color. Along the walls, ornate carvings depicted Nigerian folklore; their craftsmanship was so intricate they seemed almost alive. Plush seating arrangements in deep burgundy and gold dotted the space, paired with side tables carved from mahogany. A grand spiral staircase with wrought-iron railings swirled upward, its design reminiscent of the elaborate coral bead headdresses worn by royalty in Benin.

The man led us to an elevator tucked into a corner, its doors flanked by sculptures of Yoruba deities. He swiped a gold access card, and the elevator doors glided open. Inside, dark wood paneled the cabin, and a brass console outfitted it. He pressed a button marked 'S' for the penthouse suite.

The elevator ascended silently, and when the doors opened, I stepped into a scene that defied my imagination. The penthouse suite was breathtaking. Floor-to-ceiling windows framed an uninterrupted view of the lagoon, the horizon stretching far into the distance. Light poured into the room, illuminating a space designed to perfection. Marble floors sprawled across the expanse, polished to a mirror shine. An oversized chandelier, dripping with glass teardrops, hung from the high ceiling, casting a golden glow over the space.

On one side, a seating area with custom-made leather sofas and a Persian rug that probably cost more than my yearly income invited guests to lounge. The bar, a sleek structure of glass and chrome, stocked top-shelf liquor and crystal decanters. At the far end, an open kitchen showcased state-of-the-art appliances, though I doubted Lola ever cooked for herself.

Lola sat behind an ornate desk, her golden head wrap catching the sunlight streaming through the windows, making it glimmer like a crown. Her lips curled into a coquettish smirk as she stood to greet me. Every movement she made was deliberate and undeniably captivating.

"Dozy," she said, extending her hand. I took it and pressed a polite kiss to her knuckles. Ever the gentleman. "And who is this?" she asked, her eyes drifting to Osita.

"This is Osita. He's a friend of mine. We go way back," I said, gesturing toward him.

Osita stepped forward, his handshake firm but polite. "Pleasure to meet you, ma."

Lola chuckled, the sound low and rich. "I've had the pleasure of visiting your club," she said, her tone teasing yet genuine.

Osita nodded, his confidence unshaken. "Yes ma. I recall."

She raised an eyebrow, intrigued. "Tell me, what inspired your business model? I've been to strip clubs in Lagos before, but there's something incredibly classy about your establishment. So much so that I wouldn't even go so far as to call it a strip club."

Osita shrugged, his tone casual but with a hint of pride. "What can I say? I'm a visionary."

I stifled a laugh. The Diamond Ballot was a lot of things, but a traditional strip club it was not. On most nights, it operated more like an upscale Japanese hostess club, an idea Osita had unapologetically stolen after a summer in Tokyo. But when the occasion called for it, the Diamond Ballot could transform into a spectacle of glamour and seduction that drew Lagos' elite.

Lola leaned back, studying Osita with an appraising gaze. "Visionary indeed," she said. "I'll have to visit again soon. It's not every day you find a man with such a knack for reinvention." She walked to the bar with the confidence of someone who owned the world, or at least this penthouse. "You'll be having the scotch and soda, right?" She asked, already reaching for the tumbler.

I accepted the drink she had prepared. Taking my seat, I let the cool rim of the glass touch my lips before savoring the first sip. It hit just right.

Lola turned her attention to Osita. "And what about you?" she asked, her tone pleasant but businesslike.

"Hero," he said without hesitation. Classic Osita. His devotion to Hero beer was unwavering. *Nothing better than Igbo beer,* he would say, often followed by a half-joking lament about why Nigerians didn't export it more widely.

Lola didn't miss a beat. She reached for her phone, dialing someone with practiced efficiency. "Bring two bottles of Hero Lager to the penthouse," she said coolly before ending the call. Less than five minutes later, a server arrived with the requested beers, poured one into a chilled glass, and retreated as silently as she had come. Osita leaned back in his chair, visibly satisfied as he took a long gulp.

I walked over to Lola, lowering my voice as I spoke. "I appreciate you doing this," I said.

She smiled, her lips curling in that signature smirk of hers. "I like helping my friends," she replied, her eyes meeting mine. "You are my friend, aren't you, Dozy?"

I nodded, taking another sip of my drink. Her gaze lingered, sharp and probing, as if she were waiting for something. Finally, she broke the silence. "Aren't you going to ask me?"

"Ask what?" I played dumb, though I knew exactly what she meant.

"You've been dying to know," she said, her smile widening. "How it is that I, Lola Alakija, heiress to a multibillion-naira empire, have a stake in the Slago hustle."

I didn't answer immediately, letting the silence stretch just enough to make her think I wasn't as curious as she believed. "Admittedly," I said at last, "the thought did cross my mind."

She chuckled, the sound low and rich, like someone savoring a private joke. "The problem with having everything," she began, turning to refill my glass even though it wasn't empty, "is that you grow bored. Restless. I've run out of mountains to climb, Dozy. Slago seemed exciting to me. Not quite illegal, but definitely toeing the line."

"You do this for the excitement?" I asked, arching a brow. "Not the money?"

She leaned in closer, her floral perfume wrapping around me like a velvet glove. Her gaze locked onto mine, and for a moment, I felt the weight of her confidence, her self-assurance. Her enhanced quadragenarian bosom brushed against my lower chest, an intentional move, I was sure. Her smirk deepened as she whispered, "Do I look like I need the money?"

I couldn't help but grin, masking the slight unease her proximity brought. "Surely that's not enough to keep your attention."

There was a glint in her eyes as if she were pleased someone had refused to buy her bored rich girl act. "Yes, but you must promise this stays between us...as friends." "Friends," I echoed. "Of course. I wouldn't want to lose your trust."

She leaned in closer, her breasts rested on my abdomen. She said, "Slago is home to some of the most powerful men and women in the country." "It helps to have leverage. A girl could need a favor some day." She chuckled, proud of herself.

I nodded. The popularity of a streaming app I had just learned about surprised me. "And you've heard about the Admiral's murder?"

"And the fact you were questioned about it, yes," she said without hesitation, her voice calm like someone commenting on a mildly interesting piece of gossip.

I looked down at her, attempting to read her expression, but her face was a masterclass in ambiguity. "You knew that," I said, my tone sharper than I intended, "and still offered to help when I called?"

She tilted her head, her lips curving into a faint smile. "I reckoned you wouldn't be trying to solve the murder if you committed it," she said, sipping her drink. "Besides, you intrigue me. And intrigue, my dear, is a rare luxury for someone like me."

I narrowed my eyes at her. "This isn't just intrigue, Lola. You could be playing with fire. If your name gets dragged into this…"

"Then what?" she interrupted. "Do you think I haven't danced on the edge of scandal before? I'm an Alakija. Scandal is practically the family crest."

I couldn't tell if her confidence was genuine or a well-crafted performance, but either way, I didn't have the luxury of doubting her motives. "And what do you get out of this?" I asked, leaning back slightly.

She leaned in. "Maybe I find the thought of you owing me… delicious."

Before I could respond, the door to the penthouse opened, and a man stepped in. He was tall and wiry, his suit a shade too tight around the shoulders, his face shiny with sweat despite the air conditioning. He looked uncomfortable, the kind of man who thrived in shadows and disliked being dragged into the light.

"Elias," Lola said smoothly, gesturing toward the seating area. "Thank you for coming on such short notice."

Elias nodded stiffly, his eyes darting to me and then Osita, who sat across the room nursing his Hero beer with deliberate nonchalance. "You didn't tell me there'd be an audience, ma," he muttered, adjusting his collar.

"Relax," Lola said, her tone soothing but firm. "These are friends. They won't bite."

Elias didn't seem convinced but shuffled over to the large 80-inch TV mounted on the wall. He pulled out his phone, connected it via a casting app, and soon, the screen lit up with the interface of Slago. The bright colors and sleek design gave it an air of legitimacy that belied the murkiness Elias was about to describe.

"This," Elias began, pointing to the screen, "is the main dashboard for agents. We manage all the hosts under our umbrella through here. As you can see, each host has a customizable profile and we track their earnings, targets, and payouts."

He scrolled through a list of names, none of them real, obviously. "Slago doesn't pay hosts directly," he continued. "We act as intermediaries. At the end of each month, we receive their earnings based on the value of their rubies, convert it into cash, take our cut, and pay them the balance. I log everything here."

"And the girls?" I asked. "Do you know who they really are?"

Elias shook his head. "That's where things get complicated. Slago has strict rules about maintaining anonymity for security reasons. Most of the girls use burner numbers, secondary SIM cards, to communicate off the app. Even I don't know their real names. TequilaDream, the girl you're asking about, is no exception."

Osita snorted. "So you're telling me you pay someone every month, and you don't even know her name?"

Elias gave him a withering look. "I meet her in person at an agreed location at the end of every month. She gets her payment, and we leave it at that. It's safer that way for both of us."

"And what about... other activities?" I pressed, my tone careful. "You mentioned anonymity, but what happens when these girls engage in things the app doesn't officially allow?"

Elias sighed, glancing at Lola as if seeking permission to continue. She nodded, and he turned back to us. "Slago officially frowns on any sexual conduct. It's against the rules. But let's be real, rules are made to be broken. Some hosts use the app to find clients willing to pay more for...

extras. That's where the burner numbers come in. They can set up private arrangements without leaving a trail."

Osita grimaced, his lip curling in disgust. "And they still want to become wives and mothers after all that?"

Elias shrugged. "Most of them do. They're careful, though. They don't share personal details. The idea is to keep this part of their life completely separate from their future. A lot of these girls are playing a long game. They want the rubies, the cash, but they don't want the stigma."

"And some even find husbands," Lola added, with a touch of amusement in her voice. "There's a market for exotic beauty among certain... demographics. Most of these men are from parts of Europe and the US."

Osita rolled his eyes. "Nonsense. All those foolish beta males," he muttered. "No self-respecting man would marry a woman he met on an app like this."

I didn't disagree, though my reasoning was less moralistic. It wasn't only about self-respect, it was about knowing the truth of what you were getting into. The thought of someone being so blind, so desperate, was almost laughable.

Also, those who knew Osita well were aware of one of his more peculiar biases: his absolute disdain for interracial marriages, particularly between white men and African women. The irony was, he couldn't care less when the roles were reversed. A black man and a white woman didn't bother him in the slightest. I never quite figured out the root of his aversion, and honestly, I hadn't pressed him on it. It was one of those things about Osita. Layers of contradictions and opinions that didn't always add up. But that was a conversation for another day.

"Do you have anything on TequilaDream that might help me find her?" I asked, bringing the conversation back to the task at hand.

Elias hesitated, then swiped through his phone, casting a profile onto the massive screen. A faceless avatar stared back at us, its generic outline illuminated by metrics and graphs on the side. "This is her dashboard," he said, pointing to a series of impressive figures that demonstrated her success on the app. "She's one of my top earners. I don't know her real name, but I can tell you she's punctual, professional, and extremely good at what she does. If you're looking for her, your best bet is to be at the Lorel Hotel at the end of the month."

I crossed my arms, my mind already racing. "Lorel?" I repeated, the name clicking faintly as though I'd heard it in passing but never paid much attention. "Is that where you usually meet?"

Elias hesitated again, glancing at the screen before answering. "No, not typically. She usually prefers more private locations, but last week she contacted me and specifically asked to meet there at the end of the month. It's unusual, but she's reliable enough that I didn't question it."

I frowned. "The end of the month is three weeks away," I said, the frustration laced through my tone. That was time I didn't have, not with Detective Inspector Bayo breathing down my neck. The Admiral's murder was still an open wound in the city's consciousness, and I had no intention of waiting that long to get closer to the truth. "Is there no way to track her sooner?"

Osita, who had been quiet until now, leaned forward, resting his arms on his knees. "Elias, have you met her at Lorel before?"

Elias nodded, albeit reluctantly. "Once or twice. But only when she insisted. She's particular about her privacy, and honestly, I respect that. Girls like her don't last long in this game if they don't set boundaries."

Osita tapped his fingers on the table, his mind clearly working through something. Finally, he stood abruptly, chugging the last of his Hero beer in one go. He wiped his mouth with the back of his hand and turned to me, clapping a firm hand on my shoulder. "Alobam, I've got business to handle," he said, his tone suddenly curt and decisive. "Meet me at the club tonight."

I blinked, surprised by his sudden departure. "Wait, what? I brought you here. We should leave together."

Osita shook his head, already moving toward the door. "No, stay. Get as much information as you can from Elias. I'll find my way back."

"Osita…" I began, but he cut me off with a wave of his hand.

"Don't worry about me," he said over his shoulder. "I'll see you tonight."

And with that, he was gone, leaving me standing there with a half-empty glass of scotch and a million unanswered questions swirling in my mind.

Elias shifted uncomfortably in his seat, breaking the silence. "Your friend," he began cautiously, "he seems… intense."

"That's one word for him," I muttered, more to myself than to Elias.

I turned my attention back to the screen, the faceless avatar taunting me with its silence. Whoever this woman was, she held a key piece to the puzzle, a piece I couldn't afford to wait three weeks to obtain. My jaw tightened as I weighed my options. I was racing against the clock, sprinting through a minefield, every step a gamble.

CHAPTER 18

"Come with me," Osita said, his voice carrying a hint of anticipatory glee, like he was about to show me something he couldn't wait to unveil.

I had gone to the club to see him later that evening, unsure of what he had in store for me. Knowing him, I was instinctively cautious. I followed him through a door behind the bar. It led us to what looked like an attic, dimly lit and cast in shadows. But despite its dark, almost ominous feel, the space was surprisingly cool and clean. I felt a pang of unease creep into my chest.

"I've got something for you," Osita said, a self-satisfied grin on his face.

"What is it?" I asked, my stomach already heavy with suspicion.

There was the click of a switch, and the dim room was suddenly lit up. My breath hitched when I saw what, or rather, *who*, was in front of me.

A man, shirtless and bound to a chair. His face was slightly swollen, one eye almost shut from what I could tell was a well-placed strike. It wasn't the injuries that alarmed me though. It was the fact that I knew this man. The receptionist at the Lorel Luxury Hotel.

"Osita, what the hell?" I snapped instinctively, turning my back on the hostage, hoping he hadn't seen my face. This was *exactly* the kind of trouble Osita could put me in. I could hear Calvin tell me *I told you so*. "Why is this dude here?"

"It occurred to me when you and Elias were discussing Lorel. Well, clearly this fool sold you out," Osita said nonchalantly, like he was talking about a simple misunderstanding.

I had briefly considered the possibility, but even if the guy wanted to sell me out, I doubted he had the chance to do it so quickly. "The police found me too fast, Osita," I said. "It couldn't have been him. I didn't even give him my name." And then I remembered the grinning Bayo. Was he out there watching? Was he going to storm this place?

Osita chuckled, the sound low and knowing. "Bro, these people know everyone. People in the Lagos service industry talk. You show up in a flashy Range, and word spreads faster than gossip on social media." He was still grinning, enjoying himself.

I sighed deeply, frustration building. I walked closer to the man, feeling my conscience tug at me. I didn't care anymore if he saw my face. Thanks to him, the cops were sniffing around me. I needed answers fast.

"Who paid you to sell me out?" I asked.

The receptionist was whimpering, not even daring to look me in the eye. His posh customer-service accent had evaporated, leaving the familiar Lagos boy dialect in its place. "Oga, I swear I no sell you out," he stammered, shaking his head.

I crouched down, lowering my voice. "I'm not going to hurt you," I said, trying to sound calm. "But I can't speak for my friend over there."

Osita, ever the opportunist, grinned menacingly. He crossed his arms, enjoying his role in this little drama. "Oh boy," Osita growled in Yoruba. "You better talk if you want to leave here in one piece."

The threat was genuine enough, and the receptionist's fear was palpable. His lips trembled before he cracked.

"Na one madam!" he blurted out. "I swear, oga, I don't know her. She just showed up after you left the hotel and told me to report you to the police. She even told me where you were staying and your name. I don't want wahala."

I stood up, biting back my irritation. Typical. There is always someone in the background waiting to exploit the smallest opportunity. I moved toward Osita.

"What's going on here, bro?" Osita asked, his eyes narrowing with suspicion. "Now you know for sure someone set you up."

"I need to make a call I've been dreading," I said, heading back downstairs to the empty club.

I pulled out my phone, feeling the weight of the conversation I was about to have. It was a little past 11 p.m. Lagos time, which meant it was around 6 p.m. in D.C. The time was right. My thumb hovered over the screen before I pressed the call button. The dial tone hummed twice before the voice I expected came through, smooth and detached, like she was sitting on a throne somewhere.

"Mr. Dozy," Mmachi's voice dripped into my ear, as calm and cool as a stream at midnight.

"I'm sure you've heard by now. My condolences," I said icily, letting the sarcasm bleed into every syllable.

There was a brief pause. I could almost see her smirking on the other side of the line. "Thank you, Mr. Dozy," she said. She let out a small chuckle. This woman... unfazed by the death of her husband. She sounded more amused than anything else, as if she were talking about a mildly inconvenient business deal, not the murder of a man she once shared a bed with. The father of her child.

"My work here is done," I said flatly. "I found him."

"Yes," she replied, "but now you're the prime suspect." I clenched my jaw. There it was. The hook. I could feel the noose tightening around my neck. "Relax, Mr. Dozy. I know you didn't kill him," she cooed.

I arched an eyebrow. "And how can you be so sure? Unless..."

"Unless I had something to do with it?" she cut in, her tone unoffended by the accusation. "If I wanted Alex dead, I would not have hired you to find and bring him back to me. Your work is far from done."

I slammed my fist on the counter in frustration. "What the hell are you talking about?"

"There's more at stake here than just finding Alex." Her tone was serious now, all business. "Alex was in possession of something of mine. Certain... documents. Very important ones. He was meticulous, you see. Never let anything slip. But with him dead, I'm at risk of losing access to them. I'd prefer they didn't end up in the wrong hands."

I rubbed my temples, the weight of this new twist pressing down on me. "What in the MacGuffin is going on here?" I muttered under my breath. "How is any of this my business? I found your husband. That's all I agreed to. I'm done. I need you to use whatever remaining connections you have to clear my name. The only reason I'm not behind bars right now is because of a friend, but that'll only last for so long."

She laughed. "Your task was to return him to me alive. You're not done until I say you're done, Mr. Dozy." Her voice sharpened. "Listen to me. I've already enquired, and Alex's lawyer doesn't have the documents. Alex wouldn't leave them out in the open for just anyone to find. Whoever this woman was, the one he was supposed to marry, she might have access to them. It is possible Alex trusted her with more than a ring."

I sighed. My headache was growing stronger. Of course, the Admiral would be foolish enough to mix business with his dirty pleasures. I couldn't shake the feeling of an unseen hand, cold and relentless, dragging me further into the depths of this murky ocean. The weight of it all was pulling me down fast, and every instinct I had was screaming that I didn't need this storm brewing around me. But here I was, caught in the eye of it.

"Let me guess," I said, pinching the bridge of my nose. "You want me to dig around, find these documents, and tie up all your little loose ends?"

"Exactly." She didn't even flinch. "You're an investigator, aren't you? You find things. You found your aunt's dirty secrets. So, find the documents."

I leaned back, letting the silence stretch between us. Her words were simple, but they carried weight. She wasn't just asking me to find some papers. She was asking me to wade through more shit than I was prepared to handle. Whatever the Admiral had hidden, I was sure it was going to be messy.

But I didn't have a choice.

The police were already breathing down my neck. Bayo had me marked, and if I didn't move fast, I'd be rotting in a Nigerian jail cell before long.

"You're going to pay me more," I said after a moment of thought.

There was a pause. Then, a slow, deliberate exhale from her end. "How much more?"

"Ten thousand more."

She scoffed. "You think I'm made of money?"

"I think you're made of corruption," I shot back. "And I think you'll pay if those documents mean more to you than getting me off this case. I'm also going to need you to inform the police that you hired me to uncover and document your husband's infidelity."

"But he'd already asked for a divorce before I hired you."

"Sure," I replied coolly, "and you still hired me to dig up proof of his unfaithfulness long before that. Don't worry. I've got what you need." My mind flicked to the videos I'd seen, evidence that stretched back years before the Admiral had ever walked out on her. "So," I pressed, "do we have a deal?"

There was another beat of silence, and then, "Fine. You'll get your extra ten."

I exhaled, half relieved, half disgusted at myself for even staying on the call. But I needed that money. With Bayo on my tail, I couldn't afford to be picky.

"Good. Now tell me where to start."

"I've already given you the lead," she said. "The woman. She's involved in this more than you think. If Alex trusted her enough to run off and marry her, there's a chance she knows where those documents are. Or at the very least, where he might have hidden them."

I rubbed my chin, thinking about the livestreaming app. The ridiculous username. It was all starting to click into place. But it still felt like I was chasing shadows. Somehow,

Mmachi always seemed to be a step ahead, pulling the strings from the safety of her cushy hideout in DC.

"I might have a lead on that," I muttered. "The Admiral met his young fiancée on a livestreaming app called Slago. Her username is TequilaDream."

I heard her curse softly in Igbo, confirming what I already suspected. This marriage wasn't about love. The Admiral had fallen for a cheap romance spun out of digital lust, and Mmachi knew about it all along. There was no shock or surprise in her tone. She just sounded like she dreaded being reminded of his indiscretions.

"Track the whore down," Mmachi said. "And when you find her, those documents won't be far behind."

I didn't respond immediately. I wasn't sure I believed her. Something about the whole situation stank of manipulation. But I didn't have the luxury of walking away. Not yet. The quicker I got to the bottom of this, the quicker I could get out of Lagos for good.

"I'll get you what you need," I said, the resignation heavy in my voice. "But don't think for a second that I'm doing this for you. I'm doing it because I don't have a choice."

She let out a small, mocking laugh. "Whatever helps you sleep at night, Mr. Dozy. Just get me those documents. And remember, this mess isn't going away until you do. The police won't be your only problem."

The line went dead.

I stared at the phone for a long moment, the weight of the conversation settling into my bones.

TequilaDream. She was the next piece of this twisted puzzle. The Admiral had trusted her. Too much. But if she had the documents, that meant she also had the answers I needed to clear my name and get paid.

I let out a long breath and stood up, glancing toward the stairs. Osita was waiting for my signal, ready to continue whatever madness he had cooked up in there. But I wasn't thinking about Osita anymore.

Whoever had paid that receptionist to sell me out wanted me out of the picture.

But keeping me here? That was their mistake.

CHAPTER 19

I pulled Osita aside and showed him a screenshot from TequilaDream's profile I had taken a screenshot of earlier. Predictably, his eyes lit up like a kid in a candy store, already lost in whatever fantasies a man like him could conjure up. "Oh boy," he whistled, a low sound that carried both admiration and hunger. "This admiral had serious taste. The babe is fucking beautiful."

I rolled my eyes at him. Typical Osita. Often thinking with the wrong head. "Before I put it on your radar, did you know anything about Slago?"

Osita scoffed. "Mostly rumor but Elias' presentation confirmed a lot. The app thrives on the attention economy where people keep trying to out-gift each other just to get noticed by the streamer. And trust me, bro. You won't believe what people do on that app for a few virtual gifts."

Oh, I'd seen enough to understand just how far some of these hosts were willing to go. Although the Admiral had kept screen recordings of his private, illicit video calls with TequilaDream, I could easily assume she wasn't the only one engaging in such behavior. Some of the smaller hosts were blatant about their "cash for benefits" services, plastering their streams with messages like "PVT for 1k" or "if you want PVT, DM." They didn't bother with subtlety, often disappearing off camera but keeping their mic on letting viewers listen to the moans and sounds suggesting they were... keeping their audience entertained in a more personal way. Their phone numbers would pop up moments later, inviting anyone interested in more intimate services.

But the bigger names? TequilaDream and the top-tier hosts? They played the game differently. They were more discreet and more polished in how they handled their business. No flashing banners, no off-camera stunts. Just flirtatious glances, subtle innuendos, and an air of mystery kept the big spenders coming back for more. That's how they built their following. By offering just enough to keep you hooked, but never enough to make it obvious. It was all part of the hustle.

"Abeg oh! The babe's name is Elfreda!"

Both Osita and I pivoted to face the tied-up receptionist. The guy was craning his neck, trying to get a good look at what I'd shown Osita. His excitement had him teetering off balance.

"What did you just say?" I stepped closer, my patience fraying like a cheap suit.

"The woman in that picture. Her name is Elfreda. Elfreda Bassey. I've seen her with the Admiral at the hotel plenty of times. Her nyash dey always distract me."

Osita perked up at that, like a dog hearing the word "*treat.*"

"Damn, she get nyash? Do I need to join Slago to see the backside?"

I ignored him, feeling a strange thrill run through me. The mysterious TequilaDream. A woman I had spoken to but knew nothing of. She was real. Elfreda. This was progress.

"Where can I find her?" I asked.

The receptionist's shoulders slumped, and he shook his head. "I only ever saw her at the hotel."

I cursed under my breath, frustration simmering beneath my skin. This wasn't good enough. I was running out of time, and all I had was a name and a vague recollection of some woman with a distractingly large backside.

I looked at Osita, who was still daydreaming. "Bro, how do I find this girl?"

"She filled out a form at the hotel," the receptionist chimed in, thinking it would save him from Osita's sadistic whims. "I believe she filled in her address."

Both Osita and I locked eyes, then turned to the receptionist again. Hope flickered like a weak bulb in the back of my mind.

I took a breath, trying to process what was happening. What was supposed to be a simple job—find the old man, make him go home, get paid, and leave—had morphed into something messier. Now, I was playing private detective, tracking down clues, interrogating hostages, all while avoiding the police.

This wasn't my life. It wasn't supposed to be. My father had warned me about this country before I left for the States. His voice echoed in my mind, sharp as ever: *"Now you're leaving, don't come back. Not for anything."*

And yet, here I was.

I exhaled, forcing myself back into the present. I finally had something tangible. This Elfreda, TequilaDream. She was more than just a man's fantasy on a screen. "Where can I find this form?" I asked the receptionist urgently.

He swallowed hard. "It should be at the hotel's front desk, oga. We keep all guest forms in a cabinet at the back."

Osita's grin stretched wider. "Then we know where to start. Let's go get that form, find the babe with the nyash."

I shot him a look. This was no time for his usual playfulness, but his methods, unpredictable as they were, had gotten us this far.

— ◆ —

I convinced Osita to stay back and keep an eye on the receptionist while I made the next move. I was afraid of being spotted in the Range Rover because it might be recognized, so I borrowed one of Osita's older sedans instead. A nondescript car was less likely to get me noticed. Even so, I parked a few blocks away from the hotel, blending into the sea of vehicles, just one more shadow in the Lagosian night.

The streets were quieter at this hour, but the silence made me more paranoid. I glanced over my shoulder every few steps, feeling the weight of invisible eyes. Despite our short time together, Bayo didn't strike me as the average Nigerian cop. He appeared sharp, calculating, and was definitely still keeping tabs on me, expecting me to come sniffing around the hotel again. I wasn't about to make his job easier.

I kept to the shadows, circling the hotel, until I spotted a narrow side entrance that led into a maintenance corridor. The door creaked slightly as I slipped inside, my heart pounding in my chest. Once in, the dimly lit corridor stretched before me. I moved quietly, avoiding the main entrance. The last thing I needed was to be seen by the night staff or, God forbid, run into another cop on patrol.

The place was eerily quiet. My footsteps on the tiled floor echoed faintly, but not enough to attract attention. I walked past a janitor's closet, the faint smell of bleach hanging in the air, then past a dark, empty kitchen. The flickering overhead light barely illuminated the room, casting long, ominous shadows. I kept my body low, staying out of sight.

I reached the back of the reception area, pressing myself against the wall. Through a narrow crack in the door, I could see the front desk and a young lady sitting there, lazily scrolling through her phone. Same white shirt, same thin black tie as the receptionist Osita had tied up. But instead of slacks, she wore a black skirt that rode just above her knees. She was clearly bored out of her mind, fully absorbed in whatever drama was unfolding on her screen. Good. She wasn't paying attention to anything else, least of all me.

The shelf I needed was just behind her, filled with guest documents. If I could just slip in and grab what I needed, I could be in and out before she even noticed. But this was going to take finesse, and I wasn't dressed for a stealth mission.

I took a breath, rehearsing my movements in my head. The trick was to creep. Too slow, and she might sense someone behind her. Too fast, and the sudden shift in the air might catch her attention. I crept forward, staying low, slipping one foot in front of the other as I made my way toward the desk. The soft rustle of her skirt as she shifted in her seat almost made me freeze. Her phone screen illuminated her face in a soft glow, still engrossed, still unaware.

I made it to the shelf. The bundle of documents was thick, and I quickly thumbed through them, searching for the name "Elfreda" or any hint of a connection to TequilaDream. My fingers skimmed over the papers, trying to stay focused while the threat of discovery hung over my head like a guillotine. Finally, I spotted her form. Elfreda's name, signature, and most importantly, her address.

My heart raced. This was it. I grabbed the entire stack. It was better to have too much than too little. Then I gently backed away. The receptionist stirred slightly, her eyes still glued to her phone, as I slipped back toward the side door, clutching the documents close to my chest.

As I was about to slip out the back room, the sound of several voices caught my attention. Boisterous and slurred. The kind of sound that only came from men after one too many drinks. Instinctively, I stopped in my tracks. A bad feeling churned in my gut.

I pressed my ear to the crack in the door, glancing at the young receptionist, who was still seated at the front desk. The men stumbled in, four of them. Rowdy, unsteady, and already leering at the woman.

Four drunk men. One unprotected woman.

I clenched my jaw. I could leave. I should leave. But something told me to hang back for a few minutes. Call it instinct, or maybe just my general distaste for scum. Either way, I wasn't walking out just yet.

It didn't take long to realize I had made the right call.

One man, a thickset fellow with a greasy shirt barely holding his beer belly, leaned over the desk. "Hey babe," he slurred, his eyes running down the length of her body like she was a piece of meat on display. "You're looking very sweet tonight. Are you here alone?"

The receptionist, already looking uncomfortable, gave a nervous smile, trying to maintain some semblance of professionalism. "Yes, sir. Is there something I can help you with?"

"Help us?" another man snickered, this one lanky and swaying on his feet. "Oh yeah, baby. You can definitely help us." His buddies roared with laughter.

She glanced around the room, probably realizing what was coming. Her voice trembled as she tried to remain polite. "Please, sir. If you need assistance, I'll be happy to call..."

Before she could finish, another man reached across the desk and grabbed her arm. "Why are you acting shy? Come on now. Stop pretending." His grip tightened as he pulled her closer.

"Leave me!" Her voice was firmer now, but her fear was evident. The other men circled around, egging each other on, emboldened by alcohol and stupidity.

My blood boiled. Four against one. Even drunk, these assholes were dangerous. But I wasn't going to let this slide. I could handle four drunks. Hell, I'd dealt with worse back in the day.

I stepped out of the backroom, my footsteps heavy as I approached the group.

"Hey!" I called out. The men turned to face me, confused at first, but when they saw the look in my eyes, confusion shifted to anger.

"Who is this one?" the thickset one asked, his grip still on the receptionist's arm.

"I'm the guy who's going to give you exactly three seconds to let her go before I start breaking bones."

The men laughed, of course. They always do before the first punch. "Are you okay?" one of them sneered.

I didn't reply. Instead, I let my fists do the talking.

I moved fast, closing the distance before they had time to react. The first guy, the one holding the receptionist, was the easiest. I grabbed his wrist, twisting it sharply, forcing him to release her. His face contorted in pain just as my fist connected with his jaw. He staggered back, crashing into the counter.

The second guy, the lanky one, lunged at me. I sidestepped him easily, planting my knee into his gut. The air left his lungs in a sharp gasp, and he doubled over, wheezing.

The other two came at me together. One swung wildly, the punch sloppy from inebriation. I ducked under it and delivered a sharp elbow to his ribs. He grunted, his body folding like a cheap suit. Before he could recover, I grabbed the back of his head and slammed it into the counter. He went down hard.

The last guy, slightly more sober, tried to tackle me. Big mistake. I dropped low, driving my shoulder into his midsection, and lifted him off the ground. We crashed into a nearby table, shattering it on impact. I rolled off him, landing a few more well-placed punches for good measure.

I stood up, panting, my knuckles throbbing but otherwise unscathed. The men groaned on the floor, nursing their bruised egos and bruised everything else.

I turned to the receptionist, who was now standing with wide eyes, her chest heaving as she tried to catch her breath. She was torn between wanting to ask me what I was doing there and thanking me for stepping in.

She settled on the latter, nodding her head softly in gratitude, then quickly averted her gaze, as if silently promising she wouldn't say a word about what had just gone down.

"Go get help," I said. She nodded again, still too shaken to speak, and hurried off toward the back.

I looked down at the four idiots writhing on the floor and shook my head. "Should've taken the three seconds."

With that, I turned on my heel, leaving the scene behind me, slipping out the same way I came in. Time to get out of there before someone less drunk showed up to clean up the mess.

I wasn't in the clear yet. The corridor seemed longer on the way out, every step heavier, but the adrenaline kept me moving.

Back in the maintenance corridor, I ducked into the janitor's closet. I flipped through the pages under the dim light, zeroing in on Elfreda's form. Her address was somewhere in Marina.

Satisfied I had what I needed, I shoved the papers into my jacket and quickly made my way out the side door. The night air hit me like a slap, cool and heavy with the smell of petrol fumes. I kept my head low and hurried back to Osita's car, resisting the urge to run. Running was suspicious. I needed to look like just another tired Lagosian heading home after a long day.

Once I was back behind the wheel, I took a deep breath and exhaled slowly. I had a proper lead on Elfreda Bassey. Now, I just needed to decide whether to confront her directly or play this a little smarter.

One thing was evident: whatever this woman knew, it was going to bring me closer to the documents, and further into this damn mess.

I punched the address into the GPS and headed for the home of Elfreda Bassey, the alluring TequilaDream. The drive to Marina was long but easy enough, the night air washing over me as I sped across bridges and roads with the windows down and the sunroof open.

The complex wasn't much to look at. A stack of garden-style apartments behind an iron gate, which, given the late hour, was surprisingly wide open. In Lagos, some people never slept. Apartment 4A had me climbing the outdoor stairs to the fourth floor until I came to the end unit. The number carved into the door was so faded it looked like it wanted to forget itself. A steel security gate guarded the entrance.

I knocked.

Nothing.

I waited, listening. I swear I heard movement. I Knocked again, louder.

The door swung open, but the bars stayed between us.

"Who the fuck are you?"

She was young, with twists, wearing a black singlet and what looked like a man's boxers. Her arms showed cuts from either a hard job or a hard gym routine. Fair-skinned, pretty too, though she was working overtime to bury it. Dull eyes, a frown like it had taken root. Maybe I'd just caught her at a bad time.

But one thing was certain, she wasn't the woman I'd seen with the Admiral.

"I'm sorry," I said, keeping my voice calm. "Looking for an old friend."

"Which friend? Your friend does not have a phone?"

Her voice carried down the hall, rattling neighbors out of bed.

The longer I looked at her, the more familiar she seemed. "Wait. Have we met?"

She shot a glare at me. "Are you mad?" The door started to close.

"I'm looking for Elfreda. Elfreda Bassey."

That stopped her. Just a flicker, but enough for me to see.

"You know her?" I asked.

"I don't. No Elfreda here. Can I go back to sleep?"

"Yes, of course," I said, stalling. "My name's Dozy. Dozy Agu. Can I leave you my number if you hear from her, Miss...?"

She slammed the door in my face.

A shirtless neighbor shuffled out, scowling. "Oga, wetin be this now? Which kind nonsense be this?"

I muttered an apology and backed off, heading to my car. I sat there in the dark, engine off, waiting. For what, I didn't know.

"*That chick look suspicious to you?*" Osita's voice came through the line not long after I'd settled into the car, mid-stakeout.

"Very," I muttered, replaying her hesitation when I'd mentioned Elfreda Bassey. One second too long. Enough to show me she knew something.

"*Alobam, make I show? I fit make her talk.*"

I cringed. "How about you keep your ass put and focus on letting that man go?"

He grunted with half amusement and half irritation. I was about to push when movement caught my eye. Someone in a hoodie, shorts, and spotless Jordans stepped out of 4A. The girl. She kept her head low, phone in hand, moving with purpose.

"I gotta bounce," I blurted. "We'll talk later." I hung up and slid out of the car.

The roads had cracks and were littered with broken bottles and oil stains, and generators hummed while street vendors called out to phantom customers. Still, there were corners, kiosks, parked cars, enough cover for a man who knew how to move.

I kept back. Fifteen, maybe twenty paces. Slipping behind danfos and rusted taxis, ducking low whenever she glanced over her shoulder. She didn't spot me. Too wrapped up in her phone.

She cut through a side street where Aboki stalls leaned against each other like tired men. A dim bulb buzzed overhead, casting warped shadows across the pavement. I ducked behind a kiosk stacked with crates of empty Coke bottles, heart ticking steadily, eyes fixed on her hooded frame as she crossed toward the main road.

Finally, she hit the street. Still buzzing with life despite the hour. Petrol fumes from a nearby filling station mixed with suya smoke. The girl paused at the roadside, pulled out her phone, waiting. I needed to know who.

I edged closer, sliding into the dark mouth of an alley, pressed against a wall. That's when I heard them.

Three shapes broke off from the shadows, moving toward me with lazy confidence. One was shirtless, chest gleaming with sweat. Another in a dirty wife-beater, grin missing two teeth. The last wore a dark polo, collar popped, like he owned the street.

"*Ogbeni*," the polo one called. "*Wetin be the time for there?*"

I didn't miss the way their eyes glittered. Not curious, but hungry. They weren't after the time. But I wasn't about to stir up attention with the girl standing just meters away.

I flicked my wrist. "Quarter to eleven."

They closed in regardless. The one in the wife-beater chuckled, elbowing his friend. "*This one na oyibo oh.*"

I looked straight at them. Calm. Controlled. "*Alaye, calm down. I no want wahala.*"

They laughed like hyenas. "Ajebutter dey form Ajepako!" the shirtless one barked.

"But na wahala we bring come na," the polo one added, flashing steel. A knife glinted under the streetlight. The others followed suit with chains and blades.

No guns. Lucky for me.

The girl shifted slightly, her head cocking at the sound of their laughter. I cursed under my breath. This had to be quiet.

So I turned back to the boys. My pulse slowed. Breath evened.

"Make I hold your phone, first," said one.

I could have complied. Mmachi gave me a generous allowance, and I was sure I could get some more if someone robbed me. But stubbornness took over. I wasn't about to let these punks get a free meal.

"Una dey craze," I spat.

The first lunged. I slipped past his swing, clamped a hand around his throat, and slammed him into the wall. His knife clattered harmlessly to the ground as I squeezed until his knees buckled, then dropped him like trash.

The second came fast with the chain. I stepped into him, caught his wrist mid-swing, and jammed an elbow into his gut. The air rushed out of him in a wheeze. I twisted his arm until the chain fell loose, then cracked him across the jaw with the butt of my palm. He went down without a sound.

The last one hesitated, knife trembling just slightly. Two quick strides, a twist of his wrist, and the blade was mine. I rapped him behind the ear with the hilt, catching his fall so he hit the ground quietly.

I straightened, breath steady, scanning the street. Three bodies down, no noise, no witnesses. Clean.

Then I looked up.

The girl was gone. I caught the red blink of the taillight of a bike weaving into traffic. She'd hopped on an okada and was already scooting away, disappearing into the chaos of Lagos nighttime.

"Shit!" I spat, slamming the knife down into the gutter. I'd dealt with the touts, sure, but I'd lost the only lead I had. At some point, I needed to figure out what my next move would be.

But all that could wait. By then, I was running on fumes. Sleep played a dangerous game of hide-and-seek with me since my arrest, and I needed it badly, so I walked back to the car and went home. My body screamed for rest, my muscles protesting with every step. The adrenaline that had kept me running until now was long gone, and I was starting to feel like a dead man walking.

When I pulled up to the house, Akaneme was already by the gate. The sight of him startled me. He hadn't waited up so late since I started staying there. His expression was unreadable, but something about the way he stood there made my skin crawl.

"Are you okay?" I asked, trying to gauge the situation.

"Yes, sah," he answered in an unusual monotone. There was something off in his voice. "Good night."

Before I could say anything else, he retreated into his quarters, the click of the door echoing through the quiet compound. The lights in his quarters went out, and I stood there under the dim security lights, feeling like the world had slightly shifted on its axis.

Shaking off the weird vibe, I unlocked the front door and stepped inside. That's when the scent hit me. A thick, sweet, and lingering perfume. Pretty expensive too. The type you can smell from across a room. It hung in the air like a warning sign. My senses went into overdrive, every nerve in my body on high alert. Then, I saw it. The light in the living room was on.

I froze.

Someone was in the house.

The calm I usually held onto in these situations was nowhere to be found. I wished, for the first time since I had arrived in Lagos, that I had a gun. I moved quietly, stepping into the kitchen and grabbing the first weapon I could find. A knife. It wasn't ideal, but it'd do.

I crept toward the living room, knife in hand, every step measured and deliberate. I half-expected to find a thug ready to jump me, maybe someone sent by Chief Obidi, or the police. But when I finally reached the room, I stopped dead in my tracks, the knife falling limp at my side.

Sitting there in the middle of the living room was a woman. *Her.*

She was a sight to behold. Her skin, a rich caramel, glistened under the soft lighting of the room, like silk stretched over a body sculpted for desire. Her mint-green dress was tight, almost scandalously so, hugging her curves with precision. The fabric rippled with texture, giving it an almost liquid appearance as it clung to her ample chest, cinching at her narrow waist before flaring out over her hips. The plunging neckline, bold and unapologetic, offered more than a glimpse of the fullness of her figure.

At the sight of me, she stood. Her legs, long and shapely, were accentuated by a pair of delicate strappy heels, adding to her height. Her hair was sleek, pulled back into a long, straight ponytail that cascaded down her back like a midnight waterfall, contrasting beautifully with her skin tone. Bangs framed her face, drawing attention to her eyes. They were dark, almond-shaped, and brimming with a sultry confidence. She had the kind of face that could make men weak with just a glance, her full lips curved into a small, knowing smile, as if she had already won whatever game she was about to play.

The dress, the posture, the perfume. It was clear she had prepared for this moment, knowing exactly the kind of effect she would have. She was here for a reason, and she wanted me to know that I was the prey in this little hunt.

"Mr. Agu," she purred, her voice as sweet as the perfume that lingered in the air. "I hear you've been looking for me." I blinked, still holding onto the knife like some fool who had no idea what he was walking into. *Elfreda Bassey.* I'd finally found her. Or rather, she had found me.

CHAPTER 20

Elfreda was an enigma wrapped in contradictions. Nervous yet dripping with confidence. As she sat on the couch, her eyes didn't waver from me, watching as I offered to make her a drink. "Let me guess," I began. "You'll have tequila?" She smirked at me without a word and shook her head softly. She asked for a gin and tonic instead. It was easy enough to make. I opted for scotch and soda water as usual.

Oddly enough, the bone-deep exhaustion that had been clinging to me since the hotel had lifted. It was as though her presence, magnetic and disorienting, had somehow burned it off. I made sure not to ogle, but damn, it was hard not to. She was statuesque in a way that could only exist in magazines, social media, or, let's be real, porn. She would make anything she wore look seductive, but tonight she dressed with purpose. The tight dress, the striking color. It was a visual weapon.

When I handed her the drink, she took it with a delicate, deliberate sip, like some kind of seductress—every movement made to ensnare. I drank too, letting the scotch burn its way down my throat, attempting to keep my mind sharp. I had questions, a laundry list of them, but I wasn't about to let her see me unravel.

I leaned back on the couch opposite her, trying to look casual, maybe even a bit detached, but I was playing a part. Cosplaying as a therapist or some low-budget PI in a forgotten detective movie. "So, how did you find me, Ms. Bassey?"

She brushed a strand of her impossibly straight, artificial hair away from her face, her eyes flickering with amusement. "Word is you've been looking for me," she said, voice syrupy smooth. "Eventually, that kind of noise reaches the right ears."

"Honestly," I replied, "I was more focused on finding the Admiral." My words were sharp, intentional.

Her expression shifted slightly, something like regret flashing across her face. "Poor Alex," she breathed, looking down at her feet like the weight of it had just hit her. "I can't believe he's gone. We were going to be so happy together, Mr. Agu."

I almost groaned. She was playing the grieving widow, but I knew enough about women of her type not to buy it wholesale. Still, her vulnerability stirred something in me. A primal instinct to comfort. I hated myself for it.

"Please call me Dozy," I said, the words slipping out before I could stop them. Instantly, I regretted it. *Smooth, real smooth,* I thought. Lowering my guard to a woman like her? Amateur hour.

Her laugh was light, a little too practiced. "I meant to ask you last time," she said. "I thought your name was Alvan?"

"It is," I admitted, feeling like I was already slipping into dangerous territory. "When I was seven, I had an allergic reaction while we were visiting the U.S. My dad registered me at the hospital using my full name, Alvan Chidozie Agu.

Now, any Nigerian knows Chidozie is pronounced *Chee-doe-zee-ay*, but when this skinny white nurse came out to call me, she butchered it. Called me 'Alvan *Chai-Dozy* Agu.' My family thought it was hilarious, and I've been stuck with Dozy ever since. Only my mother still calls me Alvan."

She smiled, genuinely this time. "Let me guess, your mother gave you the name."

I nodded. "Yeah, she did. Named me after her cousin. You might've heard of him."

There was a brief flicker of curiosity in her eyes. "Alvan?" she repeated. Then, the recognition hit her like a revelation. "You mean *the* Alvan? Alvan Ikoku?" She leaned forward. "The man on the ten Naira note?"

That reaction. It always came. Most people would lose their minds at the mention of my uncle's name, as if they were in the presence of royalty. And sure, being the nephew of a key figure in the country's development should've been something to be proud of. But it wasn't. Not for me. With the way this country was falling apart, it was hard to celebrate the ghosts of its past. If anything, it felt like an inheritance of failure. My uncle's name was etched into the history books, but the Nigeria he fought for? That dream suffocated long ago.

I had always kept my distance from that part of my family history, but there I was, boasting about it to her. Why? What was it about her that made me want to impress her, to paint myself as something more than I was? The Admiral must've felt it too, that intoxicating draw, like Odysseus caught in Calypso's snare. Elfreda was the nymph, and I was fighting the urge to wreck myself on her shores. I couldn't let myself be another victim of her seductive pull.

I snapped out of it, shaking off the haze she'd put me in. "That still doesn't answer my question," I said, my tone sharpening. "How did you find this place?"

She took a leisurely sip from her drink, drawing it out like she was savoring both the liquor and my frustration. Crossing her legs with deliberate, exaggerated grace, she replied, "Akaneme told me. Alex and I used to come here in the beginning. He liked the privacy, but then he got paranoid. He worried his *ex-wife* might know about it."

I caught the faint emphasis she placed on *ex-wife*. It lingered in the air like smoke. My eyes narrowed as I mulled it over. "Akaneme contacted me and told me you were staying here after Alex was murdered and they arrested you," she added, as if this was the most natural conversation in the world.

I glanced instinctively over my shoulder toward Akaneme's quarters, silently cursing myself. All the trouble I might've saved if I'd just thought to ask him about Elfreda from the start. Then, her earlier choice of words resurfaced in my mind like a splinter, and I turned back to her, eyebrow raised.

"*Ex-wife?*" I echoed. "Last I heard, the divorce wasn't finalized."

Her lips curled into a slight smirk, a mix of amusement and something sharper, like she enjoyed dangling the bait. "Technically, you're right. But in the court of public opinion? They were over long before lawyers got involved. Trust me, Mr. Dozy, there's nothing binding about a marriage when one half is already living with someone new."

I decided to prod a bit. "And this arrangement you had with the Admiral, did it involve him taking you to the United States?"

She hesitated, and I couldn't help but feel a bit conflicted. Even if it was a scheme to leave the country and secure a better life, I'd married Jasmine for a similar reason. Who was I to judge? So, I didn't wait for her to respond. "Why weren't you having your meetings with the Admiral at your place?" I pressed, observing her. "Wouldn't that have been more discreet?"

She let out a light chuckle, trailing a finger around the rim of her glass. "I have a housemate," she said. "She's not fond of male visitors. The apartment is hers. She's sort of my landlady as well. So, the hotel was the easiest solution."

I remembered the hostile girl in 4A and nodded. Yet, I stared at her, sizing her up. Her answers were too convenient, too polished. Every word she spoke was wrapped in layers of deceit, but I couldn't quite peel them away yet. Elfreda appeared dangerous, and just alluring enough to keep me drawn in when I should've been running the other way.

But I wasn't running. Not yet.

"Elfreda..."

"Freda, please," she corrected. "If I can call you Dozy, call me Freda."

"Okay. Freda," I said slowly, leaning forward, narrowing my eyes. "Why are you here?"

There was a brief flicker of uncertainty in her eyes, just for a second, but enough for me to notice. She was slipping. I was getting closer to the truth. She parted her lips as if to answer, then stopped, reconsidering her next move.

I could almost see the gears turning in her mind, calculating the best way to play this. I waited, sipping my scotch, letting the burn fuel my focus. We were at a standoff. Her secrets against my questions.

"Fine," Elfreda finally said. "I'll be honest with you. But I need you to answer something first." Her eyes didn't leave me, her gaze as piercing as ever. "I have a question too, Mr. Agu. I mean, Dozy.why were you looking for Alex?"

I formulated an answer, careful not to give too much away. I wasn't about to mention the documents just yet. Not until I had a better read on her. "Chief Mrs. Mmachi Alex-Maduagu hired me to find him," I said, keeping my tone even. "She wanted her husband back."

Elfreda rolled her eyes and sucked her teeth, her disdain sharp enough to cut through steel. "She only wanted him back so I wouldn't have him," she spat. "She's a bitter, evil woman."

I noted her words. It was the kind of fury only a mistress could muster. The type that made side-chicks hold on to the delusion that they were somehow the victims, as if the real injustice wasn't the fact that they were messing with someone else's husband.

Elfreda continued. "Alex was meant to be with me. God declared it."

That made me raise my eyebrows. Of all the things she could have said, invoking God was the last I expected. "Declared by God, you say?"

"Of course. You see me like this and think I don't know God? That I don't go to church?"

I shifted in my seat. The thought hadn't crossed my mind. However, Elfreda didn't seem like the type of woman who would attend church, but I wouldn't say that. So, I responded with an apathetic shrug.

Elfreda stood. Her figure, in all its exaggerated perfection, came into full view as she ran her hands over her waist and hips, as if she were emphasizing the obvious. "You must look at me and think I'm some baddie for Christ," she said. "I can't help that I look like this."

I looked away, feeling an uncomfortable heat rise in my chest. "Are you going to answer my question?" I said, clearing my throat to regain composure, "Why are you here?"

She stared at me for a few moments, her eyes narrowing slightly as if measuring whether to tell me the truth or play another game. "Alex is dead," she said softly. "Someone killed him, and I don't feel safe."

"And the man the police think is the prime suspect is your best bet?" I asked incredulously.

She stepped closer, her perfume wrapping around me in a subtle yet intoxicating cloud. "I trust you, Dozy," she murmured.

I let out a dry laugh, devoid of any humor. "Trust? You barely know me," I said, studying her carefully. Her proximity, her tone. Everything about her felt calculated.

She shrugged lightly, her gaze never wavering from mine. "Alex thought highly of you," she said, her lips curving into the faintest hint of a smile. "He spoke about you with... admiration, the last time we were together."

I arched an eyebrow, the memory of Alex's goons tossing me into the ocean still fresh and infuriating. "Was this before or after he had me thrown off his yacht?" I asked, my tone laced with sarcasm.

She sighed, as though the question was an annoyance rather than a valid point. "After the Alakija luncheon," she clarified. "And besides," she added, her head tilting slightly, "I have a knack for reading people. Call it instinct, but I can tell you're trustworthy."

Her words were smooth, but they didn't sit right with me. Being someone's "instinct" bothered me, especially when that person was tangled in a dead man's web of secrets. Still, I couldn't deny the strange pull she had over me. Whatever it was, I couldn't shake the feeling that she wasn't done pulling my strings.

"When was the last time you were together?" I asked.

She hesitated, just for a fraction of a second, before answering. "A little after five in the evening. The night he passed." Her voice was smooth and deliberate. "I would have spent the night with him at the hotel, but I had promised my housemate, Candy, that I'd be home in time to help with her birthday party celebrations."

She placed a hand on her chest, the gesture almost too polished, her expression tinged with exaggerated regret. It was theatrical, like she was trying to convince me or herself that not being at the hotel that night weighed on her deeply. But it didn't sit right. If anything, it felt like a line she'd rehearsed before.

I sighed. "Running to the prime suspect doesn't exactly scream 'self-preservation.'"

She took a step back, her lips curling into that same smile. "Maybe it's because I know you're not the killer. Maybe it's because I know there's more to this story."

"Is that so?"

She nodded, her eyes shimmering with a mixture of resolve and something darker, more elusive. "I think we both know someone set you up," she said.

I flinched at the assertion, discomfort tightening my features. "And how can you be so sure?" I demanded, skepticism sharpening my tone.

Elfreda seemed almost satisfied by my reaction, as if she had anticipated it all along. She drifted over to the bar with the grace of a practiced socialite, pouring herself another gin and tonic. The ice clinked against the glass like distant warning bells. "It was Mmachi," she revealed after a sip, her back still to me. "She had Alex killed at the Lorel Luxury Hotel, and she also tipped off the police, leading them straight to your location."

At her words, a surge of anger propelled me to my feet. My fists clenched at my sides, a physical manifestation of my growing fury. "How do you know this?" I pressed.

Elfreda turned to face me, her hand raised in a gesture of peace, as though she could physically push back the tension between us. Her eyes were wide, almost pleading. "Let me tell you what I know," she said, her voice trembling slightly but sufficient to convey the weight of her words. "A week before Alex died, he told me he had something. Documents, recordings, I don't know what exactly, but he said it was enough to ruin her. He was going to use it to secure a divorce. Dozy, he was paranoid. Scared. He kept saying she'd find out about us and that he needed to move quickly. And then…" Her voice broke slightly as she swallowed hard. "She got to Alex. I can't help feeling I'm next."

Her words sent a chill down my spine. Ever since Mmachi had mentioned those elusive documents, I'd suspected they might have been a motive for her to want Alex out of the picture. She wasn't specific about the contents. Probably intentionally so. But whatever they were, they had to be explosive. Something that could bring her entire world crashing down.

Even Alex's sister, Onyeka, had hinted at Mmachi's obsessive need for control. Losing Alex to another woman, especially someone younger like Elfreda, might have been enough to bruise her ego, but losing leverage, losing the ability to keep him in line? That was a different beast entirely. And if those documents contained something so damaging it could destroy her, that would be motive enough to push her over the edge.

I clenched my jaw, piecing together the threads of what I'd learned so far. If Elfreda was telling the truth, then this wasn't simply a lover's quarrel gone wrong or a messy divorce spiraling out of control. This was premeditated. Mmachi didn't just want Alex gone, she needed to protect herself, her power, and her secrets at all costs.

And now, I realized, those costs might extend to Elfreda and, perhaps, even me.

Was I working for a murderer? The thought chilled me, but I had to be sure before jumping to conclusions. I wasn't ready to start pointing fingers without concrete evidence.

Elfreda's attempt to appear vulnerable might have fooled a less experienced man, but I wasn't just any man. Years of sniffing out lies as an insurance fraud investigator had honed my ability to see through facades. Her eyes, though wide and frightened, held a calculating gleam. It was the same look I'd seen in Mmachi's eyes, in the eyes of every other player in this corrupt game. They all had something to hide, something they desperately wanted others to believe, even if it stretched the bounds of reality.

A thought gnawed at me as I stared at Elfreda. How did I play into this supposed plan of Mmachi's? Was I meant to be the fall guy all along? It didn't make sense. Why go through the trouble of hiring a man from D.C. and paying me an allowance, flying me halfway across the world, just to frame me for murder? Surely Lagos didn't have a shortage of desperate souls or unwitting patsies willing to do her dirty work. There were an abundance of hustlers, fixers, and scapegoats in a city like this.

Something didn't add up. The pieces of the puzzle didn't fit, no matter how I turned them.

Why? Why me? Why now?

I couldn't shake the feeling that I was missing something. A critical detail buried beneath all the lies, half-truths, and veiled threats. The money, the documents, the murder, it all swirled in my head like a storm. If Mmachi was as calculating as everyone said, then there was more to this than I could see. And I hated walking blindly into anything.

No, this wasn't only about framing me. It was too convoluted for that. There was a bigger game at play, and I had no clue what my role was in it, or worse, how deep I'd already been pulled under.

"You can sleep in the bedroom tonight," I finally said. "I'll take the couch. Tomorrow, I'll take you somewhere safer while I figure this all out."

Elfreda nodded, perhaps a little too quickly, her expression unreadable. Whether she was relieved or plotting, I couldn't tell. But one thing was clear: I was in deep, and there was no easy way out. I turned away, feeling the weight of the night heavy on my shoulders. Tomorrow would come soon enough, and with it, perhaps a path through this tangled web of deceit and danger.

CHAPTER 21

Sleep didn't come easily that night, not with Elfreda in the next room. Even with the AC blasting, keeping the living room cool, I was sweating. Maybe it was the heat, or maybe it was the weight of everything hanging over me. Whatever it was, I drifted off eventually, but not into peace.

The dream came on slowly, like the fog rolling in before a storm. Soft at first, barely noticeable, but then thickening until it was all I could see. I was nineteen again, in the middle of the sun-scorched field behind my father's house in Enugu. The kind of heat that made the air shimmer and your lungs burn with every breath. And there he was. General Agu—standing tall with that military posture that demanded respect. He was watching me, his sharp eyes tracking my every move as I trained, pushing my body to the limit, testing every ounce of strength and willpower I had.

"Again," he said, flat and emotionless.

My knuckles were up, body angled, knees bent. Krav Maga was never about finesse, not like boxing or those fancy martial arts you see in movies. It was brutal, efficient. I moved through the motions, throwing quick punches followed by elbow strikes, every movement focused on disabling an attacker as fast as possible. A knee to the groin, a swift strike to the neck. It was all about survival. I clenched my fists so tight that I could feel the sweat slicking my palms. He barked an order, and I moved, blocking, striking, dodging imaginary opponents.

"Faster," I heard his voice. "You think an opponent is going to wait for you to catch your breath?"

I gritted my teeth and pressed on, muscles burning, legs heavy like lead. I threw a punch, then a kick, but my footwork faltered. My vision blurred, and suddenly, I was on the ground, breathing hard, arms splayed out, the dirt clinging to my skin. I wanted to stay down, to give in just for a second, but I felt his shadow looming over me.

"You cannot afford to be lazy, my son. In a real-world situation, you may not have the luxury of rest."

I groaned, trying to push myself up, but my arms felt like they belonged to someone else, disconnected and useless. Still, I managed to get on one knee, wiping the sweat from my brow with the back of my hand. The heat was unbearable, but that wasn't what was making my head spin. It was him. The way he loomed over me, relentless. The way his disappointment felt like a noose tightening around my neck.

"Get up. Fight." His tone left no space for argument, no room for weakness. He took a fighting stance: feet shoulder-width apart, knees slightly bent, hands up, ready. Always ready for anything, always expecting an attack from any angle.

I stood shakily, my chest heaving. "Sir, I'm going to Enugu for university," I said, sarcasm slipping into my words as I swayed on my feet. "I'm not going to Sambisa Forest."

He chuckled, but there was no warmth in it. "The world is a battlefield, my son." He circled me slowly, like a predator eyeing its prey, calculating, waiting for the moment to strike. And then, in a flash, he grabbed my arm, twisted, and before I could even react, I was on the ground again, staring up at the sky.

He loomed over me, hands on his hips, shaking his head in that familiar, disappointed way. "Whatever you do," he said, "never let your guard down."

I blinked up at him, gasping for air. "I'm trying," I muttered, but my father just kept shaking his head. His grip tightened as he hauled me up again.

"Trying isn't good enough," he shot back. "You fight. You win. You survive."

The sky above me seemed to darken, the sun disappearing behind thick clouds. The heat still pressed down on me, but it felt different now, more oppressive, more suffocating. The world started to tilt, and I felt the ground beneath me shift, slipping away.

I woke up with a start, heart pounding, breath coming in shallow gasps. The air in my living room was frigid. I sat up on the couch. My eyes darted around the room, still half-caught in the dream, expecting to see him standing there, arms crossed, waiting for me to stand up again. But it was just me. Just the cold glow of the streetlights filtering through the curtains, and the steady hum of the air conditioner.

I rubbed my face, trying to shake the remnants of the dream, but his voice echoed in my head. *You fight. You win. You survive.*

It was just a dream. But with everything that had happened, with everything still looming over me like a shadow, it felt like more than that. Maybe it was a warning, or maybe it was just my subconscious replaying all the old scars. It wasn't just a memory. Dreams have a way of filling in the blanks, adding extra details where reality was fuzzier. Certain things hadn't played out exactly as they did in real life, but the core of it was true. It was a fair representation of one of the many grueling training sessions with my father. The kind that left a mark on me deeper than the bruises ever could. Either way, I couldn't afford to rest. Not now.

I sat up, my eyes adjusting to the dim light. Elfreda was asleep in the bedroom, but I couldn't shake the feeling that something was off. That nagging sense that I was still being tested, still being pushed beyond my limits. I wasn't nineteen anymore. I wasn't under my father's thumb. But the fight... it never really ended.

The world is a battlefield, my father had said. Damn if he wasn't right about that.

I glanced at the clock. 4:38 AM. Too early to be awake, too late to go back to sleep. I grabbed my phone from the side table, thumb hovering over my mother's number. Maybe hearing her voice would help. Maybe it would remind me that there was still something soft, something normal, waiting for me on the other side of all this.

I stayed up after that. As soon as it was a little past 7 AM, I called my mother. She was always up by that time, right after her morning prayers. It was no surprise when she picked up after two rings.

"Alvan, nwam. How are you?" Her voice was warm, like a balm over my scattered thoughts.

"I'm fine, mummy. I hope you're well."

My mother sighed softly. "I thank God. Isn't it very early there?"

I paused for a second, suddenly remembering she had no idea I was back in Nigeria. I couldn't exactly blurt it out now. "I couldn't sleep," I replied. "Wanted to hear your voice." I could practically hear her smiling through the phone. "It is well, my son." In the background, I heard some playful chatter, and then two familiar voices called out, asking my mother to pass the phone. Of course, my sisters.

"Brother Dozy!" Amarachi shouted; her voice was full of energy even so early in the morning. "Good morning! When are you coming to visit?"

"Before you know it," I said, smiling despite myself.

"Just don't forget the soap I asked for," Nkechi added, ever the practical one.

"I wouldn't dream of it."

The more we talked, the more I realized how much I missed them. My sisters had always irritated me when we were younger, with their endless gossip and petty arguments. But now? Their voices were like music to me.

We chatted for a while longer, each sister filling me in on the latest drama in their lives. School, friends, whatever was trending. My mother's laughter in the background was constant, like a steady drumbeat of joy that I hadn't heard in what felt like forever. It was the perfect way to start my day.

Once we said our goodbyes, I felt lighter. I headed back to the bedroom and knocked on the door, expecting Elfreda to still be asleep. There was no response. Quietly, I opened the door, figuring she could use some more rest while I grabbed my laptop to work on a few things.

But the bed was empty. The sheets were untouched.

I cursed under my breath. Had she played me? Was there something in the room she had needed, something she'd taken while I slept?

And then it hit me. *The SD card.*

I practically leaped across the room, my heart pounding in my chest. My computer was still on the table where I'd left it. I pressed the slot where I had inserted the SD card the previous day, holding my breath tight in my lungs.

Still intact. Relief washed over me like cold water on a blistering day. The flash drive was plugged in, and the file transfer completed. I made a mental note to dig into its contents later. Just then, I noticed Akaneme passing by the window, broom in hand, performing his usual morning ritual of sweeping the compound. He didn't look my way, his gaze fixed on the ground, but I held off for a moment, waiting until he moved out of sight.

Once he was gone, I wrapped the SD card in a bit of paper and slid it under a leg of the table. A backup plan in case the flash drive somehow disappeared. Paranoid? Maybe. But I'd lost enough small storage devices in my life to make this habit second nature.

This case was already proving to be more complex than it had seemed. Even if Elfreda hadn't thought to search for the SD card, I couldn't shake the feeling that someone else might. Even if Mmachi wasn't the one who set me up, she could still be looking to cut me out and pocket my fee. Who knew whether she had someone lurking nearby, just waiting to pounce?

Fifty thousand dollars was a lot of money, after all.

Before I could fully relax, I heard soft footsteps behind me. I whirled around, instincts sharp.

There she was. Elfreda. The steam from the bathroom followed her, and beads of water trickled down her skin, glistening against her chest. She wore nothing but a small towel, clinging precariously to her curves. Her dark, dripping hair clung to her shoulders, and her skin practically shimmered under the morning light filtering through the curtains.

Her waist was impossibly narrow, her hips wide, tapering down to long, sleek legs. The way she stood, the way her eyes locked onto mine with the perfect blend of innocence and sultry intention. I'd seen this woman fully naked in videos, and yet somehow, standing there with a towel barely covering her, she managed to look even more seductive.

"I'm sorry," she said. "Did you want to use the shower?"

I could feel my face heating up. *Damn it.* She was trying to toy with me. "N-no," I stammered, forcing my eyes to the ground. "I just came to get my computer. Sorry for walking in."

I turned to leave, trying to be as casual as possible, but she stepped forward, blocking my path. Her soft chest pressed against my stomach, the heat from her skin radiating through the thin towel between us.

"It's fine," she whispered, her breath warm against my neck. "Really."

I swallowed hard. Any man with half a brain could tell what she was doing. She was offering herself up, whether as a thank you or a way to keep me on her side, I wasn't sure. Either way, it wasn't a good idea. The last time I took a beautiful woman I barely knew to bed, I woke up with a job I never wanted and a headache I couldn't shake.

I took a deep breath and shuffled past her, doing my best not to think about the curves pressed against me. "I'll go grab us some breakfast," I muttered, trying to keep my voice steady. Then I shut the door behind me, feeling the weight of her gaze even through the wood.

I couldn't afford to get distracted. Not by her. Especially not by her.

As I headed for the kitchen, my mind raced. Elfreda was a mystery, and mysteries had a way of killing you if you didn't solve them fast enough.

But for now, I needed air.

CHAPTER 22

I drove to the Diamond Ballot, my thoughts racing. Something Elfreda had said the night before kept replaying in my mind, gnawing at me. I needed Osita's help to piece it together. After the chaos of the past twenty-four hours, I didn't mind the drive to Victoria Island. The quiet hum of the car was almost like a cold shower, shaking off the remnants of whatever lust Elfreda had awakened in me.

As soon as I got into the club, Osita was lounging, cigarette hanging from his lips. The haze of smoke swirled around him in the dim light. He looked up at me, probably sensing the tension in my expression.

"What's eating you?" he asked.

"The receptionist," I said. "I need you to take me to him. I think he was keeping something from me."

Osita blinked, taken aback. "Wetin happen?"

"Elfreda showed up at my place last night," I began.

Osita's posture changed in an instant. He shot up, his cigarette falling to the ashtray. "Wait, wait, wait. How that one take happen? How did she find you?"

I gave him a quick rundown of what had transpired the night before, keeping my tone neutral but knowing damn well how bizarre the entire thing was. I also told him about Mmachi and how she hired me. There was no reason to be discreet anymore.

"There's something she said that bothered me," I continued. "She told me Mmachi set me up and tipped off the police. So what role does the receptionist play in all this?"

Osita whistled low. "The bastard must've been working with her all along. Was she the mystery woman who paid him to snitch on you?"

"Maybe. I don't know for sure so I want to talk to him again. Did you keep an eye on him? Where is he now?"

Osita cocked his head, that ever-present smirk tugging at the corner of his mouth. "Oh, you want to speak to him again?" He stood up straight, flicking the cigarette to the ground. "Follow me."

I followed him back through the dimly lit corridors of the Diamond Ballot, the smell of alcohol and perfume clinging to the walls. He led me past the main floors and up the creaky stairs toward the attic. My gut tightened the moment I stepped into that musty, confined space. The receptionist was still there, tied up and gagged, exactly as I had left him the night before.

The sight of it twisted something in me, a deep unease clawing at my insides.

I turned to Osita, my face hardening. "Why is he still tied up? I told you to let him go after we got the information."

Osita shrugged, almost lazily, like we were discussing something trivial. "I didn't trust him, not yet. Needed the night to think things over." He glanced over at the receptionist, his eyes narrowing in thought. "I was going to release him just before you showed up. Good timing."

The receptionist, tied to the chair, started whimpering, panic etched across his sweaty face. Osita removed his gag. "Please, oga, let me go. I gave you information. I've been cooperative." His voice cracked, rising in desperation.

I stood there for a moment, my gaze shifting between Osita and the receptionist. Something wasn't adding up, and that familiar instinct, the one that had kept me alive this long, started tugging at the back of my mind.

"Do you have his phone?" I asked.

Osita gave me a sly grin. "I smashed it. Didn't want him calling anyone, obviously. Why? Do you think he was communicating with Mmachi?"

My eyes moved back to the receptionist, but something kept gnawing at me. I stepped closer, eyeing his wrists, bound tightly behind the chair. That's when I noticed a silver chain watch on his wrist, glinting faintly in the low light. Nothing out of the ordinary at first glance, but something about it seemed... off. Too sleek, too modern for a basic analog watch.

I almost ignored it, but my gut told me to take a closer look.

I reached down, examining the watch more closely. It wasn't an ordinary timepiece, it was a smartwatch. Cleverly disguised in a silver case, sleek and unassuming, but a smartwatch nonetheless. The kind with its own SIM card. Essentially, it was a covert phone strapped to his wrist. My eyes narrowed as I pieced it together. This wasn't a mere gadget; it was a tool. A direct line of communication, likely with someone pulling the strings.

The receptionist's eyes widened, his lips trembling. He opened his mouth to say something, but no words came out. The guilt was written all over his face.

I stared at him, my mind racing. None of this added up. Why? Why me? What could I possibly have done to Mmachi to warrant being dragged into this elaborate scheme? I didn't know her. We had no history. Sure, I could understand why she'd want to deal with her husband. Revenge, control, whatever. But me? Was it something tied to my father? No, that didn't make sense either. The Admiral had told me she barely knew my father, despite what she had insinuated. The deeper I went, the less the pieces fit.

What the hell was going on?

Osita's chuckle broke my spiraling thoughts. "I'm sure you don't regret I kept this fool here," he said, motioning to the restrained receptionist.

I turned to him. "Elfreda already suggested that Mmachi was working with him."

From the corner of my eye, I saw the flicker of panic in the receptionist's face. His eyes lit up momentarily, then darted down. He flinched, as though I had just struck a nerve.

"That's all I need to know," Osita said, stretching his neck. "We'll find out what more he knows and finally clear your name."

But before we could press him further, the receptionist erupted.

"Motherfuckers!" he screamed. "I'll kill them all!"

The outburst was jarring, a stark contrast to the cowering, fearful man he'd been moments earlier. Something had snapped. Whatever pushed him over the edge, it was significant. Important. Before I could decide how to respond, the man surged forward, the chair's restraints clattering uselessly to the floor. My stomach dropped.

He lunged at me with unexpected ferocity, his full weight crashing into me. I stumbled back, the air knocked out of me as we both hit the ground. Out of the corner of my eye, I saw

Osita go down, the toppled chair slowing his reaction. Then the receptionist's hands were on my throat, gripping with brutal force.

I gasped, my vision blurring as his thumbs pressed against my windpipe. The sheer strength of his grip was suffocating, and panic clawed at the edges of my mind. I tried to focus, to steady myself, but the lack of oxygen made it difficult to think. My limbs felt heavy, my chest on fire.

Disoriented, I forced myself to assess the situation. The quickest way to get him off me, I decided, was to slam both his ears. A disorienting move that could buy me precious seconds. My hands twitched, readying for the strike.

But before I could act, Osita's hand moved faster than I thought possible. A blur of motion, quick and precise.

Bang!

The gunshot echoed in the attic, deafening in the cramped space. The receptionist's head snapped back, blood splattering the wall behind him as his lifeless body slumped to the floor.

I froze, staring at Osita in shock, my pulse hammering in my ears. He lowered the gun, his face cold and devoid of any remorse. "Bastard," he hissed.

I coughed, drawing in ragged breaths as I scrambled to sit up. "What the hell was that?" I rasped.

Osita looked at me, his expression unreadable. "You're welcome," he muttered.

I clenched my fists, fighting the urge to throttle him. "He was about to tell us everything!"

Osita wiped the blood splatter from his cheek with the back of his hand, looking unfazed. "Before or after he strangled you to death? He tried to kill you. This fool was no use to us."

My mind was spinning, the weight of the situation crashing down on me. I stared at the receptionist's body, the pool of blood spreading across the floor, and took a deep breath. I froze, feeling the chill of realization spread through me. I closed my eyes, inhaling deeply. Of course. It was Osita. He'd kidnapped the man, tortured him, and now the poor bastard was dead. I had been gone from Lagos for too long, and fooled into thinking Osita had softened with age, that running the Diamond Ballot had given him a legitimate life. But no. He was still the same violent cultist I remembered. The same Osita who had once decapitated a rival cult member and left the head in the school square as a warning. A story I'd prefer not to recount.

"You didn't have to do that, man," I muttered. But I already knew he'd have some justification ready.

"You just said the guy was lying through his teeth. He was part of all this shit. And who knows? Maybe that Elfreda babe is the one setting you up. Have you considered that maybe she has been working with Mmachi too?"

The last thing I needed was for Osita to get involved with Elfreda. He had a way of turning situations messier than they needed to be. If I let him near her, things would spiral out of control, no doubt about it. She might have been hiding something, but I wasn't going to let Osita sniff around and make it worse than it already was.

"Anyway," he continued. "You should go handle your business. I'll take care of the body.

A hot flare of fury took me and I smashed my fist against the wall. It should have hurt. It should have stopped me, but the adrenaline had dulled everything into a hard bright focus. "You bloody madman!" I snarled. "That was a person. How could you just kill him? What is wrong with you? This isn't your campus cult playground. You don't get to run around murdering people."

For a stupid second I forgot he had a gun. If he thought I was about to run to the police, he might have pulled the trigger. The thought steadied me like ice.

Osita watched me with that sleepy, half-amused look he reserved for children throwing tantrums. He didn't move.

After a long silence he finally slid the gun back into his trousers and closed the distance between us, slow and deliberate. I clenched my fists, ready for anything, but he made no threatening move. He stopped, letting the dead man lie between us, and smiled like he'd just finished a neat job.

"Alobam," he said. "This na my world. No come if you no fit handle am. Go home. Call if you need more help. I got you."

Cold sweat trickled down my temple. I could have throttled him there and then. Instead, I took a breath, kept my face calm, and nodded. "Okay."

I walked away, feeling like a mindless zombie, my thoughts a blur. Osita's voice cut through the haze. "Dozy," he called out. I stopped and turned to face him. He tossed something at me, and my reflexes kicked in, catching it mid-air. It was the receptionist's silver smartwatch, smeared with a few specks of blood.

Osita smirked. "You're an investigator, right?" he said, eyes gleaming with something close to amusement. "Then investigate."

As sick as I felt in my stomach, I managed to nod.

As soon as I stepped outside, the air hit me like a cold slap, but it did nothing to clear my head. I leaned against the side of the building, rubbing my temples. What had I done? A man was dead. Sure, the receptionist had crossed the line. Maybe he was part of this whole twisted conspiracy, but that didn't mean he deserved a bullet to the head. A thorough ass-kicking? Sure. Maybe a few bruises to remind him not to play both sides of the fence. But dead? That was different.

I couldn't shake the image of Osita, so casual about the whole thing, like taking a life was just another day in the office. He hadn't changed. The same Osita from university. One moment, a jokester with a wicked grin, my best friend who always had my back. And the next? A volatile, violent gangster with blood on his hands. That was the problem with him. He was unpredictable, like a fuse that burned at both ends. And now, I was in the middle of that fuse, wondering when it would blow up in my face.

I regretted ever asking for his help. It had seemed like the smart move at the time. Osita knew Lagos, its underbelly, the places where shadows had shadows. I thought his connections would lead me to the truth faster. But now the truth had come with a bullet to the head, and I was trapped in a nightmare I hadn't signed up for. I wasn't part of the murder, but it didn't matter. There was no undoing what Osita had done, and I couldn't shake the guilt.

The thought crept in, uninvited and cold: *What if Osita turns on me?*

I decided then and there to keep my distance for a while. I wasn't eager to see more death. Not like this. Not so senselessly.

I clenched my fists, staring down the street, replaying the look on the receptionist's face in my mind. Fear, confusion, maybe regret in those final moments, followed by rage as he throttled me. Did he see it coming? Did he even know he was a pawn in a game much bigger than he could understand? The bastard might have been part of this mess, but no one deserves to go out like that.

Another life snuffed out in a city that didn't blink at the sight of blood anymore.

I couldn't undo it, but I could distance myself from it. Keep my hands clean as much as possible. This whole mess was spiraling out of control, and I was in deep enough as it was. I didn't need Osita dragging me down with him. Hell, if anything, I needed to start untangling myself from his web. He was too far gone, too entrenched in this underworld, and I wasn't going to let him take me down with him.

I had to breathe. Regain my footing. And figure out how to do this without adding more names to the body count. I wasn't interested in walking over graves.

I pushed off the wall and started down the street, my mind racing with half-formed plans and growing regrets. *This mess*, I thought. *This goddamn mess.*

I slipped into the car and stared at the watch in my hand. It was password-locked, naturally. I didn't know enough about the receptionist, and I definitely didn't have the time to waste cracking the code right then. I fastened it around my wrist, making a mental note to figure it out later.

On the drive back, I called Calvin. The phone rang twice before his laid-back voice came through the speaker.

"What's up, bro?" he said.

"Dozy, how far?" Oge's voice chimed in.

"Glad I caught you both," I said, relaxing a little hearing their voices. "I need your help."

"What can we do?" Oge asked.

"I'm going to need a tiny screwdriver, and a little clip cable, the one with the needle-nosed clamps. I'm also going to need a laptop. Then please get me everything you can find on a woman named Elfreda Bassey," I said, my mind already racing ahead. "I'll swing by your hotel in a bit. I need to take care of something first."

"Got it," Calvin responded. "We'll get on it."

— ◆ —

As I pulled up to the house on Banana Island, I was taken aback by the sight in front of me. A black *Innoson* Minibus was idling near the gate, its engine purring softly. I stopped the car a short distance away, squinting through the windshield, trying to make sense of what was unfolding. Who the hell parks a bus like that in front of this kind of estate? Something was off. Then I saw Elfreda, her eyes red and puffy, streams of tears staining her cheeks, being roughly escorted toward the van by a hulking man in a black suit and sunglasses. He looked like something out of an early 2000s Nollywood film. A clichéd henchman, built like a wall, trying too hard to blend in but failing miserably. His attempt to conceal the pistol in his hand was sloppy, but that was enough to make my heart race.

I didn't have time to think. I was damn near out of time. I had come too close to wrapping up this whole mess, and I wasn't about to let it slip away. With a surge of adrenaline, I slammed my foot down on the gas pedal. The engine roared, and the tires screeched as I bolted toward them. The car jolted as it bounced over the uneven patches of the road, but I held firm, my hands gripping the wheel like a vice.

Elfreda and the goon's heads snapped in my direction. They ducked back through the gates just before I rammed into the back of the minibus, sending the vehicle forward with a satisfying crunch. The impact slammed me into the airbag, which exploded into my face like a fist. White hot pain flashed in my skull, and the world spun. A high-pitched ringing buzzed in my ears, disorienting me. My vision blurred for a few seconds, and I could taste blood where my lip had split. I forced myself to focus, blinking rapidly to clear the fog.

"Mister man, are you mad?" yelled a voice, thick with irritation.

Through the haze, I glanced at the rearview mirror and saw the suited man storming toward me. His massive frame cut through the smoke from the engine, making him look even more menacing. The bastard thought I was out cold. He reached in through the window, his meaty hand fishing for the door handle. Big mistake. The second his fingers wrapped around it, I shot my hand up and clamped down on his wrist. His eyes widened in shock just as I yanked him into the car and disarmed him in one swift motion. Before he could react, I delivered a crushing punch straight to his nose. I felt the crunch of bone under my knuckles as he stumbled back, blood pouring from his face.

But this wasn't over yet. The minibus driver, who had slumped over the wheel from the impact, suddenly moved. He staggered out, his face pale but determined, a gun now in his hand. Damn it! I didn't have time to fight them both. Without thinking, I bolted toward the house, grabbing Elfreda along the way.

"Come on!" I shouted, dragging her with me as the sound of gunfire exploded behind us.

We sprinted down the street, my eyes darting around for cover. That's when I spotted a yellow *keke napep*—a small, motorized three-wheeler used for quick trips around the city—idling nearby. I yanked open the flimsy door, practically tossing Elfreda inside before jumping in myself.

"Oga, go! Go!" I yelled at the driver, who blinked at me in confusion for a split second before slamming his foot on the pedal. The keke sputtered to life and we shot forward, weaving through the early morning traffic. The goons had already piled back into their minibus, its front bumper dangling after the crash, but still very much functional. The chase was on.

The keke bought us a few seconds of mercy, nothing more. The van behind us was faster, heavier, and driven by men who didn't seem to care whether they hit us or the traffic in front of them. By the time we reached a crowded intersection before the bridge, the engine of the keke was already whining in defeat.

I threw a few banknotes at the driver and We jumped out while it was still rolling and sprinted toward the nearest dark-yellow danfo with thick black lines running across its body. The conductor froze mid-yell, surprised to see passengers running toward him, but his eyes lit up when I shoved a wad of cash at him.

"Move," I ordered. "I'm paying for the entire bus."

That was all he needed. No arguments, no questions, no hesitation.

The driver slammed the door, stomped the accelerator, and the danfo jumped forward.

The streets of Lagos blurred past us with market stalls, pedestrians and hawkers. Everywhere was alive with the chaotic energy of the city. We tore through the intersections, narrowly avoiding collisions, but the bus was gaining on us. My heart pounded in my chest as the bus bounced over potholes and swerved past *okadas*. I could see Oshodi in the distance, its sprawling chaos waiting like a trap.

Traffic hit us hard as we entered the dense hub of Oshodi. The vehicles ahead came to a grinding halt, the blaring horns adding to the madness. We had no choice but to abandon the bus.

"Move!" I shouted at Elfreda as we bolted out and disappeared into the maze of side streets, dodging between vendors selling sachets of water and roasted plantain. We darted into a narrow alley, the sound of the bus doors slamming shut behind us echoing in the distance. The two goons were on foot now, chasing us through the labyrinth of streets. My legs burned, but the fear of being shot kept me moving.

Up ahead, I spotted a small water sachet factory. One of those tiny establishments that supply pure water to the street vendors. Perfect. I dragged Elfreda inside, the smell of plastic and damp air hitting us as we slipped through stacks of water bags. I could hear the heavy footsteps of the men getting closer.

"Stay low," I whispered to Elfreda, positioning myself behind a stack of bags. I waited, every muscle in my body tense, my breath shallow as I listened to the sounds of the men approaching. One of them knocked over a pile of crates, cursing under his breath.

I crouched behind the crates, the sound of approaching footsteps growing louder with every second. My breath came out in short, controlled bursts. I waited, heart pounding, muscles tensing, timing it just right. When the first man rounded the corner, I sprang into action, grabbing one of the heavy bags of water and hurling it with every ounce of strength I had. It hit him square in the chest, knocking him back into the wall. He stumbled, gasping for air, but I wasn't done. I surged forward, pivoting on my feet and drove my elbow into the side of his jaw with precision, the blow sending a shockwave through his skull. He crumpled to the floor in a heap.

But there was no time to celebrate. His partner was already pulling out a gun, the metallic click ringing out like a death sentence. My instincts kicked in before my brain had time to catch up. I grabbed a sachet of water from the ground. It was small, but packed with enough weight and I flung it at his head with all the force I could muster. It struck him in the face, buying me a split second as he stumbled back, firing a wild shot that echoed through the warehouse. The bullet ricocheted off the wall, slamming into the first guy's leg, a sickening scream filling the air as he hit the ground.

The gunman cursed, his aim thrown off. I didn't waste a second. I charged him, lowering my center of gravity as I tackled him at the waist. We went down hard, rolling through the wet dirt, his fists slamming into my ribs, my forearm driving into his throat to keep him from getting leverage. Desperation brought back long-dormant instincts, muscle memory kicking in from the countless drills my father had put me through. I blocked a wild swing with a swift upward palm strike, then slammed the heel of my boot into his knee, sending him howling in pain.

But he was resilient. He twisted under me, managing to throw me off just enough to get a hand on his gun again. I saw the flash of metal in the corner of my eye and reacted, gripping his wrist and twisting it sharply. He growled in pain, the gun slipping from his fingers and clattering to the ground. I drove my knee into his chest, knocking the air out of him, and in one fluid motion, grabbed the gun and pistol-whipped him across the temple. He went limp instantly, collapsing into unconsciousness with a dull thud.

The fight was over.

I stood up, breathing heavily, water dripping from my face, blood pounding in my ears. My arms ached from the struggle, but the adrenaline was still coursing through my veins, keeping me upright. The only sound was the heavy breathing of the man clutching his bleeding leg on the floor. He was whimpering now, holding his wound, eyes wide with pain and fear.

I took a step back, wiping my forehead with the back of my hand, trying to shake off the daze of the fight. I glanced at Elfreda. She was staring at me, wide-eyed, frozen in shock. She looked like she didn't even recognize me. "What the fuck is going on here?" I muttered, though the question wasn't really meant for anyone.

I bent down, grabbed the fallen gunman's weapon, then stood up straight. "Let's get the hell out of here," I said, glancing around the sunlit factory, still half-expecting more thugs to pour in. My body was still on high alert, every nerve screaming at me to move.

Elfreda didn't need to be told twice. She nodded, still pale, and we bolted for the door. We heard the man we left behind moaning in the warehouse, and we disappeared into the Lagos market.

CHAPTER 23

We walked down Marina Street on Lagos Island, the bustling heart of the city, and Elfreda was visibly shaken. She led the way, her pace quicker than usual, her eyes darting around, scanning the crowd like a hunted animal. I couldn't blame her. The events of the last hour had been enough to rattle anyone. Trust was in short supply.

I was taking her to her apartment to pick up a couple of things, and I'd put her up in a hotel where she could at least feel safe for a night or two while I figured out Mmachi's connection to the receptionist and the two men who nearly killed us.

As we waded through the crowd, the street around us pulsed with the chaos of Lagos City at rush hour. The sheer number of people reminded me that this city was a living organism, breathing, shoving, and grinding through each day. Men in suits, too heavy and ill-fitting for the relentless heat, strode past with determined looks. Women in professional blouses and skirts navigated the sidewalks, their heels tapping against the cracked pavement. And amidst the formality of office workers were the street hawkers: children in t-shirts and shorts, darting between cars, balancing trays of bread, soft drinks, and peanuts on their heads. The agberos, of course, were never far from the scene. Every corner had at least one, their singlets stained with sweat; their three-quarter shorts hanging low, swaggering through the crowd with a chip on their shoulder, always on the lookout for trouble or money. Whichever came first.

One particular agbero caught my attention. The sun bounced off his perfectly shaven bald head like it had a personal vendetta against him, reflecting a glare so bright it was almost hypnotic. For some reason, I found myself watching him for a beat longer than I should have, his bald head shining like a beacon in the crowd. The moment I turned away, a loud, unmistakable smack echoed from behind us.

Instinctively, I turned back to see the same bald-headed agbero holding his head, his face twisted in confusion.

"Who slap me for head?" he shouted into the crowd, his deep voice booming over the noise of the street. He wasn't talking to anyone in particular. He spun around in circles, looking utterly bewildered, like a man betrayed by the very air around him.

As I watched him, trying to stifle a chuckle, he finally seemed to give up his search. With an exaggerated, dramatic flair, he stretched out his arm and pointed his palm in the direction of the invisible offender, making a classic Nigerian obscene gesture one that, in this country, carried the same weight as flipping someone the bird.

I couldn't help but laugh quietly to myself. This was Lagos in its purest form. A city where anything could happen, where life had a strange rhythm that didn't make sense anywhere else. One moment, you're dodging street hawkers; the next, you're watching an agbero accuse the air of slapping him.

But Elfreda was still on edge, her body tense, her movements hurried. The enraged agbero might've been a distraction for me, but for her, the weight of the situation hadn't lifted. She had every reason to be nervous. By trying to kidnap her, it meant whoever we were dealing with wasn't just playing games. Someone was cleaning up, making sure that any loose ends—like Elfreda, like me—wouldn't be around much longer.

Seeing her apartment in the daytime, I noticed it was a worn-down complex that looked like it hadn't seen a fresh coat of paint in years. We accessed it through an iron gate that creaked like it was protesting the weight of time. The neighbors, true to Lagos form, were out on the balconies, shouting over each other in loud, animated conversations, laughter cutting through the air like a knife. It was that familiar city noise. Chaotic, unfiltered, and impossible to ignore.

A couple of kids in school uniforms dashed around the compound, already smudging their white shirts and socks with dirt. I could tell from the mess they were making that they wouldn't be walking into school looking sharp. Typical of the environment. Kids let loose long before their first class bell rang.

Elfreda didn't pay any attention to them or the scene around her. She walked straight for the staircase, head down, her body stiff with tension. I offered to wait outside while she grabbed her things, thinking she might want some privacy, but she turned to me, her eyes wide with fear. "No, come in," she said quickly. "I'm scared."

Scared. I didn't like the sound of that. Something about it didn't sit right, but I followed her inside anyway. The apartment was modest, clean, well-furnished, and comfortable enough, though nothing fancy. It had all the essential gadgets an apartment might need. Entering her bedroom, what caught my eye was the smart chandelier blinking in RGB colors, casting the room in shifting hues. It looked like something ripped straight out of a gamer's Twitch setup. A strange touch for a place that otherwise screamed low-key.

Elfreda noticed my gaze and gave a knowing nod. "I'm assuming you know I'm a host on Slago," she said. I shrugged, feigning ignorance.

"No need to pretend," she continued, a faint smirk playing on her lips. "Last night, you offered me tequila. Your tone spoke volumes. You know of my alter ego, TequilaDream."

I sighed, deciding there was no point in denying it. "I also know that's how you and the Admiral met," I said.

She looked down at her feet, her posture stiffening for a moment before those dark brown eyes were on me again, sharper now. "Is there a hint of judgment in your tone?" she asked.

I leaned against the counter and made sure to keep my mouth shut. I just knew anything I'd say in that moment would be misconstrued or come off as judgmental. My priority was getting her to a safe place, everything else came second.

She took note of my reticence and laughed bitterly, a sound devoid of humor. "Men are always going to lust after me," she said. "At least this way, I make money off it. Enough to take care of myself. Enough to help my family survive."

I raised an eyebrow. "And where are they? Your family?"

Her shoulders softened, and she let out a slow breath as she sat down. "Back in Calabar," she said quietly. "My mother and three sisters. My father's gone. It's just us. I'm the only one out here, the only one who can change anything. I promised I'd make it big and bring them to the city, where they could have a real life." Her voice cracked slightly, but she pushed on. "Alex... Alex was going to help me do that."

She stared at the floor for a moment, her composure faltering. I folded my arms, my thoughts churning. As much as I might have felt for her, I wasn't here to play the comforting friend or offer sympathy. She was a crucial piece of a puzzle I needed to solve quickly. Time was not a luxury I could afford, and I had little patience to be a shoulder to cry on.

"The Admiral knew about your situation?" I asked, my tone firm but not unkind.

She wiped a single tear from her cheek and nodded. "He felt bad for me," she murmured. "Said he'd help me get to the US and achieve all my dreams."

"Thus... the sudden engagement?" I prompted.

She nodded again. "He said it was the only way to do it right. He also suggested we be seen in ublic more often to make it look more genuine."

"For a green card," I said, more to myself than to her. The scenario struck an uncomfortable chord. I couldn't help but think of Jasmine, the woman who had once taken pity on me and made the same offer. A flood of memories washed over me, and for a fleeting moment, I couldn't judge her. Not entirely. "So, the relationship wasn't legitimate after all," I remarked, my words carefully measured. "Despite what you said earlier about loving him."

Her head shot up, her eyes blazing with anger. "He was my savior!" she snapped. "I will always love him for what he would have done for me. For my family. There is nothing fake about how I felt about him. How I feel."

I studied her for a moment, letting the weight of her words settle between us. Her hardened exterior was slipping, and beneath it, I saw the desperation that drove her. This wasn't ambition or greed, it was survival. A young woman navigating a system designed to crush her, doing whatever she thought she had to do to claw her way out.

"Elfreda," I began softly, my tone gentler now, "what you're doing... I get it. I don't agree with it, but I get it. You're trying to survive. But Alex... he's gone. You can't pin all your hopes on what he might have done for you."

She looked up at me, her gaze defiant but glassy, betraying the vulnerability she tried so hard to mask. "I know," she whispered. "But he was the first man who saw me as more than just a pretty face. He promised to help me because he believed I deserved better."

"I'm sure you do," I said. "But you can't rely on anyone else to fix this for you. If you want to make it out, you've got to find a way that doesn't drag you deeper into the mud. Putting yourself out there like this... the internet doesn't forget."

She dropped her gaze again, her hands clenching and unclenching as if trying to grasp something just out of reach. For a moment, I thought I might have overstepped, but then she nodded, just slightly. A crack in her armor, faint but undeniable.

"I just wanted a way out," she said, her voice barely audible.

I nodded. "I'll let you get your stuff together," I said. "I'll wait in the living room."

I turned and made my way to the door, pushing it open with a quiet creak. But as soon as I stepped through, the atmosphere shifted. A faint rustle caught my attention. A presence emerging from my peripheral vision. My instincts kicked in, but before I could react, a hand clamped around my arm, and with a sharp pull and a twist, I was flipped to the floor.

The impact sent a jolt through my back, but I recovered quickly, flipping myself back onto my feet. Just as I steadied myself, I turned to face my attacker only to be blindsided by a firm and precise front kick. The blow hit square in my chest, sending me flying backward and crashing into the couch with a grunt.

Before me stood a young woman, her braided hair tied back. Her posture was striking. Her front foot was pointed directly at me, her back foot angled outward at about 45 degrees, her weight evenly distributed for balance. Her knees were slightly bent, primed for explosive movement. Her hands were raised in a guard: the front hand positioned slightly forward, fingers loose but ready to snap into a strike or block, while the back hand hovered near her chin, prepared to counter. Her stance radiated sharp precision, fluid readiness, and the controlled power of someone who had spent years perfecting her art.

Her eyes locked onto mine, sharp and unwavering, filled with suspicion that felt as solid as the kick I'd just taken. There was no mistaking her training. She moved with the fluidity and power of someone who knew exactly what they were doing. And as I stared back at her, trying to catch my breath, something about her struck a chord of familiarity. Then I remembered: the girl from the previous night.

She didn't say a word, her body coiled like a spring ready to strike again. Her gaze pierced through me, unrelenting, as if she were assessing whether I was friend or foe. I raised a hand slowly, palm out, signaling I wasn't a threat. "Hold on," I said. "Let's not do anything rash here."

Her stance didn't shift, but her eyes narrowed, studying me carefully. I couldn't place where I'd seen her before, but there was something in her face and her presence that was eerily familiar. "How the hell did you get in here?" she demanded.

Before I could respond, Elfreda emerged from the back, rolling a pink suitcase behind her. She stopped in her tracks when she saw the girl. "Candy," she said, her tone a little too high, a little too strained. "You're home."

Candy didn't acknowledge Elfreda's discomfort. She just narrowed her eyes and gave a curt nod. "Why is...Who is he?"

Ah, this must be the housemate Elfreda had mentioned. The one who didn't take kindly to male guests. Her energy made sense now. There was something about her stance, about the way she sized me up, that screamed territorial.

I stood up, stretching my hand out in what I hoped would defuse the tension. "Dozy Agu," I said, trying to keep my tone casual, though the unease in the air was thick. "Freda here never mentioned your exceptional fighting skill. You pack a mean punch. I don't mean to intrude. I was just stepping out."

Candy didn't take my hand. She just looked at me, her eyes narrowing further, like she was trying to decide whether I was worth the trouble of throwing out. Elfreda, sensing the situation was getting uncomfortable, hurriedly grabbed her suitcase and nodded at me. "Could you wait for me outside?" she muttered. I wasted no time grabbing the handle of her bag and getting out of there.

Even as I waited by the taxi outside, I could hear raised voices coming from the apartment. Candy and Elfreda were arguing. The words were muffled, but the tone was clear. There was a history there, something deeper than just an aversion to strangers.

I leaned against the cab, watching the complex and mulling over the enigma that was Candy. She did not just seem annoyed or dismissive; her hostility to the presence of a man, even for just a few minutes, felt deeply personal. She was agitated, like a coiled spring ready to snap. I didn't need to be a detective to know there was a story there. Her masculine clothing, while it didn't necessarily mean anything, could hint at something. Maybe she harbored feelings for Elfreda that went unrequited. A woman as alluring as Elfreda probably had no shortage of admirers. If Candy had to watch that, time and again, it could have left her bitter, resenting every man who came near.

I stopped myself. As was constantly the case, in my stress I had begun to overthink things.

I glanced down at my phone, weighing the pros and cons of the call I was about to make. Everything I'd encountered so far pointed to Mmachi setting me up. Typically, my near-religious reliance on Occam's razor would have convinced me to stop right there. The simplest explanation usually sufficed, and all signs led to her. But something nagged at me, an itch I couldn't scratch.

It was the motive, or rather, the lack of one. The whole thing felt too elaborate, too... messy. That unanswered question had been clawing at the back of my brain, refusing to let go.

I sighed and hit the call button on Mmachi's name. The line clicked almost instantly, but no words came through. Silence, except for the faintest sound of breathing. She was there, listening, waiting. I wasn't in the mood for games.

"Someone set me up," I said flatly. "And I think it was you."

No response. Just the steady rhythm of her breathing on the other end.

"You wanted your husband out of the way the entire time," I pressed on. "You made sure I'd confront him in public places, so it'd look like I was stalking him. Then you conspired with the receptionist at the Lorel Luxury Hotel to kill him and frame me for it."

The silence lingered, stretching longer than my patience. And then her voice finally came through, calm and deliberate. "It sounds to me like a lot of things would have needed to conveniently fall in line for this supposed plan to work," she said, her tone devoid of any emotional response to my accusation.

She continued, each word measured and cutting. "For one, I would've had to be absolutely certain you'd accept my offer. What if you had turned me down? And even if you agreed, I'd need to know exactly where you'd find Alex on the very night I intended to kill him. How would I ensure that? What if you'd gotten lost or decided to take a different approach to finding him? What if Alex didn't show up at the hotel at all?"

She paused, letting the weight of her questions settle before delivering the final blow. "But most importantly," she said, "do you think I'm stupid enough to use someone who lives in the same city as I do? Someone who could be tracked back to me with the slightest bit of effort?"

I pulled the phone away slightly as the sharp sound of her clicking her tongue echoed in my ear. That familiar tsk-tsk noise. It was the kind of sound someone made when they were disappointed. It felt patronizing, like she expected more from me.

"No, Mr. Dozy," she said. "I did not set you up. Now, I suggest you stop wasting my time with your ridiculous accusations and focus on what actually matters: getting me those documents. That's the only reason I continue to pay you and tolerate these stupid phone calls."

Click. She hung up.

I stared at the phone for a moment, my face hot with a mix of embarrassment and frustration. She wasn't wrong about the holes in my accusation. It didn't add up. The plan I'd laid out required too many perfect alignments, too many variables she couldn't possibly control. It didn't sit right with me from the start, and now I knew for certain this wasn't her doing.

Whoever had orchestrated this had gone to great lengths, and I was still no closer to finding out who they were or why they'd chosen me. But my call had served its purpose. I'd ruled out Mmachi.

I took a deep breath, pocketed my phone, and clenched my fists. There was still work to do.

When Elfreda finally emerged, her face was flushed with frustration.

"You ready?" I asked. She nodded, avoiding eye contact for a moment. "I don't mean to pry, but there are dangerous people after you. Don't you think your housemate should come with us?"

She looked up at me. "Candy? She'll be fine."

"You saw what we're dealing with, Freda."

"Candy knows Taekwondo," she replied. "I've seen her take down men three times her size. Trust me, she's even more impressive than you in a fight."

I rubbed my chest, still sore from her kick earlier. I was slightly offended but chose not to ask her any more questions despite being impressed. Whatever argument they'd had wasn't my business and we had bigger problems to deal with. I opened the door for her, and we drove off in silence, heading for the hotel in Ikeja where Calvin and Oge were staying. When we pulled up to the hotel, Oge was already standing at the entrance, waiting for us. She flashed a concerned smile as I stepped out of the car with Elfreda. I introduced the two of them, and they exchanged greetings with mutual politeness, though Oge's gaze lingered on Elfreda for a second too long, trying to size her up.

Oge had already handled the logistics. She booked Elfreda a room under her own name, keeping her off the radar from whoever might be hunting her. Smart move. Once Elfreda was squared away and disappeared down the hallway to her room, Oge turned to me, arms crossed.

"You never did explain, Dozy," she said. "What exactly have you gotten yourself into?"

I exhaled through my nose, glancing away. I could dodge, maybe brush it off, but she wasn't the type to let things slide. Osita had a blind loyalty to me. He'd throw a punch first and ask questions never. But Oge? She was different. If she stuck her neck out for me, she wanted to know why. Not because she doubted me, but because she wanted to make sure I wasn't doing something stupid. She did this because she felt she owed me a debt she could not repay.

It all went back to university, the end of our first year. Exams were over, and everyone was eager to pack up and head home. Oge and I weren't exactly friends back then. We were colleagues, at best. I was the Class Rep, and she was my deputy, which meant our conversations were strictly business. Then, one afternoon, I spotted her in front of the department offices, shoulders trembling, silent tears slipping down her face.

My first instinct was to keep walking. None of my business. But something tugged at me, that damn conscience of mine, so I stopped and asked what was wrong.

She hesitated, sizing me up, then decided to take a chance.

It was the same ugly story, the one whispered in every corner of Nigerian universities. A professor with too much power and no scruples, offering good grades in exchange for sex. Some students played along, seeing it as an easy path to an A. Others hated it but felt they had no choice, living with the weight of that compromise for the rest of their lives. Then there were the ones like Oge—strong-willed, stubborn, the kind of woman who'd rather set the world on fire than let it burn her first. But even the strong break sometimes. That day, she cracked.

She never asked for my help. I was already moving before she could. My irritation alone was enough to fuel me. I paid the professor a visit, had a little *chat* with him. The specifics of that meeting? Another story for another day. But when I walked out of his office, Oge had nothing to worry about anymore.

Later, she'd insist she could have handled it on her own. I believed her. Given time, she'd have pulled a move so bold it would've left the whole university shaking. But she was still grateful. And from that moment on, she had my back. But not without questions first.

Now, here she was again, standing in front of me, waiting for an answer.

"I promise, I'll tell you everything in due time," I said. "I just really need your help. No one digs up dirt like you."

She studied me for a moment, weighing my words, then sighed. "Fine," she muttered. "I'll check on Elfreda, make sure she's settling in, then meet you at the bar." She tapped her fist against mine and walked off.

I headed toward the bar across the lobby, already tasting the burn of whiskey on my tongue.

I had barely taken a few steps when someone called my name.

"Is that Dozy?"

I looked to my left and saw Lola, dressed in a striking black and gold dress, her heels impossibly high. I was certain she'd topple over, but she carried herself with the same confidence I saw when I first met her on the Yacht, her stride smooth and deliberate. She approached with a satisfied grin on her face.

"How are you? I hope you're not stalking me," she teased.

I chuckled awkwardly. "Lola. I didn't realize this was one of your family's hotels."

She waved a hand dismissively. "Are you okay? You look a bit...beat up."

"I got a little carried away at the gym," I lied smoothly.

Her eyes sparkled with interest. "You do look like a fighter," she said. "Have you booked a room in our fine establishment?"

"No, I'm staying with a friend," I said, keeping my tone light. "This visit was impromptu."

She waved her hand again as if dismissing the idea. "Nonsense, you'll have your own room. Allow me to handle that for you."

"You really don't have to. It's fine," I started, trying to deflect.

Another wave. "I like to help my friends, Dozy," she said, then paused, her expression turning serious. "Any luck with that Slago business?"

I nodded, feeling a wave of discomfort. "Yes, I found her."

She flashed me a brief, knowing look. "You go ahead. I'll find you in a bit."

I thanked her and made my way into the bar. Calvin was there, already sipping on a cup of coffee, his usual cool, unshakable demeanor in place.

As soon as he saw me, he raised his cup. "You look like you need this more than I do," he said.

I accepted his offer and slumped into the chair across from him. He ordered me a coffee, black, no sugar. It suited the mood. I wasted no time catching him up on the morning's chaos. I left out the bit where Osita took matters into his own hands, of course—he worked in law enforcement after all and would appreciate being left in the dark on all that. Calvin listened in silence, taking mental notes like a detective unraveling a case in his head. When I finished, he took a slow sip of his coffee, the gears in his mind visibly turning.

"So, do you trust her?" he asked, finally breaking the silence.

"No," I said, shaking my head. "But I'm not sure that matters right now. She's got information I need. Could be my way out of this mess."

Calvin leaned back, studying me. "You think she has these documents?"

I sighed, running a hand through my hair. "That or she knows who does."

I set the cheap plastic watch on the table between us. It smelled of sweat and smoke, the kind of gadget you pick up in a market and regret by morning. "Did you bring the tools I asked for?"

Calvin dug a pouch from his bag and handed it over, eyebrows raised. "You sure you don't want my help? You said it was password-locked."

I uncapped a jeweler's screwdriver, the metal tip catching the light. "Cheap things talk when you play gentle." I worked the seam slow. Patience was a kind of violence that kept you from smashing what you couldn't fix. The back popped with a tiny sigh. Inside looked like a joke: tiny chips, solder pads, nothing that screamed enterprise security. A neat row of test pads winked up at me. Factory leftovers most buyers never saw. But they were the door.

Calvin was quiet for a beat, then asked, "Where'd you learn this?"

I didn't look up. "About a year and a half back I busted a guy who ran SIM-swap scams. He social-engineered telco reps, took over numbers, harvested two-factor texts and emptied accounts. He'd been studying telecoms, then dropped out of computer engineering to sell access. He said it was to pay for his mother's surgery. Desperation breeds strange skill."

Calvin whistled. "SIM-swap. That's proper cybercrime."

"Proper and ugly." I clipped a cable to the pads and hooked the other end to Calvin's laptop. "When I had him, I could've handed him to the cops. Instead, I cut a deal. He taught me the backyard tricks. Not server breaks, not state-grade stuff, just how sloppy protections on cheap devices leak crumbs: bad defaults, unencrypted caches, careless pairing. Not legal. Useful."

Calvin gave a crooked smile. "You let a fraudster school you in law-bending."

"You learn how a thief thinks so you can smell the lie." I signed into my cloud storage and pulled up the black-box program I'd been given. No command lists, just a progress bar that crawled like a wounded animal. "That's why you crack it open first," I muttered, half to Calvin, half to myself. "The program's the key, but you still need to find the lock."

Calvin nodded like an unwitting student. "And what made you ask to learn all this?" he asked.

I shrugged. "Too many times a locked device stood between me and the truth. Only recently I had to crack a phone with nothing but luck and a guessable password. It worked that time. Lucky, not clever. But these tools will make it much easier every time."

The program spat out a few lines: timestamps, a scatter of GPS pings, and several messages. Calvin leaned forward.

"Jeez... you actually did it?" he breathed.

I turned my attention to the messages now visible on the screen. They were written in a kind of shorthand, no doubt due to the discomfort of typing on a tiny watch screen while being tied up. The first one read: "*Dzy goin 2 Lorel.*" Another followed: "*tld abt woman infomant.*" But the message that really grabbed my attention was from an unsaved number, timestamped around the time I had been heading home from Lorel after discovering the Admiral's body.

"*Handle the doctor. She might talk,*" it said.

The receptionist had responded with: "*I'll take care of it. Just don't forget my mullah.*"

Calvin leaned in closer, his expression serious now. "We've got something here," he said, his eyes scanning the screen again. "That last message? It's vague, but it could be a lead."

I nodded, processing it all. The receptionist had been more than just a lackey. He was a key player, and now he was dead. I couldn't shake the feeling that there was more to this than we were seeing. Who was this mystery person texting him? And who was this woman they were talking about silencing?

I dialed the number. It was dead. A burner maybe?

"We may need to revisit this," Calvin said, breaking my thoughts.

He wasn't wrong. I had other leads to chase.

Oge joined us a few moments later, sitting down with a sigh of her own. "She's out cold," she said, referring to Elfreda. Then she eyed my busted lip. "Dozy, what the hell happened to you?"

I shrugged, giving her the short version of the scuffle. Oge's brow furrowed with worry as she listened. "You're supposed to be staying out of trouble."

Her concern was touching, but I couldn't afford to be slowed down by it. "Tell me what you found out about her," I said, steering the conversation back on track.

Oge hesitated for a moment, then nodded and pulled out her phone. "Her name's Elfreda Bassey. She's from Ibiaku in Akwa Ibom State. A recent graduate of UNILAG. A B.A. in Linguistics. First of four kids."

I nodded, digesting the information while waiting for the details that mattered. "And her lifestyle?"

Oge scrolled through her phone and then handed it to me. "She presents herself as a charitable type. Spends her time handing out food to the less fortunate in places like Ajegunle." She tapped on a video, and I watched as Elfreda stood by the trunk of her car, passing out prepacked meals to a crowd of raggedly dressed men and women. The recipients, faces worn and hungry, erupted into praise and gratitude, their voices rising in a chaotic symphony of thanks. Candy was by her side, helping to distribute the packages with a smile plastered across her face.

It was a compelling scene, one that could easily pull at the heartstrings of anyone watching. But I wasn't anyone. I'd seen too many wolves draped in the wool of public charity, parading acts of kindness to build an image. Celebrities and pseudo-celebrities staging their generosity for the camera, handing out food, clothing, or a fistful of cash in exchange for social media clout. The worst kind of engagement farming and virtue signaling.

I handed the phone back to Oge, my skepticism unwavering. "It's impressive," I said flatly, "but people like her don't do anything without an angle. What's she really about?"

"Well, despite all that, her life's far from humble," Calvin chimed in.

I looked at him, then back at Oge, who scrolled to Elfreda's Instagram page and handed me the phone again. It was all there. Pictures of exotic vacations, posing on beaches in Zanzibar, living it up in the deserts of Dubai, decked out in designer outfits, the works. She looked like your typical influencer, the kind who was either incredibly lucky or had a rich benefactor footing the bill who was always absent from the pictures.

Oge smirked. "Now we know where the Admiral's money was going."

Calvin leaned in. "Not just him. I've seen her accounts—don't ask how—and she's had deposits from plenty of people. We're talking millions of Naira. Some of them big names. Very influential."

I shook my head, not the least bit surprised. "She's a star on Slago. Always in the top ten for most gifts received."

"Pretty stupid to send money directly," Oge said. "At least Slago gives them some cover."

"Who are these other benefactors?" I asked, holding out my hand, expecting something. Documents, a list, anything. Calvin only shook his head. "Way above us, Dozy. I shouldn't have even mentioned it."

Oge and I traded a look. *Oh, shit.* If Calvin was staying quiet, it meant the names could cost him his job. Elfreda's clients went that high?

"Anyway," Calvin said, trying to wave it off. "I can guarantee you they had nothing to do with this. That's all I'll say."

I sighed and let it drop. I trusted him enough to know when not to push. Still, the pieces kept turning in my head. "The Admiral wasn't making money. Everything he gave her came straight from Mmachi."

Oge arched a brow. "His wife? That couldn't have gone over well."

"She might've stomached a mistress," I said. "But a second wife? That's different. That could've made her snap. And knowing Elfreda had other heavy-hitting clients just tells me the one thing the Admiral offered her that nobody else could... was a green card."

Calvin slid a piece of paper across the table toward me. "Check this out."

I picked it up and saw it was a bank statement. It belonged to Alex Maduagu. I looked up at him and he waved his hand as if telling me not to ask how he had acquired them as well. Calvin had highlighted several transactions on the statement, all to one name. Catherine Ughene.

"Who's Catherine Ughene?" I asked, my curiosity piqued.

Oge leaned over, unlocking her phone and pulling up an image. She handed it to me, and my eyes fell on a digital flyer for "*Mother C Prophetic Ministry Intl.*" There was a photo of a large woman in a bright, traditional outfit, smiling warmly, the epitome of a Nigerian prophetess. The woman the Admiral had been sending thousands of Dollars to. I recognized her instantly. I saw her on the yacht the night I was thrown overboard. Catherine Ughene was the so-called prophetess, Mother C!

I told them where I had seen her before and squinted at the flyer, trying to piece it together. "So, the Admiral was funneling money to this... Prophetess?"

Oge nodded. "We found videos of him attending her services. It looks like she had him completely brainwashed."

I leaned back in my chair. "Elfreda mentioned she was religious too at some point. I bet this Prophetess has her hooks in her as well."

Calvin sipped his coffee, his eyes narrowed. "Would you like me to talk to this Elfreda girl, Dozy?"

"You'll only scare her, man," I chuckled.

"That's the point!" he shot back.

Lola sauntered up to us, her usual easy smile on her face. "Oh, I don't mean to interrupt," she purred, her tone dripping with charm. She handed me a keycard, her fingers lingering just a little too long. "Maybe later we can…talk about our shared trauma. You know, the Admiral?" Her voice carried a flirtatious edge.

I could feel Oge and Calvin's eyes darting between us, confusion plain on their faces. I gave Lola a slight nod and a smirk, not wanting to give anything away.

"I'll be hosting a party this Saturday, by the way," she said casually, though her eyes sparkled with anticipation.

"Another one?" I asked, raising an eyebrow.

She placed a manicured hand on her hip and gave me a look that said I should have known better. "Of course," she replied. "Party like it's your last, my dear. You and…" she cast a quick glance at Oge and Calvin, "…your friends, are welcome to join."

She leaned in slightly, her voice dropping into a conspiratorial tone. "It has a theme, though. Roaring Twenties. So, think fringe dresses, feathers, sequins, and pearls for the ladies. Suits, bow ties, suspenders, and fedoras for the gents. Glamour, opulence, and decadence. You get the idea."

Her words conjured images out of the Great Gatsby in my mind.

She straightened, her hand still on her hip, and flashed a confident smile. "I'll be seeing you," she said, before turning on her heel and striding away, her departure just as striking as her entrance.

I cut Oge and Calvin off before they could speak. "Don't ask," I muttered, already bracing for their teasing.

I stared at the flyer once more, my instincts kicking in. I'd spent my career sniffing out lies and fraud, and this Prophetess smelled like both. "I guess I'm going to church," I said, standing up.

Oge smirked. "Be sure to pray while you're there."

CHAPTER 24

The timing was spot-on. It was a Wednesday, prime time for a midweek church service. A day Nigerian churches used to keep the spiritual momentum going. Recharging their members on hump day, encouraging a fresh wave of thanksgiving, or maybe just another excuse to pass the offering basket one more time. Sunday was never enough.

After freshening up in the room Lola had reserved for me, I borrowed a car Calvin had somehow procured. Just as resourceful as Osita, though less bloody. I made my way to Ikoyi, where the church was located. I had barely driven five minutes when a dark blue Peugeot screeched to a halt in front of me, cutting off my path. My instincts kicked in, and my hand flew to the gearstick, shifting into reverse, ready to escape. I figured I had fallen into a typical armed robbery setup.

Then, just as quickly, a Jeep appeared behind me, blocking my only way out.

I was trapped.

I wasn't sure if I had the energy for another scuffle so soon after the last one. My body still ached, and I wasn't about to tempt fate with men who might be a bit trigger-happy. I glanced at the doors of both cars, waiting for them to swing open and release hell. And then, sure enough, someone stepped out of the Peugeot. The figure was familiar. A man in dark aviators with a smug smirk stretched across his face.

Detective Inspector Bayo.

Relief and dread flooded me all at once. At least it wasn't some trigger-happy robbers. But Bayo wasn't much better. If anything, this might be worse.

He swaggered up to my window, tapping it with a ringed finger, and gestured for me to get out of the car. I did without putting up a fight.

"You've been busy," he said, sounding proud of himself.

"I don't know what you mean," I replied, trying to keep my tone neutral as my eyes darted between the other officers, all emerging from their vehicles like vultures circling fresh prey.

Bayo took off his aviators, revealing sharp, calculating eyes. "Who is she?"

"Who is who?" I played dumb. Always a good strategy in situations like this.

He grinned, enjoying himself. "We've received reports of a high-speed chase in Oshodi earlier today. Followed by a man and woman running into a pure water factory and getting into a fight. Witnesses heard a gunshot. The description of the man fits you to a T. So, I'll ask again: who is the woman?"

I could feel my pulse thudding in my neck. He had me. He had me dead to rights. But there's one thing I've always sworn by: *never underestimate the power of denial*. So, I straightened up, locked eyes with him, and went for it.

"It wasn't me," I said, quoting Shaggy like I was at a karaoke bar.

Bayo chuckled darkly, but his amusement quickly faded. "You know," he said, leaning closer, "I'm surprised you haven't tried to leave the country yet." He pulled a face like a disappointed father. "I would have enjoyed dragging you back to prison."

I forced a shrug, trying to look unbothered. "I have no reason to leave. This is my home." That was a lie, of course. I'd thought about getting the hell out of here more times than I could count. The mess with the Admiral, the police on my tail. It wasn't the homecoming I'd imagined. "Besides, you till have my passport."

What came next took me by surprise. Bayo, without warning, swung his fist into my gut. The pain exploded in my abdomen, like a sledgehammer to my insides. I doubled over, retching, one knee hitting the ground as I tried to catch my breath.

The world was nothing but searing pain.

Bayo bent down, his face now inches from mine, daring me to retaliate. He knew I wouldn't. I couldn't. Not here. Not in front of his goons.

When I didn't move, didn't flinch, he grinned like a hyena. "I see," he said, with mock admiration. "All that time in Yankee never changed you. You know there's nothing you can do. You know to behave yourself."

He wasn't wrong. This was Nigeria, where cops like him didn't just rough you up for fun, they did it because they knew there would be no consequences. No one to report them to. No higher-ups to hold them accountable. They could beat you to within an inch of your life in broad daylight, and people would just walk by, minding their own business. That's how things worked here. They hesitated only if they thought you had connections. Me? They must have figured out I wasn't connected to anyone consequential.

Bayo stood up and smoothed his suit, as though punching people was just part of his daily routine. "It looks like death follows you, Mr. Agu," he said. "First, Alex Maduagu. Then, Silas Effiong."

I wiped the saliva from my chin, wincing at the lingering pain in my gut. "Who the hell is Silas Effiong?"

Bayo tilted his head slightly, a fake look of surprise crossing his face. "So now you're acting like you don't know the receptionist from the Lorel Luxury Hotel?" His voice dripped with sarcasm.

The name made my stomach churn: Silas. I had never cared to learn his name, never asked, and now it echoed in my mind, making the air around me feel heavier. I forced myself to stay composed, to keep up the façade. As far as anyone was concerned, I had never set foot in that hotel.

I shrugged, feigning indifference, even as my mind raced. Wherever Osita had disposed of the body, he must have made it easy for the cops to find. But why? He wasn't careless. If anything, he was meticulous to a fault. He had to know the trail would lead directly to me.

I clenched my jaw, suppressing the wave of frustration rising in my chest. What game was Osita playing? And more importantly, what was I missing? Something about this didn't add up, but I couldn't let the cracks in my armor show. Not now.

"Let's not forget the good doctor." Bayo's voice sliced through my thoughts.

I raised an eyebrow, but deep down, I already knew who he meant before he even said the name.

"Dr. Onyeka Okonkwo, Admiral Maduagu's sister. An attempt was made on her life the same day someone murdered her brother.

My stomach churned again, this time not from the detective's gut punch, but from realization. Silas was the one who had to eliminate Onyeka. The text I'd seen on his watch. The one about handling "the doctor," it was obviously about her. He wasn't as innocent as I had wanted to believe. Maybe Osita had sensed it too, which is why he'd pulled the trigger without hesitation. Or maybe I was just trying to justify it to ease the guilt gnawing at me. Either way, whoever had texted Silas could be behind the Admiral's death.

I looked up at Bayo, my glare sharp. "I'm getting tired of being accused of murder."

Bayo chuckled, his smile smug. "Oh, she's not dead. In fact, she's recovering from surgery that saved her life. And when she wakes up, I'm sure she'll tell us exactly who the bastard was that shot her. Then, you and I will have this chat again. And I won't be so pleasant then."

A weight lifted off my chest, and I let out a quiet sigh of relief. I was glad she'd pulled through, but I wasn't naive. Once she woke up and named Silas, Bayo would be quick to find a way to connect him to me. And from what I could tell from my interactions with Bayo, he wouldn't stop until he did.

I wasn't out of the mess yet. Not by a long shot.

Bayo nodded slowly, as if confirming something to himself. Then he stepped back, his face hardening into a stone mask. "I dey watch you oh," he said, his tone laced with threat, before signaling to his men.

I watched as they got back into their vehicles and pulled away, the screech of tires fading into the distance. I stood there for a few moments, trying to breathe through the ache in my ribs, trying to shake off the humiliation of that gut punch. People were watching. Lagos was always watching.

I got into the car and dialed Osita. He answered almost immediately, his tone as casual as ever. "Alobam," he said. "Hope you're well?"

I glanced over my shoulder, paranoia gnawing at the edges of my composure. "They found Silas, the receptionist. I'm already being looked at."

There was a beat of silence, followed by what sounded like the snap of his fingers. "No way. That guy was never supposed to be found."

"Well, they did, man," I said. "What exactly is going on here?"

I knew Osita could sense the accusation buried in my words, but he chose not to take offense. He responded in a measured, almost thoughtful way. "Something is wrong," he finally said, his tone heavier now. "I'll get to the bottom of it. Let me get back to you."

And just like that, he hung up.

I sat there for a moment, gripping the steering wheel, my mind racing. I forced myself to take a deep breath, trying to rein in my thoughts. I couldn't dwell on this now. No, I had to stay focused, get back on track.

I needed to know what the hell the Admiral had been up to, and how deep Elfreda was involved. And I needed to figure it out fast before Bayo or someone else decided to come at me again. This time, I wasn't sure I'd be so lucky.

— ◆ —

The building was extravagant. This was no humble sanctuary for the meek and downtrodden. No, this was a monument to money. An opulent palace masquerading as a house of God. The exterior was all gleaming marble and glass, the kind of structure that seemed more suited for a five-star hotel than a church. Inside, massive screens lined the walls, and they displayed clips from past services, each one more ridiculous than the last. One particularly absurd clip had the so-called Prophetess Mother C throwing off her red high heels into the congregation. The crowd surged toward the stage as if it were Black Friday at a mall, but before anyone could grab them, a quick-handed usher scooped them up, cradling them like some holy relic.

Madness. Complete madness.

As I stood there, taking it all in, a man in a dark blue three-button suit approached me. His grin was so wide it could've cracked his face open. I'd seen that look before. It was the look of a man who saw fresh meat. A new member. A new benefactor.

"I am Brother Jeremiah," he announced, practically oozing enthusiasm. "What can I do for you today?"

I removed my shades and shook his hand, keeping my expression neutral. "Brother Jeremiah, I was hoping I could have a moment with the Prophetess. I just moved back, you know? And I could sure use a place to call home in Christ. You know what I mean?" I laid it on thick, switching to my best African-American accent. It was a bit rough around the edges, but authentic enough for someone like Brother Jeremiah. He wasn't sharp enough to pick up the cracks.

"Of course! The Prophetess would be delighted to meet you, brother!" He flashed that wide grin again before hurrying off, no doubt eager to show me off as his latest conquest.

He returned shortly, gesturing for me to follow him down a hallway that reeked of expensive air fresheners and old religious tapestries. We stopped outside a large, ornate door. Jeremiah knocked gently, and when a muffled voice from within answered, he pushed the door open, waving me inside.

The Prophetess sat behind a sprawling desk, the kind of oversized furniture meant to dwarf anyone who sat before her. Her office was just as luxurious as the rest of the church, decked out in dark, polished wood, gold-framed paintings, and shelves lined with books, though I doubted she had ever cracked one open. The smell of expensive incense wafted through the air, blending with the faint scent of lavender perfume.

She stood as I entered, arms outstretched, draped in an extravagant outfit. Bright pink and nearly as wide as the desk. The wide-brimmed hat perched on her head was the cherry on top, a bold fuchsia monstrosity that made her look like she had just stepped out of a flamboyant gospel music video.

"Hello, brother," she said in a slow, deliberate tone, as if she was speaking to a child in need of saving. "I am so happy you finally came."

I flinched. Something about the way she said that didn't sit right with me.

She noticed and, with a sly smile, continued. "Yes, brother. I saw you before you even came. God told me... a brother from America would be arriving, looking for his way. I have been waiting for you."

Complete bullshit. But I wasn't about to call her out just yet. I had a role to play.

"That's... remarkable," I said, letting a little awe seep into my voice. I took a seat in front of her desk, crossing my legs and leaning back. "I was hoping to get some guidance."

"Of course!" she replied, beaming with the warmth of a grandmother who was about to ask for your life savings. "Guidance is what I'm here for."

I nodded slowly, pretending to mull over my words. "I'm actually seeking guidance on something very specific. I'm looking for someone. Alex Maduagu. I believe he was a member of your church?"

Her smile didn't falter, but I caught the briefest flicker in her eyes. The kind of flicker you get when you're trying to keep a secret.

"The Admiral, yes. He was a good man," she said, her voice soft, almost reverent. "He was... lost when he first came to us. But God, through me, helped him find his way."

I kept my tone casual, though my mind was racing. "And were there any pecuniary benefits to this...help?"

She waved her hand dismissively, though I noticed how her fingers twitched. "Money is simply a tool, my son. God blesses those who give, and the Admiral was very generous."

"I bet he was," I muttered under my breath. "So much so that you attended luxury parties with him."

She tilted her head, her eyes narrowing ever so slightly. "Is there something else on your mind, brother?"

I leaned forward, locking eyes with her. "What I really want to know, Prophetess, is if Elfreda Bassey had anything to do with his generosity?"

Her expression didn't change, but the room seemed to get colder.

"Elfreda," she said. "She was... close to him, yes. But the matters of men and their desires... are not my concern."

"Right," I said, standing up, having heard enough. "I'm sure."

My eyes remained fixed on her, heavy with suspicion. Whatever was happening here, she knew more than she was letting on. And something told me I was getting uncomfortably close to the truth, a little too close for her liking.

I barely had time to process the sound of approaching footsteps before a sharp prick on the back of my neck made me jump. I swung around and saw two men in sunglasses and dark clothing. One of them held a needle, still dripping with a clear liquid.

Then everything went dark.

CHAPTER 25

I saw General Agu, my father, like the Ghost of King Hamlet. He stood in a sea of blood. His once-vibrant eyes, now clouded like ethereal cataracts, bore down on me, unreadable. He wore a full General's uniform. A green tunic with gold epaulets on the shoulders, each one adorned with the brass insignia of a soaring eagle. Rows of medals hung on his chest, symbols of victories and horrors I could barely comprehend. He had a belt around his waist, which held a leather holster for the sidearm. His cap, with its bright scarlet band and the emblem of the Nigerian eagle shining at its center, was cocked at a perfect angle, its brim casting a shadow over the top half of his face. He stood tall, as majestic in death as he had been in life.

His silence was deafening. But I could feel him, urging me to rise, to fight. The message was clear. He raised his fists, adopting a stance I knew well. The same stance he drilled into me over the years, his way of preparing me for a world that wasn't fair. His fists clenched tight, knuckles dark as coal. He wanted me to remember what I had forgotten in my years of chasing the American dream. His silent command: *Get up. Fight.*

And then, like the shattering of glass, I awoke.

A cacophony of voices bombarded my senses. Hundreds of men speaking Pidgin, Igbo, Yoruba, and Hausa all at once, their words a mixture of curses, taunts, and idle conversation. If there were other languages, I couldn't identify them in the chaos. But what struck me most was the undertone they all shared. Their voices were heavy with anger, violence simmering just beneath the surface.

I lay on cold, wet concrete, the smell of piss and shit thick in the air, clinging to the dampness of the walls. My singlet stuck to my skin, soaked in sweat. Grime stained my jeans. I blinked, disoriented, as I tried to make sense of my surroundings. The flickering fluorescent lights above barely cut through the gloom. It was then that I realized where I was.

This wasn't just any place. This was a Nigerian prison.

How the hell did I get here?

Bayo. It had to be. Somehow, he had finally gotten his wish.

The rabble quieted as the sound of boots echoed down the corridor. Five prison guards marched in. They wore olive-colored uniforms, their faces hardened by years of dealing with the men in this prison. One of them didn't waste any time. He cracked me across the face with an open palm, the sound reverberating through the narrow hall.

"Welcome to Kirkiri," mocked one.

I cursed under my breath. The name alone gave me chills. I'd heard of Kirikiri Maximum Security Prison before. Everyone in Nigeria had. This was a death sentence.

The noise I heard wasn't random chaos. It was the enraged outcry of men—shirtless, filthy, their bodies scarred from years of neglect and violence—who had noticed me. I could see them now, pressed against the rusted iron bars of their cells, eyes wild and burning with jealousy. Unlike them, I was in a cell by myself, a luxury they couldn't fathom. Most of them slept like sardines in shared spaces, bodies crammed into airless rooms with little more than a bucket for relief. To them, my tiny cell was a hotel room.

The blow left stars in my vision, but I didn't resist as two others grabbed me by the arms and dragged me out. I was half-dazed as they threw me face-first into a puddle of mud.

I looked up and saw the jagged edges of razor wire lining the top of a wall. This was the courtyard where prisoners were sent to be broken. I could hear the clinking of chains, the shifting of bodies. Men, too many to count, stood in a wide circle around me, shirtless and covered in tattoos, scars, and grime. I stood wiping mud from my face, trying to steady myself.

Then, a voice crackled over a megaphone, loud and emotionless.

"Whoever is first to take him down will receive their freedom and five million naira."

Freedom and money? I swore under my breath. *Shit.*

I wiped the muck from my face again just in time to see the first man charge at me. He was big, too big to move with any actual speed, but he came at me with all the fury of a bull. I braced myself, slipping instinctively into a fighting stance, fists raised, elbows close to my body.

I sidestepped the first attack easily enough, but another man was already coming at me from the side, faster than the first. His fist connected with my ribs before I could block. The sharp sting of pain shot through my side, knocking the wind out of me.

Rusty. Definitely rusty.

I winced, but there was no time to dwell on it. I blocked another punch with my forearm and countered with a jab straight to his throat. The man gagged, dropping to his knees, but I couldn't savor the moment.

By this time, the whole courtyard had come alive with chaos. One by one, the inmates had jumped in, hungry for a piece of me, their eyes wild with bloodlust. But something shifted in the heat of the moment. The frenzy of bodies, fists flying in every direction, had taken on a life of its own. In their desperation to be the one to take me down, they'd started turning on each other, clashing like rabid dogs over a scrap of meat. It was a brutal free-for-all, the sound of bones crunching and grunts of pain filling the air.

I stood there catching my breath, my chest heaving. The chaos gave me a brief reprieve, a moment to assess the situation. My muscles burned with exhaustion, but I welcomed the break. In a twisted stroke of luck, they'd thinned their own ranks. Fewer men to deal with. Fewer fists aimed at my head.

But I knew the moment wouldn't last. The wild pack would settle soon enough, and I'd be right back in the middle of it.

Another prisoner, tall and wiry, lunged at me with a jagged piece of broken glass in his hand. I caught his wrist before he could stab me and twisted it hard until I heard a snap. He screamed as the glass fell into the mud, his wrist bent at a sickening angle.

But I wasn't fast enough to dodge the next hit. A solid punch to my temple from another man behind me. My vision went white for a second, and I stumbled forward, disoriented, mud splattering everywhere. My father's voice echoed in my mind, as if chastising me for being too slow. I hadn't been in a proper fight for years. It showed.

You fight. You win. You survive.

One rushed at me, kicking me hard in the chest, sending me backward into the crowd. I rolled to the side, avoiding being stomped on, my muscles aching with every movement. The mud was thick, making it harder to keep my footing. But as I got up, instincts kicked in. A series of quick punches to a man's nose, a well-placed elbow to another's jaw. Blood and sweat mixed with the grime on my skin, and though my body ached in protest, I pushed through.

A beefy arm wrapped around my neck in a chokehold from behind. I gasped for air, feeling my vision blur again. My father's training flickered in my memory, *'drop your weight'* and I did just that, yanking down with all my strength, forcing the attacker off balance. I used his own momentum to flip him over my shoulder and into the mud with a satisfying thud.

But another man was already charging at me, swinging wildly. His knuckles cracked against my cheekbone, and I tasted blood. The hit rattled me, sending me staggering backward. My chest heaved with each breath, and the pain was becoming more than just an inconvenience. It was slowing me down.

I spat blood, gritted my teeth, and ducked under a wild haymaker, delivering a sharp knee to the attacker's gut. He folded like a cheap suit, gasping for breath. I grabbed him by his collar and slammed him into another assailant. The two fell in a heap, groaning in pain. My chest heaved. *Stay fluid. Don't get stuck. Keep moving. Keep fucking moving!*

I swung the back of my fist into another man's face, feeling his jaw give under the impact. A swift stomp to his knee dropped him to the ground, screaming. My hands throbbed from the repeated blows, but adrenaline kept me from feeling the full extent of it.

Another man tackled me from behind. I rolled with him, feeling the mud coat my skin as we grappled. I twisted, throwing him off me, and landed a brutal elbow to the back of his skull. He collapsed face-first into the mud, unconscious.

I was running on fumes now, but I kept going. A man to my right lunged with a shiv, but I knocked his arm away and slammed my forearm into his throat. He choked, eyes wide, before he crumpled to the ground.

I stood, chest heaving, my body screaming for rest. The surrounding men groaned in pain, clutching their ribs, jaws, and limbs. They lay scattered across the mud like broken dolls, their desperate hopes for freedom dashed.

I looked up, panting, my vision blurred from the exhaustion and sweat running into my eyes. And then, through the haze, I saw him.

A figure. Standing at the edge of the courtyard, wearing dark clothes and a wide-brimmed hat. He was too far away to make out clearly, but something about him was hauntingly familiar.

Before I could process it, pain exploded in the back of my skull. A nightstick. The force of the blow sent me crashing back into the mud, and everything went black. Again.

— ◆ —

The first thought that crossed my mind when I came to wasn't confusion about where I was or why I was lying, cleaned up and in clean clothes, on a comfortable bed in a room I didn't recognize. No, it was more of a tired, irritated thought. *How many more times am I going to get knocked out before I learn to stay vigilant?*

I could almost hear General Agu scolding me. He was the kind of officer who never let himself slip. While his peers aged into their ranks, growing fat and slow, my father stayed sharp. He was fit, trained in Krav Maga, and always ready for action. There were no excuses with him. If I had let myself get this rusty, he'd have dragged me to the mat and pummeled me until I remembered every move he'd ever taught me.

I forced myself up, rubbing the back of my head where the dull ache pulsed like a reminder of my stupidity. Standing by the door was a man, sinewy, tall, with muscles bulging through his compression shirt like they were trying to escape. He looked like a wrestler who could snap my neck with a shrug. He didn't speak. He just opened the door and jerked his head, signaling me to follow.

I didn't protest. The nap had been...unexpected but had left me recharged. Or maybe it was just a false sense of bravado, the kind that sneaks up on you when you've been pushed too far and want to believe you're still in control. Either way, I followed him.

We moved down a set of marble stairs, the kind that belonged in palaces, not simple homes. Every inch of this place screamed wealth and power. Traditional Igbo artifacts lined the walls. There were handcrafted fans, ceremonial staffs, and even an old, dusty rifle hanging like a relic from a forgotten war. The deeper we went, the more I understood the scale of this mansion. Whoever owned this place, whoever I was about to meet, wasn't just rich. He was *important.*

The man led me into a massive parlor, where it became clear my attempts at staying under the radar had evaporated. There was no hiding from this. Not here.

In the center of the room, seated on a lavish golden couch, was a man. *The man.*

He wore a pristine traditional attire, soft gray with fine embroidery running along the edges. Around his neck hung a thick gold chain, resting on his chest like a badge of authority. His wide-brimmed black hat gave him an almost regal, old-world gangster vibe, and a gold ring on his finger gleamed as he handled his meal. He ate from a plate of meat, *nkwobi* by the smell, and it was bathed in a rich yellow sauce, garnished with shredded leaves and onions.

Chief Obidi.

He didn't even glance my way as I approached, too engrossed in tearing into a piece of goat meat, savoring it like it was the only thing that mattered. Our entire conversation would be in Igbo. Obidi never spoke English with another Igbo unless he had no other choice. If you couldn't speak Igbo, he'd switch to English, but not without constantly reminding you that you were a disgrace, a traitor to the Igbos, he would say. Lucky for me, I was fluent.

"I'm sure you haven't had this in a while," he said, his voice deep and carrying a menace that sent a chill down my spine. "Good nkwobi is hard to find in America."

He spoke as if we were old friends, but there was no mistaking the malice behind his words.

I massaged the back of my sore head, doing my best to stay composed. "You're not wrong," I muttered. "This type of food is why I hope to take an Igbo wife someday."

He chuckled at that, a sound that felt more like a warning than amusement. "Chidozie Agu," he said, my full Igbo name rolling off his tongue with deliberate weight. "I thought the Americans would have washed away that traditional Igbo man behavior from you by now."

I met his words with a forced smile. "If I remember correctly, Chief, you once told me that being a traditional Igbo man was my greatest strength."

Finally, he looked up, his jaundiced eyes fixing on me like a hawk sizing up its prey. "You are taller," he remarked, his gaze roaming over me. He gestured lazily at the food. "Join me. This might be your last meal. Why not make it a delicacy?"

I glanced over my shoulder, assessing the room. Guards stood at every corner, all built like the man who had led me down. There were no exits, no way to escape. The room was a fortress, and Chief Obidi sat at the heart of it, fully aware of the control he held.

Reluctantly, I picked up a stool. From the corner of my eye, I saw one guard shift, probably assuming I intended to use it as a weapon, but Chief Obidi raised a hand, stopping him. His confidence was palpable. He didn't fear me. He knew I wouldn't try anything. He wasn't wrong.

I sat down next to him, washed my hands in the glass bowl set at my feet, and picked up a piece of goat meat. The flavors burst in my mouth. The tender meat soaked in spicy sauce. It was rich, indulgent, and for a moment, I forgot the danger I was in. It reminded me of everything I had missed about home, the authentic food that made my years of bland takeout back in DC feel like a punishment.

Obidi continued eating, not in any rush. He was a man who enjoyed making others wait, savoring his power over them. He spoke. "Your mistake," he said between bites, "was thinking I didn't know you were here the moment you set foot in Lagos. Every moment of freedom you've had was a gift from me, Chidozie. You were better off driving your Uber in Washington, DC. At least that job is safer."

He was the only one who ever insisted on calling me by my full Igbo name. While Osita postured as pro-Biafran, Chief Obidi was the real deal. An old-school nationalist with the power to back it up. A man steeped in Igbo tradition, one who wielded influence like a weapon.

"After all these years," Chief Obidi said, a smirk playing on his lips, "you still remind me why I wanted you in my organization. I was certain those prisoners would tear you apart."

I shook my head, wiping a mix of dried blood and mud from my cheek. "They were malnourished and weak, Chief. If they had any strength left, I'd be dead, no question." I gestured to my face, which was swollen and bruised from the hits I hadn't dodged. "I didn't exactly walk out unscathed."

Obidi leaned back in his chair, studying me with those jaundiced eyes that never missed a thing. "Still standing though, aren't you?" He chuckled, low and satisfied, like this was all some game he had orchestrated. "You've always had a way of surviving, Chidozie."

I exhaled slowly, the ache in my ribs reminding me that survival didn't mean invincible. "Surviving's one thing, Chief. But I didn't walk away untouched."

He waved a dismissive hand, as if my injuries were inconsequential. "Wounds heal. What matters is you fought, and you lived." His voice was calm, almost patronizing, as if my struggle was nothing more than a test he already knew I'd pass.

I looked down at my bloodied knuckles, still throbbing from the fight. "Let's not pretend you weren't hoping for the alternative," I muttered under my breath, but loud enough for him to hear.

Obidi's smirk widened, and he leaned forward, resting his elbows on his knees. "If I wanted you dead, Chidozie," he said, "you wouldn't have made it out of Kirikiri."

I chewed my meat quickly, swallowing hard. "I think I met a couple of your boys earlier," I said, trying to keep the tone light. "I hope the one who got shot in the leg got it checked out."

Chief Obidi paused, then turned his jaundiced gaze to the man standing behind him in a sharp grey suit. The man with silver-lensed glasses that glinted ominously shook his head once, barely perceptibly.

Obidi turned back to me, wiping his hands. "I don't know what you're talking about, Chidozie," he said calmly. "I only gave the order to bring you in after you visited Mother C."

I froze for a moment, taking mental notes. If those thugs I fought earlier weren't Obidi's men, then who the hell were they? Someone else was clearly watching me, making moves behind the scenes. This mess was getting more tangled by the minute.

But I kept my face neutral, acting as if nothing had phased me. The Chief went back to his meal, and I picked at the nkwobi, my mind racing. Racing to a memory from years ago. A set of events that invariably led me to this place.

CHAPTER 26

My father sent me to Igboland to get a bachelor's degree with the ultimate aim of getting me more in touch with my roots. Most of the time, General Agu served as a military attaché in embassies across Europe, Asia, and North America. He was a man who understood the value of a global upbringing. Exposure to different cultures, languages, and people. But a few years before retirement, something shifted in him. His mind became consumed with one burning concern: his children were Igbo in name only. We didn't speak the language, didn't know the customs, didn't understand the culture. To him, this was unacceptable. He acknowledged his role in allowing it to happen and, in classic military fashion, decided it was time to correct the course.

I'll admit, back then, it felt absurd to me. What use did I have of Igbo proverbs or village customs? They would not help me get ahead in Lagos. My father's determination seemed like nostalgia mixed with a dose of old-world fear. But in many moments since, I could almost hear his voice in my ear, reminding me that home was more than a place, it was something you carried with you.

So, with little debate, we were shipped back to Nigeria, right into the heart of Igboland.

As his first and only son, I became his special project. It wasn't enough that I returned; he was determined that I absorb all there was to know about my heritage. He would talk to me about it during dinner, on drives, even during his fitness routines. For him, this was a mission.

"All I've ever wanted was to give my children a comfortable life," he once told me. "But now I see that comfort shouldn't come at the expense of your ability to survive in this world. Life here isn't kind, and comfort can make you soft. By the time we're done, you'll understand what it takes to survive in this country. You'll know the history of your people, the weight of it, and the strength it gives you."

He paused, his eyes locking with mine in that intense way only he could manage, as though daring me to understand him in that moment. "Whenever it pleases God to take me," he continued, his tone unflinching, "you will be the strong pillar of this family."

When it came time for university, he insisted I attend one of the more prestigious universities in the Southeast. He didn't care about my protests or any objections I raised. To him, this was the best way for me to reconnect with my roots. I hated the idea, resisted it as much as I could, but he was stubborn. Military to the core. And now, looking back, as much as I didn't want to admit it, some of those lessons stuck and have been useful ever since.

Although the school I attended was considered one of the best in the country, it had its fair share of problems. No, that's putting it too mildly. It had real dangers lurking beneath its reputation. One of the biggest? Campus cults.

Walking the broken streets of campus as a wide-eyed freshman, I realized quickly that people showed interest in you for one of two reasons: either to recruit you into a *cult* or a *fellowship*. For many, it felt like a literal tug-of-war between good and evil. But after spending some years there, I learned the line between those two groups wasn't as sharp as people liked to think. Both utilized deception, both made grand promises, and both lured unsuspecting freshmen into their ranks with a sense of belonging. And once you were in? You were bound to their system. A rigid hierarchy designed to keep you in your place until it was your time to rise.

I remember attending a Sunday service of one of the more popular campus fellowships once. Underwhelming was an understatement. I couldn't stomach the idea of students, who had barely as much life experience as I did, preaching at me, telling me how to live, using God as both a punctuation mark and endorsement of their self-proclaimed authority. Maybe it was just the Catholic in me, but I found it hard to take spiritual advice seriously from anyone who didn't have the weight of priesthood behind their words. There's a certain gravity in the way a Catholic priest speaks; years of formation and tradition make you inclined to listen. But a student pastor? They had none of that.

After the service, a young woman approached me. Her name was Isis. She was dark-skinned and strikingly pretty. Modestly dressed for church, sure, but with enough flair to suggest she could pull off something more daring if she wanted. It looked like someone had assigned her to talk to me about paying tithes to the fellowship. Odd, considering it was my first day there.

I calmly explained that I was Catholic, a friend had invited me, and I paid my tithes at the Catholic church. A lie, of course. My skepticism toward Nigerian authority figures, especially in religious settings, made me wary of tithing. But her next words floored me. She smiled, thought for a moment, then said, "Well, maybe you could split your tithes. Half to the Catholic church, half here."

I was truly bewildered. The audacity of asking me to divert money from *my* church to hers struck me as wrong. I might have overreacted, but it turned me off.

So, cults or fellowships?

I elected to join neither.

Osita, though? He was a different story. Recruited right out of secondary school, Osita came in with a reputation. A reputation that led him to rise through the ranks of his cult faster than most. It wasn't long before everyone on campus knew he was not to be trifled with. People feared him. And because one of the most feared men in school respected me, it raised eyebrows. People couldn't figure it out. Why would Osita respect Dozy Agu? What did I have on him?

What they didn't understand was that a man like Osita was never just your friend. Sure, he helped me out during registration and smoothed things over for me when I needed it. But that wasn't enough for someone like him. Osita saw me as someone he could exploit, someone who owed him, someone he could control. He never said it outright, but it was in the way he treated me, the way he spoke to me. And for a while I let it slide. I kept my head down, kept my distance. I wasn't looking for trouble.

But trouble doesn't always give you a choice.

One hot afternoon after my lectures, Osita crossed a line. He didn't ask me, he demanded that I sit in for him during a French exam. Now, by this point, he had done and said a lot of things I found disrespectful, but I let them go. I wasn't looking to stir anything up with him. But that day? That day was different. Maybe it was the heat, maybe it was the build-up of all the things I had let go, but something in me snapped. I broke his nose.

He was stunned. I remember the look on his face. It was a mix of shock and anger. Of course, he tried to fight back, he had to; it was in his nature. But I was quicker. Back then, my father's drills were still fresh in my mind. Osita couldn't land a single blow. And after I finished with him, I turned my attention to his minions. Those little shadows that followed him everywhere. I dealt with them just as swiftly.

"Oh boy," he finally said, clutching his broken nose and backing away, "person wey go get you as enemy dey find trouble."

He wasn't wrong. You didn't want me as your enemy. I had inherited my father's ruthlessness. That streak of cold calculation, of hitting where it hurt most, was in my blood. That was probably why I never joined a cult. To me, they were all just pretenders. Weak men who needed a group to make them feel powerful. I didn't need that. I could stand on my own.

And that was how we truly became friends. Beneath all the posturing, Osita was a fascinating guy. Book smart, endlessly curious, and with a sense of humor that could turn any bad day around. I learned to turn a blind eye to his *extracurricular* activities, those shady dealings I didn't want to be too involved in. Sometimes, though, I had to step in when he got too reckless, when his actions veered into the unreasonable. It was exhausting, but I couldn't deny the value of having someone like him on my side. It brought a certain peace, knowing that while Osita might have been a wild card, he was my wild card.

Now, back to Chief Obidi. Our paths crossed when I was in my final year.

It was a time unlike any other at the university, with politics reaching a fever pitch that none of us had ever seen before. The rivalry between the incumbent governor and a former minister, who was looking to unseat him, had bled into nearly every aspect of life in the state. Everywhere you turned, politicians were throwing money around like confetti, hoping to curry favor and build alliances for the upcoming elections.

Concurrently, we were gearing up for our Student Union Government (SUG) elections which became more than just campus politics, they became a battleground for influence over the state's youth vote once the bigwigs took an interest, seeing an opportunity to sway thousands of students to their side.

I had no desire to get involved. As a class rep, I already had enough responsibilities on my plate, and the idea of throwing my weight behind some aspiring student politician wasn't exactly my idea of a good time. But then Osita came knocking.

"Dozy, I intend to run for SUG President," he had said one afternoon, sitting across from me under the shade of a mango tree on campus. "I need you to mobilize Year 1, 2, and 3 students. Get them to vote for me."

I looked at him, unimpressed. "Why me?"

He leaned back, grinning. "Nwoke, don't act like you don't know everyone respects you!"

I sighed. I didn't want to get involved, but Osita was persistent, and I respected him. Besides, people had already been asking me to run for SUG President. Backing my friend would ease the pressure. So, I agreed, hoping to keep my involvement as minimal as possible.

After this, candidates for other positions visited me before the elections. They came to pay their respects to secure my endorsement. They were certain that my word would carry some weight. I found the whole thing bizarre. Why would they care about what I thought? I might have been the class rep for the Department of Political Science final years, but I wasn't a political player, just a class rep trying to keep my head down. But I had underestimated the connections I had built, and the reputation I had somehow gained.

— ◆ —

Once Osita was confirmed as our candidate, the Political Science Department got involved, making the tense elections even worse. Known for having the strongest and most influential cult members on campus, Political Science typically handled the "security" during elections, which meant intimidating anyone who wasn't voting for our man.

The gubernatorial campaigns heated up, raising the stakes of our own campus elections even higher. The student body became a microcosm of the greater political battlefield outside. And in this environment, Osita's campaign was a lightning rod for chaos.

The day of the elections started like any other, with students lining up to cast their paper ballots. But I should have known it wouldn't end so simply. I voted early in the day so I could spend the rest of the day with Oge and Calvin, taking advantage of the freedom from lectures an election brought. Then I received a phone call from a third year in charge of security at one of the voting centers.

"Oga Dozy," he began frantically. "Them don dey play wayo! Osita no come dey get votes again!"

Soon after, more people on the inside of the counting process sent me frantic messages, telling me that something wasn't right. The numbers weren't adding up. Votes were being manipulated in real-time, right under everyone's noses. Osita was losing. I had to get there before all hell broke loose.

I was standing by, observing the process, when suddenly a group of cars came screeching to a halt near the voting area. The students immediately became tense, some already inching towards the exits, sensing trouble. The doors of the lead car burst open, and out jumped one of Osita's associates, Dark Snow. Dark Snow's outfit was head-to-toe black, with dark shades concealing his eyes, which matched his nickname. He looked around frantically for a moment before screaming at the top of his lungs, "Get the ballot! Get the ballot! GET THE FUCKING BALLOT!"

A few students bolted at the sound of his stentorian voice, knowing exactly what was about to go down. Chaos erupted as a group of Dark Snow's men rushed the ballot box, shoving aside students and volunteers in their path. I wanted no part of this, so I stayed where I was, out of the fray.

The whole thing was madness. Everyone knew the elections were rigged, the money and violence had seen to that. But this level of open aggression, in broad daylight, took things to a new level. And the chaos didn't stop there. The candidates running for Financial Secretary, Secretary-General, and a few other key positions were snatched off campus by masked men and held until after the elections. The campus had seen nothing like it.

And that was when I met Chief Obidi.

He was the godfather behind the sitting Governor. People said Obidi's patronage was the sole reason for the Governor's position, and with another election coming, Obidi was determined to keep his man in power. But with the student body at the university making up a fat slice of the youth vote, Obidi couldn't afford to let it slip through his fingers. Trouble was, most of them were registered back home in Abia, Anambra, Imo, Lagos, Abuja. Merely a fraction were from Enugu.

That's where Osita came in. Chief Obidi had given Osita a one million Naira bribe, hoping to ensure that if Osita won the SUG presidency, he would rally the student body to support his candidate in the state elections. He would kick off a registration drive. Before long, students would be lining up to transfer their voter cards to Enugu. The technicality of whether they were indigenes was irrelevant because of the personalities working behind the scenes. One by one, their votes would cross state lines, and just like that, Obidi would have the beginnings of an army.

But Osita wasn't enough to make this happen. Obidi had heard of me, the enigma behind Osita, the guy who seemed to have a strange hold over him. Cultists who feared nothing seemed to give me a wide berth, and that intrigued Obidi.

When we met, it was surreal. He pulled up in front of my apartment in a sleek grey Mercedes-Benz G-Class. He stepped out with the air of a man who had long since stopped asking for respect and simply expected it. He wasn't as stocky as the usual suspects in the country's political class. He was more angular, more composed. His skin was smooth for his age, his beard neatly trimmed and dyed to hide the grey that likely came with wielding too much power for too long. His hair, also darkened by dye, sat under a round brown bowler hat adorned with a feather. A pair of tinted, purple-lensed glasses rode low on his nose as he peered over them, the gesture deliberate, theatrical. His teeth were so white they looked almost artificial like they'd been scrubbed clean of every lie he'd ever told. The brown traditional outfit was tailored, pressed, and punctuated by coral bracelets on his wrist that said *chief, money,* and *you can't touch me.* We shook hands, but the moment I touched him, I felt an aura of death, a stench of iron, like blood on a battlefield. I'd felt nothing like it before. It wasn't fear, exactly, but it was enough to make every fiber of my being reject the man standing in front of me. Something about him was wrong. Very wrong.

I'd heard the stories. Everyone had. The whispers of people who crossed Chief Obidi and vanished like smoke. Some said he had a habit of sending a wreath to the family afterward, a silent 'don't test me' message. Feeling his icy grip, I wondered if I was next in line for a 'friendly warning.' The thought curdled my stomach.

"Dozy Agu," he said. "What kind of name is that?"

"It's a nickname, sir," I replied, trying to maintain a tone of respect despite the unease creeping up my spine. "Short for Chidozie."

He gave me a solid smack on the shoulder, a gesture of approval that made me wince. "*Ehen!* Now you're talking. Chidozie, *ị na-asụ Igbo*? Do you speak Igbo?"

I nodded. Back then, my Igbo was functional, though my accent was rough around the edges. But he didn't care. He immediately dropped the English. "You're someone I could use," he said, the shift in language somehow making his words heavier, more deliberate.

"Use?" I asked. "How, sir?"

He didn't answer right away. Just snapped his fingers with the precision of a man used to being obeyed. One of his guards stepped forward. He was a sinewy slab of muscle in a skintight black shirt, thick gold chain around his neck, and Versace sunglasses that hadn't been removed since they stepped out of the G-Wagon. He moved like a dancer trained for violence.

The man handed over a polished wooden box. Authentic Cuban cigars, thick and oily with a deep, earthy aroma. Real hand-rolled Habano, not the knockoffs that floated through Lagos nightclubs.

Chief Obidi selected one with care, then produced a bronze cigar cutter, slicing the cap with a practiced flick. The cigar landed between his lips like a crown jewel. A silver butane lighter, sleek, engraved, was placed gently into his palm by another attendant. He lit it himself, slowly and theatrically. The flame flared, dancing on the tip, before he drew in a long drag and let the smoke curl from his mouth like a blessing or a curse.

Clearly, he preferred it this way. The self-lighting. Probably thought it made him look more menacing.

Oddly enough, it did.

"There's no need to act like you don't know what I'm saying, Chidozie," he said. "I'm sure Osita there has filled you in."

I glanced over my shoulder.

Osita was standing by the apartment door, arms folded, his gaze sharp but unreadable. There was confidence in his posture, but a quiet tension underneath like a panther crouched in tall grass. Ready to spring if the rhythm changed. But until then, doing his best impression of a loyal spectator.

Everything in me rejected this man. I had always believed Nigerian politicians were all crooked, each one waiting their turn. Just part of the endless revolving door of who got to stuff themselves on the national cake. But Chief Obidi? He was different. I could tell immediately that anyone backed by him had to be the worst of the worst, scraping the bottom of an already filthy barrel.

The same sinewy guard returned, this time carrying a suitcase. He set it down with care, clicked it open, and Obidi pulled out five fat bundles of one-thousand-naira notes, all crisp, clean, and reeking of fresh ink and quiet power.

"This is for you," he said. "There's more to come when you've done the needful."

I didn't touch it. I watched his hand instead.

"That won't be necessary, Chief," I said calmly. "I don't involve myself in politics outside the SUG."

Obidi's face twitched, just slightly, but enough. Like a man whose gift had just been swatted aside.

"Are you mad?" he asked.

Before I could reply, Osita stepped in. He'd sidled up beside me without a sound and now reached for the cash, his smile practiced, disarming.

"Chief Chief," he said, laying it on thick with faux reverence. "Don't mind my man, Dozy. He'll do it. He's just... careful about how he collects money. But he'll come through. No shaking."

I clenched my jaw but said nothing. I knew Osita. He wasn't the groveling type. This wasn't fear, it was strategy. He was keeping things calm, trying to steer us away from bloodshed.

Obidi narrowed his eyes at him, suspicion flickering behind those dyed lashes, but after a moment, he gave a slow nod.

"Good," he said at last. "You'll be hearing from me."

And just like that, he was gone.

Silence fell for a beat before Osita looked down at the wads in his hand and shook his head.

"Alobam," he said with a half-smile. "How you wan escape this one now? Obidi no be small fry."

There were several more unavoidable and unwelcome meetings after that. Each one only deepened my resentment, stoking something reckless inside me. Until finally, I snapped. For the first time, I dove headfirst into politics, but not for Obidi. Against him.

It became personal.

I made it my mission to see that his candidate didn't get reelected. I pulled every string, called in every favor, rattled every cage that needed rattling. I wanted it loud. I wanted it public. I wanted everyone on campus to know I wasn't standing by with folded arms. I gave speeches, wrote blistering articles, stirred up debates in lecture halls and cafeterias.

Even Osita, the SUG President by then and arguably the most powerful student on campus, couldn't steer me off course. He didn't try very hard, though. He was my friend before anything else. And while he respected Chief Obidi, he didn't fear him.

Osita never feared anyone.

When the incumbent finally lost his bid for reelection, I felt a surge of relief. Obviously, I could not take all the credit, but I had played my part, and for the first time in a long while, it felt like a win. Not just for me, but for the people who dared to stand up to the political machine. But I wasn't naive. I knew a man like Chief Obidi wouldn't take a loss lying down.

Igboland was his territory. I had to leave.

I returned to Lagos to visit my father after the election. Lagos had always been his second home, the place where I'd often spend my holidays, even though my mother preferred the quieter life in Enugu. It felt like a way to reconnect with him before heading off for my NYSC year. By then, General Agu had softened. He no longer woke me up at the crack of dawn for training sessions or found fault in every little thing I did. Instead, he seemed content to enjoy my company, like I was an old friend he couldn't wait to share a beer with. I still think back on those days fondly. Moments of rare peace between us.

I served my year of service in Nasarawa State. Osita, Calvin, and Oge, ever resourceful, took advantage of the corruption within the NYSC and turned what should have been a random posting process into a sure thing. They made sure they were posted to Nasarawa as well. We had our little crew, sticking together in that quiet town, keeping each other company through the monotony of it all.

It wasn't long before the shadow of Chief Obidi stretched way beyond Southeastern Nigeria. One night, in the town of Akwanga, after returning late from a birthday party, I stumbled into my apartment, still buzzed from too much palm wine. I wasn't drunk, but the edges of my thoughts were fuzzy. I took a cold shower. It was exactly what I needed to clear my head before bed. I stepped out of the bathroom with a towel wrapped around my waist when the door creaked behind me.

Instinct kicked in. I whirled around just in time to see a man rushing at me, a gleaming cutlass raised above his head. I ducked, the blade slicing through the air where my head had been a second earlier. The man was tall, muscular, and moved with a brutal efficiency that told me he'd done this before. He swung the cutlass again, and I barely managed to sidestep it, feeling a breezy whoosh as it passed dangerously close to my chest.

The next blow caught me off guard. He slammed into me, knocking me backward. I crashed onto the floor, my back slamming against the cold tiles. I gasped for breath as the man straddled me, his cutlass raised high, ready to deliver the killing blow. My hands shot up, grabbing his wrists, struggling to keep the blade away from my throat.

Through gritted teeth, he snarled, "Chief Obidi sends his regards."

The name shot through me like ice water. My arms trembled under the weight of the cutlass pressing closer to my skin. I could feel the cold steel almost brushing against my neck. My strength was failing. The blade was inching closer.

And then, a roar filled the room.

Calvin burst through the door like a freight train, his massive frame filling the space as his eyes locked onto the man standing over me. Without hesitation, he lunged, wrapping his enormous arms around the intruder's neck in a deadly grip, lifting him clean off the ground. The man's feet kicked helplessly in the air as Calvin's forearm pressed into his windpipe, cutting off his air.

For a second, I thought it was over. Calvin's raw power should have been enough to end the fight right there. But the intruder wasn't done. Desperation fueled his struggle, and with a sudden burst of energy, he slammed his elbow into Calvin's ribs once, twice, until his grip loosened just enough for the man to wriggle free.

The intruder dropped to the ground, gasping for air, but Calvin didn't back down. He rushed at him again, trying to get his hands around the man's neck, but the intruder was faster this time. He ducked low, delivering a quick jab to his side, then grabbed a lamp off the nearby table and smashed it into his back. Calvin staggered forward, but barely flinched, shaking off the blow as if it was nothing.

The room erupted in chaos. The man grabbed a chair, swinging it at Calvin, but he blocked it with his forearm, the wood splintering on impact. The chair clattered to the floor as Calvin advanced, but the intruder darted to the side. He grabbed a bookshelf and tipped it toward Calvin, hoping to pin him down.

But Calvin was like an immovable force. He sidestepped the falling shelf just in time, reaching out and grabbing the man by his shirt. With a roar, he slammed him against the wall so hard that the picture frames rattled. The man swung his fist wildly, connecting with Calvin's jaw, but it barely fazed him. His eyes were alight with fury now, and he retaliated with a powerful punch to the gut, doubling the man over.

The intruder tried to fight back, throwing punches and kicks, but Calvin absorbed the blows, his sheer size and strength too much to overcome. They crashed into the small table by the bed, sending it flying into pieces, and knocked over another lamp, plunging half the room into darkness. The man managed to grab a shard of broken glass from the lamp and slashed at Calvin's arm, drawing blood, but it only seemed to fuel his rage.

With a grunt, Calvin caught the man's wrist mid-swing, twisting it painfully until the shard clattered to the floor. Then, with a final burst of power, he lifted the intruder off his feet and hurled him across the room. The man crashed into the dresser, sending clothes and drawers flying, before slumping to the floor, dazed and barely conscious.

Calvin didn't waste any time. He stormed over to the man, yanked him to his feet, and delivered one last punch to the face. The intruder's head snapped back, and he crumpled like a rag doll, unconscious before he even hit the ground.

Breathing heavily, he stood over his unconscious opponent, chest rising and falling with the exertion. He glanced at his bloodied arm, wiped it on his shirt, and turned to me, offering his hand like nothing had happened.

I grabbed his hand and scrambled up, gasping for air, my body shaking with adrenaline. Seconds later, Oge and Osita rushed in, eyes wide, taking in the chaotic scene.

Osita's face twisted into a scowl. "What the hell is going on here?"

"It's Obidi," I spat out, my chest heaving. "He's come for me."

The weight of the realization hit me like a punch to the gut. This wasn't over. Not by a long shot.

The following day, my father made the call. He was a man whose ear was always to the ground, and it didn't take long for him to arrange my return to Lagos. Once there, he wasted no time. He began getting me into graduate school in the United States.

My entire family came to see me off at the airport. My mother, unaware of the full circumstances that had led to this departure, was still beaming with pride as she prayed over me. My father placed both hands firmly on my shoulders, his grip strong, his eyes serious.

"You are going to make a life for yourself in another man's land. It won't be easy," he said. "But if you take everything you've learned here, you'll succeed. Our people say *aki ga-agba mmanu aghaghi igabiga n'oku.* You know what that means?"

I paused for a moment, translating the familiar words in my mind. "A palm nut has to pass through fire before it becomes palm oil," I answered.

General Agu smirked, nodding in approval. "That's right. And I'll call you every week, make sure you don't forget your Igbo," he joked, a brief laugh escaping both of us.

But then his face turned serious again. He leaned in closer, speaking low enough that only I could hear. "My son, as long as Chief Obidi lives, do not return. I will take care of your mother and sisters. Just don't come back."

What always struck me as odd was that my father never once scolded me for going against Chief Obidi. Not even a word of caution. In fact, once I noted something in his eyes, almost like a flicker of pride. It was as if deep down he admired my audacity. My willingness to stand up against the corruption that he had spent his entire career both avoiding and fighting.

— ◆ —

Ten years. Ten long years since I had left my country to escape the wrath of the man sitting across from me now, licking his saucy fingers and washing his hands in a glass bowl like some kind of monarch. Time hadn't dulled his presence. If someone had walked into that parlor, they would have thought we were father and son, or mentor and mentee. No one could have guessed the truth. We were predator and prey.

The only thing keeping me from trembling like a leaf was sheer willpower. That, and a stubborn urge not to give him the satisfaction of seeing my fear. My fingers brushed against a piece of goat meat on my plate, subtly feeling for a sharp bone. Anything I could potentially use to take the Chief hostage. But this was a man who had lived in violence longer than I had been alive. The odds of my getting the upper hand were slim. Still, desperation could make even the most foolhardy ideas seem genius.

I cleared my throat, trying to buy time. "Is Mother C an associate of yours?" I asked, forcing my voice to stay level.

Obidi smirked, not bothering to hide the amusement dancing in his eyes. "You'll be hard-pressed to find someone in this town who *isn't* an associate of mine, Chidozie."

"But Lagos isn't your turf," I countered.

He shrugged casually. "It pays to have good friends," he said. "I may not run things here like I do in Enugu, but the man who does is my biggest business partner. He lets me play in his sandbox when it suits him."

I swallowed, feeling the tension rise. "Does Mother C have anything to do with Admiral Alex Maduagu's death?" I pressed. "Do you?"

He chuckled, but the humor didn't reach his eyes. "I'm not here to answer your questions, my friend." His smile vanished as quickly as it had come, his face growing cold. He leaned back in his seat, his fingers steepling in front of him. "I'm here to ask mine. Where are the documents?"

The question made me flinch. A small reaction, but enough for him to notice. His keen eyes narrowed with predatory satisfaction.

I feigned confusion. "What documents?"

"Jackhammer!" Chief Obidi called out, and the massive goon who had led me into the room earlier stepped forward. Jackhammer. Of course, his name was something ridiculous like that. The man was a walking wall of muscle, standing there like a slab of concrete with a pulse.

"If I get even the slightest hint that you're lying to me or trying to buy time, Jackhammer here will happily put a bullet in that thick skull of yours," Chief Obidi said, as if he were talking about the weather.

Jackhammer grunted, a low, approving sound that rumbled from his chest like thunder. I raised my hands, a gesture of compliance.

"Chief," I began carefully, choosing my words with precision, "Mmachi Alex-Maduagu didn't give me the details about any documents. I haven't had a chance to look into them. I'm still investigating."

Chief Obidi waved his hand dismissively, as if swatting away a bothersome fly. "Forget about Mmachi. You visited the Admiral's sister. She claims you broke into her home and took her brother's bag. I want to know what was in it."

I raised an eyebrow, keeping my expression neutral. "Did you try to kill her?"

Obidi chuckled, the sound low and dismissive. "Try? I don't try anything. That was the work of an amateur. If I wanted her dead, she'd be six feet under by now."

I bit back the urge to remind him he'd tried and failed to kill me once before. But a glance over my shoulder at Jackhammer, standing stone-faced behind me, made me think twice. "Silas didn't work for you then?" I asked, letting the receptionist's name hang in the air.

Obidi's eyes narrowed slightly, his demeanor shifting. "What did I say about not asking questions?"

My mind raced. Lying seemed like a terrible idea with Jackhammer looming behind me, his shadow swallowing half the room. Finally, I sighed. "An SD card," I admitted, keeping my tone neutral. "That's all. I swear."

Obidi stared at me for a long, uncomfortable moment, his reddened eyes weighing the truth of my words. Silence hung between us like a blade on a thin string, ready to drop.

Then, he turned his head slightly, his question not directed at me. "Is he telling the truth?"

For a second, I thought he was asking Jackhammer to confirm my story somehow. But before I could process it, someone stepped out of the backroom.

At first, I didn't recognize him. The scraggly hair I'd grown accustomed to was gone, replaced by a neat trim and a sharp shape-up. The man replaced his usual dirty singlet and three-quarter shorts with a gleaming silver suit, just as fancy as anything Osita would wear. A cocky smirk replaced his usual servile grin.

I felt the heat of anger rise in my chest. My fists clenched instinctively as the urge to leap out of my seat and throttle him took over. But the man, no longer bound by the façade of the lowly gateman, gazed down at me with smugness radiating from every inch of him.

"He's telling the truth," he said. "I saw him retrieve it from his laptop when the girl was at his place. He must have hidden it very well. I couldn't find it when he was out."

"And there's no chance he took it with him?" asked Chief Obidi, his eyes fixed on me.

The man shook his head. "We searched him thoroughly when we grabbed him from the church." He turned to me with a malevolent grin on his face. "Good morning…sah," said Akaneme.

CHAPTER 27

I was stuck in the back of the SUV, squeezed between Jackhammer and another goon whose name I hadn't caught, but he looked just as mean. They had blank, lifeless looks of men accustomed to violence. Akaneme, now acting as Chief Obidi's lapdog, sat in the front passenger seat, dressed for a party with fancy sunglasses that he did not remove, even as the sun dipped lower in the sky.

The ride was quiet, and that was a small mercy. It was impossible to think straight in Chief Obidi's presence. His energy was suffocating, stifling any strategy before it could fully form in my mind. But here in the car, I had a chance to breathe, to think. Every scenario ran through my mind, each ending badly. I knew I was in a do-or-die situation. There was no second chance.

The anger I felt churned into something sharper, colder. A steely determination. I didn't know how, and I didn't know when, but I was going to bring Obidi down. And Akaneme? He'd regret ever crawling out of his lowly disguise. If I had to dance with every devil in Lagos, so be it. I wasn't about to back down now.

We pulled up to the house on Banana Island, and as I stepped out of the car, the cold steel of a pistol pressed against my lower back. They weren't taking any chances, and neither was I. I led them inside, keeping my steps deliberate, calm, like I wasn't trying to buy time. In the bedroom, I walked to the desk and crouched down. I held down on the table, subtly using a lot of force, then I retrieved the card from under the front leg. The second my hand closed around it, I could feel the tension in the room shift. Akaneme stepped forward, eyeing me as I handed him the card.

"I've already looked through it," I said. My voice was steady, but my mind was racing. "I couldn't find any documents of note."

Akaneme stared at the card, a slow smirk crawling across his face. He flicked his sunglasses down his nose just enough to peer over the top of them. "You think you're so smart," he sneered. "From the moment we met, you thought you were better than me."

My mind was working, still calculating. The pieces were starting to fall into place, and it was clear: I wasn't walking out of here alive if I didn't make a move soon. "What happened to the real caretaker," I asked. "Surely, it was never you."

Akaneme turned on his heel, pocketing the card as if he'd just won a prize. "You'll be joining him momentarily. Goodbye, Mr. Dozy," he said.

That's when it hit me. He was leaving. And the three men with me? They weren't here to take me back to Chief Obidi. They were here to dispose of me.

The one with the gun stepped forward, gesturing with his head. "Oya, go to the bathroom," he ordered, devoid of emotion.

I played along, trudging toward the bathroom. My heart hammered, but I moved in a measured and steady way. As soon as I reached the door, I made my move. I spun around, grabbing the wrist holding the gun and twisting it sharply. The gun went off and hit the other guy, who screamed in pain. I shoved him into the other goon, sending them both crashing into the dresser.

They didn't get back up.

I quickly grabbed the pistol and turned to face Jackhammer. He wasn't like the others. His face was a mask of pure rage, and he rushed me like a bull. I fired off two shots, but he swerved quickly, and they only grazed him, barely slowing him down. The next thing I knew, I was flying through the air, slamming into the wall.

Jackhammer wasn't human. He was a wall of muscle that shrugged off every punch, every hit I landed. My fists felt like I was pounding them into a concrete pillar. He grabbed me by the throat, lifting me off the ground, squeezing the air from my lungs. I managed to knee him in the ribs, but it felt like kicking a tree.

I was losing. Fast.

Desperate, I grabbed a lamp from the bedside table and smashed it against his head. The glass shattered, sending shards everywhere, but Jackhammer just grunted and threw me across the room. My body hit the floor hard, my vision swimming. I couldn't take much more of this.

Then, out of nowhere, a gunshot echoed through the room. Jackhammer stopped mid-step, his eyes wide in shock as blood spread across his chest. He staggered, then collapsed to the floor with a heavy thud.

I blinked, trying to make sense of what had just happened. Then I turned and saw Detective Inspector Bayo standing in the doorway, his pistol still smoking.

He pointed the gun at me, his face unreadable. "Get up! You're under arrest."

I groaned, dragging myself to my feet, raising my hands in frustration. "Are you kidding me?" I spat. "These motherfuckers were trying to kill me!"

Bayo didn't lower the gun. "Why?"

"They work for Chief Obidi!" I snapped, gesturing to the bodies on the floor.

At that, Bayo's face changed. He dropped his gun to his side, his eyes sweeping over the carnage in the room. He shook his head, muttering something under his breath. "No," he finally said. "I can't do this. I'm staying away from that man."

His reaction did not surprise me. Most people with any sense kept their distance from the Chief. But I was going to need help, and there would be no better ally than a sharp officer in the Nigerian Police Force. So, I made a decision. I told him everything. About Mmachi hiring me, about finding the Admiral, and about Elfreda. All of it.

When I finished, Bayo let out a long, weary sigh and pointed a shaky finger in my direction. "You're not a registered private investigator here," he said, his tone heavy with exasperation. "You can't keep throwing yourself into situations like this."

I didn't know what to say. I had definitely turned into some sort of shit-magnet. All I could do was shrug like an idiot and look away, unsure how to proceed. Bayo looked out the window and then back at me, his eyes not betraying his wild thoughts. He then came closer and spoke in a hushed tone. "We don't interfere with Chief Obidi, even if I believe all you've just told me."

"But…" I began, but he raised a hand to cut me off.

"Your only option now is to leave town and wait for things to cool down."

I arched an eyebrow. "Give me my passport then."

He sucked his teeth. "The Commissioner has taken custody of it. He has shown a keen interest in your case and has put a lot of pressure on me. Now that I think about it, it's possible Obidi put him up to it."

I held my spinning head. What was I to do?

"You have family in Enugu, right?" I nodded. "Go there and stay out of sight."

"Obidi is strongest in the East. I'll be in bigger danger there."

"So, you better hope that's the last place he'd expect you to go," Bayo said, looking over his shoulder again. "I'm going to need to call this in. You need to leave now!" He pulled a pistol out of his holster and dropped it on the table between us. "You'll need that if Obidi truly has it out for you. Preferably to kill yourself. You didn't get it from me."

He turned to head out, but I stopped him with a question. "Why help me?"

He did not turn to look at me as he answered curtly. "You're not the only one who has crossed paths with Chief Obidi," he said. "If he's trying to kill you, you must be one of the good guys. Now get the fuck out of town!"

— ◆ —

The compound felt smaller than I remembered, as if memory had inflated its walls to a grander size. A two-story building perched on a patch of cracked concrete, its lower half clad in mottled white, russet, charcoal ceramic tiles like a stubborn patchwork quilt. The upper walls wore a deep, weathered maroon, the paint faded where the sun beat hardest. Blue-trimmed eaves stretched out overhead, casting a narrow shadow that never quite reached the far corner, where a rust-spotted satellite dish clung to the wall like a lonely lizard.

I limped through the gate like a stranger in my homeland, each step jabbing a dull ache into my side. My eyes stayed glued to the worn ceramic tiles underfoot. I owed Calvin one for smuggling me out of Lagos in that rattling overnight bus. Twelve hours of bone-shaking roads and every checkpoint had my nerves stretched taut as guitar strings.

I halted just inside the courtyard, exhaling a breath of relief I hadn't known I'd been holding.

"Alvan nwam?"

The voice was soft but charged with wonder. I looked up. My mother wore a radiant cobalt lace dress that caught the late-afternoon light and made her look almost regal. Her skin glowed the deep, warm brown of polished mahogany, her eyes framed with gentle lines that spoke of both laughter and hard years. A cascade of coral beads rested at her throat, echoing the traditional style I remembered from my childhood. Her hands trembled just slightly at her sides, as if she weren't sure whether to reach out or simply stand in awe.

"My son?" she whispered, disbelief and joy mingling in her voice. "Is it really you?"

Something tight and broken inside me cracked at that moment. Like a child I hadn't been in years, I crossed the few paces between us and wrapped her in a stiff embrace. She clung to me like letting go would erase the last decade, as if I might vanish again. Questions hovered behind her tears. Questions I wasn't yet ready to answer. They could wait. Right now, her arms around me were the only certainty I needed.

A scuff of shoes on concrete made me pull back and glance over her shoulder. There, caught in the soft shadow of the veranda, were my little sisters, though they looked anything but little now. They'd grown into young women, wearing T-shirts and jean shorts that marked them as teenagers, not the children I'd tucked in at night before my NYSC service. They stopped and hesitated at first, clearly not recognizing me. Not long after, however, hesitation gave way to joy, and with a burst of energy they all but tackled us in a squeal of excitement.

"Brother!"

They pressed in close, a tangle of arms and laughter, and I felt the warm pulse of home coursing through my veins. The chaos of the past days all faded into the humid air.

I could finally rest.

I don't know how long I slept, but I woke with a deep, rejuvenating sigh, fully rested for the first time in months. I was in my old room, though everything looked a little larger: the single bed I'd left behind was now a queen-size guest bed. I caught my reflection in the mirror and almost laughed. Dragon Ball Z and Tech N9ne posters crowded the walls, a nostalgic throwback to simpler days.

A soft knock at the door announced my mother's return. She stepped in, eyes narrowing at the sight of me. Before I could offer a greeting, the back of my head stung from a sharp slap.

"What was that for, Ma?" I asked, rubbing the tender spot.

"How can you be in the country for a week and not even tell me, Alvan?" she demanded, perching on the foot of the bed. The slap tasted of disappointment, not anger. She reached out and rubbed my foot, her worry seeping through. "How could you do this to your family?"

I sighed. "I'm sorry, Mummy. I came for work, but I wasn't sure how long it would take."

"What kind of work?" she pressed.

I hesitated. No excuse I could muster sounded plausible. In my rush to escape Lagos, I hadn't thought past disappearing.

Leaning forward, I took a gamble. "I'll earn enough to bring you, Nkechi, and Amarachi to the States," I said. "Soon."

She paused, studying me as if she might detect a lie. Finally, she said, "Alvan Chidozie Agu, I hope you're not pushing drugs, oh."

I chuckled and shook my head. "No, Mummy."

"Is it 419?" she shot back.

"No, Mummy."

"Illegal then?"

I swallowed. "N…no, Mummy."

"But who says I want to leave, my son? This is my house. Your father built it for us. This is your home."

"Mummy, this place isn't good anymore."

"Who says so?"

"Mummy, the power cuts never end, the roads crumble beneath your wheels, these politicians line their pockets while we go hungry, and I'm sure Daddy's sisters are still acting crazy. How can I leave you here?"

My mother chuckled, the sound warm and knowing. "Alvan nwam," she began, "yes, things are hard. Your father's sisters, though they've softened a bit since the funeral, still look for ways to make my life difficult. But you mustn't let any of that rubbish strip you of who you are."

"What do you mean?"

She eyed me for a moment longer, then stood and walked to the window. Outside, a cluster of weathered zinc-roofed huts huddled under the late-morning sun. "That village down there is where your father was born," she said, pointing. "And that second house is your grandfather's place which has been passed down through four generations. This land is our history, nwam."

She turned back, placing a gentle hand on my shoulder. "You may not want to tell me details, even though I see the way you are limping, and the bruises hidden under your shirt, but I know you'll tell me when you are ready. But here's one thing you must remember: this is your home. I saw you sleeping earlier. You looked peaceful, like a man who hadn't had a proper rest in years. You belong here, Alvan. And no matter where life takes you, nothing will ever replace that."

Her words landed with a thud. For the first time in a long while, I felt the weight of the world lift, if only for a moment, by the simple truth that home wasn't just a place on a map. It was right here in her voice, in those old walls, in the legacy of our family.

"Now, come downstairs and eat. I made fried eggs. I hope it's still your favorite."

I nodded. "Always, Mummy." I hugged her. "I love you."

"I love you too, my dear. Come eat."

"I'll be right down."

After breakfast, I made my way to the back of the house, where a tile-covered tombstone sat quietly beneath the sky. It marked the final resting place of my father. I stood there in stillness, swallowed by the weight of everything I hadn't said. Everything I hadn't done. I hadn't been ready to face the grief. Or the guilt.

Here I was, knee-deep in lies, chasing shadows, trying to make sense of the same twisted world he warned me about. In a way, his teachings had brought me here. He raised me to chase the truth. To seek justice. But he never said it would look like this.

A soft hand found my shoulder.

"Brother," Amarachi said. "I almost forgot you haven't seen this before. I'm glad you're back."

I wiped a tear from my face and offered a quiet smile. She pulled me into a tight hug.

Footsteps crunched on gravel behind us. Her twin, Nkechi, had found us. Never one to miss a tender moment, she rushed in and wrapped her arms around me too.

As we walked back toward the house, the mood lightened. We slipped into the kind of casual chatter that made grief bearable.

"I hope you brought my soap?" Nkechi asked with mock sternness.

I nodded.

"I didn't ask for anything," Amarachi added, "but I hope that doesn't mean I'm not getting something."

I nodded again, playing along.

"Aha, brother," Nkechi said, eyeing me. "Why do you look so lost?"

I sighed. "It's nothing, my dear. Just trying to sort through something. Someone I know is accused of murder. I'm trying to help him because I know he is being set up. But I just cannot figure it out."

The twins exchanged a look, then shrugged in perfect unison.

"I thought you're a fraud investigator," Amarachi said, as though it was the simplest thing in the world. "Investigating the dead man shouldn't be hard for you."

I chuckled. I wasn't sure if their casual acceptance of my offhand mention of murder should startle me. "You've been watching too many true crime documentaries. Mama told me."

"It doesn't mean I'm wrong," she said with a grin. "If anybody can figure it out, it's you, brother."

She wasn't wrong. Not entirely.

I had spent so much time chasing suspects, trying to find out who hated the Admiral enough to kill him. But I hadn't truly looked at the man himself.

— ◆ —

Later that evening, I was watching an old interview online. It was a national chat show. Admiral Alex Maduagu sat across from the host in full regalia, his voice firm, his hands steady.

"Listen. My wife is the very definition of a dedicated public servant. These accusations? Nonsense. A calculated political smear campaign. That's what it is. These leeches in high office. These cowards. They just can't stomach a strong woman with her own voice, so they do what cowards do best. They tear her down. But make no mistake: Mmachi Alex-Maduagu, the mother of my daughter, is not corrupt. She is not the monster they make her out to be."

It was clear this interview came before the fall. Before the evidence surfaced. Before the whispers turned into headlines. And yet, I didn't disagree with him. She *was* a scapegoat in some sense. That didn't mean she was innocent. But it meant the story was more complicated than they made it out to be.

Still, I couldn't help but think... the truth must have broken him. Like a pastor finding out his daughter had been flashing horny strangers on Slago.

The power had cut again, and the hum of the ceiling fan died like a warning. I sat in the dark, the only light coming from my desk's rechargeable lamp. Printouts, photographs, and notes scribbled in red littered the table. A web of dead ends and bad intentions. I'd spent hours trying to trace the Admiral's last steps and pin down whatever secret he'd died protecting. Even so, the puzzle mocked me.

The phone rang.

I stared at it. The screen lit up like an omen: *Mmachi*.

I let it ring twice, three times. My thumb hovered. Then I picked up.

"Dozy," she said.

I didn't respond.

"I assume you've made progress."

"Define progress," I said, rubbing my eyes.

"You've found my property?"

There it was, like she was asking about a misplaced handbag, not something men had bled for. I leaned back in my chair and sighed.

"No," I said, "but humor me. What's in this holy grail of yours? State secrets? A recipe for immortality? Or just receipts for your sins?"

There was a pause on the line. Then she said carefully, "They're important to me. And to you. Those documents are the key to your freedom. Freedom from Nigeria…from me."

I laughed, dry and bitterly. "That so? Because from where I'm sitting, it feels more like a death warrant."

"The contents," she said, tone flat now, "are no one's business but mine."

I went quiet. I began pondering aloud, and I didn't stop.

"You know, Mmachi… folks already believe you're dirty. The government has smeared you in the papers, on the blogs, radio jingles. Even your silence is being spun into guilt. If those documents confirm what everyone already thinks, why the secrecy?"

She said nothing.

I pressed on. "Unless they don't only damn you, they damn others too."

I hit something.

I heard her breath, yet nothing was spoken. And that was enough.

I sat forward, voice low now, like I was talking to myself. "Big names. Bigger than you. Maybe men in office. Maybe the same ones who kept the Admiral on edge. Maybe the same ones who...who sought a more permanent solution."

Still nothing.

I shook my head. "You're not just a client anymore, Mmachi," I said. "You're a suspect."

A small, amused breath came through the line. "Well, look at that," she said, almost playfully. You're finally using your brain. About time. However, I suggest you use your clever mind to *find* those documents instead of being so nosy."

I leaned against the desk, jaw tightening. "And what makes you so sure I won't leak whatever I find? Hand it over to the press? The authorities?"

She chuckled, deep and velvety. "Because you're a private investigator, Dozy. Not a whistleblower." Her voice turned chilly. "And it wouldn't be very good for business if word got out that you can't keep a client's confidence."

I didn't answer. Couldn't. Beneath the layers of insult and threat... she had a point.

And that was the worst of it.

I thought I would finish this job in a week when I took it. But here I was, waist-deep in something foul and thick, and now the rules were changing. Or maybe they'd never been what I thought to begin with.

Maybe this was who I was now.

Maybe I'd finally found a trade... in the dark.

"Is it possible," I said at last, slowly, "that the good Admiral stole those documents to set you free?"

There was a pause. "I beg your pardon?"

I leaned forward, thoughts forming as I spoke. "I've been digging into the Admiral's past. The more I found, the more this started to look different. He believed you were being sacrificed. What if he wanted to show it wasn't all your fault? What if... he did it out of love?"

Mmachi scoffed, and then her voice snapped like a whip.

"Is marrying an internet whore any way to show love to your wife?" Her words cut, full of venom. "Don't waste your time trying to understand Alex's choices. That's not your job. Just find me my fucking documents."

Click. She hung up.

I'd definitely hit a nerve.

Still, she wasn't wrong about one thing. Whatever the Admiral's motives had been, I needed to stop chasing ghosts and get back to the task.

I needed to get on with it.

I stared out the dusty window at the yard. For years I'd treated this place like a ticking bomb. Too dangerous to face, too broken to fix. In America, I'd found safety in routine, in the hum of a dishwasher at midnight and the predictable click of a lock. But that safety had become its own kind of prison, one built from fear and regret.

Chief Obidi's name still tasted bitter on my tongue, a reminder of every corner I'd cut and every shortcut I'd taken to stay alive. I'd allowed his threat to dictate my life, keeping me from honoring my father's legacy, from planting new seeds in this soil.

The realization hit me like a clean punch to the jaw: I was letting Obidi win by staying away. By cowering behind a green card. By pretending that this home, my home, wasn't worth the fight.

I wiped a line of dust from the sill and felt something stir in my chest. A spark I hadn't felt since childhood, when my father taught me how to defend myself. That same voice whispered now: "*You fight. You win. You survive.*"

I crushed my fist against the sill, resolve hardening in my veins. I would return to Lagos. I would find those stolen documents and expose every crooked soul who thought they could bury the truth. I would solve the Admiral's murder, no matter how deep the rot ran. And most importantly, I would bring down Chief Obidi, piece by bloody piece.

Because fear had held me back long enough. Now it was my turn to strike.

CHAPTER 28

The bus rattled down the cracked road somewhere near the border between Ogun and Lagos. I pressed my forehead against the warm glass, still fighting the urge to sleep. Then I gasped at the sight of a makeshift roadblock. It was a damn police checkpoint. A gateway to a realm of wasted time.

The driver slowed to a shuddering halt. A tall sergeant with a peculiar Hitler mustache barked orders through the open door: "Everyone off! Don't waste my time!" His men fanned out like vultures.

Inside, the passengers exchanged worried glances. We unloaded in a single line, shuffled toward the lantern light. The sergeant's boot cracked against the earth, sending a bird screeching skyward.

They began with the first passenger, yanking open a battered satchel and rifling through his wares. A flashlight beam danced over a bundle of clothes, a tin of chin chin, then settled on a thick stack of naira notes tucked inside a book. The sergeant's grin widened as he slipped a few bills into his own pocket.

My heart thudded. I watched as each passenger, silent now, faces lined with dread, had small valuables confiscated under the guise of "security checks." A woman's gold earrings. A man's bottle of wine. Everything vanished into the palm of the sergeant.

When they reached me, I took a slow step forward. He held out his hand. "ID."

"I no get ID," I said. "I lost it."

He squared his shoulders, eyes narrowing. "Go report to our oga."

He turned to his partner, fist raised, mouth open. My pulse roared in my ears. Seconds stretched thin as wire.

I slipped a crisp $20 note from my pocket and palmed it into the sergeant's. His eyes flickered down, then back to mine. For a heartbeat, I saw greed battling protocol. He swallowed. The other officer cleared his throat.

"All clear," the sergeant grunted, stuffing the note into his breast pocket. "You can go."

We scrambled back aboard. The engine coughed to life. I sank onto my seat, ribs protesting, and exhaled the breath I didn't know I'd been holding.

As we merged into traffic, the checkpoint's lanterns receded behind us like faded stars. The bus's radio was drowned out by the mutter of disgruntled passengers.

"They say the police are our friends? Which kind of nonsense friend?" one man spat.

"Na God go punish those people. They just take my wine like that," another groaned, slumping into his seat.

I didn't join in the cacophony of diatribes because I was too busy planning my approach. Next stop: Mother C's church. I had been knocked out the last time I was there, but this time I wouldn't leave until I was satisfied.

— ◆ —

The soreness from the prison brawl and everything that had happened before it was creeping up on me by the time I made my way back to Mother C's church. My body ached from head to toe, and each step felt like walking on broken glass, but I didn't have time for rest. I had a plan, and I needed answers.

When I arrived, the church was mostly quiet, the last of the congregation filing out after the evening service. From what I gathered, Mother C had just finished a meeting in a large conference room with her church elders.

The agenda? The Prophetess's new house. Apparently, the last one wasn't grand enough for her. They also discussed the status of the university she was building, and she stressed that no members of the church would receive discounts for their children's education. It irked me, considering that it was their money paying for the damn thing in the first place. But of course, this was how the game worked. The congregation was brainwashed. They'd thank her for building the school, even as she bled them dry.

The meeting ended a little past 8 PM. The room cleared out, and soon it was just Mother C and Brother Jeremiah left behind.

I had snuck into the church offices earlier and hid in a closet, pistol in hand. When the room was quiet enough, I kicked open the closet door, bursting out like an avenging angel. I raised and aimed the pistol at both of them before they could react. Their immediate response was to scream "Jesus!" and throw their hands up, their faces contorting in fear.

"Shut up," I muttered, my voice cold, devoid of the hesitation that rattled inside me.

I took a step forward, pistol-whipping Brother Jeremiah. He collapsed like a sack of yam flour, out cold before his head hit the floor. I wasn't here for him. My focus was on

Mother C, her face already wet with tears, muttering a quiet prayer under her breath.

"I'm going to ask a series of questions," I began, my voice low and cold as I pressed the gun to her forehead, the metal chilled from the night air.

But before I could even form my first question, Mother C broke. The sight of the gun and my hardened expression was enough to crack her completely.

"Please! Please don't hurt me," she whimpered, her whole body trembling violently. "I'll tell you everything you want to know. Anything! Just... please."

I didn't say a word, waiting for her to spill. And she did, like a dam bursting under pressure.

"Alex Maduagu... he started coming to my church a few months ago. He... he was a good giver, always generous," she said, her words tumbling out in a frantic rush. Her eyes darted between me and the gun, her chest rising and falling rapidly as panic overtook her. "I appreciated his coming, and I appreciated Elfreda's inviting him. She always brought good people with deep pockets. It was good for the church, you know? But..." she swallowed hard, her voice faltering before it picked back up, "...but one day, a few months ago, a woman I didn't know came to me. She...she gave me a lot of money... too much money... and she... she asked me to have a vision."

"A vision?" I asked, my grip tightening on the gun.

"Yes! Yes!" she nodded furiously. "A vision! She wanted me to tell Alex that Elfreda was his true wife. That God had chosen her for him. She said it had to be believable to make him leave his wife."

Her voice broke into a sob, the full weight of her panic settling in. "He accepted it just like that. It was like he had been waiting for a reason... a reason to leave his wife and find another. The Admiral... he needed a sign. I gave him one."

Her words confirmed what I had already suspected, but the desperation in her voice, the sheer terror, told me there was more she was hiding.

"And who was this woman?" I asked, my tone sharper now. "The one who bribed you?"

Mother C shook her head so fast it was almost a blur. "I don't know! I swear I don't know. I had never seen her before. She didn't give me her name."

The gun pressed harder against her forehead, and I watched as a fresh wave of fear washed over her.

"Think harder," I said, the threat clear in my voice.

"She didn't give me a name!" she cried, bordering on hysteria. "But... but she dressed like a boy. I remember that. Baggy clothes, baseball cap. She... she looked like a boy, but she wasn't."

I lowered the gun just a fraction, watching as Mother C slumped in relief, her hands still shaking as she tried to wipe her tears with the back of her hands.

I stared at her, disgust crawling up my spine. She was willing to sell her "visions" to the highest bidder, and she had helped orchestrate the Admiral's downfall for a price. But she had given me what I needed. And now, I had a new plan.

"Get out of here," I muttered. She didn't wait for me to change my mind. She scrambled away, tears still streaming down her face, her breath coming in shallow gasps as she fled the room.

I holstered the gun, my mind already working through the next steps. The pieces of the puzzle were all falling into place. But it wasn't over yet. Not by a long shot.

I left the church just as quietly as I'd arrived. The police? I wasn't very worried about them. By the time anyone noticed what had happened, I'd be long gone, and Mother C wasn't about to call attention to her own mess.

The soreness in my body slowed my steps as I walked down the dimly lit street. I felt the weight of everything pressing down on me physically and mentally. I tried to flag down a taxi to take me back to the hotel, but something in the pit of my stomach told me I wasn't alone.

A car idling a short distance away caught my eye. I paused, my senses on high alert, fingers twitching near the pistol still tucked in my waistband. But the tension eased when I saw a familiar figure step out of the vehicle.

Calvin.

"Dozy," he called out. "You need to come with me."

I didn't bother asking how he had found me. The quiet determination in his voice told me that this wasn't the time for questions. I got into the car without a word.

The drive was silent. From what I could tell, we were heading towards Ikeja GRA. If I didn't trust Calvin with my life, I might have been worried.

We pulled up in front of an incomplete building. The skeleton of a mansion, with its concrete blocks and exposed cement lines still visible. No tiles on the floor, no doors, no windows. Just the bare bones of what would one day be luxury.

Calvin stepped out first, and I followed. The night air was cool, a stark contrast to the heat of the day, but the unease in my chest grew heavier with each step we took inside the building.

We made our way through the structure, the echo of our footsteps the only sound. Then we entered a back corridor that led to another building entirely. At the doorway, two men stood guard, their faces obscured by the dim light, but I knew them instantly. They were the same two thugs I had fought at the Pure Water Factory, the ones who had tried to kidnap Elfreda.

I stopped, looking at Calvin for an explanation. He merely nodded, his face calm but firm. "It will all make sense in a minute," he assured me. He stretched a hand. "Please hand over the gun."

I didn't like this. My gut was telling me to turn back, but I trusted Calvin. So, I gave him the pistol and followed him into a brightly lit room. Inside, there was nothing but a table and two chairs. Seated on one chair was a man, his posture regal, his aura commanding. He stood when he saw me enter.

He was a man in his mid-40s, wearing a traditional senator attire, white and straight from starch. His gold wristwatch gleamed in the light, and his face was framed by a perfectly trimmed beard; his expression was calm but intimidating. His dark brown eyes held mine with an intensity that sent a chill down my spine.

Calvin gestured to the man, his tone unusually formal. "Dozy, allow me to introduce you to Peter Onuoha. My boss."

Peter Onuoha. The Director-General of the State Security Service. The name carried weight, and for good reason. This was a man with a formidable background. A long, storied career spanning continents. Born in the UK, Onuoha had initially joined MI5, where he quickly established himself in British intelligence circles before deciding to return to Nigeria. Once back, he joined the army, his tactical prowess and network propelling him through the ranks. He had served as DSS state Director in Abia, Cross River, and Ondo State before finally being appointed Director-General.

Onuoha was a strategist, a fixer, and, when necessary, an enforcer.

I turned to Calvin, my mind brimming with questions. What kind of mess had I stepped into for someone like this to be involved?

Peter smirked, his gaze steady, exuding a blend of calm and restrained menace. "I believe you've met my men," he said, his distinctly English accent adding an extra edge of authority. "Shot one of them in the leg, didn't you?"

I glanced at the man in question, noting the cast around his leg. "No, sir," I replied, keeping my tone even. "I believe his partner did."

One man muttered something under his breath, irritation flickering across his face, and I had to bite back a smirk.

Peter chuckled. "Quite the cheeky git, I see."

I turned to Calvin, frustration creeping into my voice. "What is going on?"

Calvin met my gaze with a steady look. "You should know I had no idea about this operation. But after you told me about the attempted kidnapping and the scuffle, I did some digging."

"And his digging led him straight to me," Peter cut in smoothly, his tone effortlessly composed. "You've certainly been keeping yourself occupied, Mr. Agu. Barely a week back in your own country, and already you're linked to a murder, tangled with two of my men, taken on half of Kirikiri's worst, and nearly ended up dead courtesy of Chief Obidi. Would it be fair to say trouble clings to you like flies to shit? Quite frankly, had I known one as skilled as you are at armed combat was in the mix, I would have sent more capable fighters after our TequilaDream."

I felt the weight of his words but kept my face neutral. "Are you here to arrest me?"

Peter let out a laugh, sharp and devoid of humor. "Heavens, no. I'm not in the business of arrests, Mr. Agu. My business is making people disappear." He paused, giving the words a moment to settle. "It's come to our attention that you're holding onto certain...sensitive information. On behalf of the President, I'd like you to hand it over."

I raised an eyebrow, playing dumb. "What information?"

Peter sat down, his eyes never leaving mine. "Between 2010 and 2015, while serving as Minister of Petroleum Resources, Mmachi Alex-Maduagu stole an estimated ninety million US dollars."

The number hit me like a freight train. "That's got to be some kind of exaggeration."

"If only it were that simple." Peter's tone was grave. "The State managed to recover a fraction, maybe twenty million. But the rest? It's buried in offshore accounts, hidden behind shell companies, tied up in real estate bought under false names. Practically untraceable. Our intel suggests her husband, the late Admiral Alex Maduagu, held information that could unravel it all. And we suspect he passed those secrets on to his mistress, Elfreda Bassey."

"That's why you were after her," I said, realization dawning on me. This was all about money. Millions of dollars were siphoned from the country, hidden away while the masses starved.

But something else bothered me. "Mmachi told me to retrieve certain documents her husband had. She never said anything about millions of dollars."

Peter's gaze sharpened. "Did you find these documents?"

I hesitated. "Only documents I saw were on an SD card. They had banking information but nothing that screamed millions of dollars."

"And where is this SD card now?"

I thought of Akaneme, likely fuming over the shattered SD card I'd handed him. Oh yes, did I forget to mention? Before retrieving it from under the table, I'd crushed it by pressing it down. My nuclear option. I had backed up the information on my flash drive, stowing it securely back at the hotel.

The straightforward thing would have been to tell Peter where the flash drive was, hand it over, and be done with all of this. But that left too many questions unanswered: Elfreda's involvement, Akaneme's role, and the lingering question of who had killed the Admiral.

There were probably a hundred ways I could handle this situation, but as I stood there, only one option made sense.

"I don't have it," I finally said. "But I can get it for you."

Peter raised an eyebrow, intrigued but cautious. After the public brawl in Oshodi, I knew he wasn't eager to get more of his men involved in another public showdown. If I were willing to put myself out there, he'd wait in the shadows and collect.

Finally, he leaned back in his chair, arms folded. "I assume you'll want something in return?"

A smirk tugged at the corner of my mouth as the framework of a plan began to form in my mind. "You can count on that, sir."

CHAPTER 29

Calvin drove me back to the hotel, his eyes fixed on the road, but I could feel his annoyance, like a heavy weight in the air. He hadn't said much since we left the meeting with Peter Onuoha, but I knew him well enough to recognize the silence before the storm. He looked at me. It was the same look a disappointed parent gives their child in public, trying to contain their frustration to avoid making a scene. He was going to give me an earful. I could feel it.

What caught me off guard, though, was the smirk that crept across his lips.

"Do you remember that one French class back in school?" he asked suddenly, breaking the silence, his tone lighter than expected. "The time our beautiful French teacher was scolding Dark Snow about his awful record in her class? What was it he said when she was done?"

I couldn't help but chuckle as the memory surfaced. I shifted in my seat and did my best to imitate Dark Snow's fake American accent. The one he was so damn proud of. "I'm just tryna make a change."

We both laughed, the tension easing, at least momentarily.

"You thought that was the funniest thing ever," Calvin said, still grinning. "Damn near fell out of your seat."

"I take an odd level of pleasure in random moments of humor," I replied. It was true, and it was probably why I enjoyed shows like *South Park* and *Family Guy*. The more absurd and unexpected the joke, the more it tickled me. But I could feel the mirth slipping away. Calvin hadn't dipped into nostalgia for no reason; this was his way of softening the blow before getting serious. It was only a matter of time before he hit me with what was really on his mind.

Sure enough, his expression grew sober, and his voice followed suit. "Why are you doing this, man?" he asked, his tone quiet but full of frustration. "You had the chance to tell the Director-General where the documents were. You could've walked away, put this whole mess behind you."

I nodded, feeling the weight of his words. He wasn't wrong, but it wasn't that simple. "You think I'm doing this out of some egotistical need to solve the case myself?"

"That's exactly what it looks like, Dozy," Calvin replied, shaking his head in disbelief. "It's like you've got something to prove, and I don't get it. You had a clean way out. You should've taken it."

I exhaled, leaning back against the headrest, my mind whirring with everything that had gone down since I set foot back in Nigeria. Maybe there was some truth in what he was saying. Maybe I *was* driven by ego, by a desire to show everyone—Mmachi, Chief Obidi, and whoever else was playing these games—that I wasn't some pawn in their sick little chessboard.

But it was more than that. It had to be.

"Cal," I began slowly, choosing my words carefully, "this isn't just about the documents. Sure, finding them is part of it, but someone tried to set me up for murder. I can't just let that slide. This thing has been personal from the jump, and I take that shit seriously."

Calvin huffed, clearly frustrated. He glanced at me, then back at the road, his knuckles tightening around the steering wheel. "Dozy, you were in a maximum-security prison." Chief Obidi isn't the kind of guy you mess with and live to talk about it. He'll come after you again, harder this time. By defying him during the elections, you gave people the idea that there was nothing he could do. You diminished his power and made him look ridiculous. And such a man cannot look ridiculous.

I clenched my fists, feeling the familiar burn of anger rising in my chest. "That man," I growled, "kept me away from home for ten goddamn years. Ten years, Cal. I stayed away, living in exile, because of him. I couldn't even attend my father's funeral! I'm not about to just let him win. Not again."

Calvin's brow furrowed, concern etched in every line of his face. "I get that, but..."

"No, you don't," I interrupted, my voice harsher than I intended. I sighed, trying to rein in my temper. "You don't get it because you weren't there. You weren't the one who had to disappear, had to build a new life across the ocean while looking over your shoulder every day. You weren't the one whose family had to hear whispers of threats, wondering if they were next."

I could see Calvin's jaw tighten, but he didn't respond right away. I continued, my voice softer now, but no less determined. "I can't just walk away, Calvin. Not when I'm this close. I went through hell. Kirikiri, brawling with Obidi's thugs, being tossed off a yacht, and getting knocked out more times than I can count. And you think I'm going to back down now?"

Silence fell between us for a moment. The night stretched on outside the car, but inside, the tension was thick, almost palpable.

Calvin finally spoke. "I just don't want to see you get killed, bro. I don't want to lose another friend to this damn country and its corruption. And I definitely don't want to be the one who has to tell your family what happened."

I swallowed hard, the reality of what he said hitting me like a punch to the gut. He was right. This whole thing was dangerous. Hell, I knew that better than anyone. But there was something else at play here. Something more than just survival.

"I get it," I said. "But if I don't see this through, if I don't figure out who's pulling the strings and why… I'll never be able to come home. I'll never be able to look my family in the eye. I left them once to escape Obidi. I'm not leaving them again, not without making sure they're safe."

Calvin sighed, a mixture of resignation and understanding in his expression. He wasn't happy about it, but he knew there was no talking me out of this. Not now. Not when I was in too deep.

"Just don't get yourself killed, Dozy," he said finally, his voice barely above a whisper.

I nodded, though the truth was I wasn't sure I could promise him that. Not anymore.

As we drove on in silence, the severity of everything bore down on me. The thought of coming face-to-face with Chief Obidi again, with Elfreda, with the tangled web of players that seemed hell-bent on pulling me into the abyss. It all felt like too much. But I couldn't turn back now. I had gone too far to walk away.

And then, in the quiet of the car, I thought about something else. Something I hadn't even admitted to Calvin.

Leverage.

That flash drive was a bargaining chip. In a game where everyone seemed to have their hands on the scales. Chief Obidi, the Director-General, even Mmachi herself. I had nothing but my skin to bet with. And I wasn't foolish enough to think that skin alone was enough to save me in a country where power was everything and justice was an afterthought.

No, I needed something that would ensure my survival, the safety of my family, and an end to this. I needed something that made me indispensable, something that forced the hand of the people trying to pull the strings.

The flash drive was the leverage. As long as I had it, and no one knew where it was, I still had a chance to control the narrative. To turn this mess on its head.

That's why I hadn't told Peter Onuoha where it was.

And that's why I needed to see this through.

I exhaled slowly, leaning my head against the window, the warm glass pressing against my temple. Calvin didn't understand, not fully. This wasn't just about finding out who killed the Admiral, or why they tried to set me up. It was about making sure that when this was all over, I wasn't another casualty left bleeding in the street.

It was about ensuring I walked away from this whole thing with something more than just my life.

It was about making sure I walked away with the upper hand.

My eyes widened. "Stop!" I yelled.

Startled, Calvin slammed on the brakes, his head swiveling as he tried to figure out what could've caused my outburst. I stepped out of his SUV, drawn to the lighted area of the street where a man was grilling meat. The distinct aroma of suya pepper wafted through the air, rich and smoky.

I hadn't had proper street suya since I'd returned. The fancy stuff on the yacht had been a pleasant diversion, but it couldn't hold a candle to the real deal, the kind you only find on the streets.

The suya vendor, an *aboki* with a stained apron and the confident ease of someone who'd done this a thousand times, was hard at work over a small firewood grill. He sliced thin pieces of ram meat, threading them onto skewers before placing them over the open flame. With each turn, he basted the skewers in a blend of oil and spices, the sizzling sound mingling with the smoky aroma of suya pepper and charred meat. He cut the perfectly seared meat off the skewer, dusted it with brownish-red suya pepper, added chopped cabbage, onions, and tomato slices, and wrapped the pieces in greasy newspaper.

I bought a portion and took a bite, savoring the explosion of flavors. The smoky, spicy meat mingling with the crunch of fresh onions and the slight tang of tomato. The heat from the pepper hit me, but it was a welcome kind, waking me up and pulling me into the present moment. I hadn't realized just how hungry I was until that first bite.

Calvin pulled up next to me, his head poking out of the driver's window, eyebrows raised in amused disbelief. "Dozy? Really? You made me stop the car like that for suya?"

I swallowed, still savoring the spice on my tongue. "I needed this. Give me a minute. I need to make a call."

Calvin nodded, parking by the curb as I took out my phone and dialed a number I'd hoped to avoid. But given how things were spiraling, I realized I couldn't afford to be picky with my allies.

"Alobam," Osita's voice came through the phone, familiar and laced with his usual swagger. "It's been a while. What have you been up to?"

I took a deep breath, steadying myself. "Osita, we need to talk."

"Before you go, I found out why that man, I don't remember his name, the receptionist that tried to kill you. Yes. I found out how he was discovered easily. It turns out that one of my men has a side gig."

"What kind of gig?"

"Obidi. He was also working for Obidi. I've talked to him. Said he alerted Obidi, and he ordered him to tip the police off. Why would Obidi be involved?"

I cursed under my breath. "That motherfucker has been behind the curtain this whole time," I spat. "But I'll fill you in later."

He chuckled, clearly intrigued. "Go on, then. What did you want to say?"

"I'm worried about you," I began, my voice steady but firm. "The way you handled that situation with Silas... it crossed a line."

"Silas?" He sounded genuinely confused for a moment. "Who the hell is Silas?"

"The receptionist. The man you shot, Osita."

He let out a short, dismissive scoff. "Oh, that guy. What? Did you expect me to give him a pat on the back for trying to kill you?"

I sighed, trying to keep my frustration in check. "We're friends, Osita. I came to you because I needed someone I could trust, but I can't feel comfortable doing that if you're going to keep reverting to... well, your old instincts. I didn't come to you for your muscle. I came for your connections and your street smarts. I still need your help, but I need to know you will not kill anyone else without good reason."

There was a pause on the other end, and for a second, I wasn't sure he'd even respond. Finally, he spoke, his tone skeptical but intrigued. "Alobam, you know the Lagos underworld as well as I do. It's kill or be killed out here. You want me to play nice, but that doesn't work in this game."

"I get it," I replied, my tone firm but not unkind. "But this isn't just about you. If we're going to see this through, I need you to promise. No more killing, Osita."

Another silence. Then he let out a reluctant sigh. "Alright. No unnecessary killing. But if someone comes for me, I'm not just going to stand there."

"Once again, thanks for saving me," I said, letting a hint of a smile slip into my voice.

"Fine, fine," he muttered. "You've got my word. But only because it's you asking."

Satisfied, I pressed on. "Good. Because I'm going to need all the help I can get. I need Calvin and Oge on this too. This thing is bigger than I realized, and if we're going to get through it, I need everyone on board."

Osita was silent for a moment, but I could feel his smirk even through the phone. "Now you're talking. You rally the troops, and I'll keep my end of the bargain."

"Awesome. By the way, when you say you talked to the guy who betrayed you, what did you really mean?"

"*Hapụ* that one. It's not important."

As he hung up, I took a deep breath, feeling a sense of purpose settle over me. Whatever this case had become, I'd decided I was going to see it through. And with friends by my side, I had a fighting chance.

— ◆ —

I took a long, satisfying shower. In Lagos, where the air was always thick and hot, showers were a gift, more like a liquid massage than anything else. The water pounded against my sore muscles, soothing the tension that had built up over the past few days. I'd been running on fumes, bruised in places I didn't know could ache, and while I knew an actual massage would do wonders, this was the next best thing.

When I stepped out I wrapped a towel around my waist. Water still dripped down my body, but I let it. It was my way of staying cool in this sweltering heat. I leaned over to my backpack and retrieved the flash drive I had hidden in a small pouch. It had been burning a hole in my consciousness all day.

Sliding it into my laptop, I scrolled through the folders again, searching every inch of its contents. Hoping—no, praying—that somewhere within the innocuous banking files and mundane business receipts, there would be something. Something that pointed to the billions of naira Mmachi allegedly stole. But once again, nothing. No clues, no smoking gun. Just data that led nowhere.

This frustrated the hell out of me.

You know how they say an idle mind is the devil's playground? Well, that idle mind led me to something I'd never thought I'd even glance at. Slago. Before I knew it, I was downloading the app, registering under the random username "MrProof"—the first thing that popped into my head.

Once I was inside, I felt overwhelmed. Hundreds of live streams from young women all over the world, all right there in front of me. It was a digital carnival. Real people, real interaction, but with an edge that made it feel dangerously close to... well, something more. It wasn't hard to see how someone could get hooked. It was like live pornography and, for a moment, I understood how a man like Alex Maduagu could spiral into obsession.

But I stopped myself. This was not what I needed. The Admiral's descent was one path I couldn't afford to take. What I needed was sleep.

Just as I was about to shut my laptop, there was a knock on the door.

My heart rate picked up, more out of instinct than worry. I approached cautiously, the cool air still clinging to my wet skin. I'd forgotten I was wearing nothing but a towel when I called out, "Who is it?"

"It's me."

I recognized the voice instantly. Elfreda. That familiar mix of caution and eagerness washed over me. I opened the door, and there she was, standing in the dimly lit hallway, wearing a pink tank top and shorts. She smelled of sweet vanilla. I was again struck by how naturally she exuded allure, as innocence and desire clashed on her face. It was like she didn't know how *not* to be sexy, even in the simplest of clothes.

Her eyes immediately fixed on my swollen face. She took a step closer, concern softening her features as she gently touched the side of my cheek. "What happened to you?"

"I had a little run-in with... some criminals. I'm fine," I said, brushing it off like it was nothing. But her touch lingered, and for a split second, I was surprised by how much I wanted her to keep touching me.

"I heard you were out of town. I worried you'd left without saying goodbye."

"It was a short trip, as you can see."

"Can I come in?" She asked.

I hesitated. Every rational part of me screamed to keep her out, to maintain distance, but I found myself stepping aside. "Sure," I said, the word slipping out before I could think it through. She walked past me, her presence filling the room as she sat down on the couch, her hands fidgeting slightly as if something heavy was on her mind.

"Are you alright?" I asked, turning back to my laptop, though my attention was entirely on her.

She hesitated before answering. "Yes... I'm just... just still shaken."

I walked over to her, placing a reassuring hand on her shoulder. A sense of ease and solace flowed between us. "It's okay," I said softly. "This will all be over soon."

She nodded, but I could see the vulnerability in her eyes, the fear still clinging to her like a shadow. "I never got a chance to thank you," she said. "For saving me."

I smiled, trying to lighten the moment. "Don't mention it."

But something lingered in the air between us, unspoken. Something heavier than just gratitude. And I wasn't sure if it was the aftermath of everything we'd been through... or the beginning of something else.

I sat back down at the laptop, fingers moving across the keyboard in a futile search for anything that might lead me to the money. Elfreda, still sitting on the couch, shifted awkwardly but stayed quiet at first. The tension was thick, though I tried to brush it off by focusing on the screen.

Nothing. Not a damn thing.

I turned to Elfreda. She sat quietly, her eyes drifting around my room, but it didn't seem like she was searching for anything in particular. It was more like there was something she wanted, something unsaid lingering on the tip of her tongue, and she didn't quite know how to ask for it.

Then she said, almost too casually, "I was wondering… hoping you'd join me for dinner. They say the hotel's Chinese place isn't bad. My treat. A thank-you."

My radar hummed. Pretty girls with sudden generosity usually came with hooks. But my stomach was already writing its own terms.

"On one condition," I said.

She brightened. "Name it."

"We don't go to the Chinese restaurant."

That earned me a full-wattage smile. Bright teeth, bright eyes. Dangerous combination. "Whatever you want, Mr. Dozy."

— ◆ —

We found a late-night Nigerian joint that still had heat in the pots. The place smelled of pepper soup and an assortment of meats. Oliver De Coque's "People's Club" hissed from old speakers. Servers in white shirts and Ankara vests moved as if they'd practiced. The routine was drop plates, dip heads, disappear. Even though it was past midnight, the room hummed as if it were early evening with voices, clinks, and small laughter suggesting the bills were paid for that day.

I was wrist-deep in egusi, rolling pounded yam and fishing blindly for meat. Elfreda watched me over her wine like a cat at an aquarium.

"What?" I asked.

She leaned in over her plate of jollof. "How do you say 'son of the soil' in Igbo?"

"Nwa ala," I said, mouth half-full.

She grinned. "You be real nwa ala."

I bit into a turkey gizzard. "Back in D.C., this plate is a mortgage payment. I cook it myself most times. Different when someone else gets it right."

"No Igbo girl to cook for you there?"

338

I chuckled at the gentle probe into my relationship status. "Haven't had much luck with Igbo-American girls."

"Let me guess...too strong-willed for your Okonkwo sensibilities?" she said, laughing.

"Right up to arrogance," I said, chuckling at the Things Fall Apart reference.

She laughed too.

"How long were you away?" she asked.

"Just under ten years."

"You didn't come home?"

"No." It slipped out before I could catch it. "Not even for my father's burial."

Her eyebrow climbed. "Why not?"

I set the morsel of pounded yam down. "I tell myself Immigration. I'd overstayed my student visa by the time he passed. If I left, that was it. I would not be able to return for a long time." I exhaled. "It's true. Just not all of it."

She leaned in, softer. "And the rest?"

"I was scared," I said. "I let fear keep me from returning and doing what a son should do." I shrugged as if it didn't matter. It did. "That stain doesn't wash out easily."

Her hand rested on mine, light. "What were you scared of?"

I pictured Chief Obidi, one nod away from someone's last breath. I killed the thought. "Let's just eat, Freda."

The quiet that followed wasn't comfortable. It started to itch. I broke it the ugly way.

"There's something I can't get past," I said. "What you do for a living."

Her face didn't move, but the air around her cooled. "What about it?"

"Slago," I said. "Look, I think you're gorgeous, smart, tougher than you let on. But it's hard for me to... accept it."

She laughed once, with no humor in it. "I don't need you to accept me. Keep your sermon."

"I'm not preaching," I said. "I'm saying it's hard. Like men who choke on the idea of a woman's 'body count.' It messes with the head."

Her fingers toyed with her napkin, then flattened. When she spoke again, her voice had grit in it. "I did what I was supposed to do. School. Good grades. Sent out CVs till my eyes crossed. Nigeria doesn't care. The jobs that pay want you to be somebody's 'special friend.' The jobs that don't care, pay you like you're volunteering. And the rest? They go to the cousin of the cousin of a man with a title." She leaned back, found a cigarette, and lit it with a steady hand. "Slago isn't pretty. But it pays. It means I don't owe any married man a favor. I can buy what I need without begging, and nobody gets to put hands on me unless I say so."

She took a slow drag of a cigarette. The server pretended not to see. "We don't all get to japa, Dozy."

I nodded. She wasn't wrong. The Admiral and the men like him weren't victims; they paid to be fooled. They begged for it.

"I'm sorry," I said.

She gave a tired smile. "Please. It's not like you're planning to marry me."

That one landed. I shifted in my chair.

She tapped ash into a saucer and tilted her head. "Your turn. Why are you still chasing this? You haven't told me everything. We both know Mmachi's behind Alex's death. So what are you really after? What's the hidden agenda?"

"*Hidden.*" The word snagged in my mind. The Admiral was a paranoid old sailor. If he hid anything that could burn half the country, it wouldn't sit on a desktop. It would be buried in a hidden partition, a decoy file, something you only see if you know where to look.

My eyes widened before I could stop them.

I rinsed my hands in the steel bowl. "I need to get back to my laptop."

Elfreda didn't ask. She peeled off a stack of notes, tucked it under the bill, and stood. "Let's go."

— ◆ —

I quickly navigated to my system preferences, my pulse pounding. I should've thought of this hours ago. All it took was enabling hidden files. Of course. I couldn't believe I'd expected anything more sophisticated from the Admiral. A man from the generation of people that would call you into the next room to set a new ringtone for a phone because they couldn't figure it out themselves. A man who would use something as simple as his own daughter's birthday as a pin code to his phone.

The seconds ticked by as I waited for the change to take effect.

When the screen refreshed, I stared at it, expecting... well, something.

But nothing. No hidden folders. No cryptic filenames. The disappointment washed over me, tightening my chest. Elfreda's questions faded into the background noise as I stared at the screen, trying to figure out where to go from here.

I should've known better. If the Admiral was going to hide something, it wouldn't be on a plain SD card. No, he would hide it deeper, maybe even disguise it as something else. His paranoia wouldn't allow something as simple as an easily discoverable file.

He would've hidden the evidence on something he would always have on his person. I sat up straight, feeling a chill down my spine. I'd already gone through the SD card, but there was another place where I might find what I was looking for.

His phone.

It struck me as strange that he'd leave a fully functional phone stashed in a bag at his sister's place. Was he expecting trouble that night? I hadn't yet had the chance to sift through the device's internal storage since I'd copied it.

I stood up abruptly, making Elfreda jump a little. "What's wrong?" She asked, her eyes wide.

"Nothing," I muttered, my focus shifting entirely. I grabbed my bag, rummaging through until I found the phone. It had a USB-C port, so I immediately retrieved my phone's USB-C cord and plugged it into my laptop to view the files. I searched meticulously, ignoring the surface-level content. Then I did what I hadn't before. I checked for hidden files on the drive, just as I had with the flash drive.

This time, a new folder popped up. A nameless, seemingly insignificant file at the bottom of the list. I clicked on it, and my stomach tightened as the screen filled with a series of documents.

The first file I opened was a PDF. An internal memo from the Central Bank of Nigeria. It detailed suspicious transfers between government accounts and a series of private offshore entities. Billions of naira were routed through shell companies with names like *Zarah Holdings Limited* and *Lumin Commerce S.A.*

I clicked on the next file. It was an Excel spreadsheet listing over a hundred wire transfers. The recipients were a who's who of shady corporations across multiple countries: Cayman Islands, Luxembourg, Mauritius, the Dominican Republic.

Another document was a contract for the purchase of land in Dubai under an unfamiliar name: *Ginika Mofe.*

The final document... this one made my breath hitch. It was a list of politicians, bank officials, and even international companies. All the names tied to this conspiracy. People who had aided Mmachi in siphoning off the country's wealth for half a decade. It was damning. It went beyond stolen money. This was a web of corruption stretching across countries.

The actual evidence. The documents that could bring everything crashing down. And it also became immediately apparent to me why Chief Obidi wanted these documents. His name was in a lot of them.

I closed the laptop slowly, my mind spinning. I had stumbled upon a weapon; a smoking gun that implicated the untouchable. The very people Peter Onuoha likely answered to. No, this wasn't just about the money. It was about the power that came with this kind of information. The kind of power that could cripple nations and elevate individuals, depending on whose hands it fell into.

The government couldn't care less about the money; they just needed to erase any evidence that explicitly tied them to years of misconduct. It didn't matter that the citizens had always been aware of their blatant corruption, but what mattered was keeping their secrets buried. Without this, the people's protests would be little more than just ramblings.

Suddenly, so many things began to fall into place.

Mmachi Alex-Maduagu, the infamous scapegoat of Nigerian corruption, was exiled but still lived in luxury. The circumstances of her departure always bothered me. She hadn't fled in the dead of night, hunted by the law. No, she practically strolled out of the country, slipping into the shadows of the UK, Canada, and eventually the U.S., her life marked by quiet comfort, not chaos. And what had the government done to bring her to justice? Next to nothing. Hers was a name paraded in the streets, plastered on protest signs and debated in the media. She had become the face of corruption, but now it was clear, she was a diversion. The real power lay with the men on that list: ministers, governors, senators, even the presidency itself.

So why had Alex Maduagu, her husband, held onto this information? Why risk his life and his legacy for something that could destroy so many powerful lives?

I didn't have time to dwell on it. Elfreda approached, her steps feline and smooth, her hips swaying with the sort of sensual confidence that demanded attention. "You look exhausted," she breathed. "And I'm still frightened. Your friend Oge is nice, but…" She trailed off, her fingers brushing my arm, then sliding down to rest on my thigh. "You saved me once before. I feel safer with you."

Her hand moved dangerously close to my crotch. The warmth of her touch was amplified by the leftover haze of sexual tension from earlier, stirred up by the brief encounter with Slago. My body responded involuntarily, the heat rising between us almost unbearable.

"Will you keep me safe?" she asked, her voice dropping to a near-whisper, vulnerable and seductive at once. She leaned in closer, her breath warm on my ear. "Keep me safe, papi."

Papi?

Her body pressed against mine, the scent of her skin intoxicating, as she placed her lips on mine, and we found ourselves locked in a passionate kiss.

We moved together, and any thoughts of Chief Obidi, Mmachi, or even the documents disappeared like smoke in the wind. The world narrowed to just her, the feel of her smooth skin against mine, the heat between us rising until it felt like the only thing that mattered. I hadn't felt this kind of connection in so long, not since my last encounter which I could barely remember, dulled by alcohol and poor judgment. This, however, was something else. I will always remember this: her body's movements, her lips on my neck, and the warmth of her breath on my chest.

In those moments, there was no soreness, no danger. No mission. No violence. Just the two of us, entangled in a fleeting escape. Kissing her felt like therapy. Each movement felt like healing for the wounds my mind and body had suffered over the past days. My world might be falling apart, but in her arms, I could pretend for a little while that everything was fine.

A glass shattered somewhere deep within my mind, and fragments of memory began piecing themselves together, drawing me back through the moments that had led me here. The sensation was disorienting, like falling backwards into memories I'd tried to leave behind. I didn't want to think. For once, I wanted to lose myself in simple pleasure, free from the knots of suspicion. But the pull of my past was too strong, dragging me to Banana Island, to the first day I met Akaneme. Had there been signs of his deception? A tell I'd missed?

I remembered him, hunched over, meticulously scrubbing the car, greeting me with a fractured smile that didn't quite reach his eyes. And then... her. Lying in the boy's quarters, her oversized shirt swallowing her slender frame, loose-fitting jeans hanging low on her hips. She looked... familiar.

Elfreda's warmth anchored me in the present, but I tore myself away from her embrace, the siren spell of comfort snapping. The words escaped me. "It was Candy."

She laughed, a delicate sound that tried to brush my words aside. "What are you talking about? What's wrong?"

"Candy," I repeated, sharper this time. "She was there, in Akaneme's room. My first day back. How does she know him?" I tightened my hold on Elfreda's wrists, feeling the urgency coursing through me. "Do you know him?"

She winced, struggling to pull free. "Dozy, stop…you're hurting me." But I'd had enough of the lies, the pretty diversions. I wanted the truth, raw and unpolished.

Then, a soft beep sounded at the door.

I turned just as Candy stepped in, her hair drawn back, her gaze cool and calculating. She wore dark leather gloves, and something about them struck me as wrong. I took a step forward, but she moved first, her foot slicing through the air, slamming into my chest and sending me sprawling back onto the bed.

Before I could rise, she advanced, her movements swift, merciless. I barely had time to dodge the strike, her gloved fist whistling past my face, close enough for me to feel the force. She was skilled, her kicks controlled and relentless, each strike aiming for a vulnerable spot like the side of my knee, my ribs, my throat. This wasn't street fighting; her training showed in her precision, the calculated way she closed in and retreated.

I forced myself to think past the pain and deflect, shifting my stance and finding an opening to drive my fist into her side. She staggered but recovered instantly, her leg arcing up in a quick, brutal kick that nearly connected with my jaw. I ducked, using her momentum against her to push her off-balance, following up with a knee aimed at her stomach. She grunted, twisting free before I could land another hit.

But as I moved to counter, I noticed the gleam of metal on her gloves. Iron-plated. Again, she swung, and this time, her punch landed squarely on my shoulder, causing immediate, hot pain, like being struck with a hammer. Each blow left a trail of bruises, the weight behind them magnified by the metal.

I gritted my teeth, fighting past the burning ache as I blocked her next hit and drove my elbow into her ribs. She stumbled, her breath catching, and I seized the chance, pushing her back until her shoulders hit the wall. For a moment, I had the upper hand, my hand closing around her wrist as I prepared to subdue her.

But then, Elfreda cried out behind me. I hesitated, glancing back to find her pressed against the far wall, her eyes wide, hands trembling as if she didn't recognize me. That single heartbeat of distraction was all Candy needed.

Her fist slammed into my temple, a brutal hit that sent stars bursting across my vision. I staggered back into the bathroom, loosening my grip just enough for her knee to ram into my gut. The impact doubled me over, and I let out a gasping breath, letting my body go slack as if all the fight had drained out of me. She wasn't convinced. I sensed her circling around me, sizing me up for another hit.

A sharp crack struck the back of my skull. A final warning blow. I swayed, letting my head roll to one side, and allowed my body to collapse in a heap. Shadows blurred the edges of my sight, but I kept just enough focus to watch Candy as she leaned over me, checking for any sign of consciousness. Satisfied, she turned, grabbing the heavy ceramic lid from the water closet, raising it high to finish the job.

"Candy!" Elfreda's voice cut through the haze, sharp and commanding. "He's done. Leave him. We don't have time."

Candy hesitated, her eyes narrowed and lips twisted in doubt, before she finally lowered the lid with a reluctant grunt. "Fine," she spat, "but we better not see him again."

I stayed limp, listening to their footsteps recede, waiting until the door clicked shut. Only then did I let my eyes crack open, the dim light of the bathroom filtering back into focus. Holding onto my head, I took in the surrounding air. There was a unique mixture of perfumes, floral and sweet, lingering like a whispered confession.

CHAPTER 30

I allowed myself a few hours of solid sleep. When morning rolled around, I took my time, savoring a hot shower that washed away the tension from the previous night. Refreshed, I slipped into something more polished. A light gray blazer with a casual cut that framed my shoulders comfortably. Beneath it, a white crew-neck T-shirt, understated but sharp. Dark, well-tailored chinos paired with white low-top sneakers completed the look. I looked myself over in the mirror, noting how I seemed like a man trying to keep cool under the relentless Lagos sun and the scrutiny of those who were watching my every move.

As I adjusted the lapel of my blazer, my eyes fell on my laptop resting on the table. Someone took the Admiral's phone, but the flash drive remained plugged into the USB port. Just as I'd expected. Elfreda had taken it. I'd noticed her observing me with a little too much interest the previous night, her gaze lingering in a way that hinted at more than just curiosity. I didn't want to believe she'd betray me, but my instincts had been nagging me. And Candy? Her involvement was unexpected, though in hindsight, it made perfect sense. Sometimes, once you see the first piece of a puzzle, the rest falls into place.

Just then, my phone buzzed. Calvin.

"I guess you needed the sleep," he said, with a hint of amusement in his voice. "You sold that hit like a pro wrestler."

I chuckled, though my ribs still ached. "I might have faked it, but don't get me wrong, she packed a punch. Probably helped me fall asleep faster."

"You were right about the accomplice. As soon as Elfreda led you out of your room, she made her way in with a keycard to search the place. Left shortly before you returned."

"No doubt alerted by Elfreda," I said. "I'm not surprised she fought me the moment she could. I could tell from the day she met me she didn't like me."

"Oh, you know the accomplice?"

"Goes by Candy. Elfreda's housemate. Any word from Osita?"

"Not yet," Calvin replied. "But Oge is on her way back from the hospital. She will be with you in thirty."

The line went dead.

I glanced at the laptop, feeling the weight of what I'd been avoiding. There was something else I had to do, something I'd kept pushing aside. One thing I'd learned as an insurance fraud investigator was that real progress often required stepping into uncomfortable territory. You can't get to the truth by staying in your comfort zone.

I turned back to my laptop, clicked open the folder, and braced myself as the videos loaded. Each clip was the same. About a dozen of them, each one more explicit than the last. The Admiral was there, while Elfreda taunted and teased, asking for gifts on Slago, that cesspool of financial exploitation masquerading as entertainment. Each time he promised her something extravagant, she'd raise the stakes, inching closer to his wallet, and further into his fantasies.

"Don't forget to do me *dorime* later," she purred in one clip, her eyes glinting.

From my brief dive into Slago culture, I knew *dorime* was slang for when a *gifter* sent massive sums to their favorite host. A ritual of indulgence. These women loved to be pampered, and the sad men who worshipped them were only too willing to oblige.

Six videos in, the tone shifted.

Elfreda wasn't alone this time. Another woman appeared in the frame. She was light-skinned like Elfreda, curvy, but visibly shy, avoiding eye contact with the camera. She sat on Elfreda's lap, hesitant, as though unsure if she belonged there.

"How was your Dubai trip?" the Admiral asked, eyes wide, a needy hunger written all over his face.

"It was fine," she cooed, blowing him a kiss. "Thank you for funding it, papi." Her flirtation seemed to melt the Admiral, a grown man undone by a simple gesture.

"I'll be in Abuja in two weeks," he stammered. "I'll fly you to meet me there."

Elfreda grinned, exchanging a look with the girl on her lap. A look that held secrets. "That would be nice," she replied, her fingers tracing the girl's arm. Then she leaned into the camera. "Do you want to watch us play, papi?"

The Admiral's face trembled with anticipation, his need as raw as it was pathetic. "Yes, baby. Please."

Elfreda glanced at her companion, a sly smile spreading across her lips. "You've been so good to me, papi. So, my girlfriend and I want to give you a little... gift. Are you ready?"

I took a closer look, and it hit me. The girl in the video was Candy. Her shy, almost demure presence was a stark contrast to the tough, hostile persona I'd encountered in real life. In this recording, she was someone else entirely.

I watched them—Elfreda and Candy—come together for the Admiral's entertainment, fulfilling a fantasy as old as it was clichéd. The Admiral's face, positioned in the screen's corner, twisted in blissful agony, savoring every second. I paused the video, realization settling in.

They weren't just housemates. They were lovers.

It explained the bond I'd sensed between them, the fierce loyalty Candy had displayed, and the jealousy of Elfreda's male guests. I'd suspected an attraction, but nothing this explicit. But then another question gnawed at me: Where did Akaneme fit into all this?

— ◆ —

Oge stood by her car outside, her expression a blend of suspicion and faint amusement. She wore a light blue blouse tucked into a flowing white skirt that caught the morning breeze, pairing it with her usual white tennis shoes. A pair of large brown sunglasses shielded her eyes, catching the light as she watched me approach.

At the sight of me, she shook her head knowingly. "I heard you had an eventful night."

I offered a brief smile, but it faded quickly. "Give me a break. How's Dr. Okonkwo?"

"She's stable. We talked for a few minutes."

"Did she think I had something to do with her condition?"

"Possibly, but I disabused her of that idea. I also explained Obidi's involvement. Calvin has a few men looking out for her now. She also positively identified Silas and Akaneme as the two men who came to her house looking for her brother."

I nodded. Confirming suspicions always felt good. "Thank you for doing that. Any word from Osita?"

"He called a little over an hour ago. The ladies stopped by their apartment in Marina, grabbed their luggage, and left almost immediately. They might leave town, but Osita is still following them," she replied.

I nodded, thinking aloud. "I have a hunch about where they're heading. My guess is Akaneme's place."

"The gateman?" She asked, arching a skeptical eyebrow.

I considered it, remembering Akaneme's exaggerated hunched posture, the broken, fake teeth, and his overly animated pidgin, a stark contrast to the polished, English-speaking gangster I'd encountered at Chief Obidi's mansion. The pieces didn't quite fit; there was no way that bumbling gateman act was genuine.

"He's connected to Candy somehow," I said, piecing it together as I spoke. "Elfreda's housemate. There's something between them."

Oge put a thoughtful hand on her chin. "She wasn't on our radar," she murmured, her eyes narrowing as if seeing the problem unfold.

My mind drifted to the previous night when the four of us—me, Osita, Oge, and Calvin—had huddled together, going over all the evidence, brainstorming every angle we could think of. Our plan was iffy, and Oge had made sure to tell us. Judging by the look on her face now, she had more concerns to raise.

"Did you find the documents?" She asked, her gaze turning slightly skeptical.

"I did, actually," I said, trying to sound casual. "They were hidden in the phone's internal memory. I hadn't gotten around to checking it before."

She raised an eyebrow, not buying my nonchalance. "So, they weren't on the flash drive?"

I sighed, rolling my eyes slightly. "Let's move on, Oge."

She shook her head, undeterred. "No, no... So, your entire plan hinged on the flash drive having those documents. And it didn't. You only thought to check the phone at the last minute. What was the backup plan if the documents weren't there?"

I shrugged, trying to deflect. "I'd have bluffed. Acted like I had them."

She gave me a look. "And hoped Elfreda would steal it without checking first?"

I raised my hands in mock surrender. "Look, we put the plan together a few hours before it went live. It was never going to be perfect."

She chuckled, but there was a hint of exasperation there. "You're not exactly making a strong case for yourself as a private investigator."

I snorted. "I was never a private investigator. I worked on insurance fraud cases. This... murder, conspiracy... intrigue... it's not my area. The most exciting cases I handled were things like catching cybercriminals, staged carjackings or people setting their own homes on fire for the payout."

Her smile faded, her face turning thoughtful. "This Akaneme, he's working for Chief Obidi?"

"It sure seemed like it," I replied, memories of his smirk and smooth demeanor at Obidi's mansion flashing through my mind.

"Did Mmachi know?"

Her question stopped me short. I hadn't considered that. If Mmachi knew about Akaneme, then she'd been playing me from the start. But if she didn't... it opened up a whole new set of questions. Either way, the answer to that question could crack this case wide open, and I felt it would reveal an even darker side to this twisted game.

Oge's phone buzzed, interrupting our conversation. She answered. "Osita? Are they still together? Yeah, he's here. Okay." She shot me a sharp look as she handed me the phone.

"Odogwu," I said. "You got something for me?"

"Alobam," Osita's voice came through, low and brimming with the kind of excitement only he could muster when on the hunt. "They've been running around since morning. They first stopped at a local market, then picked up something at a travel agency in Ikoyi. Now, they're holed up with some guy at a house in Ifako."

Akaneme. I'd guessed as much. "Text me the address," I replied, my mind already racing through the possibilities. "I'm on my way."

I ended the call, returning the phone to Oge. "I need you to do me a favor. Dig up any information you can find that might link Mmachi to Chief Obidi. If you can't turn up anything on the usual channels, see if Detective Inspector Bayo might lend a hand."

Her brow furrowed slightly, a flash of doubt crossing her face. "Are you sure we can trust him?"

I hesitated. "No, not entirely. But I trust your instincts. If you sense he's playing us, pull out. I'll handle the rest."

She gave a determined nod, her expression softening just slightly. "Be careful, Dozy. This thing… it's starting to feel bigger than all of us."

I forced a wry smile, trying to shake off the unease that had started to settle in my gut. With that, I turned and headed for the car, my mind already planning the confrontation ahead.

— ◆ —

I arrived in Ifako as quickly as I could, maneuvering through the winding roads and crowded streets of this unpolished part of Lagos. Unlike the opulent facades of Banana Island or the bustling commercial heartbeat of Marina, Ifako had a rougher charm. Here, the streets were alive with market stalls, hawkers calling out their prices for roasted corn and fried plantains. Keke Napeps weaved in and out of lanes, nearly colliding with each other, while yellow danfos lined the roads, loading passengers and blaring their horns. The air carried a faint mix of petrol fumes, street food, and the humid scent of rain lingering from the night before. This was Lagos stripped down to its essentials. No pretenses, just people grinding and surviving.

Osita was waiting by the gate, leaning casually against the wall, a smug smirk tugging at his lips. He looked less flamboyant than usual, blending in with the environment in a muted button-down and jeans, though the glint in his eye suggested he was just as ready for action as ever.

"Been busy?" I asked, stepping up to him.

He chuckled, nodding toward the house, a two-story structure hiding behind a high, imposing wall crowned with broken glass, a common sight in neighborhoods where everyone knew you couldn't trust anyone. "What do you think's going on in there?"

I allowed a wry smirk, the pieces already falling into place in my mind. "I can only imagine." I glanced at Osita, noting the dangerous excitement in his eyes. If things were about to go sideways, an unhinged Osita was precisely the backup I wanted. "Shall we?"

Without another word, we moved in. Osita got to work on the security gate, a thick, rusted iron barrier built to withstand Lagos' reputation for break-ins and burglary but no match for The Diamond Ballot's owner. With a practiced flick of his wrist and an assortment of picks that seemed to appear from thin air, he went to work, his fingers moving with the precision of a seasoned locksmith. In seconds, the gate clicked open, and he turned his attention to the front door, cracking it just as smoothly.

Once inside, we found ourselves in a dimly lit living room. The furniture was minimal with only bare essentials and nothing that screamed wealth or status. A flickering bulb cast shadows across the cracked walls, and the faint scent of mildew clung to the air. But our attention quickly went upstairs.

Osita moved to go up, but I raised a hand, stopping him. I wanted to hear what they were saying. Information was power, and I wasn't about to let a careless move blow our cover.

"Freda, you were supposed to poison him," came Akaneme's voice, low and insistent, laced with frustration. Hearing it sent a chill down my spine, but I forced myself to stay calm. "Chief Obidi is willing to reward me handsomely for getting rid of that fool."

Osita shot me a sideways glance, eyebrows raised in disbelief. His expression said it all: *What the fuck?* I gave him a slight nod, acknowledging the narrow escape I'd had with Elfreda back at the hotel. She'd been inches away from carrying out this very plan. I made a mental note to be a damn sight more careful from here on out.

Then Elfreda's voice drifted down, with a hint of disinterest. "We already stand to make two hundred thousand dollars for getting him the documents. There's no need for any more bloodshed."

Just then, Candy's voice cut in, full of suspicion. "Are you sure you haven't fallen for him?" Her tone was sharp, almost accusatory. "I always suspected you might. AK, I almost finished him. She stopped me!"

Elfreda scoffed, but her confidence faltered for just a second. "I'm not so easily seduced, C. I'm the one doing the seducing." Her words might have sounded strong, but there was a hesitation that gave her away, an uncertainty that belied the cool exterior she'd tried to maintain.

I turned to Osita, gesturing toward the stairs. He nodded, his face taking on a serious glint. With a steadying breath, we ascended, ready for whatever lay behind that door, prepared to confront the tangled mess of lies, betrayal, and danger waiting just beyond our reach.

That was enough for me. The surge of adrenaline coursing through my body gave me the strength to kick the door open, wood splintering as it crashed against the wall. Inside, the scene was pure chaos. Elfreda, Candy, and Akaneme all scrambled to cover themselves as I stormed in, followed by Osita.

Akaneme, completely naked, made a wild lunge toward the dresser—no doubt going for his gun—but Osita was on him like a predator on prey. One swift kick to the mouth sent Akaneme sprawling to the floor, blood gushing from his lips. He planted his Beretta firmly against the side of his head.

"Mister man," Osita said, pressing the barrel harder against Akaneme's skull, "if you try any rubbish, I will blast you now."

Akaneme's hands shot up in surrender, the fight gone from him as quickly as it had appeared.

Elfreda and Candy huddled beneath a blanket that barely covered their naked bodies, a pitiful attempt to shield themselves from our gaze. They looked vulnerable, uncomfortable, but I wasn't here to humiliate anyone. I bent down, gathering their scattered clothes from the floor, and tossed the bundle in their direction. They scrambled to get dressed, movements hurried and tense, finally settling down with the weight of defeat etched on their faces.

I sat down on a chair by the dresser, my eyes flicking between Elfreda and Candy, occasionally glancing at Akaneme bleeding on the floor. This wasn't a moment for pity. This was a moment of reckoning. There was something almost methodical about the way I painted a fuller picture in my mind. The details now crystalizing, coming together like the final pieces of a puzzle.

Candy stared at me, her eyes narrowed into a venomous scowl, clearly furious that I'd bested them.

My attention shifted to Elfreda, who sat there silently, her eyes cast downward as if hoping to escape the inevitable. "You should know," I began, "I never trusted you." I paused, allowing the tension in the room to build as everyone, even Akaneme, now struggled to keep their breath steady. I had played my cards right so far, and now it was time to lay the rest on the table.

I leaned back, giving them all a long, hard look. The room felt stifling, thick with tension, each of them on edge. Candy scowling, Akaneme on the floor bleeding with Osita's gun pressed firmly against his head, and Elfreda trying hard not to meet my eyes. Perfect.

I crossed my arms, letting a tense silence fill the room, before I finally spoke. "So, let's start at the beginning, shall we?"

My eyes locked onto Elfreda's, and I saw the flash of guilt she tried to bury. "Admiral Alex Maduagu, a revered figure in Nigerian high society, known for his integrity and commanding presence. His marriage to Mmachi, once a power couple's union, began to crumble when her corruption became public knowledge. The scandal tarnished their image, but that was only the beginning."

"Somewhere along the line, Alex uncovered evidence of Mmachi's illicit dealings. Evidence that didn't just implicate her but also exposed a web of corruption that ensnared nearly everyone in the political elite. This wasn't blackmail; it was insurance; her leverage and final ace in the event her allies turned against her. Mmachi had built her empire on power and manipulation, but Alex had found the one thing that could bring it all crashing down."

I paused, watching their reactions. No one moved.

"Now, here's what bothered me. This wasn't the type of man who'd just run off with incriminating evidence for a quick payday. Everything I knew about Admiral Maduagu suggested that he, despite his sexual weaknesses, was a man of principles, someone who'd stare down the most ruthless dictator without flinching. He defied Abacha, for God's sake. So why did he steal the documents?"

A flicker of understanding crossed Elfreda's face, but she kept quiet.

"He felt depressed. Broken. And in his lowest moments, he stumbled onto Slago Live, a place where desperate souls meet even more desperate souls. He needed a distraction, maybe even a bit of comfort." I looked directly at Elfreda. "That's where you come in." Her shoulders sank. Candy's face twisted in irritation, but she stayed silent.

"You saw a man in need, and he became just another meal ticket to you, didn't he?" I asked, my voice unmasking my disdain. "But something shifted the moment you got on that first video call with him, didn't it? On Slago, everyone hides behind the veil of their anonymous usernames, a façade of mystery and detachment. But once you saw his face, you recognized him. Admiral Alex Maduagu. A man of status.

Wealth. Power. And in that instant, your approach changed. You saw an opportunity; a way to climb higher. So, you hooked him," I went on. "But it wasn't just you, was it, Elfreda? No, you were in a polyamorous relationship. A twisted love triangle. You had Candy, your loyal and jealous girlfriend. And you had him." I gestured to Akaneme. "An ambitious man forced to eat the scraps of the underworld, desperate to claw his way into something bigger." Akaneme's mouth twisted into a sneer, but he didn't say a word. Osita's gun pressing into his skull might have had something to do with that.

"Things escalated. Elfreda drew him deeper, not just with promises of love, but with a vision, a prophecy from the so-called Prophetess, Mother C, which made him believe you were the woman for him. A match made in heaven, right?" I chuckled darkly. "Of course, that prophecy came at a price, didn't it, Candy? A little bribe slipped to the good prophetess to make it all seem real. It was absurd, but the poor fool fell for it. You had him."

Candy's jaw tightened, defiance flashing in her eyes. "You don't know anything," she shot.

"But that wasn't enough for you, Akaneme, was it?" I said, my gaze turning to him. "Elfreda here became the Admiral's most trusted confidante. At some point, he must have told her about these incriminating documents. So, you and Candy saw an opportunity to make money. But most importantly, you saw an opportunity to impress Chief Obidi, maybe secure a better position in his organization. And the way to do that? Get those documents." I turned to the ladies again. "Then you lured Alex to Lagos with promises of the time of his life. A chance to live out his fantasies with you two. The lure of a threesome was too good for him to resist, no matter how 'born again' he'd become."

I took a step closer to Akaneme, enjoying the look of discomfort on his face. "But you got sloppy, didn't you? You tried to rob him with the help of your friend, Silas, the receptionist of the Lorel Luxury Hotel. Only problem was, the Admiral was more resourceful than you thought, and he got away."

Osita nudged Akaneme with the gun, urging him to speak. Finally, Akaneme muttered, "To hell with that Silas."

Osita smacked him on the back of the head. "Don't speak ill of the dead, fool."

"And that's when the Admiral got paranoid," I continued. "He decided to hide the documents somewhere safe, so he gave them to the other person he could trust. His sister, Dr. Onyeka Okonkwo. Now, I know you were desperate. So desperate that you and Silas tried to shake down Dr. Onyeka. Of course, I didn't know at the time, but she told me about you two. Two terrifying men who showed up asking about her brother. You wanted to know if he'd handed the documents over to her. But she convinced you she had no contact with him."

Candy scoffed, trying to look unimpressed. "You're just connecting dots that don't exist."

I ignored her. "Before that, the Admiral went on to the yacht for the Governor's wife's birthday soiree, where I met him for the first time. It was also the first time I saw you, Elfreda."

I could see Elfreda's face soften with a hint of regret.

"Then we met again at Alakija's luncheon. He wasn't very clear, but it was obvious he was in pain from an earlier encounter. When I saw his body, the coroner told me he had a bruised rib from a few nights before he died. That was you guys. And that night, he returned to the hotel. And here's where things got messy. Now, I wouldn't have pieced this together if you hadn't come after me, Candy." I shot her a pointed look. "Your perfume has a very distinct lavender scent. Elfreda's is more vanilla. I smelled that combination in the hotel room where I found the Admiral's body. The same mix I smelled when you attacked me. It told me everything I needed to know. It was pure luck, but I'll take luck any day."

Candy's face paled, her confidence evaporating.

"So, I figured you were both there that night," I continued. I turned to Elfreda. "Tell me what happened," I said, softer now, almost coaxing.

Elfreda swallowed hard, her voice trembling. "Yes... we were there. We'd... been together, and then Candy got pushy. She started demanding the documents. Alex was confused, asking why she cared. Then Akaneme showed up. Silas must have given him the key."

"Then what?" I pressed.

Her eyes dropped to the floor. "Akaneme started hitting him, trying to force him to tell us where the documents were. But Alex wouldn't break. He told us that only one person knew where they were..." She hesitated.

I leaned in, demanding the truth. "Who?"

She looked up at me, her eyes haunted. "You. He said you were the only one who could figure it out."

I felt a strange pang. A mix of respect and bitterness. The Admiral, even in his last moments, had chosen to taunt his enemies with the idea that I held the key. Maybe he thought I was smart enough to figure it all out, or maybe he just wanted to throw one last wrench in the works.

"He knew he was done," I murmured. "So he laughed, didn't he? He mocked you."

Akaneme's eyes flared with anger, and Elfreda nodded. "He was... ready to die. I tried to stop Akaneme, but he was too far gone. He shot him."

"You bitch!" spat Akaneme. His outburst was rewarded with a swift kick to the gut. "Shut your fucking mouth!" Osita commanded.

I turned back to Elfreda. "After the Admiral was dead, Akaneme wanted me gone too, didn't he?"

She nodded, a tear slipping down her cheek. "He tipped off the police. Chief Obidi was supposed to send one of his men to collect you, find the documents, and then... then..."

"Kill me," I finished, the cold reality settling in.

"Yes." Her voice was barely a whisper. "Akaneme knew about Chief Obidi's grudge against you. He figured that if he couldn't get his hands on the documents himself, he'd still win favor by handing you over to Obidi."

I nodded, processing her confession. "In his paranoia, Akaneme then sent Silas to take care of another loose end. Onyeka, the Admiral's sister. She had seen your faces and could easily identify you."

Elfreda buried her face in her hands, her whole body shaking with the weight of what she'd done.

I stepped back, feeling the surge of righteous anger simmering beneath my calm exterior. "You thought you could toy with a man's life for some quick cash, that you could walk away unscathed."

Akaneme, who had been silent until this point, spat at the floor, his voice venomous. "Enough of this Sherlock Holmes shit. Tell us what you want."

I raised an eyebrow, surprised by the eloquence of his outburst despite the venom in his tone. Before I could respond, Osita stepped forward and delivered a swift kick to Akaneme's face, his boot connecting with a sickening thud.

"This man," Osita growled, standing over Akaneme, who was now holding his bleeding mouth. "You don't want to know what I can do if you open that mouth of yours without permission again."

Akaneme groaned in pain, nodding silently, blood dripping from his lip. His arrogance had crumbled just like the others.

I stood up, putting both hands in my pockets. "Your plan was simple," I said. "Effective, even. But you made a fatal mistake." I paused, letting the words sink in. "I was ready to walk away. I found the Admiral, and whether he was dead or alive, didn't matter to me."

I drew a long breath, forcing the anger down as I looked at Elfreda. "I even believed you were with him for a green card and I was fine with that. If anyone understands what it takes to get out of here, it's me. But your mistake..." My voice dropped. "...was fucking with me."

Not long after, the three of them were being loaded into a police car. Elfreda walked past me, her gaze briefly meeting mine before she looked away, her expression unreadable. She was taken by a rather imposing and well-built policeman into a black SUV on her own. Getting the VIP treatment even to prison.

Akaneme, his face swollen from Osita's well-placed kicks, limped along with two officers holding him up. It was Candy who lingered, her eyes burning with venomous hatred as she stopped in front of me. For a moment, I thought she might try something reckless, maybe a swift kick with those deadly legs of hers.

Instead, she leaned in slightly. "Obidi knew about the documents," she hissed.

"What?" I blinked, the weight of her words hitting me like a freight train.

"Long before the Admiral ever told Freda about them," she continued, her tone dripping with bitterness. "Obidi put the word out through his network. Two hundred thousand dollars to anyone who could find the documents. He knew about them much earlier than any of us did."

Before I could respond, a policeman shoved her forward, forcing her to move. She shot me one last glare over her shoulder before disappearing into the vehicle. I stood frozen, her words echoing in my mind.

I retrieved my phone and called Calvin. "Bro," I said. "I need a favor. Put me in contact with the Director-General."

CHAPTER 31

The docks at Marina were silent, save for the soft lapping of water against the pilings and the faint scent of petrol in the air. The oppressive humidity of Lagos at night clung to everything, but even that couldn't weigh down the tension that filled the space.

A black Mercedes-Benz SUV rolled up, flanked by two other sedans with blacked-out windows. From the front passenger seat of the SUV, a man in a black suit and rimless glasses stepped out, his eyes scanning the area like a hawk assessing its territory. The man was methodical, making sure no one else was present before moving toward the back door of the SUV. As the window rolled down, the familiar curl of cigar smoke escaped into the night. There sat Chief Obidi, a red chief's cap on his head and a cigar lit between his fingers, its ember glowing faintly in the darkness.

"Akaneme isn't here?" Chief Obidi's gravelly voice inquired, the tip of his cigar lighting up as he inhaled.

The suited man shook his head in response.

That was my cue. I stepped out from the shadows of an empty shipping container. "Chief!" I called loudly enough to carry across the lot. "We need to talk."

I was dressed sharply in a double-breasted black pinstripe suit that hugged my frame with precise tailoring. A crisp white shirt peeked beneath, paired with a sleek black tie, while a white pocket square and a single red rose on my lapel added a bold touch of elegance. Completing the ensemble was a white fedora tilted slightly forward, casting a shadow over my face, giving me an air of mystique.

Immediately, more men stepped out of the vehicles, firearms raised and aimed squarely at me. I raised both hands slowly, palms open in a gesture of surrender, keeping my expression calm, even indifferent. My right hand held a phone, which I made sure was plainly visible.

As soon as their eyes locked onto the device, I noticed a flicker of unease ripple through the group. Chief Obidi's face tightened for a moment, then morphed into something unreadable. He opened the door of his car and stepped out, his movements deliberate, his piercing gaze fixed on the phone in my hand.

"Chidozie," he greeted. He gave me the once-over, then raised an eyebrow. "What is this you're wearing?"

I smirked, brushing off the tension in the air. "I've got a party to attend after this," I replied nonchalantly. "The theme is the Roaring Twenties."

Obidi's lips curved in a small, knowing smile. "Alakija's party," he said, the mention of the name adding an edge to his tone. His sharp eyes darted back to the phone in my hand. "Is that what I think it is?"

I took a step closer, just enough for him to hear me clearly without having to shout. "And it's yours," I said, "if you leave me alone. I want to walk these streets without fearing you're around every corner."

Obidi let out a low, amused chuckle. "I would say that's a more than acceptable peace offering." He extended his hand, palm open. "Give it to me."

I hesitated, eyes narrowing slightly as I studied him. "You said something when we last met, Chief."

He frowned, clearly annoyed at the delay. "I said a lot. Now, give me the phone."

I smirked, my grip on the phone tightening. "You said I was better off driving Uber in DC. Said it was a safer job." I paused, watching the shift in his expression. "How did you know I was an Uber driver, and how did you know I was here on a job?"

There was a beat of silence. Chief Obidi's men exchanged uncertain glances, their fingers twitching on their triggers. And then, Obidi chuckled again, this time with more weight behind it. "Smart boy," he said, with a touch of pride in his voice. "Always been a smart boy."

"Zarah Holdings Limited," I said, watching his face for any flicker of recognition or surprise. "That's one of the shell companies used to move dirty money. And guess who's listed as business partners on deals involving this Zarah Holdings? You and a Ginika Mofe. I had a friend look into it for me. Before she married the Admiral, Mmachi's name was Mmachi Ginikanwa Okeke, and her mother's maiden name was Oluwatoyin Mofe. Not exactly the most creative alias, is it?"

Chief Obidi's expression remained unreadable, but I could see a muscle twitch in his jaw.

"The documents on this phone," I continued. "They tie you and Mmachi together in a way that's impossible to deny. Years of shady deals, bribes, money laundering, all funneled through that company. Every layer of corruption, carefully hidden under the façade of Zarah Holdings, is now on full display."

He scoffed, trying to play it off. "You think you've got me all figured out, do you?"

I held his gaze, unflinching. "Zarah Holdings is a ticking time bomb. And I'm holding the fuse."

Chief Obidi's amusement faded, his cigar dangling loosely from his lips as his eyes sharpened. "Are you trying to blackmail me, Chidozie?" His voice was low, dangerous. "In case you've forgotten, there are several guns pointed at your head."

I met his gaze, unflinching. "No blackmail, Chief. I just want to know the truth. Did Mmachi tell you I was coming back to Lagos?"

Obidi took a slow, deliberate drag from his cigar, considering his next move. Finally, he let the smoke trail out, his eyes cold. "Admiral Alex Maduagu absconded with Mmachi's documents. She contacted me to find him and retrieve them, but he was too connected. I couldn't bring any harm to him without enraging certain…personalities. At least, not directly."

I clenched my fists, the anger simmering just below the surface. "And how do I come in?"

"Well, I got you your job," he said, "I recommended Mmachi hired you."

I raised an eyebrow, but before I could speak, he pressed on. "The way you dealt with your aunties. I'll admit, it impressed me. Overnight you went from a loudmouthed student activist to a shadowy godfather pulling strings from afar. I trusted you would be able to handle it. My only condition was that you came back. I even paid for your plane ticket."

What I did to my aunts—something I've kept buried—was meant to stay a secret. But in certain circles, secrets never stayed still. They moved, whispered across tables, and traded like currency. Circles with men like the Chief on one side of the law, and Onuoha on the other. I wasn't sure it was a reputation I wanted. Maybe it was one I needed.

His words hit me like a punch to the gut. My chest tightened as I realized. "So, Mmachi gave me up," I murmured to myself.

Obidi nodded, his grin widening. "I let you play detective, but you were always going to end up in my hands. I merely decided to wait and see. If you had found the documents, I could have killed two birds with one stone. I didn't have much faith in Akaneme and his stupid girls. You were the smart and resourceful one."

The weight of everything came crashing down. All the manipulation, all the deceit. It was possible that Mmachi had never intended to pay me. I was the pawn in a larger game, one that had been orchestrated by the person I thought I was eluding.

"And by getting the documents, you save her and yourself from exposure?"

Chief Obidi guffawed. "What stupid exposure? No, with the documents, I gain even more power. You've seen the names in there. It gave Mmachi the opportunity to live anywhere outside the country without fear of government retribution. Imagine what I could do with that kind of power. She never told me what was in the documents. If not for Akaneme's little girlfriend, I never would have known."

I exhaled slowly, regaining control over the torrent of emotions swirling in my mind. Then, I looked up, a smirk tugging at my lips. "You know," I said, "I'm so lucky I made a new deal."

Obidi's expression changed, his brow furrowing in confusion. "What new deal?"

"You recently told me it pays to have good friends," I said. "I couldn't have said it better myself."

Obidi's impatience showed in the way he took another long drag from his cigar, smoke curling like a warning. "My friend, will you speak up? What are you talking about?" he snapped.

"I recently made the acquaintance of a man with considerable influence," I said. "A man who represents the interests of men and women of even greater influence."

Obidi's face tightened. For a moment he looked puzzled, then the name settled on him. "O... Onuoha," he said.

"Something tells me the people he answers to won't be thrilled to hear you tried to get leverage over them," I added.

Obidi swallowed hard, then smirked as if to steady himself. "And who's going to tell them? You, Chidozie?"

I spread my hands in mock surrender. "No, Chief." I reached out and tilted the phone toward him; this time the screen was lit and an active call was on. His smirk froze. I pressed speaker.

Voices exploded from the handset, urgent and layered in different tongues. One barked, **"An gama da kai a wannan ƙasa"**—*You are finished in this country.* Another hissed, **"Bịa, Obidi. Ị ga-anwụ taa!"**—*Come, Obidi. You will die today.* A third screamed, **"Kò ní dáa fún ẹ"**—*It shall not be well with you.*

The cigar dropped from Obidi's fingers and smoldered into ash on the concrete. For the first time, the practiced composure cracked. He tried to laugh it off. It was a small, brittle sound. But the tremor in his hands betrayed him.

"Never speak so plainly to a man with a phone," I said.

As if on cue, the deafening wail of police sirens filled the air, accompanied by the blinding flash of red and blue lights cutting through the darkness. Within seconds, an army of police vehicles had surrounded the docks. Officers poured out, weapons drawn, shouting commands as they closed in on Obidi's men like a swarm of hornets. I took a step back, letting the chaos unfold, then slipped into the shadows.

But I wasn't the only one moving under cover. Out of the corner of my eye, I caught sight of Chief Obidi, flanked by one of his hulking henchmen, darting between two rows of stacked shipping containers, attempting to escape through the maze of steel.

I took off after them, weaving through the narrow passages, the pounding of my footsteps swallowed by the clang of metal as I closed in on them. Obidi's henchman turned, spotting me, and charged with a growl. He swung a thick arm at my head. I ducked, feeling the wind of his fist whip past my face, then retaliated with a punch to his gut, feeling the hard impact as he staggered back.

But he recovered fast, swinging again, this time connecting with my jaw. My vision momentarily blurred as I stumbled back, but I steadied myself, anger flaring. I grabbed the closest weapon within reach: a rusted iron bar lying by the edge of a container. I swung it in a low arc, hitting him hard in the shin. He yelped in pain, dropping to one knee. Seizing the opening, I drove my elbow down into the back of his neck, sending him sprawling forward.

Just as I thought I had him, a shot rang out. I barely had time to react, diving sideways as the bullet whizzed past me. Obidi was standing a few feet away, pistol raised, his expression cold and unflinching. Before I could scramble to my feet, he aimed again, his eyes locked on me.

In the split second, I threw myself backward just as Obidi pulled the trigger. The henchman, still struggling to stand, took the shot meant for me. He collapsed with a pained gasp, his eyes wide with shock.

Obidi took a step back, his face twisted in anger as he targeted me once more, but suddenly there was a shout from behind.

"Drop it, Chief!"

I glanced over my shoulder to see Bayo and Calvin advancing, guns drawn, their faces grim and determined. They wore bulletproof vests, their figures imposing as they closed in.

Obidi hesitated, his eyes darting between me and the officers. Bayo's voice cut through the tension. "It's over, Chief. Put the gun down now."

For a moment, it looked like he might try to make a final desperate move. But with a resigned scowl, he let the gun fall from his grip, the clatter of metal against concrete echoing in the stillness.

Calvin stepped forward, cuffing Obidi's wrists with swift efficiency, and Bayo moved to secure the area. I took a deep breath, steadying myself as the reality of the moment settled in. Obidi's empire, the years of corruption and bloodshed, all brought down to this single, shattering defeat.

Detective Inspector Bayo approached me, his bulletproof vest strapped tightly. He turned to Obidi, who was now in cuffs, his face a mask of anger and begrudging respect.

"Chief Obidi," Bayo said. "You're under arrest."

Obidi sneered. "For what?"

Bayo glanced at me. I met his eyes and smirked, satisfied. I tossed him the phone. "That contains everything," I said. "Every dirty dealing, every corrupt transaction he's had with

Mmachi Alex-Maduagu. I'm sure you'll find enough there to bury him."

Obidi's eyes flashed with fury, but there was something else too. Admiration. He stared at me, his jaw tight. "You think you've won? Have you forgotten I'm not the only one implicated by those documents? You think they'll let them see the light of day? Are you mad?"

I stepped closer. "You've said it many times. I'm a smart boy. I know I've won."

The police led Chief Obidi away, his once untouchable reign crumbling before him.

Bayo turned to me, lowering his weapon. "Thank you for your help," he said. "This better be enough to put him away."

I nodded. "It will be."

Bayo smirked. "I'm not the kind of cop you think I am, you know."

I chuckled. "You punched me in public and claimed there was nothing anyone could do about it."

Bayo shrugged. "It was a fact. At least now I'm trying to make things right." He looked at me curiously. "What's next for you?"

I took a deep breath, feeling the freedom I hadn't felt in years. "I have family to visit," I said.

He eyed my outfit with a raised eyebrow. "Is there a reason you're dressed like Clark Gable?"

I guffawed, shaking my head. "Detective, I was pretty sure I was going to stay pissed at you, but knowing you can name-drop Clark Gable just earned you a pass."

My gaze shifted to Chief Obidi, now sitting sullenly in the back of a police vehicle, his hands cuffed and his aura of invincibility shattered. "I needed him to know," I said, "that I don't take him seriously anymore."

The detective smirked. "That's one way to make a statement."

I adjusted my cufflinks and gave Obidi one last glance before turning to leave. "Now, if you'll excuse me, I have a billionaire heiress' invitation to honor."

Without waiting for an answer, I turned my back. Calvin fell in beside me, our shoes ticking down the dock as we left the stink of the water and Obidi behind. Or so I told myself.

A shout split the air. "What do you mean he wasn't on the force?" Bayo was carving up a uniform at the gate. He spun on me, face drenched in sweat. "The 'policeman' who took Elfreda Bassey was not a police officer. He drove a black Prado. Tinted windows and no plates."

My stomach dropped.

"Elfreda," he said. "She's gone."

EPILOGUE

I spent two blissful weeks back in Enugu with my mother and sisters to make up for my previous brief visit. Convincing them that the bruises scattered across my body were from a minor accident was no easy feat. It was a delicate dance, and I had to perform it flawlessly to keep their worries at bay, especially my mother who I know did not believe me and just chose not to press me. What followed was pure bliss. After everything I'd been through, I craved my family's presence more than I could ever express. Being back home, free from fear, paranoia, and the constant tug of hidden agendas, felt like I was finally regaining a piece of myself I hadn't realized was missing.

Meanwhile, Candy and Akaneme remained in police custody as the weight of evidence against them pushed the wheels of justice forward. Police recovered the murder weapon, a Beretta 92, from Akaneme's home. As if the case needed further reinforcement, Dr. Onyeka Okonkwo positively identified Akaneme and Silas as the men who had sought out her brother and confirmed that Silas was the one who shot her. With these revelations, Akaneme now faced life behind bars for murder and attempted murder, while

Candy awaited trial on charges of complicity, blackmail, and conspiracy. They'd dug their graves, and there was no climbing out.

Still no sign of Elfreda. I wondered if I would ever see or hear from her again. I wasn't even sure how upset I was that she had gotten away somehow. I hadn't trusted her from the start so her betrayal wasn't much of a surprise. But my pride was hurt. I made a mental note to find her someday. But I was in no hurry.

My family saw me off at Akanu Ibiam International Airport, Enugu. I'm not one for tearful goodbyes, but I lingered at the gate longer than I should've, trying to memorize their faces before the PA system chased me down the jetway. I flew into Lagos and holed up two more nights at the Opal Heights, courtesy of Lola. She'd taken a shine to me and wouldn't take no for an answer. The spa knocked the road out of my bones and the noise out of my head. I felt at peace again.

Osita and Oge took me to the Murtala Muhammed International Airport in Lagos. Calvin had pulled some strings to get them access to the gate. We spent those hours laughing, reminiscing, and, true to form, studiously avoiding any mention of how much we'd miss each other.

Osita, as usual, wore something flashy but toned down by his standards. It was a brightly patterned shirt under a tailored blazer, a hint of his usual flamboyance. He laughed loudly at one of Oge's jokes, his face full of life, but my mind wandered as I looked at him. He would keep living dangerously; that much was certain, and it gnawed at me. I worried that one day, a call would come, and it would be about him ending up on the wrong side of a gun. But as much as his lifestyle made me uneasy, I'd long since accepted who he was. Osita was always going to play with fire; it was in his nature. Still, he was my friend, for better or worse.

Oge, in contrast, was a calming presence. I didn't worry about her. She was both grounded and sharp. The next time I returned, I was certain I'd be coming back for her wedding. The thought made me smile. At last, I could look forward to such moments without the shadow of Chief Obidi looming over me.

As the boarding call echoed through the terminal, I stood to gather my things. Just as I was about to head toward the gate, a man in a gray suit approached us. It was Calvin. "Someone would like a word with you, man," he said.

I understood immediately and followed him without saying a word. He led me to a private lounge, and there, seated like some kind of royalty in another finely woven deep-blue senator outfit, was Peter Onuoha. The subtle embroidery on his collar and cuffs caught the light as he looked up at me with that infuriatingly satisfied smirk, a look that told me he thought he had orchestrated this moment to perfection.

"Mr. Dozy," he greeted, his voice smooth but laced with mockery, "leaving us before we could finish our arrangement? The phone you handed over to the police didn't have the complete information we needed."

I took a deep breath, walking toward him slowly. "Thank you for letting me have these last two weeks," I said. "I needed them."

He nodded, acknowledging my words with a glint of warning in his eyes. "I assumed you were aware that you were being watched."

"I'm more conscious of tails these days," I replied, reaching into my jacket's inner pocket and pulling out a portable SSD. "The phone I gave Detective Inspector Bayo was sufficient to take down Chief Obidi. Everything else? It's in here."

Peter's hand reached for the SSD, but I held it back just enough to remind him who held the leverage here. He smiled thinly. "Naturally," he said. "You'd prefer I honor my end of the bargain."

I handed the SSD to Calvin, who plugged it into his laptop and began verifying its contents. After a few moments, he gave Peter a nod of confirmation. Satisfied, Peter reached into his pocket, pulled out his phone, and tapped a few keys. My phone buzzed shortly after. I checked the notification. Two hundred thousand dollars transferred into my US bank account. My fee. The sum Mmachi owed me, plus a lot extra for the trouble. It wasn't a fortune compared to what the government stood to recover, but it was more than enough for me.

The sight of that number brought a surge of satisfaction. I glanced at Calvin, sharing a brief, triumphant look before turning back to Onuoha. "And Chief Obidi?" I asked.

"He's never leaving prison," Peter replied, his gaze dropping to the SSD. "He thought he could control the narrative, hold on to power with this information. But he crossed too many lines. Ticked off the wrong chaps." He looked up at me, a glint of menace in his eyes. "You didn't by any chance make a copy of these files, did you? Your relentless sense of justice wouldn't have driven you to, say, slip a copy to the press?"

He stepped closer, his gaze hardening.

I shook my head. "I was recently reminded of Umaru Dikko," I replied. "Waking up in a crate isn't on my bucket list. I know what you're capable of."

This made Peter chuckle. He adjusted his cuffs and looked at me appraisingly. "You know, we could use someone like you in the Service," he said casually. "Your friend seems to think so too." He nodded toward Calvin.

I glanced at Calvin, who gave a subtle nod of encouragement. But I chuckled, shaking my head. "I appreciate the offer, but I'm done playing in the shadows."

Peter's eyes held a glimmer of something. Maybe disappointment, maybe just calculation. "You could go far in this line of work," he said, as if extending one last invitation.

I smiled. "I've got a family to think about."

He shrugged as though my refusal were inconsequential. "Suit yourself." He extended his hand, and I shook it firmly but briefly. "On behalf of the Presidency, thank you for your service." Then, with a nod of appreciation to Calvin, I turned to leave, only to stop myself. I looked at him over my shoulder. "Were they able to locate Elfreda Bassey?"

Once again, as if unbothered, Peter shrugged. "The girl was more resourceful than she led on," he said. "Our poor departed Admiral wasn't the only man caught in her seductive web. If I can't determine who helped her escape, it means I'm not allowed to know. Which means…"

"It's above your pay grade," I finished. Peter shrugged again.

"You're free to hang around for a while longer. You could make finding her your new case? I cannot guarantee you wouldn't be stepping on a few big toes, however."

I thought for a few minutes. Remembered the statuesque young lady from Calabar who had played all of us from the beginning. My very own Irene Adler. "Some other time, maybe," I said and left the lounge, heading back to the gate where Osita and Oge were waiting.

As I rejoined them, I turned to Osita. "I'll pay you for your services, as promised," I said with a grin. "And Oge, count on a generous donation to your nonprofit."

They exchanged a playful look before laughing, and just as Calvin joined us, we all shared a warm group hug. Our own quiet farewell.

As I finally stood at the boarding gate, I felt a weight lift. Nigeria would always be home, but for now, I was ready to leave it behind. There was still one last thing to take care of, one last piece of unfinished business lingering in the back of my mind. But as I took a deep breath and walked toward the plane, I knew that whatever it was, I'd face it on my terms.

— ◆ —

I stood before the imposing wooden door of Mmachi Alex-Maduagu's opulent Northwest DC home, my knuckles throbbing from the series of sharp knocks I'd just delivered. The cool fall air should have calmed me, but it didn't. Nothing could. I could feel the heat of everything that had led me to this moment simmering beneath the surface, a volatile mix of anger, frustration, and, perhaps, the faintest hint of triumph. This was it. The lies, the betrayals, the deaths. It all came down to this.

The door swung open, and Adaora appeared, her scowl etched deeply into her youthful face. She sized me up, a flicker of irritation crossing her gaze.

"You again?" she muttered, not bothering to hide her disdain.

"Is your mother home?"

She didn't bother answering. She simply turned, leaving the door ajar. I took a steadying breath, stepped inside, and closed the door behind me.

There she was, Mmachi, standing in the center of her meticulously designed living room. She wore an elaborate black traditional outfit: a blouse and wrapper with vibrant, intricate patterns, and a headscarf that made her look regal. She held a composed posture, with her hands folded neatly in front of her, appearing every inch the dignified matriarch. But her eyes told a different story. They were sharp, assessing me with a mix of defiance and resignation. She already knew. The walls had closed in around her, and the endgame was here.

"Mr. Dozy," she greeted me. "You're welcome."

"Ma'am."

She held my gaze, her facade slipping just enough for me to see the faint cracks. I could tell she was running out of strength to maintain the performance. The enormity of her actions, the havoc she'd unleashed on her own family, was bearing down on her.

"I heard about Chief Obidi," she said, her voice softer now, tinged with something close to fear. "I suppose you're here for me next."

I didn't answer right away. Instead, I let my gaze drift around the room, taking in the opulence, the carefully chosen furniture, the lavish decor. All of it felt hollow, suffocating even. Wealth and power, yet none of it seemed to bring her peace. She fidgeted under my silence, the self-assurance she wore like armor beginning to chip away.

"I can still pay you." She said. "There's no need for revenge."

I turned my attention to a large family portrait on the wall. Admiral Alex Maduagu stood in his pristine white navy uniform, looking proud, a quiet dignity radiating from him. Beside him was a younger, radiant Mmachi. Her warm cocoa skin glowing against the dark backdrop, glossy braids swept up beneath a crimson headband, and an off-shoulder ruby dress textured with subtle, swirling patterns. A cascade of chunky coral- beads draped around her neck, the very image of a beautiful Igbo maiden. They looked happy, untouched by the darkness that would later consume them. I felt a pang of something close to sadness: a family once bound by love, now shredded by greed and corruption. A tragedy that could have been avoided. "Did I ever mention that I'm an avid reader?" I said, more to myself than to her, still gazing at the portrait. She didn't respond, unsure if it was a rhetorical question.

I turned to face her, catching the wary flicker in her eyes. She was on edge now, waiting for whatever I was about to say next.

"The trouble with Nigeria is simply and squarely a failure of leadership. There is nothing basically wrong with the Nigerian character. There is nothing wrong with the Nigerian land, or climate, or water, or air, or anything else. The Nigerian problem is the unwillingness or inability of its leaders to rise to the responsibility, to the challenge of personal example, which are the hallmarks of true leadership." I said it like a Shakespearean monologue, every word deliberate. "The great Achebe."

I watched as she absorbed them, her gaze faltering.

"When I think about the corruption that plagues our country, I remember a story my mother used to tell me when I was a child," I continued, my voice soft but unyielding. "It was about a magic tree. A tree that could grant any wish, so long as you truly knew what you wanted. A poor man, desperate to change his fate, discovered it deep in the forest. He wished for wealth. Enough to escape hunger and the shame of his poverty. And the tree gave him riches beyond his wildest dreams."

I walked toward the kitchen, helping myself to an apple. The crunch echoed in the quiet room, unsettling her. "But the man's heart was restless," I said, taking another bite. "His hands, once empty, began to crave more. He returned to the tree, asking not just for wealth, but for power. He wanted the world at his feet. And the tree granted his wish again. Yet, it still wasn't enough. His greed grew until one day the tree, tired of his endless demands, took everything back in an instant. He had nothing left, and his heart felt as empty as his hands."

I leaned against the counter in front of her. "Your insatiable greed, it's what led you here," I said. "Like the man in the story, you kept taking, until there was nothing left to give."

Her expression crumbled, the mask of power and poise slipping as she took a shaky breath. "Mr. Dozy, I...I was desperate. I needed..."

"I don't think you were always this way," I cut in, my tone softened by the slightest edge of regret. "I think at one point you had principles; a sense of duty. But somewhere along the way, you lost sight of it all. The money, the power—they became more important than the people you once loved. And that's the tragedy here. It didn't just destroy you; it destroyed your family."

Her lips trembled, but she didn't respond. She knew I was right. She knew what she had become.

I glanced back at the portrait of her and the Admiral. "You let your ambition and greed consume you. You chose power over loyalty, and now your husband is dead. Your daughter barely recognizes the woman who was once her hero. All that wealth, all that influence, and you've lost everything that truly mattered. You could have left a legacy to be proud of; something more than this hollow empire built on lies."

I watched her shoulders sag. She was no longer the untouchable powerbroker, the feared mastermind. She was just a woman who had gambled everything and lost.

I tossed the apple core into the trash, feeling an odd sense of closure. "You've lost whatever protection those documents gave you," I said, turning toward the door. "You're out of moves."

I paused at the threshold, giving her one last look. "Good luck," I said.

Stepping outside, the crisp night air hit me, and for the first time in what felt like years, I could breathe. The weight on my shoulders lifted, the shadows that had clung to me finally starting to dissipate. Was it all over? I wasn't sure. But I'd closed this chapter, and for now, that was enough.

As I headed for my car, a heavy question clawed its way into my mind, one that had been quietly gnawing at me since starting this whole mess: had I, in some twisted way, been part of the reason kleptocracy thrived in Nigeria? Not just a bystander, but an enabler. I thought about corruption, that plague that seeps into the cracks of every building and every institution, like rot under peeling paint. It's in the schools where grades have a price, in the homes where a little lie greases the wheels, in the markets where honest deals are a rare commodity. Even the churches, places that should be sanctuaries, have their own unholy handshakes in the dark.

The system had turned into a monstrous thing with too many heads, a hydra fed by everyone's quiet acceptance that integrity is just a romantic notion, and a dangerous one at that. If honesty had its day, everyone had something to lose. It's a delicate web, and every player in it knows their role, afraid to pull too hard on the strings lest the whole thing come crashing down around them. I was just one man, and one man alone couldn't hope to take it all apart.

But then again, I wasn't about to roll over. Not entirely. I lied to Peter Onuoha. Of course I'd kept a copy of the evidence tucked away for a rainy day, in case I ever found a way to use it that might actually make a difference. Because as much as these documents could expose the people in power, they'd barely scratch the surface of the whole diseased machine. People like them; they're just a cog in the wheel, easily replaced by someone with a handshake just as firm and a conscience just as filthy. No, taking them down now might make headlines, might even shake the ivory tower for a week or two, but in the end, worse people would replace them.

I couldn't play hero, not yet. But that didn't mean I'd quit the game.

What was next? I had two hundred thousand dollars in my account, a green card, and the opportunity to bring my family over from Nigeria at last. No more threats, no more games. I could finally live without constantly looking over my shoulder.

Maybe, just maybe, I could go several months without opening another job application.

About the Author

Kevin Obike is a Nigerian-born writer of noir mysteries and mythological fantasy. Under his own name, he introduces readers to Alvan "Dozy" Agu in *The Dead Man's Dame*—a hardboiled detective story set against the restless backdrop of Lagos and Washington, D.C. Under his pen name, Kevin C. Noel, he pens *The Ambler Accounts*, a series of sweeping fantasy novels that reimagine myth and history.

Educated in Italy, China, Nigeria, and the United States, Kevin draws inspiration from his international upbringing, weaving stories that reflect the complexity of culture, politics, and human ambition.

He lives in Maryland with his wife, where he is at work on new stories across both his worlds.

For more, visit **kevincnoel.com**

More from the Author

Writing as Kevin C. Noel

The Ambler Accounts

- *Children of Semyaza*
- *Army of Shimshon*
- *ZAK* (novella)
- *The Last LeGrey* (novella)